ITALIAN LESSONS

Books by Peter Pezzelli

HOME TO ITALY

EVERY SUNDAY

FRANCESCA'S KITCHEN

ITALIAN LESSONS

Published by Kensington Publishing Corporation

ITALIAN LESSONS

PETER PEZZELLI

KENSINGTON BOOKS
http://www.kensingtonbooks.com

KENSINGTON BOOKS are published by

Kensington Publishing Corp.
850 Third Avenue
New York, NY 10022

ISBN-13: 978-0-7582-2050-9
ISBN-10: 0-7582-2050-2

First Kensington Trade Paperback Printing: October 2007
10 9 8 7 6 5

In memory of my father, Pasquale "Pat" Pezzelli

PART ONE

CHAPTER I

Had he chanced to glance out his office window just a few minutes before noon, Professor Giancarlo Rosa might have seen, off in the distance, a solitary figure making his way across the near-deserted campus of Rhode Island College. It was the last week of May; commencement had already come and gone, and most of the faculty, save for those teaching a summer course, had vanished along with the students. The few laggards, Rosa among them, were busy collecting their things, finishing up last-minute paperwork, and doing whatever other odds and ends that required completion before staff members could escape to their own summer retreats. With no immediate plans for his vacation, and nothing particularly urgent on his agenda for the day, the professor of music was in no great hurry, so at the moment he was sitting at his computer, perusing the online edition of *Il Centro*, an Italian newspaper. Behind him a recording of Clementi sonatinas played on a little CD player atop the filing cabinet—or more precisely, atop a stack of papers, manuscripts, books, and other paraphernalia that teetered precariously atop the cabinet.

As absorbed in his reading as he was at the moment, the world outside his window held little interest for him. Not that it would

have mattered even if he had just then taken a notion to look outdoors. Had he caught a glimpse of the person off in the distance, a
young man of twenty-two years, Rosa would most likely have
taken little note of him. There was nothing out of the ordinary
about the young man's appearance that would have caught his attention, no immediate indication that his journey across campus
was tending in any definitive way toward the building in which
Rosa sat, and certainly nothing to convey any augury that his path
and that of the professor would very soon intersect.

For his part, the young man strode across the campus with an
air of great purpose, though with a slight but perceptible limp, the
remnant of an unfortunate though not terribly serious mishap on
the rugby pitch some weeks earlier. His ankle had been unceremoniously stomped on while he lay defenseless on the ground at the
bottom of a ruck, a pile of players struggling to obtain possession
of the ball. The injury had not yet completely healed—every step
was a small reminder of the incident—yet he took little notice of
it. He was in a hurry, and the small discomfort was of little concern. Not completely certain of the exact location of his ultimate
destination—the building housing the college's music department—
he paused as he passed the soccer field and track oval, and gazed
ahead at the cluster of structures before him to get his bearings.

It was a warm, pleasant day with just the hint of a breeze whis-
pering across the grounds, nudging the light brown hair hanging
down over the young man's brow. Above, the brilliant blue of the
noonday sky was unbroken save for a smattering of puffy white
clouds gathering on the horizon far away to the west. It was the
type of day best given to lounging beneath a shady tree, or perhaps
taking an excursion to the beach or enjoying some other form of
outdoor recreation, but the young man had more serious pursuits
on his mind. He oriented himself toward what he felt certain was
the appropriate building and continued on.

By the time the young man reached the side entrance to the
building, ascended the stairs to the third floor, and poked his head
out into the corridor to ascertain whether he had come to the

right place, Rosa had already turned away from his computer. The professor was now standing at his desk, collecting into stacks the various papers and notebooks he intended to take with him. Two of these he gathered into his hands and dropped into a cardboard box destined for the backseat of his car. Taking the box into his arms, he turned and walked headlong out of his office door just as the young man, who had followed the lively strains of the piano music down the corridor, was about to walk in. Only the agility of the young man, who managed to twist himself to the side at the last moment, saved the two from colliding.

Taking little notice of the newcomer, now pressed against the wall, Rosa muttered a perfunctory apology as he squeezed by, consolidated his grip on the box, and started on his way down the corridor.

"Professor Rosa?"

Rosa stopped and turned around, wondering if perhaps he had inadvertently ignored a student from the semester just passed. His students occasionally stopped by his office for one reason or another before heading home for the summer—though usually well before this late date—but, he realized, this young man was not one of them. Dressed as he was in shorts and sneakers and an oversized polo shirt bearing the insignia of some club or team, he looked like any other student Rosa might have encountered on campus, but his face was unfamiliar. He was a sturdy sort, Rosa noted, with a thick neck and rugged shoulders. An athlete, no doubt, but there were many on campus, and Rosa paid little attention to sports.

"Yes?" he finally said, eyeing the young man skeptically.

"Excuse me, you don't know me, Professor Rosa," he said in a respectful but urgent voice, "but my name is Carter, Carter Quinn. I was wondering—that is, if you had just a minute—if I could talk to you."

"Well, Carter, Carter Quinn, you've already started talking," Rosa noted with a bit of acerbity, which his foreign accent had a way of accentuating, "so I suppose whether or not I have a minute is now a moot point."

"Actually," said the young man with a sheepish smile, "it's just Carter Quinn. You know, one 'Carter,' not two."

"You should learn to speak more precisely."

"Well, in a way, that's why I'm here."

"Really?" said Rosa. "And how might that be?"

"I want to learn how to speak Italian."

"You're in the wrong place," Rosa told him. "This is the music department. The foreign language department is in the next building over."

"Actually, I called them already this morning," said Carter. "They're not offering any introductory classes this summer. But the woman I spoke with—I think her name was Patricia—she said I should try getting in touch with you before you left for the summer. She told me that you come from Italy and that sometimes you give private Italian lessons, so I took a chance that I'd find you here. I would have called first, but she said not to bother because you almost never check your voice mail."

"Hmm," Rosa grunted. "That sounds just like Patricia."

"Then it's true, you do give lessons," said Carter.

"Yes, sometimes I give lessons," Rosa admitted, somewhat impatiently. "Sometimes, but not always—and not to just any stranger who walks through the door, I'm afraid."

"I never really made it through the door," Carter observed. "Does that help?"

"Not really," Rosa replied. "Forgive me, my friend, but I don't think I'll be giving any lessons this summer. If you look around, perhaps in the yellow pages, I'm sure you'll be able to find someone who can help you. Now, if you'll excuse me, I'm a little busy at the moment."

With that the professor turned and continued on his way down the corridor to the stairwell and out to his car. Looking up into the sky as he crossed the parking lot, Rosa took in the warmth of the sun and the touch of the soft breeze. He had not realized just how lovely a day it had turned into. That morning, he had brought with him a bagged lunch, intending to eat it at his desk while he finished his work. Now, breathing in the warm, pleasant air, the idea of taking a few minutes to enjoy his meal outdoors seemed to him a much better option. He stowed the box in the backseat of his car and headed back to his office.

To his surprise, when Rosa climbed the stairs and stepped out into the corridor, he found Carter Quinn sitting on the floor outside his office. Seeing the professor approach, Carter jumped to his feet, an apologetic but hopeful expression coming to his face.

"I still haven't walked through the door," he said, nodding to the office.

His arms crossed, Rosa shot him a look of consternation. "Mister Carter—"

"Um, Quinn," he said, clearing his throat.

"I beg your pardon."

"It's Mister *Quinn*," he said affably, "but of course you can call me Carter."

"Mister Quinn, who are you? Are you a student here at the college?"

"No," Carter explained with a shake of his head. "Actually, I live in North Providence, just a little ways up the street off campus. But I just graduated from UNH last week."

"New Hampshire seems like a long way to go to obtain an education when you have a perfectly fine college right next door," Rosa pointed out. "Pardon me."

Rosa stepped past him and into his office. His back to the door, he went to his desk and continued organizing his papers.

"Just needed a change of scenery, I guess," said Carter with a shrug, lingering outside the door. "It's a nice place."

"So I've heard," said Rosa with an air of detachment. He hoped that an attitude of indifference on his part would discourage the younger man and entice him to go on his way. Undaunted, however, Carter stood there, lingering in the corridor just outside the door. His persistence piqued Rosa's curiosity, and so, against his better judgment, for he had no intention of changing his mind on the matter of the Italian lessons, the professor said, "And what did you study there in New Hampshire, Mister Quinn?"

"Financial management."

"And for what purpose?"

"Purpose?" Carter said. "I don't know. I guess because I want a career in business."

"A career in business," repeated Rosa with a mildly derisive laugh. "That's like saying you want a career in breathing. What is it that you truly want to do with your life?"

A moment passed before Carter replied. "I dunno," he finally admitted. "I'm working on that one."

"After four years of college, you're still working on it? What were you doing all that time? Daydreaming?" said Rosa. He looked back over his shoulder and nodded at the insignia on Carter's shirt. "I'm guessing you are an athlete, yes?"

"I played football," said Carter with another shrug. "And some rugby in the spring."

"A scholar athlete," Rosa noted, turning back to his desk again. "Tell me, which were you more of, the former or the latter?"

"I studied pretty hard . . . sometimes," he answered, sounding less than convincing, and even less convinced. "But sports were important to me, too, I guess."

"Sports often are to people," said Rosa with a sigh. "Too important in my opinion, but in your case I suppose I could understand why. Financial management doesn't sound like the stuff to stir one's academic passions."

"Seemed like a good idea at the time."

"And why are you coming to me now?" asked Rosa. "Didn't they have any Italian courses at your university for you to take?"

"Oh, sure they did," said Carter. "But it wasn't until just a few weeks ago that I decided to take a trip to Italy sometime this summer."

"I see. And just what was it that inspired you to do that?"

At this question the young man grew ill at ease. He shifted his stance and looked down at his feet.

"It's hard to explain," he said after a time.

"Try."

"Well, it's just that lately I've become really interested in Italian culture," he offered. "I'd like to learn more about it, so I thought studying the language would be the best place to start."

At this pronouncement, Rosa paused and looked once more over his shoulder, eyeing the young man with a look of bemusement. He chuckled to himself as he turned around and leaned back against the edge of the desk, his arms folded.

"So tell me," he said in a far gentler voice than he had thus far used to address the young man, "what was her name?"

"What do you mean?" said Carter, his face reddening.

"Please, Mister Quinn," said the professor with a dismissive wave of his hand, "let's not play games. When and if I agree to invest my time in teaching, I do it only for people who I believe are truly motivated. Otherwise it's a waste of my time and their money. Now I know some might construe what I'm about to say to you as less than politically correct, but when a young woman comes to me and tells me that she wants to learn to speak Italian because she is interested in studying Italian culture, I usually believe that this is her true intention, because more often than not, this is truly the case. On the other hand, when someone such as yourself comes to me and says that he wants to speak Italian because he is interested in studying Italian culture, more often than not what he is really interested in studying is an Italian woman. So, Mister Carter, Carter Quinn, I'll ask you again. What was her name?"

A long pause ensued. From what Rosa could see from the pained look on his face, the young man was feverishly turning the question over and over in his mind. At last he dropped his arms to his side and heaved a weary sigh, as if all the energy that had driven him to that place had suddenly left him.

"Elena," he finally said, speaking the name in an almost reverential voice.

"Elena," Rosa repeated upon hearing this confession. "A beautiful name. I trust it belongs to a beautiful young lady."

"Very," Carter murmured. Then, squirreling up the side of his mouth, he sighed again and added, "How did you know? I mean, is it that obvious?"

"How did I know?" scoffed Rosa, throwing his hands up. "Tell me, what is it that drives a man to leave his home and seek his fortune? Hmm? What is it that makes him want to conquer the world? What is it that finally roots a man in one place, or that can just as easily uproot him in the blink of an eye? What makes him come and go? My friend, for better or worse, it's *always* a woman. Trust me. It is just one of the simple facts of life."

"Yeah, well, I don't know how simple all of this is," muttered Quinn.

Rosa stood there for a moment, rubbing his chin thoughtfully, before gesturing to the chair across from his desk. "Sit," he told him, "and tell me how you came to know this Elena."

Surprised that his confession had brought him an invitation into the professor's office instead of immediate ejection from his presence, Carter stepped tentatively inside and sat down in the chair.

"Where do I begin?" he said disconsolately.

"Begin at the beginning," suggested Rosa. "Tell me about how you first met, or better yet, how it was that you first saw her."

"That's easy," said Carter, looking past Rosa with a faraway gaze. "I can remember it like it was a minute ago. It was during a rugby match over in Newport—the New England collegiate tournament. I was carrying the ball, and when I got tackled I ended up flat on my back, trapped at the bottom of a ruck. There must have been ten guys on top of me, all fighting for the ball, and one of them, probably one of my own teammates, had his knee jammed into my midsection. So besides getting crushed, I could barely breathe. I tried screaming, but nothing came out. It was like being born. I was in agony, and I thought it would never end, but then the ball suddenly came loose and everyone unpiled, leaving me there on the ground while they all ran down the field. I sat up to catch my breath, and I was just about to pick myself up and go running down the field after them when I saw her standing there on the sidelines, looking straight at me, smiling."

"What did you notice about her?" asked Rosa, studying the young man's expression.

"Everything," said Carter dreamily, reliving the moment in his mind. "But not just about her. All of a sudden it was like time had stopped, and I became aware of all these things I never bothered to notice before. How sweet the grass smelled, and how soft it was. How warm the sun felt on my face, and how colorful the uniforms of the players and the clothes of all the people on the sidelines looked. And how beautiful the sky and the clouds were, and how the trees swayed in the wind. It was like everything suddenly came into sharp focus. And Elena was right there in the middle of it all."

"What did she look like?"

"How can I describe her?" sighed Carter. "She was the most beautiful girl I ever met. She had this long wavy hair like strands of gold, and her face was like the one in that famous painting you see all the time of the girl standing inside the clam shell. You know the one I'm talking about?"

"*The Birth of Venus*," said Rosa. "I've seen it. But I believe it's more like a scallop shell."

"Whatever," said Carter with a dismissive wave of his own. "It's a shell. Anyway, she looked at me and smiled, and all of a sudden I forgot about the match and the guys running down the field and the pain in my gut. I couldn't take my eyes off her. It was like nothing else in the world mattered to me anymore except her."

"Hmm, I would say that you got hit by the thunderbolt," chuckled Rosa. "It happens."

"Yeah? Well, that wasn't all I got hit with. Two seconds later the ball came bouncing back my way and I was right back in the thick of it. I got whacked but good. But you know, I played the rest of the match in a fog, not feeling a thing. Everywhere I ran on the field I kept looking back to see if she was still there, you know, to make sure I hadn't just imagined her."

"And then what happened?"

"The match ended and she was gone," said Carter. "I figured she must have been a mirage, but then I saw her again a little while later on the other side of the field. I couldn't help myself, so I just walked straight across the field—right where another match was going on—because I had to talk with her."

Rosa gave a little laugh and turned back to his desk. He started to sift through the remaining papers stacked there, stuffing those he wished to take with him into a leather satchel. "And how did that first encounter go?" he asked over his shoulder.

"I felt so at ease when I went up to her, like I'd known her my whole life," said Carter, full of wonder. "And I could tell that she felt the same way, too. The way she smiled and told me her name after I introduced myself. The way she looked at me and touched my cheek on the spot where I had gotten kicked in the face. The way she laughed because I didn't seem to care about it. And when she talked, her voice, it was like she was singing. You know?"

"I suppose," said Rosa.

"Anyway," Carter went on, "I could tell from her accent that she was a foreigner, so I asked her, and she told me she was from Italy. She was an exchange student at Salve Regina."

"Hence your newfound fascination with Italian culture," the professor noted. "What happened next?"

"We ended up walking a little ways up the side of the hill next to the field," said Carter. "We sat down together to watch some of the other matches and just started talking. Actually, she did most of the talking, which was fine with me because I was happy just listening to her—even if her English was a little shaky."

"What did you talk about?"

"The weather," shrugged Carter. "Small talk. Then she asked about the rugby matches, so I tried to explain to her what was going on down on the field. After a while she started telling me about Italy, and how nice it was this time of year where she lived, and how I should come and visit it someday."

"And where would that be?"

"A town called Roccasale," the young man replied.

"Roccasale?" said the professor, suddenly turning to the young man, an eyebrow arched in curiosity.

"She said it's a little town not far from someplace called Pescara, wherever that is," said Carter. "Have you ever heard of it?"

Rosa stood there for a moment, rubbing his chin as he considered the question.

"Yes," he said thoughtfully after a time. "I have heard of it. Very interesting." Then, resuming his former impassive expression, he asked, "So, how long did this blissful interlude go on?"

"Not long," said Carter miserably. "Our next match was about to start, so I had to leave her to go warm up with my teammates. Before I went back to the field, I told her it would be nice to see her after the match. She said she thought it would be nice, too, but friends were coming to pick her up because she had to get back to her dorm to get packed. Turns out she was flying home to Italy the very next day."

"Ah," sighed Rosa. "And so . . . ?"

"And so nothing," griped Carter. "I didn't know what to say. All of a sudden my teammates were coming up to me, nagging me to get back to the field to get ready, and she just smiled and waved goodbye. 'Ciao, Carter,' she said. And that was it. I haven't seen or heard from her since. I know it's crazy, but now, no matter what I do or where I go, I can't get her out of my head. I can't think straight about anything. It's like my whole world has come to a stop, and it won't start again until I see her—at least one more time."

"And so am I to understand that your idea is to learn Italian and go to Italy in search of this girl?" said Rosa.

"That's pretty much it," Carter replied, as if this plan sounded perfectly reasonable.

"Seems a little half-baked," Rosa opined. "Tell me, exactly what would you do if you were to see her again?"

"I don't know," admitted Carter. "Maybe try to explain to her how I feel about her. Find out if she feels the same way—and in my heart I know that she does. I *know* it. But you see, that's why I need to learn to speak Italian—so that I can be sure she understands me, and that I understand her. That's why I came to you today, because I need someone who really knows the language. Will you help me?"

"Mister Carter—"

"Quinn."

"Mister Quinn," said Rosa. "Your story is quite touching, very heartfelt, but I was very much in earnest when I told you that I wasn't planning on giving any Italian lessons this summer. I would like to help you, truly I would, but—"

"Yeah, okay," said a disconsolate Carter before Rosa could complete the sentence. "I understand." With a dejected nod, the gesture of a desperate man who, not finding the help he needs, simply moves on to continue in search of it, he got to his feet and started for the door.

Rosa was prepared to watch him go, but then found himself raising a finger into the air. "*Aspett' un attimo*," he said, bringing Carter to a halt. "Wait."

The professor paused, heaved a long sigh, and passed his hand over his face as he eyed Carter with a look of mild annoyance. "If you give me a telephone number where you can be reached," he finally said, "I will give it some consideration over the next day or two."

Carter's face lit up.

"Don't get your hopes up," Rosa quickly added. "I make no promises. It is my vacation time, you know, and I was looking forward to a nice rest. Maybe I will, and maybe I won't. If I decide no . . . then perhaps at least I can help you find someone else."

"Whatever you can do to help me would be great," enthused Carter, excitedly searching through his pockets for a pen. "You won't be sorry."

"I'm sorry already," observed the professor. He took a pen from his desk and handed it over.

Later, after Carter had gone, Rosa stood at the window and watched him make his way back across campus until he was out of sight. He stayed there for a time, gazing out into the distance, his thoughts turning over and over inside his head. At last he turned away from the window and shook his head.

"Roccasale," he muttered.

Then he reached for the bottle of water and the paper bag resting on the corner of his desk and headed outside to eat his lunch.

CHAPTER 2

"Ciao, Giancarlo!"

Giancarlo Rosa was sitting on the ground, his back up against a tree, eating his lunch while he looked out at the track that circumnavigated the soccer field. There little clusters of people were walking or jogging round and round together beneath the midday sun. Rosa rather enjoyed watching them from the cool of the tree's shadow. The inherent monotony of their journeys had a way of lulling him into a daydream, and he was staring out at them, his thoughts far away, when he heard the familiar voice. He looked to his side and saw, approaching him, the woman to whom it belonged.

"Ciao, Patrizia," he called back, nodding a greeting to the woman as she drew close.

"What a beautiful day," said Patricia, beaming him a smile from behind her sunglasses as she sat down in the grass beside him. "And what a nice spot to have lunch."

Dressed in burgundy running shorts, a faded Rhode Island College shirt, and sneakers, she looked ready to join the others out on the track. Indeed, as youthful looking as she was, she might easily have passed for a coed instead of a member of the faculty.

"Can I offer you something?" said Rosa.

Patricia lowered her sunglasses enough to reveal a pair of playful, inquisitive blue eyes. "Hmm, what's on the menu?" she said, leaning closer.

"I have some olives and half of a roasted pepper and provolone sandwich left," he replied.

Patricia laughed, and pulled her sunglasses up onto the top of her head.

"What is it with you?" she teased him. "Whenever I see you at lunch, you're always eating prosciutto or provolone or mortadella or something else. Haven't you ever heard of just a plain old peanut butter and jelly sandwich?"

"Sorry, I tried that once," said Rosa, feigning a shudder. "It was not an experience I wish to relive."

"You're a finicky eater."

"I was born that way," he said by way of explanation before adding, "So, you are not interested in the sandwich?"

"Thanks, but I'm going to be running soon," said Patricia, feigning a shudder of her own. "I'm sure it's delicious, but roasted peppers probably wouldn't be the best thing for me to eat right now."

"Suit yourself," said Rosa, helping himself to a bite of the sandwich.

Patricia stretched her legs and arms straight out before her and folded her upper body forward until her head was a few inches over her knees. She took a deep breath and then slowly exhaled while she held the position.

"Tell me, why do you run, Patricia?" said Rosa, looking away to the track. "What is it that makes everyone want to go out there and run around in circles all day long?"

"It's good for your body," she answered, easing back. "Even better for your head. I like the track. You can go for miles and miles if you want and never have to worry about anything, about traffic or getting lost. And if you go far enough, you start to forget everything, whatever's on your mind, all the things you've been worrying about. It's really very relaxing in its own way. You should give it a try sometime."

"Someday, perhaps," he said with little enthusiasm.

Patricia smiled and bent forward again, this time sliding her hands down to her ankles and stretching out completely until her head rested on her knees. Holding there, her back and arms perfectly extended, she looked at him for a moment.

"Did that student I talked with ever get in touch with you?" she said after a time.

Rosa gave a grunt and swallowed the last of his sandwich. "Ah, Mister Quinn, I presume," he said, flicking the crumbs from his fingers.

"That's the one," she said brightly, a twinkle in her eye as she raised herself back up.

"He accosted me outside my office just a little while ago. And he told me what you said about me and my voice mail."

"Well, it *is* true, isn't it?" she chided him. "It's terrible, you know. You never check your messages. Or if you do, you almost never return the calls."

Rosa gave a shrug, as if to say that it really made no difference.

"I really wish you had recommended him to someone else," he groused.

"Why do you say that?" laughed Patricia. "I thought you enjoyed giving private Italian lessons. You always said it was a nice change of pace from teaching music all the time."

"Yes, but for once in my life I was looking forward to having absolutely nothing to do for the summer. I've been feeling burnt out lately. I'm tired, and I need a rest. It's been a long year."

"Well, if that's the case, you can always just say no."

"That's what I did."

"Really?"

"Well, at least at first," admitted Rosa. "To be honest, he didn't seem like the type I wanted to teach."

"Why not? Was there something wrong with him?"

"No, nothing, not really," he said. "It's just that he's a rugby and football player, and well—"

"Ah, he's a jock," said Patricia. She opened her legs into a V and reached out to grasp the tips of her running shoes. "You don't like athletes," she added, pulling herself forward.

"It's not that I have anything against them," said Rosa, looking away once more to the track. "It's just that my experiences with them in the classroom haven't always been so good. Too often their heads are on the playing fields instead of in the classroom. And many of them seem to do the least amount possible to get by. It's very disappointing sometimes. I just don't like wasting my time if they're not going to do their part, that's all. Anyway, I only enjoy teaching students who show some motivation. Otherwise it's not worth it to me."

"So you sent this student packing, I assume," said Patricia.

"Well, I had planned to," he answered, "but then I told him that I'd think about it."

Patricia got to her feet, came to his side, and reached out to the tree. Placing her hands against it, she leaned forward to stretch her calves. As she did so, Rosa found himself hard-pressed to resist the natural instinct to let his gaze follow the sleek lines of her slender arms and legs, already pleasantly tanned from her daily visits to the track.

"So, why the second thoughts?" she asked with an air of nonchalance, leaning closer to the tree, deepening the stretch, and further accentuating the contours of her leg muscles.

"His persistence, I guess," Rosa answered with a sigh, doing his best to look away. "He's very anxious to go to Italy."

"Oh? Why is that?"

Rosa gave a little laugh and rolled his eyes.

"He's in love," he told her.

Patricia smiled as she looked down at him. "Why do you laugh like that?" she said. "What better reason could someone have for going to Italy?"

"Hmm, I don't know," Rosa admitted. "But I'm sure there must be at least one."

Patricia eased out of the stretch and stood upright. Placing one hand against the tree for balance, she reached down for her ankle and pulled her foot to her backside to stretch her thigh.

"You know, you should go home to Italy yourself someday," she said. "I often wonder why you have never gone back."

"It's a long story," he said. "And not a very interesting one. But in any case, why would I go back there when everything I need is right here in America?"

"Maybe you need more than you realize."

"Maybe," said Rosa. He gazed off into the distance for a time before saying, "So, how far will you run today?"

"I don't know," said Patricia, now stretching her other quad in the same way she did the first. "Three or four miles, maybe a little more."

"Is that far enough to forget all your troubles?"

"For a few minutes at least," she replied, "but never completely."

With that she lifted the sunglasses from the top of her head, shook out her short brown hair, and put the sunglasses back on properly, hiding her eyes from him once more.

"Will you go to Sheffield's party tomorrow night?" she asked.

"I think so," he answered. "Probably."

"So, that means we don't have to say goodbye yet for the summer."

"No, Patrizia. Not yet."

"Good," she said with a nod and a smile. "In that case, I'll let you finish your lunch in peace." At that, she turned away and started off to the track. "Ciao, Giancarlo," she called over her shoulder.

"Ciao, Patrizia," he called after her. Then, letting himself drift back into the daydream in which she had found him, he settled back against the tree for a time and watched her trot out to join the others, all of them still going round and round, farther and farther, but never going anywhere.

Later that same afternoon, after he returned to his office and finished collecting his things, Giancarlo drove home beneath suddenly darkened skies. The smattering of clouds that had dotted the western horizon earlier in the day had by this time burgeoned into a towering mass of billowing gray-white mushrooms. Advancing inexorably toward the east, it was quickly engulfing the sky and the sun as it approached.

When he pulled into his driveway and stepped out of the car, Rosa cast a glance up at the menacing skies. From off in the distance came the low rumble of thunder, and the leaves on the trees were beginning to stir in that fretful way they often do before the coming of a storm. A single heavy drop of rain plopped against the pavement, a warning that it would be best not to dawdle carting his papers into the house. Wasting no time, he grabbed his satchel and the box from the backseat, and hurried up the front walk. After a moment of fumbling with the keys, he unlocked the door and stepped inside.

It was a small, single-story house where Rosa lived, modest but more than sufficient for the needs of an unmarried man living alone. The foyer in which he stood led into the heart of the house, giving way on one side to a charmingly cluttered living room walled with bookshelves and dominated by a lovely old baby grand piano inundated with piles of sheet music. Beneath the piano hid a guitar, a violin, a flute, and a variety of other musical instruments, all in their cases, stowed haphazardly atop one another. The remaining space was taken up by a couch and a chair flanking a low round coffee table, upon which lay an assortment of books waiting to be read. Further along, off the opposite side of the foyer, came two bedrooms, one where Rosa slept, the other a study of sorts with a small desk, a personal computer, a small sofa, and a television. Around the corner, past the bathroom and down the short hall, came the kitchen, through which one could reenter the far end of the living room or continue on to the back door, which opened to a small screened-in porch looking out to the backyard.

Rosa set his things on the floor and hastened about the house, lowering the windows before the rain came. One look out at the now-swaying trees and the blackening sky was enough to convince him that it wouldn't be long in coming. When the last of the windows was secured, he went to the kitchen and stood at the sink, gazing out at the gathering tempest. A thrill of anticipation surged through him. The crackle of lightning, the ferocious boom of thunder, and the sight of the wind and rain whipping down from the sky had always fascinated him, ever since he was a small boy growing up in Italy's Abruzzi mountains. Each storm was to him a dazzling symphony of sight and sound, no two ever exactly the same. The power of nature to compose such spectacles at will awed him, filling him with a delicious sensation of terror and delight, not unlike what a child might experience on a carnival ride. And so it was with great eagerness that he looked out with watchful eyes, awaiting the opening strains of this new opus.

It was not to be, however. As often happens, particularly in New England, the sky suddenly changed its mind. Just when it seemed as if the storm was about to erupt in all its spectacular fury, the winds went quiet and barely a drop of rain fell against the window. The dark clouds, so full of menace just a few moments earlier, gave a few desultory grumbles as they rolled by, but that was all. They seemed as disgruntled by the sudden cancellation of their performance as Rosa, who stood at the window, hands on hips, looking out with keen disappointment as the storm slipped harmlessly away. Feeling strangely let down, he turned away from the window and slouched to the living room in search of solace. There he pushed aside some of the papers and books piled on the piano bench and sat down.

There were in the stacks of sheet music about him on the piano innumerable selections he might have chosen to play as he sat there contemplating the keyboard, some the work of the classical masters; others, sonatas and concertos he himself had composed early in his career. Before him, on the piano's music stand, lay his last work, a sonata in A he had started composing years ago but for some reason along the way had one day become incapable of seeing through to completion. Subsequent efforts to press forward with it, or with any other new work for that matter, proved fruitless, and the unfinished pages had remained there on the piano ever since, gathering dust while they awaited inspiration to return to their creator.

And so, unable to write anything new, and no longer interested in playing the old, Rosa sat there for a time, gazing straight ahead, before inevitably turning in frustration to the only thing left to him. Reaching out over the keyboard, he began to play scales and arpeggios, basic piano exercises to improve one's playing technique that he had first learned as a child, though now he played them not to improve, but simply to preserve. Not knowing what else to do, he played them over and over, major and minor scales, parallel and contrary motions, his fingers running up and down the keyboard, back and forth, their journeys always beginning and ending at the same place, always in motion, but never really going anywhere. On and on he played them, over and over again, until finally, after a time, Giancarlo Rosa began to forget about his troubles.

CHAPTER 3

Pain.

Carter Quinn felt it first in his legs, and then in his lower back. He squeezed his eyes shut, trying to force himself to ignore it, but the burning agony was growing more intense with the passing of every fraction of a second. It was overwhelming him. Beads of sweat rolling off his forehead, he gulped down a breath of air and tried to focus. Before long, though, the pain had spread like wildfire to his chest and shoulders and lungs. His vision blurred, and his pounding heart felt like it was about to explode. He was dying. Hating to surrender to the inevitable, desperate not to give in, he did the only thing he could think of.

He screamed.

It was no ordinary scream. It was more like the howl of a wild beast, the release of dark primal forces hiding somewhere deep within. Had he somehow been able to hear it from outside of himself, Carter would not have recognized the blood-curdling sound as something of his own. It was as if it belonged to someone, or something, else. Whatever its source, whomever it belonged to, the scream had the desired effect. Carter arched his head back and slowly, agonizingly, extended his legs, hoisting the bar resting across his shoulders, and the stacks of iron plates it carried, to its acme. The final repetition of his squat workout complete, he set the bar down with a crash on the squat rack and backed away. His legs going wobbly, he staggered to a nearby bench and collapsed on it, oblivious to the other gym patrons, who had momentarily paused their workouts to gawk at him. Satisfied to see that someone had not just died beneath a pile of metal plates, they turned back to their own workouts, and the room soon regained its former hum of activity.

Gazing blankly at the floor, Carter rested there on the bench, elbows on knees, head drooping forward, until a towel flew across the room and caught him full in the face.

"You, Carter Quinn," said the flinger of the towel, "are one sick mother."

"Oh yeah, Jimmy?" panted Carter, taking the towel and wiping it across his brow. "What makes you say so?"

"You work out like an animal," Jimmy laughed. "That's what makes me say so."

"I'm just trying to get in shape."

Jimmy opened his arms wide and gestured at the rest of the gym. "Hey, take a look around you," he said. "Everybody's in here to get in shape, but nobody else tortures themselves like you do. You're the only one that's trying to kill himself. It's sick. Whatta you do it for, anyway?"

Carter shrugged, and flipped the towel around the back of his neck.

"What can I say?" he replied. "The fall rugby season's only a couple of months away. I've gotta be ready if I want to play for Providence this year."

"Trust me, you're already ready. But this is something different. There's gotta be some other reason you come in here every other day and hurt yourself the way you do."

Feeling a little recovered, Carter puffed out a breath and straightened up. "I dunno," he said with a shrug, "I guess I just like it."

"What, the pain?"

"Yeah, I guess."

Jimmy tilted his head and gave his friend a look of incredulity. "Let me tell you something, Quinnie," he said, wagging his finger.

"Nobody in their right mind likes pain. I don't care what the psychologists tell you."

"It's not so much that I like it," explained Carter. "I just like what it does for me."

"What does pain do for you?"

"It makes me forget things."

"What kinds of things?"

"I don't know," said Carter, mocking his friend's expression. "I can't remember."

"You're such a loser," Jimmy needled him, shaking his head. "You know, if you want to forget things, drinking would be a lot easier."

Carter laughed, and tossed the towel back at his friend. Satisfied that he had stressed his leg muscles to the fullest possible extent on this particular occasion, he picked himself up and went into the adjacent room to see how well he might torture his upper body.

Later, after he had finished his workout, Carter threw on a dry T-shirt, stuffed his gear into his gym bag, and walked out with Jimmy. It was a warm, pleasant evening—a soft breeze was puffing out of the south—and the two stood on the sidewalk for a few minutes, contemplating how to make the best of what remained of it. Carter let out a contented sigh as he watched the cars zooming back and forth, many with their tops down, radios blaring. Summer was in the air; it wouldn't be long in coming.

Jimmy nudged him and nodded to the establishment across the street. "What do you say, a couple of beers before you go home?"

A couple of beers later, the two were still sitting at the bar, watching the Red Sox play on the television overhead. An empty bowl of bar mix sat on the bar between them. Jimmy reached into it, scratching the bottom for the last few crumbs.

"You know," he said, stuffing the bits into his mouth, "it speaks well of you that despite your four years of higher education, you still lower yourself to hang around with your knucklehead friends who barely made it out of high school."

Carter took a sip of his beer and chuckled.

"What can I say?" he said with a smile. "I like the feeling of superiority it gives me hanging around with mental midgets."

"Hey, you'd better watch out for us mental midgets, my friend," Jimmy warned him. "Trust me, God likes ignoramuses like me. That's why he makes so many of us. We got you egghead guys *way* outnumbered. Don't ever forget that."

"Now there's a sobering thought."

"So tell me, Mr. Superior," Jimmy went on. "What are you gonna do now with all that college knowledge you've got stored up in that brain of yours? You got a job on Wall Street lined up yet?"

"Not exactly," replied Carter, "but I'm expecting the offers to start pouring in any minute now."

"So what are you planning to do in the meantime?"

"Not much," said Carter. "For the time being, I start working a construction job on Monday."

Jimmy shot him a look.

"Construction? Are you crazy? You've got a college degree. Where's swinging a hammer gonna get you?"

"Just as far as Italy," said Carter. "That's all I'm worried about right now."

Jimmy slapped his hand to his forehead. "Oh no," he groaned. "Don't tell me you're still all hung up on that Italian broad you were going on and on about the other day after you got home. I figured that whole thing was just some daydream of yours."

"Figured wrong, Butch."

"Carter, be serious. You're not going to Italy."

"I am being serious," he said. "And I am going to Italy."

Carter stared at the television set for a moment, but without really seeing the action, for his mind was somewhere else.

"Listen, I don't know how to explain it," he finally said, turning back to his friend, "but I have to do this. It's like I don't have a choice. You don't know what's it's been like for me this past month. I can't get her out of my head. It's like nothing else in the world matters to me anymore. But what's really weird is that ever since I met her, I want to be better."

"What do you mean 'better'?"

"I mean better. Better at everything. A better person. Stronger. Smarter. Nicer. I don't know, just better. Anyway, I can't think straight about anything but getting there to see her again. All joking aside, that's half the reason I've been banging the weights around like I've been lately. It's the only thing that clears my head."

"Well, it hasn't cleared your head enough, if you ask me. So tell me, what are you gonna do? Fly all the way across the ocean and start traipsing around trying to find this chick? You don't know anything about Italy, and you don't speak a word of Italian."

"I'm working on that," said Carter, raising his finger.

"Oh, really? What have you been doing? Watching Lidia cook?"

"No, bean brain, I've got a teacher lined up—well, at least almost lined up. He's going to give me lessons."

"Italian lessons?"

"No, Chinese lessons."

"Very funny," said Jimmy. "So, who is this teacher, and what do you mean he's 'almost lined up'?"

"He's a music professor over at RIC," Carter explained.

"I thought you wanted to learn Italian."

"He's from Italy," said Carter, impatiently. "He gives private Italian lessons to people in the summer . . . sometimes."

"What do you mean 'sometimes'?"

"Well, I've only met him once, but he's kind of a pain," said Carter. "I guess he's kind of particular about who he teaches, because when I asked him to give me lessons, he said he'd have to think about it."

"What's to think about?" said Jimmy. "What is he? Some old geezer?"

"Nah," said Carter with a shake of his head. "I'd say he's late forties, maybe early fifties."

"That's old in my book," opined Jimmy before downing a gulp of his beer.

"Honestly, I don't care if he's as old as the hills," said Carter.

"Somebody at the school told me he's the best Italian teacher around, so that's good enough for me."

"And what happens if this guy doesn't come through for you?" said Jimmy. "Then what are you gonna do?"

"I haven't gotten there yet," Carter admitted with a shrug. "I'll worry about that when I do. For now I'll just wait."

"And do what?"

"Get in shape," Carter reminded him. "The fall rugby season's coming, remember?"

"Of course, how could I forget?" said Jimmy, rolling his eyes.

"You should come out and give it a try," said Carter. "You work out enough. Why not put it to good use? Don't give me that look."

"Carter, please, let me explain something to you," said Jimmy, still giving him that look. "I happen to like my face just the way it is. See this nose? I don't want it bent sideways. And I don't want my ears to look like two hunks of cauliflower. I work out for one reason and one reason only."

"And that would be?"

"The beach," he replied.

"Oh, right," Carter kidded him. "I forgot, the chicks just fall all over you when you show up on the sand and take your shirt off."

"Hey, you'd be surprised," said Jimmy, flexing both arms. "I have to stay strong to be able to swat them away. Speaking of which . . ."

Jimmy nodded to the entrance, where two attractive young women were just walking in. The two sauntered past them on their way to a table on the other side of the bar. Natural instincts being what they are, Carter could not stop his eyes from watching them. He was discreet enough, however, to at least turn away and observe their passing reflections in the mirror behind the cash register. Jimmy, however, unabashedly bid them a good evening and eyed them longingly as they ambled by, turning their backs to the two young men.

"Now that's what I'm talking about," said Jimmy with a nod

and a wink. He rubbed his hands together with glee. "Come on. What do you say we go over and say hello."

"Uh-uh," grunted Carter.

"What do you mean 'uh-uh'?"

"I'm being good this summer," said Carter.

Jimmy looked at him as if he hadn't understood.

"Good for what?" he asked.

"I'm doing it for Elena. No fooling around."

"Elena shmalena," said Jimmy with a dismissive wave. "I don't know what kind of spell that chick put on you, but I can tell you that right now she's five thousand miles away on the other side of the Atlantic doing God knows what with God knows who, so forget about her."

"Can't do it, Jimmy," said Carter, shaking his head.

"But why not?" he cried.

"Because, I told you, I'm trying to be better, and I don't want to waste my time on something that's meaningless."

"Waste your time?" said Jimmy incredulously. "*Meaningless?*" He sighed, and shook his head. "Wow. Whatever you've got, man, you must have it bad. But all I can say is, suit yourself. As far as *I'm* concerned, I've got all the time in the world right now, and wasting a little of it with one of those two fine ladies—preferably both—sounds just fine to me."

Later, after Jimmy had gone off to waste some time, Carter left the bar and drove home alone. When he pulled into the driveway, he sat there for a moment and gave a yawn before reaching for his gym bag. Worn out as he was by his workout, the effect on him of the relatively modest amount of beer he had consumed at the bar was considerable. The heavy weight of fatigue had settled on him, and suddenly all he wanted was to crawl into bed and close his eyes. Carter had not mentioned it to Jimmy, but the forgetfulness of sleep was the one other thing that cleared his mind. He stepped out of the car and started for the house.

"Hey, could that be the one and only Carter Quinn?" came a voice from the house next door.

Carter stopped and looked across the yard to the house's darkened front porch. There, in silhouette, he saw the figure of a young woman stand and come to the side railing.

"Hey, who's that?" he called back amiably. "There's no way it could be Sheila Mahoney. She's been gone for years and years."

Carter dropped his bag and walked across the grass to the side of the porch just as the young woman leaned out into the pale glow cast by the streetlight on the corner. He was right, of course, it was Sheila—but looking up at her as he drew close to the porch, he realized that this was not the same Sheila he had once known. Thinking back, the last time he could recall talking to her for any length of time was a million years ago, in high school, and even then it was only in passing. In those days, Sheila was still just a shy, awkward, skinny girl with short stringy hair, glasses, and a mouthful of dental work. The two of them had grown up next door to each other, gone to the same grammar school, attended the same church. After eighth grade, though, Sheila's parents sent her to a Catholic high school, while Carter went on to North Providence High.

A typical boy growing up, Carter had through the years assiduously ignored the meek little girl next door who had an unnerving way of gazing at him with affectionate eyes whenever they crossed paths. Now, though, the contrast between the image in his mind of the girl he once knew and that of the barefoot young woman standing before him on the porch could not have been more striking. Gone were the eyeglasses, and the once stringy hair, now dark and silky, fell long and luscious about her shoulders. Her cut-off jeans and tank top clothed the gentle curves of a woman's torso, and her arms and legs, no longer skinny, were now simply slender and graceful. It might have taken twenty-two years, but Sheila Mahoney had finally blossomed.

"Hi, Carter," she said, revealing with her smile a set of perfect teeth easy to see even in that dim light. She leaned over and rested her elbows on the porch railing. "Long time no see," she said. "How have you been?"

"I'm doing great," said Carter, returning her smile. "But wow, look at you. You're all grown up!"

"Oh, so you noticed," she said with a hint of playful sarcasm, pushing her hair back away from her face. "How nice."

"Hey, I'm sure a lot of guys have noticed," he told her. "So, when did you get back from school—Wheaton, right?"

"Right. A few days ago. How about you?"

"Last week."

"Heard you made All-America in football."

"Ha!" Carter laughed. "You must have heard that from my mother. It was second team, All-*Conference*. There's a big difference."

"Not to her."

Carter folded his arms and shook his head. "It's weird, isn't it?" he said.

"What?"

"We live right next door to each other, but in four years of college, I don't think I've seen you four times."

"I've seen you," she said. Then, before he could ask when, she added, "So, how did you like college?"

"Loved every minute," Carter sighed. "Kind of hated to leave it behind. How about you?"

"I loved it, too," said Sheila, "but by the time this last semester came around, I was ready to move on."

"You obviously didn't belong to a fraternity," Carter kidded her.

"Oh, God," she laughed, "don't tell me you were a frat boy."

"Hey, what's wrong with frat boys?" he laughed in return.

Sheila did not answer right away, but instead smiled and gazed at him for a time with an expression not unlike the ones Carter had seen so many times in the past. Somehow, though, this one was different. It radiated more self-confidence, as if she knew that she was in complete control of the situation.

"So, what are you doing here?" she said at last. "I thought you would be staying with your parents down at their beach house. My mother told me that they've already moved down to Charlestown for the summer."

"Yeah, their last kid is finally out of college," Carter replied, "so they figured they could leave me home and get an early start on their vacation. Imagine the nerve."

"So how come you're still hanging around in the city?"

"I've got things to do," he said, a bit evasively.

"Career things?"

"Not exactly," he answered. "I haven't really figured that part of things out yet. How about you. Any plans?"

"I'm going to France," she said.

"A trip to France? Nice. That a graduation gift from your parents?"

"Well, in a way, I suppose," she said. "I'm leaving in August to go there for a year to study. It's a graduate program in international relations."

"No kidding," said Carter, very much impressed. "How did you manage that? Do you speak French?"

"Minored in it."

Sheila went on to tell him about the program and how studying in France had always been a dream of hers. She loved French culture and had jumped at the chance to apply for the program when she first learned of it from her advisor. As she spoke, Carter looked up and listened without interrupting, for he was rather enjoying himself. It was still quite astonishing to him that this Sheila and the one he thought he had known were one and the same. He would have been content to let her do all the talking, but after a time, she stopped and turned the conversation toward him. What, she wondered, were his plans for the immediate future? The question caused Carter some unease, and he stood there awkwardly for a moment before letting on that he was thinking about doing some traveling of his own around the same time as she was—perhaps to Italy.

Sheila smiled.

"Well, you know," she pointed out, "Italy and France are right next to each other." Then she gave a little laugh, and in it Carter heard the echoes of the little girl he once knew.

"What's the matter?" he said. "Why are you laughing?"

"I was just thinking," she said, "but wouldn't it be funny if after all these years of living next door without seeing one another that someday we met up in Europe?"

"I guess stranger things have happened," he mused. It *was* a funny thought. But just then he thought of Elena, and his cheeks went hot. As idle as the conversation might have been, he was suddenly deeply ashamed of himself for having let it distract his thoughts from their real purpose. He felt as though he had betrayed Elena in some way.

Perhaps sensing the sudden change in his mood, Sheila looked at him in an odd way before lifting her elbows off the porch railing and standing up straight.

"Well, it's getting late," she said, giving her arms a gentle stretch. "I guess I'd better be getting inside."

"Yeah, me, too," said Carter softly.

"I'll be home all summer," she told him. "Maybe we'll see each other again."

"Good night, Sheila," he said.

"Good night, Carter."

A short while later, Carter stood at his bedroom window, looking out at the house next door. As always, he was thinking about Elena, but then his thoughts turned to Sheila, and then to the two women in the bar, and then to the long, hot summer yet to come. Carter's life at the moment was nothing more than a bundle of unanswered questions. Of one thing, however, he was quite certain. The straight and narrow path he had pledged to tread on his way to Italy would be one fraught with peril.

CHAPTER 4

The annual party at the summer home of Henry Sheffield, dean of the college, was one that never failed to live up to Giancarlo's expectations, if for no other reason than his expectations for it were never exceedingly high. That this was so was in no way due to any shortcomings on the part of Sheffield or his wife, Amanda. Indeed the two were lively, gracious hosts, and their South County home, perched as it was on a little hill overlooking Narragansett Bay, was a lovely spot for the pre-solstice gathering. The inevitable clambake, catered by a firm out of Wickford, was, if one enjoyed steamers and lobster, always well done; the cocktails flowed easily; and the jazz trio usually engaged for the evening—a piano player, bass player, and drummer—kept spirits high without forcing the party-goers to converse in shouts over the music and into one another's ears. It was as convivial an affair as one might hope to attend.

For Giancarlo, however, the whole thing was something of an ordeal. Even though, in his heart, he truly liked most of those in attendance, by the time June rolled around each year, he had seen quite enough of his fellow faculty members and looked forward to a prolonged absence from the groves of academe to renew his fondness for their company. Giancarlo was also one of those people who never seem to acquire the knack for small talk, and he dreaded situations in which he was forced to make it. Doing so usually required more effort than he seemed able to muster, and he often came across as aloof simply because when he had nothing of particular interest to say, he preferred to leave things at that and say nothing. Nevertheless, despite his aversion to such affairs, Giancarlo felt obligated to show up at the Sheffields' house every year, the first Thursday after commencement, to do whatever he could to help celebrate the close of another academic year.

On this particular evening, as he often did at parties, Giancarlo stationed himself in a corner, in this case out on the veranda overlooking the bay, where he could watch the proceedings while maintaining his distance. He lingered there on the fringes by himself, content to sip his drink and nod an occasional hello to the other guests as they came to and from the lawn below. For the most part, though, he simply leaned against the railing and stared out at the darkening ocean, his eyes and thoughts fixed on some unspecified point far away on the horizon while he listened to the music. It was at such a moment that Patricia discovered him.

"Here you are, Giancarlo," she said, suddenly emerging from the crowd.

At the sound of her voice, Giancarlo straightened up and turned away from the railing to look at her. The contrast in her attire from when he had seen her the previous day out by the track was quite pronounced. Though still officially spring, it was a comfortably warm night, and Patricia was wearing a light summer dress, and wearing it exceedingly well. As she came over to him, Giancarlo could not help but notice how the fabric of the dress moved with her, accentuating the slender figure beneath in a very pleasant way.

"Ciao, Patrizia," he said.

"I was beginning to think that you decided not to show tonight," she said. "What are you doing, hiding out here all by yourself?"

"Watching," Giancarlo replied, nodding over his shoulder to the ocean, "and waiting."

"Watching and waiting for what?"

"There," said Giancarlo after a moment, pointing to the east, where a faint, thin glow had just appeared on the horizon.

"What is it, the moon?" said Patricia, gazing out with him.

"Yes," he said. "I love watching it rise, especially when it comes up over the ocean, the way the moonlight dances on the water as it gets higher and higher in the sky. It's quite magical."

Patricia turned her eyes to him and smiled. "My, I didn't think you were the type to notice such things," she said playfully.

"I notice a lot more than I let on," he replied.

"So, tell me," said Patricia. "What are your plans for the summer? Did you make up your mind yet about your prospective Italian student?"

"As a matter of fact I did," said Giancarlo. "I decided this afternoon that I would call him tomorrow and tell him no. I'm really just not in the mood for it right now."

"No? Oh, that's too bad," she said with a pout. "When you said that you were thinking it over yesterday, I was sure you were going to give him a chance. I was hoping you would." Then, with a mischievous gleam in her eye she added, "Maybe you'll reconsider. It would be a nice gesture to love, you know. Just think, what's to become of that poor young man now?"

Giancarlo was considering how best to reply when he saw their host walking across the veranda in their direction. A burly, jovial man, Henry Sheffield gave the two of them a warm smile as he drew close.

"Well, there you are at last, Giancarlo," said Sheffield, reaching out to shake his hand.

"*Benvenuto a casa nostra.* Did I say that correctly?"

"Perfectly," said Giancarlo with a little laugh. "But you still need to work a little more on your accent. You haven't quite gotten it yet."

Sheffield huffed and looked at Patricia with mock indignation. "You know, he tells me that all the time. It's really quite annoying." Then, turning back to Giancarlo, "But I'm glad I finally caught up with you before the evening got too late. I was telling Patricia just a few minutes ago that I saw you from across the yard when you first arrived at the house, but that I hadn't seen you since. Tell me, what's he been up to, my dear?"

"Moon watching," said Patricia, nodding out to the ocean.

"Ah, one of my favorite pastimes," said Sheffield, looking out to the horizon. "And it looks like tonight's show is just beginning."

Sure enough, the top edge of the moon had just nudged itself over the horizon, casting its soft orange glow across the sea. Sheffield stood there for a moment, staring out at the sight.

"You know, that's something I never get tired of watching," he said in a faraway voice. Then he smiled and looked back at Giancarlo. "So, *Professore*, will you play for us tonight?"

Giancarlo looked down at his drink. "Sorry, Henry," he replied softly. "I'm afraid not."

Clicking his tongue, Sheffield turned to Patricia and shook his head.

"Did you know," he told her, "that when he came to us twenty years ago, Giancarlo was without doubt the best piano player and the most talented composer anyone had ever seen here?"

"Yes, I have heard that," said Patricia, turning her gaze to Giancarlo, who was still contemplating his beverage.

"I used to always be able to count on him to play for us whenever we had a get-together," Sheffield went on. "It was wonderful, until one day—poof. He suddenly decided to stop playing in public. Now he won't even give piano lessons anymore—and I have to pay someone else to come and play at my parties."

"I know how you feel," said Patricia. "I once tried to get him to teach me to play, but he turned me down."

"I didn't actually turn you down," said Giancarlo, clearing his throat.

"Ha," scoffed Patricia. "You said 'perhaps some other time,' which for you means never."

"She has you on that one," said Sheffield, smiling at Giancarlo's obvious discomfiture.

"I think it's going to be a full moon tonight," said Giancarlo.

"Yes, I think you might be right," said Sheffield, taking the bait. "I'd love to stand here and watch it come up with you two, but I seem to have misplaced my drink, and I feel quite naked without it."

"I'll get you a new one," offered Patricia. "I need to powder my nose, anyway, so why don't you stay here and keep Giancarlo company until I get back."

"What a doll you are," said Sheffield. "A gin and tonic, please. And very easy on the tonic."

"Gin and gin it is," said Patricia over her shoulder.

"Patricia," Giancarlo suddenly called before she had gone far, for he had just then noticed something different about her.

She stopped and turned around.

"Did you cut your hair?" he asked.

Patricia cocked her head to one side, mocking his curious expression.

"So, he does have eyes after all," she huffed. She gave a sigh and shook her head. "Well, at least maybe that means there's hope for you yet, Giancarlo."

With that she turned and walked off into the crowd. Sheffield gave a little sigh as he watched her go.

"Now there goes one delightful creature," he said wistfully. He paused, and eyed Giancarlo for a moment before saying, "She's in love with you, you must know that. Anyone with eyes can see it."

"Oh, I'm sure you're mistaken about that," said Giancarlo uneasily.

"No, I'm not, my friend, and you know it as well as I," said Sheffield. "What's more, I know that you think well of her, too. What puzzles me is why you keep pushing her away. It worries me. What is it that keeps you from letting someone into your life? I've known you many years, but I still haven't been able to discern it. It must be a very heavy anchor you're carrying around inside you, whatever it is that holds you back."

Giancarlo shrugged and gave a sigh of his own.

"You know, it's not for lack of trying, but these things just don't seem to ever work out for me, Henry," he said. "People always end up getting hurt. I'm tired of it. What you said is true. I do like Patricia. But things will just end up like they always do, and she'll get hurt just like the others."

"You know, Giancarlo," said Sheffield kindly, "sometimes it hurts someone more to never at least be given the chance."

Giancarlo made no reply, but instead looked away, his eyes and mind inevitably drawn back across the shimmering bay to just above the horizon, where the full moon was now aglow, hovering there like a distant beacon.

CHAPTER 5

"Giancarlo!"

Awaking with a start, unsure of just what it was that had suddenly roused him from his sleep, Giancarlo opened his eyes and stared at the ceiling. His vision slowly adjusting to the dimness of the room, he rolled his head to one side and looked over to the window. There a thin band of morning sunlight was slipping through the tiny gap between the drawn curtains, stretching out like a cord to the side of the bed. The angle at which the light fell across the bedroom floor told him that it was well past dawn. The digital alarm clock on the bedside table glowed eight fifteen, confirming his assessment of the hour. He yawned, and stretched his legs beneath the blanket.

Up to that point, Giancarlo had been immersed in a rather curious dream about the ocean. In the dream he had been sitting on a beach by the water's edge, looking out at the windswept waves tumbling toward him. This in itself would not have been so strange except that he was sitting there at an upright piano, feverishly trying to think of a song to play as the waves crashed far out from shore. Before he could summon up a tune, the surf came rolling in with a great surge, washing over his feet as he tried to step on the piano pedals. As the water rushed back out, eroding the sand beneath him, the piano listed to one side and began to sink. Giancarlo heard a loud thump and looked up to the top of the piano, where a smiling Patricia, still wearing her party dress from the previous evening, was standing atop a surfboard. "Come on!" she was calling down to him. "You should really give this a try!"

It was just at that odd juncture that Giancarlo had suddenly awoken. Now, with the memory of the dream rushing away from his consciousness like the broken waves rushing back to the sea, he propped himself up on an elbow and cocked his ear toward the door, straining to hear. From out on the front stoop came the sound of voices followed by a series of loud knocks.

"Giancarlo!" someone called again.

Giancarlo recognized the man's voice as that of his cousin Anthony. His cousin's wife, Celeste, was no doubt with him. Giancarlo gave a groan, slid his legs out from beneath the covers, and set his feet on the floor. With another yawn he pulled on his robe and pushed his feet into his slippers.

"*Aspetta, mannaggia*—I'm coming!" he cried at hearing another series of knocks.

As expected, Giancarlo found Anthony and Celeste standing on the front step when he finally opened the door. The two were one of those annoyingly happy couples whose entire married life seemed to be one long, incessant, uninterrupted conversation, never a quiet, contemplative moment between them—or for anyone else who happened to be near. They had been jabbering away the whole time they waited for Giancarlo to come to the door. As soon as the obligatory good mornings and exclamations of relief that they had indeed found him at home were complete, the pair clamored into the front hall of Giancarlo's formerly tranquil domain.

"Giancarlo, *cosa fai*? What are you doing still in your pajamas?" exclaimed Anthony with a click of his tongue. "I thought you were always up at the crack of dawn."

"We were sure that by now you would have been up for hours with the coffee already made," Celeste chimed in before Giancarlo could respond. She held up a string-tied box. "See, we brought some goodies from the bakery to have with it."

A bit groggy, for he still had not completely shaken the sleep out of his head, and somewhat shellshocked by this early morning assault on his auditory senses, Giancarlo regarded the box with a vague expression. "That's very nice of you," he said to Celeste with a yawn. "But why are you here?"

Rolling her eyes, Celeste gave an exasperated huff and turned to her husband. "He didn't get our message," she said with a shake of her head. "I told you that was probably what happened."

"Of course he got our message!" cried Anthony. "I called three times. He just didn't listen to it. He never listens to his messages!"

This pronouncement led to a brief exchange between the two regarding the comparative merits of answering machines and voice mail, and the appropriateness for Giancarlo of a new digital answering machine as a Christmas gift come December. Unable to offer his own opinion on the matter—even if he had wanted to do so—Giancarlo stood there and watched in pained silence as the debate continued without him. When at last he could absorb no more of this particular line of discourse, he simply turned away and beckoned for them to follow.

"Things haven't changed much in here," observed a disapproving Celeste as they passed the untidy living room.

"Really," nodded Anthony. "The Rhode Island Philharmonic Orchestra could come and play here, with all the instruments he has laying around."

"They're performing here next week," said Giancarlo with as much sarcasm as he could muster in his drowsy state. "I'll get you tickets."

With that he trod on toward the kitchen. Once there, Celeste insisted that the two men sit at the table while she made the coffee for them. Giancarlo had no objection to being treated like a guest in his own house, so he pointed out where the coffeemaker and filters were to be found and settled into a chair across the table from his cousin

Celeste went to work, moving about the kitchen as if it were her own. Seeking mugs and a plate for the pastries, she opened one of the cabinets and peered inside. "What you need," she opined as she closed the cabinet and opened the one next to it, "is a good woman. Then you could get things in order around here, the way they should be."

"I kind of like things around here just the way they are," offered Giancarlo.

"That's because you've lived too long all by yourself," she said. "You don't know any better. Isn't that right, Anthony?"

"I dunno," her husband shrugged, giving Giancarlo a wink. "Sometimes living alone doesn't sound like such a bad idea."

"Ha!" his wife scoffed. "You wouldn't last a week without me."

"That's what women always say," Anthony sighed. "They think we're all babies."

Before Giancarlo could comment, the couple went off on a tangent about the virtues of matrimony over bachelorhood. Was it good for a man to live all alone for so long? Who would look after him when he got old? Where would he go? What would he do? There was nothing for Giancarlo to do but pretend to listen while he waited for the coffee to finish brewing.

"So, tell me," he said when a pause in the conversation mercifully offered itself to him. "What brings you two here today? And why was it necessary to start banging on my front door like you were trying to knock it down?"

"*Ayyy*, we rang the bell ten times and you still didn't answer," Anthony told him. "The car was in the driveway, so we knew you must be inside sleeping."

"Yes, and I might still have been," noted Giancarlo through yet another yawn. "I got home a little late last night."

"Out celebrating the end of school till all hours?" chuckled Anthony.

"Something like that," he replied, his thoughts drifting back to the party. Not that he was anyone's idea of a night owl, but Giancarlo truly had stayed out quite a bit later than the sensible hour at which he normally retired to bed. When the jazz trio quit playing and the caterer began to clean up, Giancarlo thanked the Sheffields and filed out with the other guests, intending to head straight home. It was Patricia who had, with no small amount of good-natured pleading, coaxed him into tagging along with some of their colleagues who were planning to stop at an all-night diner to re-hash the party over a quick cup of coffee before heading their sep-arate ways. There is no such thing as a quick cup of coffee when a group of academics, especially those returning from a soiree at the dean's residence, sits down to gab. To no one's surprise, least of all Giancarlo's, the waitress was called upon more than once to refill their cups as the hour grew later and the conversation louder and more boisterous. Despite Patricia's best efforts to keep him en-gaged in the confab, Giancarlo inevitably found his attention flag-ging, his eyelids growing heavy. When at last he could no longer keep up a good face, he abruptly stood, bid everyone a good night and a good summer, and headed out to his car. Patricia followed him out and, after extracting a promise from him to keep in touch during the weeks ahead, gave him a quick, awkwardly accepted kiss on the cheek. "See you in September, Giancarlo," she had told him, a hint of sadness in her voice. Then she turned quickly away and hurried back to rejoin the others. Left alone in the darkness, he had wearily climbed into his car and driven home, filled all the while with a strange sense of loss that he could not quite compre-hend.

Now, sitting at the table, the rousing aroma of the coffee just starting to waft through the air, Giancarlo passed a hand over his stubbled cheek and looked over to Celeste, who had found the right-size plate and was just opening the box of pastries.

"So, what did you bring from the bakery?" he asked her, nod-ding at the box.

"Eh, just some biscotti, a couple of cannoli, and some sfogli-atelle," she said, laying each of the pastries onto the plate before setting it on the table. "You two help yourselves," she told them. "The coffee will be ready in a minute."

Anthony gave a nod to his cousin, who in turn gestured for him to help himself first. Anthony selected a cannoli, while Gian-carlo opted for one of the sfogliatelle, a shell-shaped puff pastry filled with ricotta. Before long the coffee was poured, and Celeste joined them at the table.

"So, tell Giancarlo about our trip," she said, taking one of the biscotti and dunking it into her coffee.

"You two have been traveling?" said Giancarlo.

"That's why we're here," said Anthony. "We just got back from Italy last week."

"What a nice trip we had," sighed Celeste. "Rome, Capri, Sorrento, and then up to Perugia and Florence. We went all over before going to Abruzzo."

"Ah, Abruzzo," said Giancarlo matter-of-factly. "I guess it really *was* quite a trip."

"Yes, we spent a few days in the *paes'*," Anthony added hurriedly at seeing the drawbridges of disinterest go up in Giancarlo's eyes. He paused, and gazed at his cousin, hoping perhaps to see if this particular pronouncement would stir some emotion in him, some inclination not to retreat into himself, as he always did whenever the subject of his hometown arose. If it had such an effect, Giancarlo's faraway expression did not betray it, and a rare but awkward silence fell over the three.

At last Celeste reached out to Giancarlo and patted his hand. "They were all asking for you, you know," she said in a gentle voice.

Giancarlo gave a shrug and looked down at his mug. "They always do," he said before taking a sip.

"Yes, they do," said Anthony thoughtfully before adding, "And that reminds me . . ." He reached into his jacket pocket and withdrew a small package, the size of a paperback book, wrapped in brown paper and tape. "I was asked to give this to you," he said, sliding it over to Giancarlo.

Giancarlo turned the package over in his hands, judging the heft of its well-padded contents, before putting it aside.

"Don't you want to open it?" said Celeste eagerly.

"Perhaps later," said Giancarlo. "For the moment I'd prefer another piece of pastry." He reached to the plate and took one of the biscotti.

Celeste cast a questioning glance at her husband. The latter simply shrugged, and nothing further on the subject of the package was said.

"So tell me," said Giancarlo, forcing a smile for their benefit. "Where else in *L'Italia* did you two travel?"

Later, after his two visitors had gone on their way, Giancarlo showered and dressed, intending to go about his business the rest of the day. There were in the house a number of long-neglected plumbing and repair issues crying for his attention, and Giancarlo had decided some time ago to devote the beginning of his summer vacation to addressing them. Not that he was at all handy when it came to this particular line of endeavor. To the contrary, he knew next to nothing when it came to home repairs. His plan for the start of that day had been to peruse the yellow pages for a contractor to handle these chores for him.

Although he tried his utmost to focus himself on the pressing needs of his domicile, Giancarlo found his thoughts inexorably drawn to the kitchen and to the small package still resting unopened on the table. It seemed that no matter where he went in the house, he felt its tug, and he passed the morning in a state of distraction. By midday it was clear to him that there was no point in trying to ignore the inevitable, so he sat down at last at the table and ripped open the package.

Inside, carefully tucked within thick layers of packing material, Giancarlo found a familiar cloth pouch. He held it for a moment, considering its soft, slightly frayed material before loosening the cord that held it closed. He turned the pouch over, and out into his hand slid the pocket watch he knew he would find inside. Giancarlo sat there for a time, brooding over the timepiece, running his fingers over its gold cover, etched with a delicate design. He opened the watch and regarded the face, which displayed a young couple standing by a horse drinking from a well. Once upon a time, when the watch was in working order and was wound properly, it would play a tune while the man bowed to the woman and the horse dipped its head to the water. A turn of the knob on top produced no such result, confirming his suspicion that the watch was still broken, as it had been for many years.

Giancarlo heaved a heavy sigh and lay the watch back down on the table. He stood and went to the window. There he stayed for quite some time, staring blankly off into the distance, turning things over and over in his mind, his thoughts racing back and forth across the vast ocean that separated the continents. When at last he brought his ruminations home to a conclusion, an idea came to him, and he realized that there was at last a possible solution to what was vexing him. His mind made up, he went to his study and retrieved from his satchel the piece of paper on which was scrawled the phone number he sought. He picked up the phone, dialed the number, and waited until the recorded message of the answering machine he had reached finished.

"Mister Carter," he said when he heard the beep. "This is Giancarlo Rosa. I'm calling to see if you are still interested in Italian lessons."

CHAPTER 6

The position of construction laborer was not one Carter Quinn had ever envisioned as a serious career option during his four years of college study. He liked to think that despite his less-than-inspired efforts in the academic realm, he was meant for something greater than stacking sheets of plywood, lugging about heavy equipment from place to place at a work site, and sweeping bent nails and other debris from sawdust-covered floors. Nonetheless, such was the description of the duties he was called upon to perform that Monday morning working for R & D Home Construction, his first post-graduation employer. Ron and Dave, the two principals of the little firm—and the only other workers—took on Carter in spite of his lack of carpentry skills, or more likely because of it. His educational background in finance, as impressive as it might have looked on a résumé, was of no value whatsoever to them. What they needed was a sturdy, reasonably intelligent man with two good arms and a strong back, one who didn't mind hard, simple work and who would follow instructions without complaint.

In this last regard, they could not have hoped to find a more suitable candidate than Carter. Construction, the young man quickly discovered that first morning on the job, especially for someone in so lowly a position as his, could be grueling, spine-warping, mind-numbing labor. There seemed no end to the calls for him to move this stack of boards from that place to another, or to cart that pile of gravel away from the foundation, or to clean up that area in the back right away. From the moment he set foot on the property to start work in the morning till the moment he walked off it at the end of the day, Carter Quinn worked harder and shed more sweat for a day's pay than he ever had in his entire life.

Still, despite the long, arduous hours, Carter went about his duties with as light a heart as any man walking. There was something about this line of employment that, for the time being at least, suited him just fine. Yes, the work was hard, the hours long, and the pay only middling, but at least he was toiling away outdoors in the open air beneath the brilliant sunshine. He was not confined in some cubicle, chained to a desk, staring at a computer monitor, a small cog in some corporate machine, never seeing any tangible result for his efforts other than a paycheck at the end of the week. Though some, like his friend Jimmy, might have looked upon his labors as ignoble and unbefitting one who had spent his formative years preparing for a more prestigious career, it was honest, straightforward work with rewards of its own. For one, Carter was an athlete and he liked being part of a team working toward a simple though not easily attained goal, in this case the construction of a two-story house. For another, there was, at the end of the day, no question about what he had been a part of or what had or had not been accomplished. The fruits of his labors and those of his bosses were there to be seen in plain view. It was an immensely satisfying feeling, and Carter reveled in it. Of primary importance to him, however, was that this job had the very great virtue of being one from which he could, with easy conscience, walk away in three months' time.

And so it was that Carter had gone cheerfully about his duties that day, his thoughts inevitably drifting to Elena and his soon-to-come encounter with the Italian language. The call from Professor Rosa that previous Friday afternoon had left him in searingly good spirits, which carried him through the weekend and that first day on the job. Upon hearing the professor's message on his answering machine, Carter had of course immediately called him back. When at last they spoke, Rosa had made it clear that he was not one to waste his time, and so he had made Carter a simple offer: They would meet at the professor's home on Monday evening after work for a single lesson, a test of sorts. If things went well enough, they would make arrangements for the continuance of his studies. If not, then all bets were off. Rosa was, in effect, giving Carter one single chance. This proposal was more than acceptable to Carter, for a chance was the only thing he was asking for.

Upon returning home after such a first day of work as the one Carter experienced, a less-fit individual would most likely have collapsed in exhaustion onto the couch the moment he stepped into the house. Carter, to the contrary, bounded up the stairs on seemingly fresh legs. He stripped and jumped into the shower, the day's exertions already a distant memory by the time he washed himself of the dirt and grime. His appointment with Professor Rosa was scheduled for six o'clock, and Carter already knew better than to dare arrive late. When he was finished showering, he threw open the curtain and grabbed a towel. Running it frantically across his head and body, he hurried into the bedroom to get dressed. Within a mere few minutes, he was bounding back down the stairs and out to the car.

Despite driving the whole way with the windows wide open, Carter's hair was still damp and matted when he pulled up to the house at the address Professor Rosa had given him. It was, he saw, a small, unassuming home, simply landscaped with a brick walkway leading across a neatly trimmed lawn to the front doorstep, which was flanked by two well-pruned shrubs. As he made his way up the walkway, Carter heard the sound of a piano playing inside. Oddly repetitive, what he heard was not the melody of any particular song that he could recognize, but there was something hypnotic about it nonetheless. When he reached the front step, he paused, and listened to the intricate music. So precise and error-free was the playing that he could not be quite certain as to whether he was listening to a live performance or a recording. Whichever was the case, the music abruptly stopped the instant he pressed the button and the doorbell inside chimed. A few moments later, the front door swung open.

"*Buona sera*, Signor Carter," the professor greeted him, gesturing for Carter to come inside.

Carter had been quite anxious about making good at this first lesson. Still, he could not suppress a smile as he came into the house. "It's Quinn," he reminded Rosa. "Carter Quinn."

"Ah, *scusami*, Signor Quinn, Carter Quinn," the professor replied, the slight gleam in his eye letting the younger man know he had said this in jest so as to break the ice a little. He nodded at Carter's damp head. "Has it been raining?" he asked.

"Just got out of the shower," Carter explained.

"Good," said Rosa. "Hopefully that means that you come to me a *tabula rasa*."

"I'm sorry?" said Carter.

"A clean slate," Rosa explained. "That is always the best way to begin something new." Then he gestured for Carter to follow and led him into the living room.

Carter let his eyes roam about the room as he walked in, his gaze taking in the bookshelves lining the walls, the musical instruments tucked all about, and of course the piano at the heart of it all. He lowered himself into the upholstered chair by the coffee table, noting while he did so the ornate globe behind the couch adjacent to the chair. Flanking the globe were two statuettes, miniatures of famous pieces of sculpture, one of which Carter thought he recognized, but only vaguely. It was of a young man with a slingshot draped over his shoulder; the other statuette was of a woman playing a harp. There were, he saw, a few other such pieces here and there on the bookshelves around the room, as well as a pair of paintings, both mountain landscapes that Carter took to be scenes of Italy. All in all, looking about at his surroundings, the room had to him the aura of a very small museum or some ancient library or perhaps the study of a philosopher from a bygone age.

"Saint Cecilia," said Professor Rosa, nodding to the statuette of the woman playing the harp as he installed himself on the couch across from Carter. "The patron saint of music. The other of course is David."

"I think I've seen that one before," mused Carter. "But I'm not sure where."

"I'm sure you have seen an image of it at one time or another," said the professor with a certain air of pride in his voice as he cleared a space on the coffee table between them. Then, suddenly quite animated, speaking with fierce conviction, he went on, "Or at least I certainly *hope* you have. If you don't know it already, the influence of Italy and Italians is everywhere in our world, in every field you can imagine. That statue is only one example. You name it: Art, literature, science, architecture, music, politics, religion, sports. There is nothing that Italian culture has not touched in some significant way. Forget the Sopranos and the Corleones and all those other misbegotten notions of what some people in this country have come to think of as Italians. Yes, those types of people exist, but they are aberrations, no more indicative of all Italians any more than sharks are indicative of all fish. Italians all over the world are heirs to a rich, beautiful culture that has given the world the likes of Giotto, da Vinci, Michelangelo, Dante, Boccaccio, Machiavelli, Galileo, Marconi, Fermi, Caruso, Fellini, Pavarotti, Sophia Loren. The list goes on and on and on!"

"And I thought all they gave us was pizza and pasta," quipped Carter.

"Ha, don't laugh," said Rosa, wagging a finger at him. "Just think, where would this world be without Italian cooking?"

"I don't know," Carter chuckled. "I'm pretty much a meat-and-potatoes guy myself."

"That will change when you go to Italy," the professor assured him, then added, "But to first things first. Your desire to know the language."

At this Rosa sat back, rubbed his chin, and eyed Carter thoughtfully. Up to that point, Carter had been rather enjoying the exposition on the virtues of Italian culture. It had put him at ease. This sudden silence, however, unsettled him, and he felt the butterflies flocking in the pit of his stomach once more.

"Tell me," Rosa finally said. "Have you ever studied another language?"

"In high school," said Carter. "I took a few years of Spanish."

"I see. And how did you fare?"

"Not all that great," admitted Carter, sensing that candor in this matter would work more in his favor.

"I'm not surprised," said Rosa. "I suppose you learned by memorizing lists of vocabulary words and studying over and over again the conjugation of verbs."

"How else is there to do it?" Carter asked.

"Ah, a good question," said the professor, holding up a finger. "Do you remember that clean slate I mentioned before? For starters, that is what you need more than anything else. Think about it. If you wish to study a language, you must forget everything you have learned. You must become a child again, with a child's clear mind, no preconceived notions of anything." Rosa leaned forward and tapped the cover of a book on the table. "And so, when I point to this and say *libro*, I need for you to think *libro*, nothing more or less, just as a child would. You must take it to heart, believe it with all your might. I don't want you to sit there thinking, Ah yes, *libro*—that must mean 'book.'" He pointed to the chair. "*Sedia*." To the table. "*Tavolo*." To the window. "*Finestra*. You must forget that you know the names of these things, and relearn them all over again. You must let me guide you through the language, step by step, piece by piece, just like a parent guides a child. This is essential, for if you cannot be led, I cannot teach you. Do you understand?"

Carter swallowed hard. It was beginning to dawn on him that his foray into the Italian language might be a more rigorous undertaking than he had first envisioned. For a fleeting moment he questioned whether he would be equal to the task. Just as quickly, he thought of Elena, and all doubts flew away, for he knew that he had to try. And so, taking a deep breath, he nodded yes.

"*Va bene*," said the professor, nodding solemnly in return. "In that case, let us begin, Carter Quinn, and see just how much you can be taught."

CHAPTER 7

"So, what do you think?" said a hopeful Carter.

They were still in the living room. An hour had passed, completing the time allotted for this qualifying exam of sorts. Now the young man was anxious to hear the verdict—and Giancarlo was quite ready to render it. All the same, Giancarlo did not reply right away, but instead sat there for a time, pensively tapping a pencil against the pad on which he had been taking notes from time to time during the session.

"Tell me again," he finally said, holding the pencil still for a moment. "How many years of Spanish did you say you took in high school?"

"Three," Carter answered. His eyes showing concern, he cast a worried glance at the notepad.

"I see," said Giancarlo, scrutinizing the young man with a narrowed gaze while he scribbled another note. "And what kind of grades did you achieve?"

"C's, mostly," Carter admitted with a nervous shrug. "Honestly, I don't think I learned all that much." Sensing, perhaps, that his first performance in Italian had also not been quite up to standards, he began to look a bit crestfallen.

"Hmm," grunted Giancarlo, tapping away once more with the pencil, only now against the tip of his nose, something he often did when slipping deep into thought. Then, settling back as he turned things over in his mind, he fell silent again for a few moments.

"Very interesting," he finally said under his breath, more to himself than to Carter.

Carter slouched back in his own chair and squirreled up the side of his mouth in an expression that conveyed deep disappointment. "That bad?" he said, glumly.

Giancarlo gave a little laugh and tossed the pencil onto the table. "Oh no," he answered with a shake of his head. "It was not bad at all. Actually, you did quite well—better than I had expected."

"Better than expected" was something of an understatement, and Giancarlo well knew it as he replayed in his mind the hour of teaching just passed. He had begun, as always with a new student, by touching his ear and telling Carter, "*Ascolta!*" (to listen). Without speaking a word of English, he proceeded to point out various objects in the room, naming them in Italian as he went. *Libro, tavolo, quadro, porta, penna, carta,* and so forth. He named them again, this time telling Carter, "*Ripeta!*" and gesturing for him to repeat what he had heard. It was a very simple exercise, but an essential one, as it would form the foundation upon which he would lay the future bricks of the language when and if he continued to teach the young man.

It did not take very long to erase any doubts Giancarlo might have had in this regard. As the lesson progressed, he gradually introduced the definite and indefinite articles, to see if Carter would grasp the difference between *il libro* and *un libro (the* book and *a* book). He did so with little effort, allowing the professor to eventually move on to the demonstrative pronouns, *questa* (this) and *quella* (that). It wasn't long before Giancarlo, instead of pointing to an object, simply asked in Italian what this or that was, and Carter would respond accordingly. Now and then he would struggle and stumble over the words, but eventually he would also correct himself with little prompting.

And so it was that the two had raced along through that introductory lesson, from one set of basic words and phrases to another, pausing only occasionally for a moment of rest or perhaps for a sip of water. From the outset, Carter had followed his teacher's lead, watching and listening with eager, wide-eyed intensity, his attention never wavering. When called upon to speak, he did so without hesitation. His pronunciation was not always perfect—at this point pronunciation was not a great concern—but he displayed remarkable recall and readily repeated every word that he had heard. He questioned nothing, but simply tried to absorb everything his teacher sought to convey. Giancarlo might have called it by a different name, but he recognized right away that Carter possessed one essential quality, one just as important as innate ability.

He was coachable.

"Better than expected," said Carter, suddenly quite buoyant. "That's good, right? I mean, you'll let me come back, won't you?"

Giancarlo considered the question for a moment before saying, "That depends."

"On what?"

"On you," said Giancarlo, aiming the pencil in the young man's direction. "Yes, you certainly seem well able to learn, but ability is not everything. Are you committed to doing this? That's what I need to know. Do you have the discipline, the motivation? This is no easy undertaking you're contemplating here. What you want to accomplish will be exceedingly difficult. To learn enough of a foreign language in such a short time, and then to fly across the ocean and not make a spectacular fool out of yourself in front of that young woman? This is going to take as much effort as or more than any you've ever given to sports to prepare yourself."

Carter leaned forward and looked him squarely in the eyes. "Tell me what I have to do."

"What you must do for the next three months," said Giancarlo, "is eat and drink and sleep the Italian language. For starters, one lesson per week is not nearly enough. I recommend three—no less."

"Done," said Carter without hesitation. "What else?'

"You must immerse yourself in the language at every opportunity when you're not here," Giancarlo told him. "The more you hear it spoken, the more you try to speak it yourself, the more it will register in your brain, even if at first you don't comprehend what is being said. This will require dedication and discipline and a little imagination. I have some tapes I can give you, some books to look at, but you must also look elsewhere, perhaps at the library. See what they have. Language tapes, Italian movies, music, whatever, it doesn't matter, just so long as they are speaking Italian. As a child you learned English because every corner of your world was saturated with it. If you want to learn Italian, you'll have to do the very same thing. Can you do all this?"

"I don't know," Carter confessed after a moment's pause. "I really don't. But I know that I have to try. And I will give it my best, everything that I have. I can promise you that."

Giancarlo sat back and folded his arms. "In that case, Quinn, Carter Quinn, I suppose I have no choice but to take you at your word."

Carter smiled. "So, what comes next?" he said.

"You come back on Wednesday," said Giancarlo. "And then we will begin."

CHAPTER 8

Carter dug his toes into the sand and gazed out at the ocean. It was a warm, lazy Sunday, and he was sitting alone on Narragansett Beach. He wouldn't be alone for long, of that he felt reasonably certain. This being Rhode Island, it was inevitable that he would, at some point that afternoon, encounter at least one friend or acquaintance strolling by along the shore. Rhode Islanders loved the ocean, and Narragansett Beach was a port of call when summer came. It was not quite officially summer, of course—the solstice was still a week away—but you could not tell that to the beachgoers who had flocked to the shore that day to soak up the sunshine. It had been a cool, damp spring, as springs generally were in southern New England, and the advent of some warm, dry weather was all it took to lure people to the beach.

At this date in June, the water was still quite chilly. Now and then a brave soul would sprint across the sand and take a quick plunge into the bracing surf. Those who did so rarely stayed in the water for long. More often than not, they popped up out of the waves, emerging with eyes and mouths wide open from the shock of immersion, and retreated with great haste to their beach blankets to find the warmth of a dry towel. Save for a few toddlers who seemed to love frolicking at the shore's edge regardless of the water temperature, only the surfers took to the waves for any length of time, and then only when arrayed in their neoprene wet suits.

Carter yawned as he watched the surfers bobbing up and

down on their boards just out past where the waves were breaking. His first week as a construction laborer had left him more than a bit worn. Added to that, he had stayed out quite late the night before, enjoying a few libations with friends on the deck of the Coast Guard House, a local nightclub perched atop a rocky point jutting out into the bay. Carter had gone there alone, but soon bumped into several old teammates from his high school football team. The lot of them had taken turns at the bar, buying rounds for one another, talking and laughing the night away, while occasionally pausing in their revelry to flirt with the young women squeezing by through the crowd. It had been a pleasant evening out, one that stretched well past midnight before Carter finally bade his friends good night and made his way home to his family's little beach house a few miles down the road.

Now, sitting there on the beach, Carter turned his gaze away from the surfers and scanned the crowd around him. Looking about at the people reclining on the sand, he recognized some of his fellow patrons at the bar from the night before. He chuckled to himself, for there were many, he was sure, who were still feeling the ill effects of staying out too late and drinking far too much. Carter breathed deeply and gave a contented sigh. He loved the beach. The air thick with the salty scent of the sea. The incessant roar of the waves tumbling to the shore. The touch of the ocean breeze, and the feel of the warm sand on his feet. He loved staring out across the bay, watching the sailboats and ships come and go. And his eye, of course, was invariably drawn to the females, the way they ambled by so smoothly, almost in rhythm, smiling from behind their dark sunglasses. He could not help but watch them as they padded across the sand and stretched out on their blankets or beach chairs in the most delightful way, their well-lotioned skin glistening in the sun, their faces turned upward to receive its warmth. Looking at them made him think of Elena, and he wondered if, perhaps, somewhere across the great expanse of sea, she was sitting on a beach, as well, enjoying the same brilliant sunshine. Then it occurred to him that Italy was six hours ahead of the

United States. Her day would just be coming to an end. Carter imagined her pulling on a skirt over her swimsuit, tossing a beach bag over her shoulder, and walking away barefoot as the sun slipped toward the horizon. The thought of her brought a smile to his face.

Thinking of Elena reminded him of his Italian studies in general and his first week of lessons in particular. Things had not gone quite as he had anticipated. When he'd first contemplated the study of the Italian language with a private tutor, Carter had no preconceived idea of what type of experience he should expect, just a vague notion that it ought to be a lighthearted, pleasurable undertaking. He knew next to nothing about Italy, or Italians, but the thought of it and them conjured up in his imagination enticing visions of wine, red and delicious; of pasta and cheese and olives and bread; of gondolas slipping along beneath moonlit skies; of violins and accordions; and of course of romance. When he thought of Italy, he thought of Elena, and so could only marvel at what type of country it must be that it could produce such a beautiful creation as she. Thinking of being there with her made him happy, so it stood to reason that studying her language, the thing that would bring them together, would make him happy, as well.

The weaknesses in this line of syllogistic thought had become quite evident early on that previous Wednesday evening after he had sat down to begin his first official lesson with Giancarlo Rosa. The professor quickly disabused him of any notion that this course of study was going to be a pleasure cruise of any sort. If anything, it was more to the contrary.

It was all business.

Carter had arrived on time, just barely, after a long hard day of construction work. He was tired and hungry, but excited nonetheless, to finally be starting his preparation for the journey to come in three months' time. During the forty-eight hours since he had last come to the house, Carter had faithfully listened to the Italian language cassette Rosa had lent him, playing it over and over again, repeating the words and phrases as prompted. He listened to the tape when he awoke in the morning. He listened again during his lunch break, later after dinner, and again in bed just before he dozed off for the night. True, he had yet to make a trip to the library or video store to track down some Italian movies or other media, as Rosa had suggested, but still he felt as well prepared for the lesson as one could reasonably expect.

Rosa had greeted him cordially enough when he showed up at the door. He ushered him into the living room, where the two sat across from one another at the coffee table. Even though he had never before taken private language lessons of any type, it struck Carter as a bit odd to find only a pad and a pencil on the table. For some reason he had expected something more elaborate now that the professor had taken him on as a student: a book, a dictionary, perhaps some pictures with Italian labels under various objects. Something. Considering the cost of the lessons—and it was considerable—he had expected a few bells and whistles to go with the show. He would come to learn, however, that there was great virtue to be found in simplicity, and that what he was paying for was not a show. It was the real thing.

"Remember what I told you," Rosa had instructed him with great gravity before they got started. "When you sit in that chair, you must become like a child again, and learn as a child would learn. You understand, yes? Very well. Now, *ascolta!*"

And so the lesson had begun.

At first they had spent a short while reviewing the words and basic phrases Carter had learned two days earlier. Before long Rosa moved on, introducing him to new words, the names of other objects around the room, and in particular the verbs *essere* (to be) and *avere* (to have). Carter focused with all his might, listening to every word, struggling to keep his mind from wandering, for Rosa demanded concentration every moment. He was like a coach, constantly pushing, cajoling, bullying, anything to keep his athlete motivated and moving in the right direction. Now and then the professor would grow impatient, waiting for a response, and Carter very quickly grew accustomed to the sight of him rapping his pencil against the pad with one hand while gesturing with the other for him to *"ripeta, ripeta!"*

Although he had at times felt a bit overwhelmed, Carter could not help feeling that things had, for the most part, gone fairly well that first lesson. They had moved steadily along—that was, at least, until they came to the personal pronouns. Carter readily grasped *io* (I) and *tu* (you), but for some reason, perhaps fatigue and the gnaw of hunger in the pit of his stomach, the third person threw him. From beneath the coffee table, Rosa had produced a page with black and white drawings of people in various situations. One depicted some children waiting for a school bus; another showed a gentleman and a lady sitting at a café; a third, a police officer directing traffic. He kept pointing to the men and boys, saying *"lui"* this or *"lui"* that. Carter did his best to understand, but he was confused, and he found himself wondering, Who's Louie? Which one is he? At last he shook his head and asked, *"Chi è Louie?"* (Who is Louie?)

Rosa, of course, heard, *"Chi è lui?"* (Who is he?) He persisted in pointing to the various pictures, saying in Italian, "He is a policeman. He is a husband. He is a boy." Meantime, Carter persisted in not understanding, and his professor grew visibly agitated. For the next several minutes they went back and forth, confusing *lui* and *Louie,* the two of them sounding for all the world like Abbott and Costello doing their "Who's on First?" routine. This went on for quite some time, until a puzzled Rosa finally stopped and gaped in exasperation at his student. Then, unexpectedly, his expression changed to one of bemusement as it dawned on him just what the trouble had been. He looked to be on the verge of bursting out in laughter, but instead he simply gave a little smile and, departing from his method, explained in English that *lui* meant *he,* not the name Louie, thus breaking the logjam.

Carter's ego was one not easily bruised, but his face had reddened as the long-delayed understanding of this obvious trifle dawned on him.

"No, you mustn't be embarrassed!" Rosa had admonished him

on noting Carter's pained expression. "The greatest mistake one can make, particularly when trying to speak a new language, is to be *afraid* to make a mistake. Don't worry about it when you do. Take it with good humor. Trust me, it is far from the end of the world. You will discover, in fact, that people generally find it quite charming when a foreigner makes an honest effort to speak in their native tongue and trips up now and then while doing it. Italians, in particular, will love you all the more for it."

Rosa's words bolstered his pupil's shaken self-confidence to some degree, and after a brief pause for both to catch their breath, the lesson had continued. Now, though, as he sat there on the beach recalling the incident, Carter felt his face flush again ever so slightly. He was not a perfectionist by anyone's definition, but he was extremely competitive when it came to anything to which he committed himself. He hated looking bad, and the sting of the memory was enough to prod him to work all the harder, to ensure that it didn't happen again anytime soon. With that thought in mind, he reached for his cassette player and headphones to listen to the next in the series of Italian tapes Rosa had lent him. It was just then, as he was about to pull on the headphones, that he saw Jimmy, beach bag and chair under his arm, parading down the beach in his direction.

"Ugh, I should have known," Carter moaned in jest when his friend unceremoniously walked up and dropped his chair and bag beside him in the sand. "Just when I was beginning to enjoy being alone."

"C.Q., what's the matter?" replied Jimmy. "I just drove all the way down here from Providence. You're not happy to see me?"

"Does it matter?"

"No," said Jimmy, shaking his head. He turned and looked longingly about at the many young women sunbathing nearby. "Just look at this scenery," he said in delight. "You have definitely scored a prime spot here. It would be rude of you not to share it with a friend."

"Well, if you're gonna stay, why don't you at least sit down and stop staring at everybody before you embarrass me," suggested Carter.

"With pleasure," said Jimmy. He unfolded his chair and sat down, his head turning back and forth, as if he could not decide where to look first. He stopped just long enough to notice Carter fumbling with the cassette player. "What's that you're listening to?" he asked.

"My Italian tapes," said Carter. "They help me learn."

"So you're sticking with the Italian lessons and your plans to go to Italy, eh?" chuckled Jimmy.

"Uh-huh," grunted Carter with a nod.

"So tell me, how's it going?" asked Jimmy. "You learn how to say anything good yet, like, I don't know, maybe something like, 'your place or mine'?"

Carter laughed and gave a shrug. "I'm getting there," he said. "Takes time, you know."

"Yeah, sure. And what about this professor? What's his deal?"

"He's all right," said Carter, "but I gotta tell ya, it's like spending an hour and a half with Henry Higgins three times a week, if you know what I mean."

"Henry who?" replied Jimmy, evidently not knowing exactly what he had meant.

"Never mind," chuckled Carter. "Why don't you just go back to staring at the scenery, and let me listen to my tape?"

With that Carter pulled on the headphones and gazed out at the water, where a small boy was having the time of his life chasing the waves as they slipped back to the ocean before rolling once more toward the shore, chasing him back the other way. Carter smiled at the sight and closed his eyes. Then, imagining himself to be a child again, he reached for the cassette player and pushed the PLAY button.

CHAPTER 9

Giancarlo loosened the cord of the cloth pouch and let the pocket watch slide out into the palm of his hand. He sat there for a time at the kitchen table holding the watch up to the light, studying the delicate design of its exterior before opening the cover to examine the interior. Though he tried to forget about the presence of the timepiece in his house as he came and went from day to day, he nonetheless often found himself brooding over it, as he was doing now. At the moment, he was reflecting on his decision to take on Carter as a pupil. Giancarlo had reasons of his own for making this choice. As he turned the matter over in his mind, however, it occurred to him that his initial motivation in continuing the lessons had, at least in part, been replaced by something else.

Curiosity.

The truth of the matter was that Giancarlo simply did not know what to make of his new pupil. To be sure, Carter was not the first highly motivated student to come his way, and certainly not the only one to pursue his study of the language with enthusiasm and dedication. Indeed, the same could be said of virtually all the people Giancarlo had ever taught. He demanded it as a prerequisite above all others before he even considered taking on someone new. What intrigued him about Carter was the rapidity with which he seemed to learn. He had covered more ground in his first week of lessons than most students achieved in a month or more. It was uncanny. They flew from one lesson to the next, rarely needing to cover the same material twice. Giancarlo would have liked to flatter himself by crediting his teaching skill with this result, but he knew better. Whatever his academic abilities might have been in other subjects, Carter was obviously gifted with a distinct ear for language.

Ironically, it was a gift that Carter did not seem to realize he possessed—and one of which Giancarlo was hesitant to apprise him. There was an earnest modesty in the way the young man approached his lessons that Giancarlo believed served him well. Taking nothing for granted, he came to every session well prepared and eager to work and learn. Giancarlo could not have known it, but these were the very same traits Carter had always displayed as an athlete and the reasons he had made the most of his God-given talents on the playing fields. Just as his former coaches had once taught him to stretch and push his body to achieve its greatest potential, Giancarlo was now teaching him to stretch and push his mind. And Carter, he realized, was a young man who did not mind being pushed to his limits. To the contrary, he seemed to relish it. In short, he was tough.

In light of this toughness, Giancarlo had taken a sterner, more unforgiving approach with Carter than he might have used with another pupil, for he wanted him to make the most of his abilities. And so he pressured and prodded him, demanding nothing less than complete concentration from the start of each lesson to its finish. He eased off only when they hit the occasional snag (like the *lui* incident). Lest Carter become discouraged from his teacher's constant haranguing, he sprinkled in just enough praise to bolster his confidence without letting him become cocky. The results to this point had been astonishing. But how far, Giancarlo wondered, could he push him?

Giancarlo tucked the watch back into its pouch and, leaving it there, got up from the table. He went to the living room and parted the curtain. It was just after six o'clock and still Carter had not arrived. This irked Giancarlo somewhat, not so much because he himself was punctual to a fault, but more so because he was simply eager to get started. Contrary to his prior expectations, he was actually quite enjoying these lessons. Not knowing how else to channel his growing agitation from waiting, he went to the piano and began to play his scales.

It wasn't long after that the doorbell finally rang. When Giancarlo opened the door, he found an apologetic Carter standing out on the front step, a white paper bag in his hand.

"Mi dispiace il ritardo, Professore," said Carter, expressing regret for his late arrival. He stepped inside and held up the bag before adding in explanation, *"Ma ho molto fame.* I'm really hungry, so I had to stop and get something."

At hearing this, Giancarlo became very much annoyed with himself. He ought to have understood from the start that the young man would be hurrying to each lesson after work, tired and hungry, barely a moment for something to eat. Too many years of solitary living had eroded his social graces, and so it had never occurred to him to have on offer at least a little something to sustain his student throughout the session.

"Entra, entra," replied Giancarlo, waving him in. "Go sit, and I will bring you something to drink with it."

When he returned from the kitchen with a carafe of water and a glass, Giancarlo found Carter standing at the piano, leaning over the bench to look at the sheet music on the music stand.

" 'Sonata in A by Giancarlo Rosa,' " he read aloud, sounding most impressed. "I heard the piano when I came to the door. Is this what you were playing?"

"No," replied Giancarlo uneasily, setting the carafe and glass on the coffee table. He went to the piano and reached for the music. "What you heard were just exercises," he said, folding the pages shut. He tossed them in the pile with the others, and gestured for Carter to take his seat.

"I didn't know you wrote music," said Carter, once installed at the coffee table. "I suppose of course that it makes sense that you would, I mean given that you are a music professor."

"Some of us do, some of us don't," said Giancarlo distantly, sitting down across from his student. "I don't any longer."

"Why not?" asked Carter innocently. "If what you write sounds anything like those exercises, it must be awesome."

"You're forgetting your meal," said Giancarlo, reaching for the carafe. He filled the glass and placed it near Carter. "What did you bring to eat?"

"Just a burger and fries," said Carter. He reached into the bag, extracted both, and began to unwrap the hamburger. The bun was overflowing with shreds of dried-up lettuce and some sort of sauce oozing out of the sides.

Giancarlo looked on aghast, his face suddenly taking on an expression of acute dismay. He had a pronounced aversion to fast food of all types, and the sight of this talented student about to consume it right before his eyes produced a visceral response that was exquisitely painful.

Upon noting his teacher's obvious discomfiture, Carter paused before taking a bite. "Something wrong?" he asked.

"No," replied Giancarlo at first. Then, "Well, actually, yes. But it's not your fault. It's just that I can see that I will have to teach you a little bit more about Italian culture than just the language."

"Like what?" Carter asked, sincerely curious.

"Well, a little bit about food wouldn't hurt," his teacher replied as delicately as possible. "You see, there are things one eats, and there are things one shouldn't eat unless it's a matter of dying of hunger. And then there are yet other things that one doesn't eat even if it does mean dying of hunger."

Carter broke out in a smile. "Are you telling me that you disapprove of fast food?" he asked with something of an impish look as he took a chomp from the hamburger.

"What I'm telling you, *Signor* Quinn," intoned Giancarlo somberly, like a father counseling a wayward son, "is that I will forgive you this one time for eating that in front of me, but you would do well not to do it again."

"Okay," chuckled Carter amiably as he gobbled down some of the fries. "I get the message. But if it would make you feel better right now, I could just toss the rest of this in the trash."

"No, that won't be necessary," Giancarlo told him. "Let's just say that I will endure it just this once as a proper penance for my lack of good manners—and leave it at that."

The next time Carter came to the house, Giancarlo was ready for him. As he opened the door to let him in, he noted that his pupil had come empty-handed, not a hamburger or french fry to be seen. He quite rightly surmised that Carter had arrived in much the same famished state as he had two days earlier. Unbeknownst to Giancarlo, he had managed to gobble down an apple in the car en route to the house, but it had not been nearly substantial enough to satisfy his hunger. Worse still, the weather had grown very warm and humid, and he was looking quite drained after his day's labors. And so it pleased Giancarlo to note the look of relief on Carter's face when he walked into the living room and discovered, set out on the coffee table, a small bowl of olives, a block of cheese, and a bottle of San Pellegrino water along with two glasses and some paper napkins. The young man sat down in the chair by the table and eyed the items with great interest.

"*Assaggia*," said Giancarlo cordially, gesturing to the olives and cheese as he took his seat. He took one of the olives, bit into it, and pulled out the pit, which he deposited onto a little plate set next to the bowl for just this purpose. Then he reached for the knife and lopped off a piece of the cheese, which he offered to Carter. "*Assaggia del formaggio*," he said.

Carter gladly accepted it, took a nibble, and then quickly swallowed the rest of it with apparent gusto.

"*Ti piace la mozzarella?*" said Giancarlo, asking him if he liked the cheese.

"*Si, molto*," nodded Carter.

How could he not like it? The mozzarella cheese was soft and moist and delicious, perfect for someone who was hot and tired.

"*Assaggia un oliva*," said Giancarlo, gesturing once more to the olive bowl.

It required just a few moments more of prompting before Carter began to understand that he was being introduced to the verb *assaggiare* (to sample or taste). In saying "*assaggia*," his teacher was inviting him to try some of the olives.

Carter reached into the bowl and picked out one, which he consumed in a twinkling. Then he reached for another while Giancarlo poured them both a glass of water. Carter downed a gulp of the water and sat back for a moment.

"*Grazie*," he said with a weary sigh. Then, not knowing the phrase in Italian, he added, "That really hit the spot."

"*Prego*," replied Giancarlo. He settled back, as well, for a moment and looked at Carter with a thoughtful gaze. "You are tired from your work, yes?"

"Yeah, a little," Carter admitted. "It's hard, but I kind of like it—not that I plan on doing it for very long. But it's okay for now."

Giancarlo gave a little laugh.

"What is it?" said Carter.

"I was just thinking about how much people take for granted in this country," he replied.

"What do you mean?"

Giancarlo took a sip of water.

"Where I grew up," he began, "if you were fortunate enough to secure a good-paying job, you stayed with it for your whole life. More often than not, the job was one someone else, probably your father, arranged for you. So you see, in a way, a path got laid out for you almost from birth, and you tended to deviate very little from it because it was safe and predictable. It's like that in Italy, and in most places, believe it or not. People tend to take the safe, certain way in life, because otherwise the risk of failing and looking bad is too great—and to look bad is the worst thing that can happen to you when you're Italian."

Giancarlo paused, and took another sip of water.

"Here in America, on the other hand," he went on, "people don't fear uncertainty so much, and they fear failure even less. You change from one job to the next like you're changing channels on the television. If you get tired of working for other people, you can try to start your own business, with hardly a moment's thought about the risk. Look at how many businesses fail after only one year, and almost none make it past three. America is a land full of failures, and I say that only because that is what makes it great. In this country, when your dreams crash and burn all around you, you're expected to simply learn from your mistakes, pick up the pieces from the wreckage, and start all over again. There's no shame in it. And if you're tired of your job or of running your own business, well, then you can go back to school at night and learn how to become a lawyer or a doctor or an architect or whatever you like. If you're willing to work, there are no preconceived notions about what you can become or how far you can go. Trust me, it's not like this in other parts of the world. It's the main reason so many people come to this country—to be free of the old ways of thinking about themselves."

"But not everybody comes," Carter pointed out, "or probably even wants to come."

"That's because this place is not for everybody," explained Giancarlo, wagging a finger. "America is a beautiful country, and I have come to love it dearly, but we live in a tough, competitive, demanding society here. This holds true in virtually every aspect of our lives. For all the abundance we enjoy, these things exact a toll, one that many people in other countries would just as soon not pay. So they stay right where they are and err on the side of caution, because that's the safe way through life."

"I never thought of things that way," said Carter when Giancarlo had finished. "I mean, life here doesn't seem all that tough to me."

"That's because you were born and raised here," said Giancarlo. "It makes a difference." He paused, and let out a breath. "But in any case, enough of my hot air. Now that you've had a little to eat, *ti senti meglio?* Do you feel better? Got a little bit of your strength back?"

"*Si,*" said Carter with a smile. "*Grazie.*"

"*Bravo,*" said Giancarlo. "So in that case, we can get back to business."

With that he picked up his pencil and tapped it against the table, bringing the class to order.

"*Va bene,*" he said, reacquiring his taskmaster's voice. "*Adesso parliamo in Italiano!*"

CHAPTER 10

Carter's head hurt.

It had been another long, hot day on the job at R & D Home Construction, and he was feeling like a wet rag. With the car windows wide open to let in the breeze, he drove home from work, sipping a bottle of water while listening to the latest Italian tape Professor Rosa had lent him. Along the way, he decided to stop at a video store, where he rented an Italian-made movie. His plan was to watch it that night after catching a quick workout at the gym. As he mulled over his itinerary for the evening, he began to understand why his head was throbbing. It wasn't just the heat and the daily physical work that were getting to him, but also the concentration and mental energy he was expending to learn this new language. Between his construction labors and Italian lessons, though he enjoyed both immensely, he was beginning to feel like he was back in his football days, going through pre-season double sessions again—and Giancarlo Rosa was as tough on him as any football coach he had ever played for. It was a rigorous routine, more difficult than he had expected, but Carter also understood that, just like for football, he would have to work at his Italian lessons before he could play in Italy. This little bit of cranial discomfort was simply an inevitable part of his preparation.

Driving along, though he tried his best to keep up with the Italian tape, his thoughts turned to Elena. As he often did, he tried to rewind in his mind the memories of their brief encounter that day on the hill by the side of the rugby pitch. He dissected every second he could remember of the brief time they'd spent together, every word that had passed between them, looking for clues— something she'd said, a gesture, a laugh, anything at all—that would tell him more about her. As always, he soon found himself simply dwelling on the shape of her lovely face, her smile, her hair, and the indescribable color of her eyes. In the end these things still mesmerized him, just as they had that moment he first laid eyes on her, and told him everything he felt he needed to know.

When Carter approached his house, he caught sight of Sheila Mahoney walking down the front walk of her house to the mailbox at the edge of her yard, near the street. Looking quite pretty in a conservative skirt and blouse, she most likely also just returned from work. As Carter passed her and pulled into his driveway, she gave him a smile and waved before opening the box.

"Hey, Sheila," he called to her, returning the smile, when he stepped out of the car. "How's it going?"

"No complaints," she called back.

She took the mail from the box, flipped the lid closed, and strolled across the yard to him. She stopped at the edge of the property and stood there for a moment, assessing his rather grimy appearance, before nodding to his sweat-stained shirt.

"Long day at the office, dear?" she asked, batting her eyes with feigned sweetness.

"They all feel pretty long these days," Carter chuckled. "Not that I'm complaining, either. At least I'm getting paid."

"It does make having a job worthwhile," she noted. "I take it you're still working on the chain gang."

"Oh yeah," shrugged Carter. "But construction's not so bad. It'll do for the summer, before I finally have to find a real job. How about you?"

"At the bank," she said with a shrug of her own. "It's boring, but like you said, it'll do for the summer."

She paused, and gave him that familiar look of hers.

"Still planning to go to Italy in September?" she asked. "I remember your saying something about that the last time I saw you."

"That's the plan," nodded Carter. He held up the Italian language cassette. "That's why I've been taking Italian lessons."

"Ha, language tapes!" laughed Sheila suddenly. "That explains it."

"Explains what?"

"It explains why sometimes at night, especially when it's late and really quiet, I can hear you walking around inside your house, talking out loud—but I can never understand what you're saying. Every time it happens I wonder, is he on the telephone, and who is he talking to at this hour?"

"Oh, God," groaned Carter, his cheeks going red. "I'm so sorry. Am I really that loud?"

"Don't worry," she assured him. "Now that I know what you've been doing, it's actually kind of cute. Though I was beginning to get worried that you were going schizoid."

"No, I'm still relatively sane," he assured her. "And I promise to be quiet tonight. I'm just going to sit on the couch later on and watch this Italian movie I just rented before I go to bed."

"I wouldn't have taken you for a foreign film afficionado."

"I'm not," said Carter with a shrug. "It's just that my teacher says it'll help me learn the language."

"He's right," Sheila nodded. "What did you get?"

Carter showed her the DVD box.

"Hmm, *Satyricon*," she read. "Do you like Fellini movies?"

"I couldn't tell ya," chuckled Carter. "I just picked out the first Italian movie I saw in the foreign film section. Why, have you seen this one?"

"Oh yes, I've seen this, and some of his other films," she told him.

"How are they?"

"They're . . . Felliniesque," she replied after a moment's search for the right word. Then, despite a rather noncommital expression that conveyed a distinct lack of conviction, she added, "You might like this one—maybe."

"Can't hurt to try, right?" said Carter.

"I suppose not," she said.

Carter hesitated for a moment. He was eager to head inside and get changed for his workout, but at the same time he was once again enjoying talking to her.

"So, how go the plans for France?" he asked at last.

"*Tres bien!*" Sheila said brightly. "The only thing I'm waiting for is my passport. Can't leave home without that. I was hoping it would be in today's mail."

"Your passport?" said Carter, getting a nervous stab in the pit of his stomach. "Do you need that to go to France?"

"Of course, silly," she laughed. "And you're going to need one, too, if you want to go to Italy. Haven't you applied for yours yet?"

"It never even occurred to me," Carter admitted, inwardly berating himself for having overlooked such a necessity. "I thought all I had to do was book my flight on Expedia and I'd be all set."

Sheila clicked her tongue and shook her head.

"Not the way it works," she said. "I wouldn't wait too long to do it, if I were you. They say it can take up to six weeks for them to send it to you after you apply, unless of course you want to pay a bunch extra to get it done quicker."

"Six weeks," muttered Carter, wiping his brow with the back of his arm. It was nearly the end of June. Six weeks would mean the middle of August, dangerously close to the time he was planning to leave. He let out a sigh. "I guess I'd better get moving on that," he said.

Sheila gazed at him for a time, no doubt noting the look of concern on his face.

"Do you know how to go about applying for it?" she asked.

"No clue," Carter confessed.

Sheila smiled and held up a finger.

"Wait here a minute," she told him. "I'll be right back."

With that she left him there and walked off into her house. A few minutes later she reemerged with some sheets of paper in hand. By this time Carter had drifted across the Mahoneys' front lawn and was waiting for her at the bottom of the steps to the front porch. Sheila walked out, sat on the top step, and gestured for him to come up and take a seat next to her. Acutely aware of his sweaty, disheveled state, Carter obeyed but sat down at a discreet distance so as not to totally offend her with his odor. Nonetheless, Sheila leaned closer to show him the paper she had just printed out for him.

"Here, look, it's easy," she said, her shoulder touching his as she pointed to the paper. "I printed this off the State Department Web site. It tells you everything. You see, you have to do it in person."

"Don't tell me I have go to all the way to D.C. to get this," said an alarmed Carter.

"No," Sheila laughed. "You can do it right at the post office, where I applied. But the first thing you need to do is have someone take a passport photograph of you."

Sheila went on to explain the entire procedure, which was not at all complicated but had to be done completely and correctly, she warned him, else the application would be denied. Carter did his best to pay attention, but as she went down the list of items, her head leaning close to his, he found himself increasingly distracted by the smell of her perfume and the scent of her hair. Instead of looking at the paper, his eyes were inevitably drawn to her.

It was a discomfiting situation.

For her part, Sheila glanced up at him only occasionally as she talked away, making sure that he understood everything, looking for all the world as if she were totally unaware that she was having an effect of any kind on him. Someone observing the pair, however, would most likely have perceived otherwise.

"And that's all there is to it," said Sheila when she was finally finished. "Got it?"

"Yeah," nodded Carter. "It doesn't sound like it's as big of a hassle as I was afraid it was going to be."

"Nope," said Sheila, handing him the papers. "But like I said, don't wait too long." Then she frowned and nodded toward his house. "Now go home," she told him, "and take a shower, because you really reek right now."

"Sorry about that," laughed Carter, getting to his feet. He walked down the steps off the porch and turned to her. "I promise I will, but first I have to go the gym, so there's no point in doing it right now."

"In that case I'm not coming over to watch that movie with you tonight," she said, batting her eyes once more for him.

This remark caught him off guard, for he could not recall having invited her to watch it with him.

"Maybe some other time," he found himself saying just the same.

"Maybe," she said.

"Anyway, thanks for this," said Carter, holding up the papers she had given him.

"*De rien,*" she replied.

Carter smiled, nodded a goodbye, and started back across the yard. When he reached his driveway, he stopped and looked back to her. She was still sitting there on the porch steps, her elbows resting on her knees.

"*Lei è una brava ragazza!*" he said with a flourish.

Sheila smiled at him.

"I don't know what that means," she said, "but I like the sound of it."

With that she nodded a goodbye of her own, got to her feet, and went inside.

Carter watched until she had gone in before turning to go about his own business. Then he hurried into the house to get changed for his workout, surprised to discover that suddenly his head did not hurt anymore.

CHAPTER 11

Giancarlo sighed, and gazed out the window. Outdoors, a steady rain was falling from a charcoal sky. It was inevitable that the run of gorgeous weather they had been enjoying would come to an end, but he had hoped that it might continue for at least one more day. He had awakened that morning with all good intentions of spending some time out back, tending to the flowerbeds and pruning the bushes. Not that there was a great amount of work to be done there. His little backyard was a neat, unpretentious affair. He paid a boy from the neighborhood to cut the grass once each week—Giancarlo had better things to do than push a lawnmower—but caring for the shrubs and gardens he reserved to himself. These were small and easily managed, adding just enough color to the surroundings to break up the monotony without causing him too much trouble. Though he found the brief time he devoted to tending to them somehow soothing, Giancarlo was not an enthusiastic gardener by any means. He liked to keep things simple in the garden, the same way he tried to keep everything in his life.

Turning from the window, Giancarlo considered his options for the day. He was not one to go out and stand in the rain, no matter how much the gardens might have required his attention. Just the same, the prospect of spending the day in the house held little appeal. He gave a sigh and chanced to looked into the living room. His thoughts turned to Carter and the rapid progress he had been making in his Italian lessons. It occurred then to Giancarlo that it would not be long before his pupil outran the introductory course of study that he had originally anticipated would last the summer. Very soon he would need to make plans for more advanced lessons, and to acquire materials suitable for them. This line of speculation led him to the inevitable conclusion that an excursion to a bookstore was in order. It was a happy resolution to his deliberations, for it gave his day a new purpose. Giancarlo went straightaway to the front hall closet. The gardens, he told himself as he pulled on a raincoat, would have to wait for better weather. Till then at least the flowers would not need watering.

Later, at a nearby Barnes & Noble, Giancarlo stood between a pair of shelves lined with magazines of every description. Clutching under his arm the little paperback Italian-English dictionary he had picked out at the reference section, he perused the selection of Italian magazines and newspapers on offer, hoping to find something of interest that would not present too much of a challenge for Carter. He had just flipped open the cover of *Gente*, an Italian equivalent of *People* magazine, when from the corner of his eye Giancarlo saw someone come into view at the opposite end of the aisle in which he was standing. Instinctively he turned his head, and he saw an attractive woman with short blonde hair reaching for a magazine. Dressed in snug-fitting jeans and a T-shirt, a raincoat draped over one arm, she happened to look his way at just that same moment. The two briefly regarded one another, turned quickly away so as not to stare, and then looked back again, the light of recognition suddenly coming to the eyes of each.

"Giancarlo, is that you?" said the woman.

"Hello, Claire," he replied softly, returning her smile.

The two approached one another and exchanged kisses on the cheek.

"My God, how long has it been?" said Claire when she pulled back from him.

"A long time," said Giancarlo, nodding. "A very long time."

It had in fact been over ten years since they had last seen one another. Once upon a time, in what now seemed centuries ago, the two had been lovers. They had first met, just as on this day, quite by accident. Giancarlo had gone into his local bank, requesting to see the manager to dispute an overdraft charge on his checking account. The manager was at the time occupied with another matter, and so Giancarlo was directed to his assistant, who turned out to be Claire. Giancarlo was immediately taken with her, and in the course of explaining his grievances regarding his checking account, he found himself inviting her to finish the discussion over dinner. Claire had obviously been as equally taken with him, for she readily accepted, and so the affair began. They were together for nearly two years, the relationship bringing Giancarlo as close to happiness as any he had ever had. Just the same, it came to a dismal end, as had all the others before and since, when inevitably she had asked for a commitment, something that Giancarlo had never been able to give. It was a painful separation for both of them. Still, it ended amicably enough, and the two had gone their separate ways with little rancor.

Now, as he stood there looking at her, Giancarlo was struck by how much time had passed. How odd, it seemed to him, that in such a little place as Rhode Island, their paths had not crossed again much sooner. Then it occurred to him that perhaps somewhere along the line they had, and he simply had not been paying attention. This would not have surprised Giancarlo; his thoughts were often far away from wherever he happened to find himself at any given moment.

"I didn't recognize you at first," he said. "It must be because you're wearing your hair much shorter these days."

"I know," Claire sighed, playfully flicking a few strands with her fingers. "Sometimes I miss wearing it long, but this length makes life a little simpler. It's so much easier to take care of."

In bringing her hand to her hair, Claire revealed a wedding band, which Giancarlo did not fail to notice. It really should have come as no surprise to him. Time had gone by since they were together, and Claire had moved on. What else could he have expected? All the same, the sight of it caused him a momentary ache. Why, he was not quite sure.

"It still looks good on you, whatever its length," he assured her nonetheless. "In fact you look wonderful."

"Thanks," she said with a smile. "So do you." She paused, and nodded to the dictionary and magazine in his hand. "What are you reading these days?"

"Oh, these are not for me," Giancarlo replied. "They're for a student of mine who is planning a trip to Italy."

"That's right," said Claire. "I forgot that you give Italian lessons during the summer."

"Keeps me occupied," he said with a shrug. "How about you? What brings you out to the bookstore on such a dreary day?"

Claire gave a shrug of her own. "Besides shopping, where else can you take two little girls on a rainy day?" she said.

For a moment Giancarlo did not understand. Then Claire lifted the coat draped over her forearm and showed him the two smaller raincoats lying beneath.

"Children?" he said with great surprise. "Yours?"

"Two daughters," Claire beamed.

"But where are they?" said Giancarlo, looking about.

"They're in the back, listening to the storyteller. I've just been wandering around the bookshelves to pass the time. Come on, I'll show you." She took him by the elbow and led him to the end of the aisle. "See them there?" she said, pointing to two little girls, one perhaps five years of age, the other a year or two older. With their blonde hair and sweet faces, the two sisters were the very image of their mother.

"They're beautiful," Giancarlo whispered to her. "You're very lucky, and I'm very happy for you."

"Thanks," she whispered back.

Giancarlo was about to ask her if she would like to join him for a cup of coffee while she waited, but just then the story time came to an end and the two children began to look about for their mother.

"Oh well, time to go," she said, turning suddenly to him. She reached out, and the two shook hands. "It was good to see you, Giancarlo."

"It was good to see you, too, Claire."

Giancarlo had truly meant what he said. He really *was* happy for Claire, and for the new life she had found. What he could not account for was the persistent dull ache of sadness he felt growing within as he watched her hurry off to her children. It was an old, empty feeling, one that haunted him from time to time. It grew only worse when Claire waved goodbye to him before shepherding the girls out of the store. And then of course he understood. His encounter with her had reminded him of the ordinary pleasures of everyday family life that seemed, for whatever reason, to lie perpetually beyond his grasp. Regrets can be a heavy load to bear, and these were settling in on him. Nonetheless, he smiled and waved farewell.

Afterwards, when he had finished paying for the dictionary and the magazine, Giancarlo paused at the door and looked out at the rain-swept parking lot, where the sky above was as dark and bleak as his mood had become. He turned up his collar, stepped outside, and trudged off through the puddles, wondering all the while where he should go or what he should do next. It was a problem that vexed him from time to time in his solitary existence.

The simple life, he well understood, was one not always easily lived.

CHAPTER 12

The rain persisted, washing away the rest of June.

For the better part of a week, a dreary gray shroud hung over the region, the precipitation coming in intermittent waves, sometimes as a drizzle, at other times as an outright downpour. The dry, pleasantly warm weather that had prevailed the whole month of June was soon but a memory, and the temperatures hovered well below their norm for this time of year. Seasoned New Englanders of course were unsurprised by this turn of the elements. It had been an unusually dry month, so it stood to reason that sooner or later nature would find a way to make up for the shortfall of rain. Why she had felt it necessary to do it all at once was anyone's guess. But she was a fickle lady, nature, and she did everything at a time of her own choosing. There was nothing to be done for it other than wait for the dark clouds to wear out their welcome with the sky.

Despite the cool, damp weather, as he sat there in the living room of Giancarlo Rosa, Carter felt a sheen of sweat forming on his brow. From the time he first sat down to begin the lesson through that very moment, *il Professore*, as Carter liked to address Giancarlo, had been cracking the whip. It was Wednesday, the first week of July. There would be no lesson that following Friday, for it fell on the Fourth of July, so it seemed his teacher was intent on reviewing everything he had taught Carter since the very first day he came to the house. The days of the week, the months of the year, the hours of the day, what to say and do in a restaurant and a bank, how to ask for directions, numbers, the names of the colors, a seemingly endless stream of nouns and verbs and adjectives he had learned.

All of it.

"*Ripeta!*" Giancarlo would command him, impatiently tapping his pencil against the table when his student did not respond to a question in quite the right way.

"*Pensa!*" he told him, imploring Carter to think.

On and on it went in this way, Giancarlo drilling him on everything they had covered, and Carter struggling all the while to keep pace, his brain scouring its every corner to find the right words. It was an exercise that required in its own way as much effort as any he had ever put forth in the gym or on the playing fields, and he felt physically tired when at last Giancarlo stopped, sat back, and eyed his student for a moment, the briefest hint of a look of satisfaction coming over his face.

"*Bene,*" the professor grunted, eyeing Carter with a look of approval, as might a coach whose player has worked hard in practice and was now beginning to show signs of real promise.

Carter himself was suddenly filled with a sense of accomplishment as he thought back over the volume of material they had just reviewed. It had been barely a month since he began his Italian lessons, but he had worked very hard and learned—at least so he thought—a great deal. Still he was curious about where he stood, for he had no way of knowing how his performance compared with that of the other students his professor had taught. He sat there for a moment, considering how best to put the question into words.

"*Faccio progresso?*" he finally said in a tentative voice, asking if he had made progress.

"*Enorme!*" cried Giancarlo, throwing his hands up in a rare gesture of enthusiasm that conveyed to Carter that the strides he had thus far made in the language had been great. It was the first time he had seen *il Professore* so animated. "Yes, you are doing exceedingly well," his teacher added in English. "A very good start."

Surprised and somewhat abashed as he was by such an enthusiastic outburst from his normally stern-faced teacher, Carter did not know quite how to respond in either Italian or English.

"Nothing to it," he finally said modestly. "It's easy with a good professor."

"*Grazie,*" said Giancarlo, acknowledging the compliment with a solemn nod of his head. Then he wagged a finger at his student. "But don't get overconfident," he warned him. "You have a long way to go and much more to learn before you're ready for this trip you are planning to Italy."

"I'll make certain," Carter vowed.

"*Bravo,*" said Giancarlo.

With that the professor took a deep breath, let it out, and rubbed his chin thoughtfully, evidently turning over something in his mind. Carter had come to recognize this gesture as a clue that the introduction of some new word or concept was in the offing. He took a deep breath of his own and waited for what came next. To his surprise, Giancarlo suddenly pushed himself away from the table.

"*Basta,*" he said, standing. "*Basta di pasta, andiamo ad Aosta!*"

"Enough of pasta, let's go to Aosta?" translated a curious Carter. "*Che significa?*"

"It doesn't mean anything, not really," chuckled Giancarlo. "It was just something silly my father always liked to say whenever dinner was finished and it was time to take the dishes away. For you and me, I suppose it means it's time to take a little break, *prendere un piccolo intervalo. Capito?*"

Carter nodded to show that he understood.

"*Lei prende un caffe?*" Giancarlo asked him.

Carter ordinarily did not drink much coffee, but the offer of a cup seemed like a good idea given the dismal weather. "*Si, per piacere,*" he replied.

A few minutes later, Giancarlo returned from the kitchen with two steaming cups of coffee. He set the cups on the table, slid one over to Carter, and went back to the kitchen. He returned with a small plate on which rested some biscotti.

"*Assaggia*," he told Carter, gesturing to the plate. "You can dunk them in the coffee, if you like. This coffee of course is a little weaker than what you would drink in Italy, but it will do."

While Carter sampled the biscotti, Giancarlo took a quick sip of coffee before reaching down to the couch beside him. He soon produced a map, which he unfolded and laid across the table. It was a wrinkled old chart, its browning paper fraying at the edges, the creases almost at the point of tearing.

"*La carta dell'Italia*," Giancarlo announced. "The map of Italy. It's always good to know more than just the language before you visit someplace new, so I thought a little geography lesson would be of use."

"Yes, it would," said Carter with keen interest. He put his cup of coffee aside and leaned closer to get a better look.

"We'll begin here, at Rome," said Giancarlo, tapping his pencil on the map.

With Carter watching and listening, Giancarlo pointed out Milan, Venice, Naples, and the other major cities. Italy, he explained, was divided into regions, somewhat similar to America's states, each with its own capital. The regions were organized into provinces, and the provinces in turn into municipalities, the towns that dotted the map around the larger cities. As detailed a map as this one was, it still could not show the innumerable *frazioni*, the little hamlets and villages surrounding the municipalities. Giancarlo went on to discuss the topography of Italy. He described the Apennines, a mountain chain that ran the length of the country, and the Alps and the Dolomites, which separated Italy from the rest of Europe, to the north. As his hand roamed across the map, Giancarlo would pause now and then to point out a popular tourist destination or some place of historical interest—and there were many, Carter discovered.

It was all very interesting, and Carter paid close attention. Just the same, as *il Professore* rambled on, he found his thoughts wandering to Elena. He was truly grateful for the detailed overview of the country, but in truth there was at the moment only one place in all of Italy about which he really wanted to learn. When at last Giancarlo paused, Carter could not keep himself from asking the question that was foremost on his mind.

"Roccasale?" he asked. "Where is it?"

Giancarlo clicked his tongue and shook his head, though from his bemused look it was plain that he had anticipated the query.

"*Sempre la donna*," he harrumphed. "Always the woman."

"Sorry, *Professore*," shrugged Carter. "But I really need to know."

"I thought as much," replied Giancarlo. Then he leaned over the table and lowered the tip of his pencil onto the map. "It is here," he said, tapping a region in the approximate center of the country, "in the east of Abruzzo. First you find Pescara, here on the Adriatic coast. You see? And then you go inland this way, toward the mountains." As he said this, Giancarlo moved the pencil a short distance across the map, until it came to rest on a little dot labeled ROCCASALE.

"So that's it," said Carter, unaware that he was smiling from ear to ear. He looked up at his teacher. "Have you ever been there?"

"Oh yes, I've been there," said Giancarlo matter-of-factly.

"Tell me, what is it like?"

Giancarlo jutted out his chin in a look of ambivalence and gave a shrug. "A typical town for that area. Nothing out of the ordinary, I would say," he replied. "Not very big, but not so small, either. It has a nice piazza, if I remember correctly. You can see the mountains in the distance. It's a bustling place, though. There used to be several restaurants and one or two small nightclubs. I went there occasionally with my friends when I was young."

"Really?" said a surprised Carter. "Where did you grow up?"

"Here, in a place called Castelalto," replied Giancarlo, tapping a spot on the map further west toward the center of Abruzzo. "It's a little place, a *frazione*, too small to be drawn on the map."

"Hey, that's not far at all!" exclaimed Carter.

"Eh, the mountains of Abruzzo are deceiving. It is only an inch or two on the map, but trust me, it is farther than it looks," Giancarlo assured him. "From Roccasale you can see the mountains. In Castelalto, you're in them. It's the real Abruzzo."

There was an air of mystery to the way his teacher spoke of his native land, one that piqued Carter's curiosity. "What's it like, the Abruzzo region?" he asked, hoping to draw him out.

Giancarlo sat back and gazed blankly past Carter, his eyes fixed, the young man supposed, on some image within his own mind. "Wild," the professor replied in a faraway voice after a few moments of contemplation. "Wild and beautiful, and welcoming in a great many ways. But also harsh and unforgiving in others. It took the Romans a hundred years and three wars before they could control it, you know."

Giancarlo paused for a moment, still staring off into the distance before coming back to himself.

"But as you can see," he resumed, "the coast borders the Adriatic Sea. Many beautiful places and beaches there. But most of Abruzzo is in the mountains. Tall, rugged mountains, some almost ten thousand feet high, like the Gran Sasso. And there are beautiful parks, thousands upon thousands of acres. I spent much of my youth hiking and exploring all around my hometown. I loved hiking in those days."

"Hey, I loved hiking, too," enthused Carter. "Back when I was in the Boy Scouts, we used to go up to New Hampshire and hike in the White Mountains all the time. It was great."

"Then you will certainly love the Abruzzi mountains," nodded Giancarlo.

"It sounds like an awesome part of the world," said Carter. "Whatever made you leave it and move to America?"

It was an innocent question, one for which Carter had not really expected an answer of any substance, but for some reason it seemed to throw Giancarlo, who suddenly seemed a bit unnerved.

"Oh, there were many reasons, I suppose," the professor said evasively. "As I told you once before, there is a lot that people take for granted in this country, opportunities that just aren't available for people in many parts of the world, especially in little villages far off in the mountains of Italy."

"Like what?" pressed Carter with sincere interest.

Giancarlo gave a little cough to clear his throat.

"Different things," he replied vaguely. "I was a musician and composer, you see. Intellectually and culturally, I suppose I just felt attracted to America. That was why I left."

"Intellectually and culturally?" said Carter.

"Yes."

Carter sat back and folded his arms. He regarded his teacher with a skeptical gaze before breaking out in a mischievous smile. "Okay," he said slyly. "So tell me, what was her name?"

"I beg your pardon?" said Giancarlo.

Carter was at heart still the imp he had been as a little boy. There was simply no way for him to pass up this golden opportunity to give his mentor a playful dig.

"Let me see, what was it you once told me?" he said, striking a comically authoritative air, not unlike that of the Cowardly Lion. "What is it that roots a man in one place, or that can just as easily uproot him in the blink of an eye? Hmm? What makes him come or go? My friend, for better or worse, it's *always* a woman. So tell me, *Professore*, what was her name?"

Carter had meant it all in good fun, and he had fully expected Giancarlo to accept it as such. He realized straightaway that he was quite mistaken in this regard, for the older man suddenly fixed him with a stony, withering glare that made the hairs on the back of his neck stand on end. In all his life, Carter had never seen a man's face transform itself in such a way, and never so quickly.

"And as I *also* told you," said the professor coolly "you have a great deal to learn before you go to Italy." With that he abruptly took the map and began to fold it up, an icy silence falling over the room.

Carter did not need to be told that this day's geography lesson had officially ended. At a loss for words as to why this harmless jest had provoked such a response in his teacher, he sat there quietly, wondering if it might not have been so much what he'd said but how he'd said it. Perhaps, in making the friendly joke, he had overstepped his bounds and come across as disrespectful. This was certainly not his intention. Just the same, he felt quite bad that it might have been interpreted as being so.

"Um, *mi dispiace*—" he began to say by way of apology.

"*Niente*," Giancarlo cut him short. He paused. His demeanor softening ever so slightly, he put the map aside and added, "It was nothing. Let us get back to business."

And so the Italian lesson continued, but with little of its former enthusiasm on the part of student or teacher. An awkward feeling still prevailed, and it hung there in the air like a thick mist that dampened their spirits. Though both did their best, it soon became clear that there was little more progress to be made that day, and so it was just as well that at last Giancarlo decided to end things a few minutes early.

When it came time to leave, Carter collected his jacket and made his way to the door with little fanfare. "So, see you next week?" he asked tentatively, for suddenly he was not at all certain that this would still be the case.

"Yes, of course," said Giancarlo tersely with a dismissive wave. "Monday afternoon. Be prepared."

"Hey, I'm an old Boy Scout," Carter reminded him with a smile. "I'm always prepared."

He hoped a bit of levity might help the situation, perhaps lift the dark cloud that had inexplicably descended over the proceedings. From the dour look still on his teacher's face, he judged that the desired result had eluded him. Not knowing what else to say, he tugged on his jacket, wished his teacher a pleasant Fourth of July, and then went on his way, perplexed by the puzzling turn of events. Of one thing, however, he felt quite certain. His teacher had been entirely correct. There obviously did remain much that he needed to learn.

CHAPTER 13

"**S**ounds like you struck a nerve," said Jimmy.

"You think?" chuckled Carter.

The two were in the gym. It was Thursday, the day before the Fourth of July, and Carter had just recounted the curious incident that had taken place the previous evening at his most recent Italian lesson. While he rested between sets of bench pressing, he watched his friend, who was standing before the mirrored wall, a forty-pound dumbbell clutched in each hand. Keeping his elbows tucked against his sides, Jimmy hoisted the weight in his right hand to his chin and slowly let it back down to his side before doing the same with the left hand. Thus he alternated back and forth, puffing out his breath with each repetition, all the while keeping careful watch on the reflection of his biceps in the mirror. He squeezed out several repetitions on each arm before dropping the dumbbells back onto the rack. His gaze still fixed on the mirror, he brought his clenched fists toward his midsection and flexed his arms, turning from one side to the other to get a good view of each.

"My hero," joked Carter in a high-pitched voice that sounded more feline than feminine.

"Hey, if Arnold were here, he'd be eatin' his heart out," said Jimmy, unfazed by Carter's teasing. He looked over his shoulder. "So what do you think the problem was with this teacher of yours?"

"I dunno," shrugged Carter. "But you had to see it. One second everything's all fine and dandy, and then the next—*whoosh!* I don't know how to explain it, but it was like the guy stuck his head in the icebox and freeze-dried his face. I mean, it felt like the temperature in the room all of a sudden dropped fifty degrees."

"Yep," Jimmy nodded. "Like I said, you definitely struck a nerve. I've got an uncle like that. Nicest guy in the world, talkative, funny—that is, until he gets pissed off about something. Then all of a sudden he turns into Mr. Freeze. Doesn't say a word, but you better duck because one of his looks can take your head off."

"That's just the way it was yesterday," nodded Carter. "The guy reacted like I said something about his mother. I actually felt kind of bad about it after. I mean, I kind of like the guy. He's tough, but he's all right. I didn't mean to insult him."

"Bah, don't worry about it," huffed Jimmy. "Guys like him and my uncle are all the same. They just get moody and miserable sometimes for no reason."

"Maybe," said Carter with a shrug. He lay back onto the bench and stared up at the bar resting on the rack. "But for a second there, I thought I was going to have to find a new Italian teacher—and that would have put a major hole in my plans."

Jimmy came over to spot Carter for his next set of bench presses.

"You're still dizzy over that broad?" he said with a click of his tongue as he took his place at the end of the bench near Carter's head. "What's that all about, anyway? I still haven't been able to figure it out."

Carter started to reach up toward the bar, but then let his arms drop down to his sides. He lay there for a moment, staring into space.

"Let me ask you something," he said at last to Jimmy. "Have you ever been standing someplace, maybe out on a sidewalk in the city, and you look up and see a really sharp-looking girl looking at you from the window of a bus or a car, or maybe she's just walking by with someone else?"

"Yeah, sure," said Jimmy.

"And she just mesmerizes you, right?" Carter went on. "And suddenly you think, Wow, could she be the one?"

"The one what?" said Jimmy.

"The *one*," said Carter. "You know what I'm talking about— that one girl you've been waiting for your whole life."

"Actually, I've been hoping for *more* than one," his friend replied. "But that's just me."

"Whatever," sighed Carter in exasperation. "Anyway, so there you are. You stop and you look back at her and your eyes meet for a second, and all of a sudden all these possibilities start running through your head. It's like you can see your whole life opening up ahead of you, and you think maybe you should just go after her, just get on that bus and see where it takes you. But before you can make a move, the bus drives away or the car passes or you lose her in the crowd, and it's over forever. Happens all the time, right? So you move on and just forget about it, and you never know what could have been. Well, this time, I don't want to forget about it and just move on. I wanna get on that bus. I want to know what could be. And that's why I've been studying Italian, because when I get to Italy, I want to know for sure."

"I can see that," said Jimmy, scrunching up his chin, "except you're not getting on a bus. You're getting on a plane."

"Plane, bus, makes no difference."

"It does when you're flying halfway around the world to a place you've never been, hoping that *she's* the one."

"Come on," said Carter. "Are you going to tell me that it's never happened to you, that you've never felt the same way at least once?"

Jimmy gave a sigh and shook his head.

"Let me tell you something, Quinnie," he replied. "There are some things in life that you just can't have, no matter how good they look and how bad you want them, or think you need them. That's just the way it is. So I don't worry about those things. If I can't have them—if that bus you're talking about pulls out of town—then hey, I just stop and take a look around to see what else there is right here next to me that maybe I've been overlooking. You know, when that bus goes, it usually leaves something pretty good behind. You just gotta keep your eyes open. That's my philosophy."

"Sure, you're all talk now," chuckled Carter. "But watch, someday it will happen to you. And then you'll be coming to me for Italian lessons."

"Yeah?" said Jimmy, rolling his eyes. "Well why don't you start right now by telling me how to say 'shut up and do your next set of benches' in Italian?"

Carter gave a laugh, then he reached up and lifted the bar.

CHAPTER 14

The next day, having awoken later than he had planned, Carter pulled on a pair of shorts and sneakers, and hurried out the door. It was a warm, sticky morning, and he was anxious to get a good run in before it grew more so. Carter disliked the muggy weather that inevitably came with New England summers, but as he started out onto the road and jogged at an easy pace past the neighborhood houses decorated in red, white, and blue, he was pleased to see that at least the rainy skies had finally cleared. The dark clouds had all disappeared, and now the sun was very quickly burning off the morning haze. There was no need to listen to the day's weather forecast; it was going to be a hot one. Carter breathed deep of the heavy air and quickened his stride.

A half hour later, after rounding the corner at the top of the street, Carter sprinted the rest of the way home and came to a stop at the base of his driveway. There he doubled over to catch his breath, the perspiration streaming out of every pore as he rested his elbows on his knees.

"The winner by a nose!" came a voice from nearby.

Carter straightened up and saw Sheila Mahoney on the top step of her front porch, where she was standing on tiptoes, arms outstretched, as she tried to insert the end of a flagpole into a bracket mounted above her. The young woman was not quite tall enough, and she was having some difficulty, for the weight of the flag wrapped around the opposite end of the pole made it an awkward reach. With each attempt, the heavy end of the pole inevitably listed down toward the ground, flipping the other end up before she could set it in the bracket.

Seeing her struggle, Carter hurried over to help.

"Let me do that for you," he offered.

He took the flagpole from her, set it with ease in the bracket, and unfurled the Stars and Stripes.

"There, how's that?" he said, admiring his work. He wiped the sweat from his eyes with his forearm and turned back around. It was then that he took a good look at her for the first time.

Dressed in shorts and sandals and a bikini top, her brown hair falling about her shoulders, Sheila stood there smiling at him in such an easy, natural way that Carter found it difficult to resist doing the same. She was quite prepossessing, and seemed only to become more so every time he encountered her. It unnerved him. All the more disquieting was his unsettling certainty that she knew this as well as he.

"Thanks," she said, batting her eyes playfully. "It seems I'm always relying on the kindness of strangers."

"No sweat," said Carter, giving her a nod.

"Not from what I can see," Sheila replied.

"It is getting hot," admitted Carter, wiping the perspiration from his brow with the back of his hand. He gave a little cough to clear his throat. "Looks like you're going to the beach," he said, trying very hard not to stare at her slender figure.

"Nope," said Sheila, nonchalantly adjusting the shoulder strap of her top. "I'm just going out back to catch a few rays for a little while. Then I'm going to a cookout later on, maybe watch the fireworks downtown. How about you?"

"Heading down to my parents' house," he told her with a shrug. "They're doing their usual cookout. I'll probably watch the fireworks tonight at the town beach."

"Sounds like fun."

"Happy Fourth of July, Carter," came a familiar voice from inside the house. It belonged to Sheila's mother, who just then happened to pass by the screen door.

"Hi, Mrs. Mahoney. Happy Fourth to you, too," he called back in.

Mrs. Mahoney didn't linger, but instead went straightaway to some other part of the house. "Tell your parents I said hello," he heard her call.

"I will," he replied.

He turned back to Sheila.

"Well, I guess I should get going," he said after a moment's hesitation. "Have a nice Fourth, Sheila."

"You, too," she said

Carter started back down the porch steps.

"Hey, by the way, how did you like *Satyricon*?" said Sheila before he could go far.

Carter turned around and gave her a rueful smile.

"It was—what did you call it?—Felliniesque," he replied, rolling his eyes. "Now I know why they call them *foreign* films."

Sheila laughed.

"They're not all like that," she assured him. "Next time ask me first. I'll recommend something you might like better."

Carter did not reply, but instead smiled and nodded goodbye.

The telephone was ringing when he went back inside his house. It was his mother, calling to give him a list of things to pick up for the cookout before he drove to their beach house. As he listened to her, the handset of the portable telephone nestled between his shoulder and ear, he rummaged about the kitchen counter for a pen and paper with which to write everything down. He had just found both when he chanced to look out the back window. Through a break in the bushes that separated the Quinns' backyard from the Mahoneys', he caught a glimpse of Sheila. She appeared to be spreading a towel across a lounge chair out on their back deck.

"Right, five big bags of ice," he said into the phone, scribbling on the paper while straining to get a better view of what she was doing. The break in the bushes was small, however, and to his annoyance, Sheila stepped out of sight. His curiosity piqued, Carter took the paper and pen, and walked out of the kitchen.

"Okay, what else?" he said to his mother as he headed to the staircase.

Once upstairs, he went to the bathroom window, which afforded the best possible view of his neighbors' backyard. There, only half listening to his mother, Carter pressed his forehead against the screen of the open window to see what he could spy.

The maple tree in the backyard partially obscured his line of sight. Just the same Carter could plainly see Sheila as she kicked off her sandals and wriggled out of the shorts she wore over her bikini bottom. She sat on the edge of the chair, opened a bottle of suntan lotion, and squeezed some out into her hands. With long, deliberate strokes, she spread the lotion all across her arms and legs. Distracted by the smooth, sensual motion of her hands, Carter did not quite hear the next item on his mother's list.

"Say that again, Mom," he said, trying to pay attention, and failing in the effort.

Maddeningly, Sheila just at that moment tossed the suntan lotion aside, turned the chair in the opposite direction, and raised its back. She drew in her legs and settled down onto the chair, so that all Carter could see of her was the top of her head and the tips of her toes. Disappointed he gave a sigh, went to straighten up, and in the process struck his head with a rather loud knock on the bottom edge of the raised window. The impact gave him a jolt and jarred the telephone from his hands.

"Yeah, Mom, I'm still here," he said once he had retrieved the handset. "So, what else did you say we need?"

Later, after he had hung up the phone, a much annoyed Carter stripped and went back into the bathroom. He stood in front of the mirror and passed his hand over the painful welt on the back of his head. For a few moments he stayed there, considering the bump and the circumstances that had led to it. His thoughts suddenly turned to Elena, and his head felt all the worse.

"Nothing less than you deserved," he grumbled.

Then he pulled open the shower curtain and turned on the cold water.

CHAPTER 15

It was a truth acknowledged—if not universally, then at least by a consensus of his friends and relations, particularly those of the female persuasion—that by virtue of his being in possession of a comfortable home, a respected profession, and yet a moody, temperamental disposition, Giancarlo must be in need of a wife. There was no other explanation, so went popular opinion, for the air of self-imposed exile that seemed to perpetually shadow the man like a gloomy gray cloud. It followed him everywhere, throwing a shroud over the sun's every attempt to let the light shine through, and it was generally held with great conviction that only the care and comfort of a good woman would be able to dispel it.

Such being the case, the procurement of a suitable mate for Giancarlo had long been the subject of considerable deliberation and debate. With the passage of time, the discussions and telephone calls and whispers behind backs had taken on a greater sense of urgency, lately approaching something close to outright alarm. True, Giancarlo was still very much in the prime of his life, but he was teetering on the brink of spending his remaining years in permanent bachelorhood. Left to his own devices, he might very well stumble over the edge of the precipice and fall into the clutches of that dread fate.

Something had to be done.

And so it was that whenever an opportunity presented itself, all efforts were made to foist upon Giancarlo a woman it was hoped might be capable of helping him to finally find the answers and settle down once and for all. Despite the careful vetting of potential candidates, none to date had succeeded in ensnaring his heart. This long run of failure was a source of great consternation to all concerned, but they remained nonetheless undaunted in their cause.

Giancarlo was of course quite aware of the machinations going on all about him. Though he found it tiresome at times, he was not completely without gratitude for them. There was, he understood, a certain wisdom in the attempts of his friends and relatives to guide him toward a life of matrimony, for in truth he felt no particular resistance to it. Deep inside, though, he also knew that, at least for the time being, contentment lay down some other path that had yet to reveal itself to him, if indeed it ever would. Until it did, he could only wait. Meantime, he accepted these matchmaking efforts on his behalf with stoic forbearance, as he did that afternoon at the annual Fourth of July cookout at the home of Anthony and Celeste.

Giancarlo waited until late in the afternoon to make his appearance at the festivities. He had guessed, quite rightly, that the patio area around the swimming pool in Anthony's backyard would be a frying pan earlier in the day. Sure enough, by the time he arrived at the house, many of the adults and all of the kids had already changed into their swimsuits and jumped into the water to cool off. There was talk and laughter and splashing and fathers tossing kids into the air while mothers pleaded with children to please be more careful and not run around the edge of the pool. As if this din was not enough, the music of John Philip Sousa, George M. Cohan, and others blared out from speakers set up in the living room windows inside the house. It was an appropriately raucous affair.

Dressed in slacks and a polo shirt, and having left his swim trunks at home, Giancarlo had no intentions of testing the water that day. Instead, taking care not to get splashed, he maneuvered his way through the crowd around the pool toward Anthony, who at the moment was stationed at the grill, over in the far corner of the yard. There, arrayed in a white chef's apron and a Red Sox cap, he was busy at work grilling up some marinated lamb chops. The sight of his cousin gave Giancarlo cause to smile, for he knew that there were few things Anthony enjoyed better than cooking for the masses at one of his legendary cookouts. The afternoon breeze, however, was kicking up, and a gust of wind had just nudged the smoke into Anthony's face, briefly sullying his high spirits. Muttering some unmentionable remarks about the smoke and the infernal regions from which it had apparently sprung, he whipped off his cap to fan it from his face just as Giancarlo approached. At seeing him, Anthony gave a cough to clear the smoke from his throat and waved a greeting with the tongs he was using to turn the lamb chops.

"Ayyy, there he is, *finalmente*," said Anthony amiably. "We were beginning to think that maybe you weren't coming."

"I had a few things to do earlier," offered Giancarlo. "Sorry I'm late."

"Don't be sorry," laughed Anthony. "Just grab a plate and have something to eat. We have enough here to feed the Turkish army."

Anthony gestured to the table set up beneath the awning of the little pool cabana. There the rest of the feast was laid out. Giancarlo well knew that hot dogs and hamburgers alone would never have done. And so, besides these, he was not surprised to find that those in attendance had also been treated to platters of steak and sausage and barbecued chicken, along with bowls of pasta and potato salads, and grilled zucchini, summer squash, and other vegetables. There were roasted red peppers, oranges sliced and drenched in olive oil, stuffed mushrooms, and more—all this before even considering the red, white, and blue cupcakes, the assorted cookies and pastries, and the enormous cake decorated like an American flag.

"Go ahead, make yourself a plate, Giancarlo, and then we'll talk," said Anthony. He looked about for his wife. "Celeste, Giancarlo is here!" he called. At catching her eye, the two exchanged furtive looks. "Why don't you get him a beer to have with his food," he suggested. Then, turning back to Giancarlo, "Go on, Giancarlo. Celeste will take care of you."

When he had filled his plate, Giancarlo made his way back past the pool over to the grassy part of the yard, where some of the men and children were playing bocce. He had just settled down onto a lawn chair to watch them while he ate when he saw Celeste coming over to him, a bottle of beer in hand. Beside her walked a woman he had never before seen, but to whom he was quite certain he was about to be introduced. She was not an unattractive woman by any means, but just the same, as the two drew nearer, Giancarlo gave a barely audible groan. For a few brief moments, he had hoped against reason that perhaps on this day he might have been spared this dreary ritual. Such was obviously not to be the case, for Celeste looked quite determined. He put his plate aside and stood.

"Giancarlo, we're so glad you came," said Celeste, beaming a smile as she handed him his drink. She made no pretense about her intentions, but got straight to the point. "I wanted you to meet a friend of mine. Giancarlo, this is Ann."

Inwardly Giancarlo sighed, but the proprieties had to be observed.

"Hello, Ann," he said, forcing a smile. "Happy Fourth of July."

"So, what did you think of Ann?" asked Anthony a few hours later.

They were alone together in the backyard, chatting while Anthony closed up the grill. Evening had fallen, and the rest of the guests had made their way to the front of the house with their blankets and chairs. The front lawn offered a perfect view of the fireworks display, scheduled to go off at nine from the town park a few streets over. Everyone was anxious to secure a comfortable spot on the grass before the first rocket went up. It wouldn't be long.

Giancarlo considered his cousin's question for a moment, try-

ing to decide how best to frame his response without giving of-
fense. He gave a little cough. Ann was a perfectly charming lady, he
had found, but in his estimation a bit too anxious to please. She let
on early in their conversation that she was a fan of the Rhode Island Philharmonic Orchestra and attended their performances regularly. Her appreciation of music, Giancarlo could only surmise, was
considered a prime qualification by those involved in this latest
matchmaking foray, for it seemed the two had nothing else in
common. Nonetheless he'd listened politely as she talked on and
on, eventually learning that she had been divorced for two years,
but with no children from the marriage. Though she dwelt on it
for but a moment, this last fact seemed to trouble her more than
she let on. He felt sorry for her because of it, but not enough to in-
spire in him any notions of helping her in that regard. In the end
he had excused himself so that he might try some of the lamb
chops Anthony had put out on the table. Ann had offered to make
a plate for him, but he politely declined, and the two had mercifully drifted apart for the remainder of the day.

"She's a very nice person," Giancarlo finally said.

"But?" said Anthony expectantly.

Giancarlo hesitated.

"Well, it's just that she was . . . I'm not sure how to say it, but I
guess what I mean to say is that she seemed a bit . . . I don't know
if this is the right word, but—desperate?"

"Ha! I knew it!" cried his cousin. "I told Celeste the same
exact thing just this morning, but would she listen to me? Nooo.
'No, no, Anthony, you've got her all wrong,' she told me. 'I think
she's just what Giancarlo needs.'"

"I appreciate the thought," Giancarlo offered in apology.

"Nonsense, don't give it another thought," intoned Anthony,
with a wave of his hand. "I'm glad you saw things the same as I did.
You have to be careful with women like her. Yes, yes, they can be all
sweet and pretty and nice to talk to, but you have to watch out, because they're like drowning swimmers. They always need to latch
onto someone—anyone. If you get too close, they grab you and

crawl all over you, and before you know it they pull you right down under the water with them."

"Well I wouldn't go quite that far," chuckled Giancarlo, though he well might have.

"Ayyy, I know all about these things," Anthony assured him. "Trust me, you're better off keeping your distance from that one." He paused, and looked at Giancarlo with sympathetic eyes. "But you know," he said, shaking his head, "Celeste and the others will just keep digging up new women to fix you up with until they find the right one—or until you get on the stick and find someone on your own. It's just the way they are."

"I know," said Giancarlo with a shrug. "But just for the record, I am doing my best."

Anthony gave a little laugh and patted his cousin on the shoulder. "You're a tough one, Giancarlo Rosa," he said. "No question about it."

Just then the first rocket of the fireworks display lit up the night sky with an enormous boom, prompting oohs and aahs from the gathering out front. It seemed a fitting close to the subject, and the two men walked around the house to watch the rest of the show.

Later, when the fireworks were over and Giancarlo had driven home, he sat at the kitchen table ruminating, as he often did at night, about the day's activities. A warm breeze was puffing through the window, and from off in the distance came a cracking of firecrackers, like a burst of gunfire. Giancarlo turned to the window and listened for a moment, trying to guess from exactly which direction the sound had come, but he heard it no more.

For some reason, as he gazed out the window, his thoughts drifted moodily to his last Italian lesson with Carter. Thinking back, he very much regretted his dreadful behavior of that afternoon. It was inexcusable. He had known full well that the boy was just kidding him. Why had he reacted so? It would not have surprised him if the young man had chosen to never return. Dejected by the thought of it, he passed a hand across the back of his neck, turned from the window, and reached for the cloth pouch sitting in the center of the table that held the gold pocket watch. Sliding the watch out into his palm, he stayed there for a time, turning the watch over and over again, his thoughts as always carrying him to some other place and time, until at last they carried him back to the inescapable present.

He gave a sigh.

"Her name," he murmured, tucking the watch back into its pouch, "was Antonella."

CHAPTER 16

Carter awoke abruptly on Monday morning, a stab of panic shooting through his gut. He thought for a moment that perhaps he had overslept and was in danger of being late for work, but the clock on the bedside table read only five fifteen. The alarm would not go off until six. Had he so chosen, he might have closed his eyes and tried to fall back to sleep for the remaining forty-five minutes, but instead he sat up and rubbed his eyes. He had been having a troubling dream, one that he had in varying forms from time to time, and he knew from experience that there was no point in lying back down; sleep had flown away from him for the rest of that morning.

In this particular version of the dream, Carter had been back at school. It was the end of the semester, and he realized with dismay that he had not done any of the reading for his classes. Exams were coming, and he had that terrible sinking feeling inside that he had let himself get so far behind that there was no possibility of his catching up in time. Were he to fail his exams, he would not be able to play his senior year of football, nor would he graduate, letting down his teammates and his coaches and, worst of all, his parents. Such an outcome was unconscionable to Carter, and the dream had filled him with deep regret and self-recrimination at his imagined laziness. It was a great relief to awaken and discover that all of it had taken place in his sleep-shrouded mind. All the same he still felt as though he had been put through the wringer.

Turning to the window, Carter looked out and saw that the sun had yet to burn off the soupy morning haze that had prevailed the past few days. There was not a stitch of breeze to be had, and all was still outdoors, save for the drops of dew dripping from the leaves on the trees. It was quite warm in his bedroom, uncomfortably so. Wearing only his boxer shorts, Carter had passed a fitful night's sleep atop the sheets. He had left every window on the second floor wide open, and the ceiling fan above his bed had whirred all night, but still he felt a fine sheen of sweat across the top of his chest and the back of his neck. It was going to be another steamy day.

With a yawn, Carter pulled his legs over the side of the bed and set his feet on the floor. He rolled his neck around and stretched his arms, conscious all the while of the lingering nervous twinge in the pit of his stomach. He took a deep breath and let it out slowly, hoping to dispel the feeling, but still it remained. Why, he wondered, did he have such dreams? Had he not just graduated from college and put all those worries about exams and papers behind him? He puzzled over it, until his gaze fell upon the little cassette player and headphones lying on the floor beside the bed. Then he understood. Inside the player was the latest Italian tape his professor had lent him. It was the last in the series, and he had meant to listen to it that previous night before going to sleep, but he had been too tired to do so. In truth, he had put aside his Italian studies and done nothing but sleep late and relax on the beach over the weekend. Carter truly enjoyed his Italian lessons and had lost none of his fervor to learn the language, but he was growing weary from the daily grind, and the three-day respite from construction work and his studies had come at a propitious juncture. He had needed the rest.

Nonetheless, sitting there on the edge of the bed, Carter now regretted the lost time. He had promised his professor that he would come prepared for his lesson later that day, but he had instead frittered away three precious days. It was already July 7. Officially, summer was barely three weeks old, but time had a way of taking flight in July. Look the other way for a moment and it would be gone. There was, as Giancarlo had told him, much that remained for him to learn and little time to do it. From here on in Carter knew he could not afford to let any more days slip through his fingers. With that nagging thought in mind, he arose, vowing to apply himself all the harder in the weeks to come.

When he arrived at Giancarlo's house later that evening—after his usual mad dash home to change after work—Carter was relieved to find his professor in much better spirits than when they last parted company. Giancarlo came to the door and greeted him with what appeared to be sincere cordiality.

"*Buona sera,* Signor Quinn," he said, waving him inside. "*Entra!*"

"*Buona sera, Professore,*" answered Carter, glad that the black cloud that had descended over their last meeting had apparently lifted. He stepped inside and started down the hall into the living room, where they normally met.

"*No, aspetta,*" said Giancarlo, bringing him to a stop. Gesturing for Carter to follow, he led him through the house past the kitchen and out to the screened-in back porch. The porch was simply furnished, with a rattan sofa and two chairs flanking a small table, upon which rested a pitcher of iced water, two glasses, and a plate of bread sticks. Outdoors the breeze was picking up, and the early evening air filtered through the screened windows just enough to make it a more comfortable setting for their talk than the stuffy confines of the living room.

"*Fa un po più fresco qui,*" explained Giancarlo, motioning for him to take a seat. "It's a little cooler here than inside."

"Works for me," agreed Carter. He sat down at the table and eyed the pitcher of water.

"*Prenda,*" said Giancarlo, gesturing for Carter to help himself.

"*Grazie,*" replied Carter. He poured a glass of water and slid it over to Giancarlo before filling the other for himself. He downed a gulp of water and gave a sigh of relief.

"A hot day at work, I would imagine," said Giancarlo.

"Oh yeah," chuckled Carter. "There's no air-conditioning in my office at work."

"Bah, air-conditioning," huffed Giancarlo with a dismissive wave. "Perhaps it's a good thing for the sick and the very old, but for a healthy person I think it's much better to just let your body adapt to the weather. This going from hot to cold and cold to hot is no good."

"You're probably right," shrugged Carter. "But lately it seems like I just go from hot to hot. A little cold now and then wouldn't hurt."

"You'll get used to it," Giancarlo assured him. He reached for his glass of water, took a sip, and sat back. "So, I trust you had a pleasant holiday," he said, eyeing Carter thoughtfully.

"Not bad," said Carter with a shrug. "We had our traditional family cookout at my parents' beach house on the Fourth. That was fun. Other than that, I mostly just hung out by the shore and took it easy the rest of the weekend. Nothing special."

Inside, Carter cringed a little, for he was certain that his professor was about to inquire as to whether he had kept up his studies over the past five days. He knew it was silly for him to be concerned. After all he *was* paying for the lessons out of his own pocket. Just the same, he could not help feeling like a schoolboy who had just brought home a bad arithmetic test for his mother to sign.

"That's good," said Giancarlo instead. "In that case your mind should be well rested and ready to get back to work." He picked up a pencil and tapped it against his notepad. "So, where did we leave off last time?" he said, perusing his notes.

"We were talking about Abruzzo, I think," said Carter, hazarding a reminder of their last meeting.

"Ah, yes, so we were," said Giancarlo. "And we'll return there again some other time, but for now you need to concentrate on taking your understanding of the language to the next level. The easy part is over."

"That was the easy part?" said Carter with a little laugh.

Giancarlo simply nodded and reached over to the sofa, from where he produced the Italian-English dictionary and the Italian magazine he had purchased that rainy day in June. He placed both on the table and slid them over to Carter.

"From now on, the real work begins," he said. "I hope you are ready."

"Do I have any choice?" joked Carter.

"No."

Carter took a deep breath and let it out.

"In that case, I guess I'm ready," he told his professor. "So, where do we begin?"

"Where we always begin," answered Giancarlo. "At the beginning." Then he touched his ear and said, "*Ascolta!*"

CHAPTER 17

As his Italian professor predicted, in the days to come Carter found himself working harder than ever. The focus of his studies steadily shifted from simply listening and responding to reading and analyzing, which, at least in the beginning, proved quite tedious. The *Gente* magazine was the first of several Giancarlo gave him to read. It was a struggle at first, for he encountered many words and verb forms to which he had yet to be introduced, and he found himself wearing out the pages of his Italian-English dictionary so much so that before long, the paperback cover was creased and tearing away from the glue binding. This embarrassed Carter—he did not want it to appear that he did not know how to take care of his books, especially one that had been given to him—and he did his best to keep it out of sight during his lessons. As it turned out, Carter need not have worried. One evening Giancarlo happened to point it out and noted with approval that the little dictionary was quickly becoming *rovinato* (ruined). That it appeared to be ruined by use, he said, could only be taken as a positive sign.

As time went by, Carter noticed that his lessons were becoming less formally structured and more free-flowing and conversational. The subject matter of the publications he read—they were mostly celebrity magazines—did not seem to matter very much, and indeed they interested him little. What counted was that he understood most, if not all, of what he read. With practice, reading gradually came a little easier, for Carter discovered that most of the articles in the publications he read tended to use many of the same words. He began to suspect that, just like the newspapers and magazines in this country, most of what he was given to read was probably written at a very modest grade level.

All the same, at this stage of the game, it was all quite challenging enough for him. There were some verb conjugations, for example, over which he was perpetually stumbling, particularly the conditional and the imperfect subjunctive. His questions about these often served as starting points for the dialog between teacher and student. At the beginning of each lesson, Giancarlo would patiently explain and re-explain how and when each verb tense should be used. A brief discussion of whatever topic or person a particular article might have addressed usually ensued. Invariably, though, the conversation would move on to other subjects. Be it politics, life in America, art, movies, or even occasionally sports, Carter discovered that there wasn't much about which Giancarlo did not have an opinion. While carefully guiding the conversation so that it stayed within the confines of Carter's growing vocabulary, Giancarlo would encourage him to speak about his own opinions. In this way, he made his pupil stretch what he had learned further and further.

Carter enjoyed these talks immensely, and in many ways his lessons became more enjoyable, more relaxed and easygoing. In others ways, however, they became just the opposite, for Giancarlo was becoming more demanding with the passing of every session. In the early days, for instance, he rarely corrected Carter's pronunciation. What seemed to matter most back then was that Carter recall the appropriate words he needed to speak and that he pronounce them only reasonably well. Now, however, Giancarlo hopped on every error, impatiently tapping his pencil at the sound of the slightest mispronunciation or most minor emphasis on a wrong syllable. It was a bit disconcerting at times, but it gave Carter a greater sense of urgency about his lessons and made him focus that much harder. This disciplined approach bore fruit, and to the continued amazement of his professor (who took care not to reveal it), Carter's knowledge of the language grew by leaps and bounds.

A source of frustration for Carter, however, was his inability to put his burgeoning language skills to use outside of his lessons. Sometimes he would drive through Federal Hill, a predominantly Italian-American section of Providence, and stop at a bakery or market, hoping he might chance upon someone with whom he could converse. The old neighborhood was changing, though, and he was just as likely to encounter there someone of Hispanic or Asian origin as someone of Italian descent. Even then, on those occasions when he chanced to overhear snippets of conversations in Italian, the words he heard were often completely unintelligible to him. They *sounded* Italian, but like no Italian he had yet to hear.

"Don't even try to understand them," counseled Giancarlo one evening when Carter took the opportunity during a break in his lesson to bring up the subject. "What those people were most likely speaking wasn't really Italian, but a mishmash of Italian dialects and American English."

"What sort of dialects?" asked Carter, quite intrigued.

"Oh, there are of course many permutations of the Italian language," he replied. "You must understand that Italy over the centuries has been subject to one invasion after the other. Hordes of different people descended on the country from all over Europe and Asia, the Middle East, and Africa."

"I guess they must have come for the food," said Carter with a sly grin.

"Perhaps," said Giancarlo, trying not to dignify the remark with a response, "but in any case, many of them came and stayed, settling all over Italy, in different regions, where they left their marks on the language."

"Sounds interesting."

"Oh, it truly is," said Giancarlo. "It's a course of study all in itself."

"So, do these dialects still exist?" asked Carter.

"Very much in some parts of the country, and not so much in

others. For instance, as you know, the proper way to say 'let's go' is *andiamo*. In some places, though, they say *dammo* or *gammo*. When you go to Abruzzo you might hear people say *live* for 'olive' instead of *oliva,* as you would say it in proper Italian. Words are changed like that all over the place. A letter is dropped here, a couple are added there. It happens a lot."

"That's weird," chuckled Carter.

"No, not really," said Giancarlo. "That's just the way languages are. They have a life of their own. They're always changing, never stagnant. When cultures mix, one language can borrow from the other, and different people can speak the result in many different ways. And they all have their little idiosyncrasies. Think about the way people speak English in this country. People say things like 'whatcha doin' or 'I wanna go.' Around here, that sweet, fizzy beverage you buy at the store is called soda, but in other places it's pop, and in others it's tonic. There are all sorts of words like that, and very often different ways of pronouncing them all around the country. Think about the phrase 'atta boy.' As an athlete, I'm sure you've heard that a million times. You know what it means, but how would you explain it to a foreigner?"

"That's funny," said Carter thoughtfully. "I've never really thought about things like that. You just seem to know what people are saying without it being explained."

"That's because you've grown up in the culture," said Giancarlo, "surrounded by the language. It comes as natural to you as breathing the air. It's the same in every culture. And it's the same in Italy, and that's why there are a great many dialects."

Carter paused to consider this last statement. "If that's the case," he asked after a moment's consideration, "how will I possibly understand them all?"

"You won't," said Giancarlo flatly. "So there's no point in even trying. The most important thing to remember is that no matter where you go in Italy, most people will understand *you* if you speak proper Italian."

"Sounds like I'll have my work cut out for me when I go," said

Carter, suddenly feeling a little concerned in this regard. "Do you think by the time I leave I'll know enough to get by?"

"Oh yes," said Giancarlo, nodding confidently. "That is, if you continue as you have, and try to work a little harder."

"A little harder?" laughed Carter. "Hey, I'd study more if I had more time."

"An interesting choice of phrase," noted Giancarlo, narrowing his gaze at him. "How would you say it in Italian?"

Carter furrowed his brow for a moment.

"*Se avessi piu tempo, studiarei di piu?*" he offered, as always uncertain as to whether he had used the subjunctive and conditional properly.

Giancarlo sat back and nodded his approval.

"Atta boy," he said.

CHAPTER 18

One morning, Giancarlo decided on a whim to take a ride to his office at the college, something he rarely did in the summer. His aim was to spend an hour or two there perusing the online editions of the various Italian newspapers he liked to read from time to time. It had been several weeks since he had last read any of these, and he was curious to learn just what the latest comings and goings were in his native land. Had he been willing to shell out a few extra dollars every month, Giancarlo would have been able to do all the Internet reading he might like from the comfort of his own home. Born and bred with an exceedingly frugal nature, however, he refused to pay for high-speed access and contented himself instead with a dial-up connection. It was painfully slow, but by and large adequate for his purposes. Giancarlo was not one to communicate very often through e-mail, so for the few hours a month he might otherwise spend reading online, it hardly seemed worth the extra expense. In any case, it was a good excuse to get out of the house, and the faster connection in his office would more than make up for the time spent in the car.

It was a perfect summer day, warm and dry and sunny, the kind you get only in July. The winds had shifted over the past few days, chasing away the heavy humid air that had recently dominated the weather. In its place a refreshing blast of dry air had blown in from the northwest. His car windows wide open to take in the pleasant breeze, Giancarlo drove up the hill that led to the center of campus and navigated his way to the Performing Arts Center. When he stepped out of his car, he turned his face for a moment to the brilliant sunshine before glancing off into the distance. There he saw the dome of the State House and the tops of the buildings in downtown Providence. It was really quite a lovely view of the city, but one of which, for some reason, Giancarlo seldom bothered to take notice. He pushed the car door shut and headed across the parking lot to his office.

"Ciao, Giancarlo!" came a familiar voice from behind him before he had traversed far.

He turned and saw someone walking after him. It took a moment for him to realize that it was Henry Sheffield. At first Giancarlo had not recognized the dean, for he was dressed in shorts and a T-shirt instead of the tie and jacket in which he was normally attired. Giancarlo waved a greeting and waited for him to catch up.

"Good to see you, Giancarlo," said Sheffield when at last he caught up to him, and the two shook hands. "What a surprise it is to find you here. It's so strange, but I was just thinking about you a little while ago. I had an idea that I was planning to discuss with you, but I thought for sure we wouldn't see you on campus until you made your usual grand entrance the first day of classes. What on earth brings you here on such a beautiful day? You should be out someplace enjoying it."

"If you want me to lie, I'll tell you I've come to do some work," said Giancarlo easily. "But the truth is—"

"Ah, please don't tell me the truth," protested Sheffield, playfully putting up his hands in a defensive gesture. "It's such a pleasant day, and I'd really rather not ruin it just yet by hearing the truth about anything. I'm in a bit of a hurry at the moment, in any case, so why don't you save it for now, and we'll talk about it over lunch—my treat. You can catch me up on what you've been up to this summer, and I'll tell you what it is I've been thinking about."

A time to meet was agreed upon, and the two went on their separate ways.

All was quiet in the music department when Giancarlo finally made his way down the corridor to his office. Every door on the hall was closed, and the stale, hot air trapped inside had a musty scent, like old books. The first thing he did upon entering his office was throw open the window to let in some fresh air. With no cross ventilation, it helped only a little, but it was better than nothing, and in any event, he wasn't planning to stay there long. And so Giancarlo settled in at his desk, turned on the computer, and set about searching the Web to see what news of interest there was to be had from across the Atlantic.

Later, at the appointed hour, Giancarlo shut down his computer and ambled across the campus to meet Henry Sheffield at the café in the student union. There both men ordered simple tossed salads for lunch, Sheffield because he was trying to trim off some extra pounds, Giancarlo because there was nothing else in particular on the menu that appealed to his finicky palate. The two took their trays and found a table by the window.

Giancarlo cast his eye about the largely empty room. During the fall or spring, the café was ordinarily quite crowded during the lunch hour, and tables by the window were at a premium. Save for a handful of summer students and one or two faculty members, none of whom he recognized, the café was largely empty now. He turned and looked out the window to the quad, where, not surprisingly, several students were lounging on the grass, enjoying the gorgeous day, while a few others tossed around a Frisbee. Giancarlo watched them for a time with envious eyes. They all seemed so carefree. He tried to think back and remember a time when he himself had been so, but none came to mind.

"Gee, you're a cheap date, Giancarlo," said Sheffield, bringing him back to the present. He opened a little packet of diet ranch dressing and squeezed it out across the top of his lettuce and tomatoes. It covered very little, and with a look of consternation, he tossed the empty pack into the top of the salad's plastic container. "Are you sure that's all you're going to have?" he added. "They make a decent egg salad sandwich here, you know."

This last remark he made with a sly grin, for he knew Giancarlo well.

As he pondered with indifference the packet of Italian dressing for his own salad, Giancarlo caught the mischievous gleam in his friend's eye. He put the unopened packet aside and gave a grunt.

"Henry," he said soberly, "I think you already know that I am not going to even dignify that last comment with a response."

"Ha!" laughed Sheffield. "Just the type of response I expected. It's good to see that some things never change. So, now you can tell me the truth. What are you doing here today, skulking about the campus?"

"Well, I wouldn't call it skulking," chuckled Giancarlo, picking at his salad. "Actually I just came to do a little reading online to catch up on the news in Italy."

"Still haven't broken down and gotten yourself a high-speed connection at home, eh?" Sheffield chided him.

"Afraid not," Giancarlo admitted, "but it's on my list of things to do."

"Yes, and I'll believe that when I see it," chuckled his friend. "So, tell me what you have been up to this summer."

"Not all that much, I'm afraid," replied Giancarlo, "other than giving some Italian lessons."

"Italian lessons?" said Sheffield, eyebrows raised. "I thought you had given that up, at least for this year. What was it you said to me at the end of this past semester? 'I'm tired, and I'm taking the summer off to do absolutely nothing and go absolutely nowhere.' What happened to change your mind?"

Giancarlo gave a shrug.

"The young man who came to me for lessons was quite enthusiastic about it," he offered by way of explanation. "It was hard to tell him no. Just the same, at first I wasn't going to do it, for exactly the reasons you said." He paused for a moment and looked away to the quad. "But I don't know," he went on, "I'm glad I did it now. It hasn't been the chore I thought it was going to be. Actually, I've rather enjoyed it. He has worked very hard and made a great deal of progress, a remarkable amount really."

Giancarlo was telling the truth. He truly had been enjoying the lessons. Carter's enthusiasm, however, had been only part of his own motivation in taking him on as a pupil. Giancarlo had reasons of his own for doing so, but those were his own affair. He decided that he had said enough on this subject.

"How about you, Henry?" he asked. "What have you been doing to keep yourself occupied so far this summer, and what is this idea you said you wanted to talk to me about?"

Sheffield gave a little cough to clear his throat and shifted uneasily in his chair, making Giancarlo suspect that in some unexpected way he was about to be put on the spot.

"Here's what I was thinking," his friend said, leaning closer. "The other day we were knocking around some ideas for the upcoming year, and the idea of holding a benefit concert put on by the music department came up."

"It just came up?"

"Well, actually, I brought it up," Sheffield admitted.

"I thought so," said Giancarlo. "And who exactly would this concert benefit?"

"We haven't gotten that far yet," he replied. "But there's no shortage of organizations we might help. People helping the homeless, cancer research, scholarship funds, or maybe the proceeds could go to support music programs in public schools. Who knows? It's really just a matter of using our imaginations. In any case, it would be a nice way for us to give a little something back to the community, and it wouldn't be bad for public relations, either."

"Sounds like a nice enough idea," said Giancarlo.

"I'm glad you think so."

Sheffield paused for a moment.

"Anyway," he continued cautiously, "we thought it might be nice if some of the faculty as well as the students performed."

"I'm sure there would be no shortage of volunteers," said Giancarlo with equal caution.

"Here's the thing," said Sheffield, cringing a bit. "What we— what *I*—thought would make the night extra special would be if perhaps, well, if perhaps *you* were to perform again for us. Maybe even consider composing a little something to play for the occasion."

At this suggestion, Giancarlo went cold inside.

"Henry, please," he said, shaking his head, "you know that I don't—"

"Now don't go and say no right off the bat," said Sheffield with a huff. "All I'm asking you to do is think about it. Come on, it could be wonderful. It would do you good."

"But Henry, you know that I don't play in public anymore," said Giancarlo. "And I haven't written anything new in years."

"Well maybe this could be the spark that gets you going again," he said. "It could be just the thing you need. Maybe you can recapture some of that fire you used to put in your music."

"I'm afraid that fire went out a long time ago," sighed Giancarlo.

Sheffield sat back and rubbed his chin.

"Look, Giancarlo," he said gently, "if this concert comes off, it won't happen until the spring, so you have lots of time to think it over. Just keep an open mind about it, that's all I'm asking right now. Don't say no; just say maybe."

Giancarlo was opening his mouth to just say no, but Sheffield did not give him the chance.

"Or, if you won't say maybe," he added quickly, "then don't say anything at all right now, and we'll discuss it in the fall. How's that?"

Giancarlo's only response was a low grumble of distinct displeasure, to which Sheffield gave a smile.

"By the way," the dean asked, deftly changing the subject, "if you're not going to use that Italian dressing, I'll take it."

Giancarlo handed over the packet.

"Thanks," said Sheffield, tearing open its corner. "So, how about those Red Sox?"

When he returned home that afternoon after lunch, Giancarlo walked out front to the mailbox, where he found amongst the bills a postcard bearing a picture of sand dunes by a beach. The card was from Patricia. He walked back to the house and sat on the front step to read it.

> *Giancarlo,*
>
> *Spending a few days with friends out on the Cape. Heard a great piano player last night at one of the hotels nearby. Made me wish I could play, which of course made me think of you and those piano lessons you promised me. Hope you're enjoying the summer!*
>
> *Patricia*
>
> *P.S. See, I'm keeping in touch. Your turn now.*

Giancarlo sat there on the step, absentmindedly turning the card over and over in his hands before finally tucking it back in with the rest of the mail. He looked about the yard and considered the shrubs and the flowerbeds out back, which were still very much in need of attention. Tending to them might have been just the thing he needed at that moment to distract his mind, but his heart was simply not in it. He was now very much preoccupied with Sheffield's invitation to play at the concert, with Patricia's postcard, and even with the upcoming Italian lesson scheduled with Carter for that evening. Suddenly Giancarlo had a vague, uneasy feeling about things that somehow, in some strange way he could not explain, time and circumstances were slowly drawing a lasso about him, preparing to drag him off to some unknown place he would rather not go. He disliked that feeling more than he could describe, and so he retreated into the refuge of his home, hoping he might escape it at the piano.

CHAPTER 19

Carter stood in the kitchen, guzzling down a glass of water. When it was empty, he turned on the tap again, eyeing the clock on the stove as the glass refilled. It was almost six o'clock, and he was expected to be on the rugby pitch by six thirty that evening for the start of practice with his new club. The club had begun training together the previous week to prepare for the start of the fall season. Fortunately for Carter, practices took place on Tuesday and Thursday nights, so they did not conflict with his Italian lessons. Just the same, the addition of this extra commitment had further crimped his already-crowded schedule. Now, save for the weekends, it seemed he did not have a free moment to himself anymore.

Carter glanced at the calendar hanging near the telephone on the wall. July was flying by. The month, he noted with equal measures of excitement and anxiety, was almost gone. The days and his Italian lessons were passing fast, and Carter wondered where the time had gone. Looking back, with the exception of a few precious days on the beach, the summer to that point all seemed a blur of work and lessons and study. The addition of rugby practice to his weekly agenda only compounded that feeling, but Carter had no reason to complain.

Carter had discovered the sport of rugby just that past spring, during his senior year of college, but already he loved it. Up till then, Carter had played football at one level or another practically from the time he could walk. As he progressed from the peewee leagues to high school and finally into college, the football season came to be the focal point around which he built his world. Being a football player was for him an important part of his identity. It gave him discipline and a sense of purpose and belonging that seemed to make everything else in his life better.

And so it was that the end of his collegiate football career came as something of a trauma to the young man. It left a great void in his psyche. When Carter took off his helmet and pads for the last time, packed his kit, and walked out of the locker room, he felt as though a great part of him had died, and he grieved much for it throughout the cold winter months that followed. Without a clear goal to train for, the careful discipline with which he had led his life suddenly fell apart. He stopped working out and taking care of his body, and instead took to carousing with his friends till all hours. He cavorted with women and ignored his studies, and was very close to throwing away his chance of graduating on time. Then one Saturday morning, after a particularly late night of revelry that left him passed out on the vestibule floor of a fraternity house other than his own, Carter was roused from his slumbers by a stiff kick in the ribs. Dry-mouthed and bleary-eyed, he looked up and beheld two of the fraternity's brothers gloating over him.

"You're a mess, Quinn," one of them had said with disgust.

"Really," the other had agreed with a supercilious air. "It's about time to pull yourself back together, don't you think?"

Not at all certain of his precise location at that particular moment, Carter had sat up and squinted at his two tormentors through bewildered red-rimmed eyes. Far too hung over to respond with anything other than a groan and gurgle, he gaped at them in dumb silence until the two simply shook their heads, gave him a few choice comments to consider, and left him there in a heap.

Later, as he was trudging back across campus, his head weighed down by an anvil of pain, a forlorn Carter had happened to pass a playing field where the university's rugby club was out practicing. Despite his sorry condition, he stopped for a moment to watch. Carter had heard about rugby before, but had never seen it played. Standing there alone on the sidelines, watching the players run through their drills, hearing their captains barking out instructions, he felt a familiar longing tugging at his insides. He found himself staying there for the remainder of the practice session, trying to get a sense of what the game was all about. Rugby, so it had seemed to him, was an odd amalgam of soccer and muckle football. It all seemed a little out of control, but something about it intrigued him and made him forget for a time about his splitting headache. And so, when practice was over, he approached one of the team's captains and inquired about giving the sport a try.

It was not long before Carter carved out a niche for himself on the team. His size and speed made him a perfect flanker, one of the pack of forwards whose job it was to fight for possession of the ball. Carter was a hellion on the field. With no experience and very little knowledge of the rules of the game, he often did the wrong thing, but for every error he committed he more than made up for it with his aggressive play. He was a fearsome, fearless tackler, and regardless of the situation, he always played his heart out. The discovery of the sport, the camaraderie, the brutally tough play, the teamwork, had all exhilarated Carter. It was pure joy, and it had the effect of bringing order and discipline back into his life. His elation was only furthered when he learned that there were amateur rugby clubs throughout New England for which he might play when his college days were finally history.

Life, he learned, could go on without football.

Now, after having practiced with his new club for just two weeks, Carter had already made a strong impression on his captain and teammates. He was a promising player, always hustling, never afraid to be in the thick of the action. His enthusiasm was contagious, and it soon became obvious that he was the kind of player who, simply through his example, could make everyone around him play better. All of that, however, would take a little seasoning, and his teammates tried to cajole him into forgoing his trip to Italy so as not to miss the first few matches of the fall campaign.

There was of course no chance of that happening, mused Carter as he downed the second glass of water. Rugby certainly occupied an important place in his plans for the immediate future, but it was still secondary, as were all other considerations, to his quest to find Elena again. As much as he sensed the swift passage of the days, Carter also could not escape a different feeling, one that told him that in some other way time had stopped for him and would not go forward again until his mission to Italy was fulfilled. Till then all else in his life had to stop and wait, like a clock in need of winding. Just the same, Carter understood that no matter how *his* life might have bent the passage of time, rugby practice would begin without fail in thirty minutes. With that in mind, he left the glass in the sink, grabbed his kit, and hurried out the door.

After practice, Carter returned home much later than he had planned. He had decided to stay at the rugby clubhouse to drink a quick beer with his new teammates. He had meant to come straight home, for he had a short story by Pirandello to read to prepare himself for the next day's Italian lesson. Just the same, he had found it hard to leave. Lately he had been living a hermit's life, and he welcomed the opportunity to blow off a little steam with friends. The time had passed quickly, though, and it was nearing midnight by the time he drove down the street to his house. He pulled into the driveway, parked the car, and ambled across the lawn to the house, his rugby kit slung over his shoulder. As he mounted the steps to the porch, Carter discovered a sizable manila envelope waiting there for him at the foot of the front door. He dropped his kit and stooped down to pick up the package. It was surprisingly hefty. Holding the envelope up to the porch light, he saw a short message written on its side that read:

* * *

Happened to come across these. Saved them from a high school trip to Italy. Thought they might come in handy in case you get lost over there.

S.

Carter sat down on the front step. He opened the envelope and, much to his surprise and delight, found within an assortment of brochures and guidebooks to Italy. He eagerly took one out and flipped it open. The book contained a pullout map of Rome showing the location of the Vatican, the Colosseum, and other places of interest. Another book showed the sights of Venice, and a third was about a museum in Florence. There were many others. It was a wonderful collection. As he sifted through it all, it occurred to Carter that, other than finding Elena's hometown on the map and intensely studying the Italian language, he had done next to nothing to prepare himself for where he would go and what he would see on his journey through Italy. Sheila had been right—these books would indeed come in handy.

Carter smiled. It was a very thoughtful gesture on her part, and he felt a warm sense of gratitude glowing inside. Standing, he looked over to the Mahoneys' house, hoping he might knock on the door to say thank you right away, but from the darkened windows it appeared that everyone had already turned in for the night.

Carter felt a stab of regret. If he had come straight home from practice as planned, he might have been there when Sheila came by. Now he would have to wait until their paths crossed again before he could thank her. There was of course no guarantee of this happening any day soon. Lately he saw very little of his neighbor, and when he did, she seemed every bit as squeezed for time as he. More than likely Sheila was just as wrapped up in the preparations for her year in France as he was in readying himself for his trip to Italy. He stood there for a time, wondering what he should do. He supposed that he could call her on the telephone the next day to say thank you, but for some reason this idea made him a bit apprehensive. He puzzled over the matter a bit further until he decided in the end that, if all else failed, he would simply write a note of his own to her and leave it in her mailbox. Till then there was nothing else to do, so with a yawn he collected his things and went inside to see how much of Pirandello he could read before he dropped off to sleep for the night.

CHAPTER 20

*"**P**rendiamo un piccolo intervalo?"* said Giancarlo.

"Si, d'accordo," agreed a relieved Carter.

It was the evening of the next day. The two were sitting on Giancarlo's porch, where they had been discussing at length the Pirandello story Carter had been assigned to read. As Giancarlo had anticipated, it had been a challenging exercise for his pupil. He knew that the tale contained many unfamiliar words and old expressions, most of which Carter would find no mention in his little Italian-English dictionary. Such being the case, it had been difficult at times for the young man to follow the flow of the narrative and appreciate the story's subtle humor. Giancarlo understood all this and patiently went through the story with him sentence by sentence, and occasionally word by word, but it proved to be a tiresome effort for both student and teacher. Just the same, Giancarlo had persisted, for he felt that this introduction to Italian literature was a worthwhile exercise that would pay dividends in the future. But after nearly an hour, even he had to agree that enough was enough. It was time for a little break.

For a moment the two sat back and relaxed. It was a tranquil, pleasant summer evening. The brisk late afternoon breeze that just a short while earlier had been shaking the leaves on the trees out back like pom-poms had abruptly settled down. The air outside had now grown quite still, but nonetheless it was full of sound: the chirping of the birds as they hurried back and forth from the grass to their nests, the laughter of children playing nearby, the low rumble of a lawn mower somewhere farther off in the neighborhood.

"So, what is that you brought with you tonight?" said Giancarlo at last, nodding to the manila envelope at Carter's side. "Something to eat?"

"No, no hamburgers tonight," chuckled Carter. He opened the envelope and let the guidebooks Sheila had given him slide out onto the table. "I thought I'd show you these tonight. Maybe get some ideas from you about where I should go while I'm in Italy."

"*Eccellente*," said Giancarlo, nodding his approval as he reached out to take one of the books in hand. "How did you come by all of these?"

Carter gave a little cough to clear his throat.

"*Un amico*," he said a bit sheepishly. "A friend gave them to me."

Giancarlo cast a skeptical eye on Carter, for by now he knew his student well enough to know when he was being told only part of the story.

"*Un amico* or *un'amica?*" he asked, slyly stressing the final vowel to determine with certainty whether Carter was referring to a male or a female friend.

"*Un' amica*," Carter admitted with a shrug, confirming the latter.

"Hmm, *that's* interesting," said Giancarlo as he settled back again and pretended to look over the book he had taken.

"Oh, it's not like that," said Carter hurriedly, anxious, it seemed, that there be no misunderstanding. "She's just a friend from the neighborhood who knows I'm going to Italy."

Giancarlo looked up with an expression of feigned innocence.

"I was referring to the book," he said with a smile.

"Oh, of course," said Carter.

"Have you had a chance to look any of these over?" said Giancarlo, sliding the book back across the table.

"I flipped through a couple of them last night," said Carter, now more at ease. "I noticed they talk a lot about churches."

"Oh yes," nodded Giancarlo. "If you do any sightseeing at all, you'll most certainly find yourself traipsing through plenty of churches."

"Why's that?" said Carter.

"Why?" replied Giancarlo with eyebrows raised. "Don't you know that Italy has the most beautiful churches in the world? In them are some of the greatest works of art the world has ever seen."

Carter shrugged in a way that conveyed that this was all news to him.

"I was a finance major, remember?" he said. "I was never big on art."

Giancarlo shook his head sadly.

"Your education has been sorely lacking, my friend," he said with a click of his tongue. "I think this trip to Italy will be a good thing for you."

With that Giancarlo fell silent for a time and gazed out the window, his mind lost in thought while he tapped his pencil against the tip of his nose. Before long, though, he came back to himself and gave a little laugh.

"What is it?" asked Carter. "What's so funny?"

"Oh, nothing really," Giancarlo replied. "I was just thinking about Italy and all the churches. The country is over ninety-five percent Catholic, you know. Just about everybody is Catholic. They have churches everywhere, but just the same, hardly anyone ever goes to mass."

"Really?" said a surprised Carter. "Why not?"

"That's a little hard to explain," confessed Giancarlo, rubbing his chin. "Like everything else in Italy, the reasons are a little complicated. Italians have an odd sort of relationship with their church. You see, on the one hand, everyone there gets baptized, makes their first communion, gets confirmed, and gets married in the church. And then when they die, they all want to get buried by the church. It's an important part of their lives. Italians know all the prayers and all the hymns and all the saints. They embrace all of that, and truly take it into their hearts. On the other hand, though, Italians hate hard-and-fast rules of any kind, especially when it comes to how they live their lives, so because of this they have this strange way of keeping the Church at arm's length. Like I said, it's a little hard to explain, but there are a lot of things like that in Italy. Everything is not always the way it seems. There are many shades of gray there and not so much black and white, if you know what I mean. In any case, I think if you really wanted to truly understand it, you would have to live there for a while."

"That's interesting," said Carter after a moment's contemplation. "So how about you? Are you a churchgoer?"

"No, not in a long time," admitted Giancarlo with a harrumph. "I'm afraid that God and I haven't exactly been on speaking terms for quite a while."

Now it was Carter's turn to chuckle.

"What's so funny?" asked Giancarlo.

"I was just thinking that you'd better not let Mama Quinn hear you say that," he said.

"Oh, why not?"

"Because she'll drag you by the ear to confession, and then make you go to mass every day for a month!"

At that the two men shared a laugh.

"Well, your mother certainly sounds like a good woman," said Giancarlo.

"Oh yeah, she's tough," he nodded.

"Most good women are," said Giancarlo. "But they don't always show it."

With that he tapped his pencil against his notepad, letting Carter know that it was time to get back to work.

Later, when the lesson was over and it was time for Carter to be on his way, Giancarlo walked him to the front of the house and opened the door. Carter stepped out onto the stoop, where he paused for a moment and turned around.

"So what do you think, *Professore*," he asked. "Would it really be worth my time to visit some of those churches, even when I know next to nothing about art?"

"Don't worry," Giancarlo told him. "It doesn't matter how much you know about art. It only matters that you are human. Trust me, the pictures in your books don't begin to do those places justice. When you go there and see them in person, some of what you find will be so beautiful it will make you want to cry."

"Hey, I don't cry easily," chuckled Carter with mock bravura.

"Perhaps not, my friend," said Giancarlo with a shrug. "But I suspect that when you go to Italy, you may discover that your heart is just a little softer than you imagine it to be. But you can always take that up with God when you get there."

CHAPTER 21

August came, and July was soon a memory.

What had started for Carter as just a dream back in May was quickly taking on the shape of reality, looming larger and larger on the horizon just ahead. As the days went by and the date for his departure to Italy drew inexorably closer, it felt to him as though time had suddenly accelerated simply by virtue of his having flipped the calendar over to the next page. It was like he had been paddling a canoe all summer down an easy-flowing river, unaware that the quiet water beneath was gradually pulling him along faster and faster until all at once, without warning, he had found himself on the rapids. Now there was no way to escape its irresistible pull, and Carter had the strange sensation that all he could do was hang on, let the river take him where it might, and try to steer a safe and steady course until he reached his destination—which he fervently hoped was not the falls.

It was at once exhilarating and unsettling, but August had always been a month of mixed emotions for Carter. Ever since he was a boy, he had looked forward with great anticipation to the end of August and the start of the new football season. Just the same, he loved the summer—the lazy days at the beach, the soft nights, the tranquil feeling inside that it would go on forever—and it saddened him to watch its final days beginning to slip away from him. He was of course thrilled at the prospect of very soon setting off to find Elena, but the approach of autumn still brought a nervous twinge to his stomach and filled him with a sense of regret that somehow he had frittered away his time in the sun and left too many things undone.

One evening, after returning home from his Italian lesson, Carter was moodily considering these things as he lay stretched out on the love seat on his front porch. His head propped awkwardly against the wooden arm on one end, his legs dangling over the top of the other, he stayed there for a time, gazing blankly at the darkened sky. It was a cool night, another reminder that summer was on the wane and fall would not be long in coming. He had just decided to go inside to watch a pre-season football game on the television when from next door came the sound of a screen door banging shut. Carter looked over to the Mahoneys' house, where he saw Sheila descend the front steps. At seeing her walk across her front yard in his direction, he pulled in his legs and sat up straight.

Dressed in shorts and a lightweight hooded sweatshirt, a paper bag clutched in her hand, Sheila crossed the driveway and walked up to the porch.

"Hey there, stranger," she said, giving him a nod. "Long time no see. Feel like a little company for a few minutes?"

"Sure thing," said Carter with a smile. "Come on up and join me. I'm having another exciting night here listening to the crickets."

"Hey, I love the sound of crickets," she said. "I could listen to them all night."

"Then you've come to the right place," said Carter, sliding over to make room for her on the seat.

Sheila sat next to him, set the paper bag at her feet, and pulled out a bottle of beer. She twisted off the cap and handed it to him.

"Wow, this is service," said a surprised but pleased Carter. He looked at the bottle and back at Sheila. "I hope you're not going to make me drink alone."

"Don't worry," said Sheila, drawing a second bottle from the bag. "I came prepared."

She twisted off the cap and held up the bottle.

Carter eyed her for a moment, trying to read her expression.

"We drinking to anything special tonight?" he asked at last.

"How about to life after college?" she offered.

"That's good enough for me."

At that the two clinked their bottles together, and they each took a sip. For a time they fell silent, until Carter gestured to her sweatshirt.

"A little cool tonight," he said.

"Fall's coming," said Sheila. "Can you feel it?"

"I can," nodded Carter. "I don't know when it happened, but today I could feel a change in the air. All of a sudden it had that little bit of crispness in it."

"I know what you mean," smiled Sheila. "It makes you want to go to the mall and buy some sweaters and corduroys."

"Exactly!" laughed Carter. "It's weird, isn't it? I mean, it's still the middle of August. It'll probably be ninety degrees tomorrow, but suddenly it feels like summer's all over."

Sheila smiled, a little sadly, he thought, and nodded as if to say that she felt the same way. Then she pushed a strand of hair away from her face and looked into the distance for a few moments, allowing Carter to study the profile of her lovely face, her slender neck, and the long dark hair falling about her shoulders.

"Got your note," she finally said, turning back to him. "Thanks."

"No, thank *you* for all those books on Italy you gave me," said Carter in turn. "That was really nice of you to do. I would have thanked you in person, but these days it seems that I never see you anymore."

"I know. I've been a little busy getting ready for France," said Sheila. "It's been kind of crazy. I've had so much to do."

"I bet," said Carter. "I mean, things have been crazy for me and I'm just taking a little vacation. You're going for a whole year."

"Sometimes going on a shorter trip can make it harder, believe it or not," she chuckled, "at least when you're trying to decide which shoes to pack."

"I'm figuring on wearing sneakers most of the time," said Carter. "Other than that, I haven't given much thought to what else I'll be packing."

"Well I hope you at least took care of your passport," she said with a hint of concern in her voice.

"Oh yeah," said Carter. "I sent the application in way back when you told me what to do. It should come any day now."

"Good," said Sheila. "Now make sure you put it in a safe place when it does."

Sheila went on to lecture him on the importance of carefully guarding his passport while he was away, for he would need it wherever he went if he wished to find a hotel room, exchange money, rent a car, or, most importantly, get on the plane for the return flight home.

"Trust me," she warned him. "If you lose your passport, you're in for the hassle of your life. I know people it's happened to."

"Don't worry," he assured her. "I'll be careful."

Carter stretched out his legs and settled back. He was enjoying this impromptu rendezvous, and his gloomy mood of just a few minutes earlier had lifted. Carter took another sip of his beer and nodded to Sheila's house, from which he could hear the voices of her parents within.

"So how's Mrs. Mahoney doing?" he asked with a grin. "She okay with letting her little girl go across the ocean all by herself for so long?"

"Oh, my mother's doing fine with it," laughed Sheila. "It's my father who's really nervous. I keep telling him not to worry, but he won't listen. How about your parents?"

"Sort of the same, but just the opposite," he told her, rolling his eyes. "My mother's been making buttons ever since I started talking about going to Italy. If I even bring up the subject, she goes into convulsions."

"Hey, don't make fun of her," said Sheila, giving him a nudge. "She's just worried about *her* little boy."

The two of them laughed, but something in Sheila's eyes told

Carter that she was worried about him, as well. He would never have admitted as much, but for reasons even he did not quite understand, somehow this pleased him.

"So, how about your father?" Sheila asked. "Is he worried, too?"

"Ayyy, you know my father," jested Carter. "He just told me to go and get it out of my system so I can come home and get a real job instead of swinging a hammer."

Sheila gave a little smile and raised her bottle to her lips.

"What is it that he thinks you need to get out of your system?" she asked, giving him a sideways glance before taking a sip.

"Who knows," said Carter with a shrug, even though he had understood his father's meaning perfectly. Something in Sheila's tranquil gaze led him to believe that she had understood him equally as well. This caused him a moment's unease, as he was quite certain that she was about to press him further on the subject. Instead, to his relief, she suddenly looked down and reached into the paper bag.

"Almost forgot, I brought you something else," she said, pulling from the bag a small, thin package wrapped in plain brown paper and tied with red, white, and green ribbon. She handed it to Carter.

"What's all this?" he said.

"Oh, it's nothing," she replied softly, "just a little going-away present."

"But I'm not going away for another couple of weeks."

"I know," Sheila answered, her eyes growing a bit sad, "but you see, *I'm* leaving tomorrow."

"*Tomorrow?*" said Carter. "So soon?"

"I'll have a lot to do when I get there," said Sheila with a shrug.

It made sense of course, once he thought about it, that Sheila would need to go to France a little early to give herself some extra time to settle in before school started. Nonetheless the news that she was leaving the next day, that this would be the last they saw of each other for who could say how long, had caught Carter off guard. He had just assumed that they would be leaving for Europe at more or less the same time, and that there were plenty of days left before they said goodbye. Now that the moment had come upon him so unexpectedly, he found himself strangely crestfallen and felt a sad, sinking feeling in the pit of his stomach. Despite it, he forced a smile.

"Wow, I guess you must be excited," he managed to say.

"I am," she told him, "in a frantic sort of way, if you know what I mean." She nodded to the package in his hands. "Go ahead, open it."

Carter carefully untied the ribbon and opened the package. Inside he found a DVD box, which he held up to the light.

"*Cinema Paradiso*," he read aloud.

"It's one of my favorite foreign movies," said Sheila. "It's all in Italian, which I thought you'd like, since you're studying the language, but you can also watch it with subtitles if you want. Anyway, I thought you might enjoy it a little more than that last movie you rented."

"I doubt I could enjoy it any less," noted Carter, a rueful smile curling his lips at the thought of his last encounter with Italian cinema. Then, looking at her with grateful eyes, he added, "But I'm sure I'll like this one. Thanks."

"*De rien*," she said, fixing him with that old familiar gaze of hers.

Carter smiled warmly.

"In Italian you'd say *prego*," he told her.

"*Prego*," she said, returning his smile.

Carter looked down at the DVD and turned it over in his hands for a moment.

"Feel like watching some if it?" he offered.

"I'd love to," said Sheila, "but I can't. I have a lot to do in the morning, so I need to finish packing tonight. Besides, the ending always makes me cry."

"Oh no," said Carter, playfully feigning a groan. "Don't tell me you got me a chick flick, and now you're going to make me watch it all by myself."

"Don't worry," she told him. "It's not a chick flick, honest. It's just a really sweet story. I know you're going to like it." Then Sheila looked down at her hands and gave a little sigh. "Anyway," she said, looking up again, "I'd love to stay and watch it with you, but it's getting late."

With that she took a last sip of her beer, dropped the bottle back into the paper bag, and began to stand. Carter got up, as well, and walked with her to the edge of the porch. There the two stood very close for a time, neither, it seemed, knowing just what to say. Carter looked up into the sky, where the moon was now beaming down on them with its soft light. The night, he noticed, had suddenly grown very still. Even the crickets had quieted, almost as if they were all listening and waiting to see what would happen next.

"So, what time do you leave tomorrow?" he said at last.

"I'm heading to Boston at around three," she told him, "but my flight to Paris doesn't leave till a little after seven."

"Gee, I wish I could be here," he said awkwardly, "you know, just to give you a hand with your luggage or whatever."

"It's okay," Sheila reassured him. "I knew you wouldn't be home from work yet. That's why I came over tonight."

"I'm glad you did," he told her. "It really was nice. I don't know why we never managed to spend some time together earlier this summer." He gave a half smile before quickly adding, "And I'm not just saying that because I got free drinks and a movie out of the deal."

"It was my pleasure," said Sheila. "Next time it will be your treat."

Carter nodded in agreement.

"I'd like that," he said softly.

"So would I."

Carter knew that it was time for her to leave, and it struck him how disappointed he felt at this moment's coming. He stood there rather stupidly, trying very hard to think of something appropriate to say, until suddenly, with complete and natural ease, Sheila reached out and took his face in her hands. Carter felt himself go weak as she stretched up to him, brought her face to his, and kissed him gently on the cheek.

"See you someday, Carter Quinn," she whispered. "Don't forget me."

"I won't," Carter promised, his head bowed. "Goodbye, Sheila."

"In France they say *au revoir*," she told him, tapping him under the chin.

"And in Italy they say *arriverderci*," countered Carter.

Sheila smiled.

"I like the sound of both," she said.

With that she pulled away from him, descended the steps, and started back across the yard to her house.

"Hey!" Carter called after her.

Sheila stopped and looked over her shoulder.

"Send me a postcard one of these days," he said.

"I will if you will," she answered. Then she went on her way.

Carter stayed there and watched until Sheila had reached her front door and gone into the house. When the door closed behind her, he felt somehow empty inside, as if he had just lost something that he knew he might never find again. It made his heart grow heavy, and he turned to go inside, puzzled to realize that suddenly he was thankful that before long, summer would finally be over.

The next day, a sullen Carter went about his duties at the construction site with little of his usual enthusiasm. His altered disposition did not go unnoticed by his bosses, who playfully needled him throughout the day in the hope that he might reveal just what it was that had darkened his mood. These efforts came to no avail, and the two concluded that their young employee must have been suffering the ill effects of a late night out on the town. Not wishing to discuss the subject, for he was as much at a loss about it as they were, Carter said little to dispel that notion.

Later that afternoon, when he returned home from work and

stepped out of the car, Carter glanced across the yard to the Mahoneys' house, half expecting to see Sheila come strolling out of the front door on her way to the mailbox. By that late hour, he knew full well that she was already at the airport in Boston, waiting to board her flight. The thought did little to bolster his spirits, so he turned and walked out to his own mailbox to see what the mailman had brought that day.

Carter opened the box and pulled out the stack of envelopes inside. He gathered the mail into a neat bundle and brought it all to the front step, where he sat down for a moment to sift through it. Most of it was bills and junk mail addressed to his father or mother, and he was just about to bring it all inside and leave it on the kitchen table when he happened to spy an envelope addressed to him. At the sight of the return address, Carter felt a rush of excitement. At once he forgot all about the blues that had dogged him since the night before, and he eagerly ripped open the envelope and pulled out its contents. For the first time all day, Carter let himself give in to a smile.

His passport had arrived.

CHAPTER 22

Giancarlo opened his eyes.

A moment of uncertainty passed before he realized that he had dozed off on his study couch. Sitting up quickly, he glanced at the clock on his desk, puzzled to discover that it was late in the afternoon. Giancarlo had spent the first part of the day tending at long last to the much-neglected flowerbeds and shrubs in his backyard. When he had finished, he came back inside, showered, and prepared himself something to eat. After lunchtime he decided to lie down, intending to rest his eyes for no more than a few minutes, for there were things he wanted to do before Carter came to the house for his lesson that evening. Instead he had fallen into a deep, dreamless sleep, which had stolen away the afternoon hours and left him feeling more groggy than refreshed.

Rolling his neck and shoulders about to shake out the cobwebs, Giancarlo picked himself up and walked through the house to the front window. Across the street some children were laughing and shouting as they chased one another around his neighbor's house, while others rolled about the street on skateboards. The days, he noted as he watched them play, had grown noticeably shorter. The sun was already falling away to the west, while the trees cast long shadows across the lawn. Giancarlo rubbed the back of his neck and turned from the window. It annoyed him that he had slept so long. Carter would be coming to the house soon, and he was not yet ready.

Giancarlo went into the kitchen and sat at the table with the pencil and pad he had used all that summer to document Carter's lessons. For a time he flipped through the pages, following his notes, marveling still at how far the young man had come since he first appeared at his office door three months earlier. It was remarkable. Carter had achieved so much in such a short time that it had been a challenge to stay one step ahead of him from lesson to lesson. Looking back, despite his apprehensions at the beginning of the summer, Giancarlo realized that he had enjoyed the experience more than he would have ever expected, and he felt a certain pride in his student's achievements.

The summer, however, had run its course. It was Friday, the next to last week of August, and two days earlier Giancarlo had let Carter know that his lesson that evening would be the last. It made sense that they finish up now. Carter was scheduled to leave for Italy the following weekend. He would no doubt be too preoccupied with his preparations in the week ahead to make any additional lessons of value, and with Labor Day looming large on the calendar, Giancarlo himself would be busy getting ready for the start of the fall semester. It was better this way.

Giancarlo flipped through the pad until at last he came to a blank page. Taking the pencil, he scribbled some notes, reminders regarding some finer points of grammar, diction, and other subjects he hoped to cover during this final lesson. After a time, he paused to consider a different matter, one that had nothing directly to do with the Italian lesson, but that involved Carter nonetheless. It was a small business, trivial in a way, but it was something that had weighed on his mind all summer long. Tapping his pencil against the pad, Giancarlo turned the thing over in his mind. When at last he brought his ruminations to a resolution, he scribbled a few more notes to himself and tossed the pencil onto the table. A glance at the clock confirmed that the time had almost come to finally wrap things up. And so, with a yawn, Giancarlo rose from the table and went to the bathroom to throw a little water on his face to rouse himself before the doorbell rang.

For his part, Carter could not have felt more wide awake and refreshed. He was in fine spirits, and he drove along on his way to Giancarlo's house with the windows wide open and the radio blaring. The day had already seen the end of his construction career, a cause for celebration in itself. Carter had truly enjoyed his time as a construction laborer, for he liked his bosses, Ron and Dave, and he had learned much from them on the job. Just the same, he would not miss those long, grueling hours toiling away like a slave beneath the scorching summer sun. In a way, he felt a similar sentiment toward his Italian lessons. Despite his teacher's relentless badgering and occasionally cantankerous moods, Carter had come to like and respect him. Still, he had grown weary of his studies. With the day of his departure now drawing so near, he was glad to be done with them and more eager than ever to strike out on his own and put all he had learned to the test.

When he arrived at the house, Giancarlo opened the door wide and ushered him in with a sweeping gesture.

"*Buona sera*," he said. "*Entra!*"

"*Buona sera, Professore!*" replied Carter.

By now Carter felt quite at ease in the house, and he began to walk straight in toward the back porch.

"*Aspetta*," said Giancarlo, bringing him to a halt. He nodded to the living room. "*Parliamo qui dentro stasera.* Let's talk inside tonight."

With that he left Carter and walked off to the kitchen.

Carter went into the living room and took his seat at the little round coffee table, upon which he found an open bottle of red wine and two glasses. While he waited for Giancarlo to return, he looked about at the books and the piano and the musical instruments still all strewn about the room. It all brought back to mind that nervous day in May when he came to this house for the first time. It seemed so long ago now, and the memory of it brought a smile to his face.

Giancarlo soon returned carrying a plate holding a stick of dry abruzzese sausage, a wedge of cheese, olives, and some sliced bread.

"*L'ultima cena,*" he joked as he set the plate on the table and sat on the couch. "The last supper, for the last lesson." He nodded for Carter to help himself, while he took the bottle and began to pour, explaining as he filled their glasses that the wine was a typical one from the Abruzzo region. He passed a glass to Carter and raised his own. "*Salute,*" he said.

"*Salute,*" replied Carter, as he had been taught, raising his glass before taking a sip. Carter had always had a preference for beer—and a decidedly uneducated taste in wine—so he was pleasantly surprised to discover that he quite liked the taste, and found that it complemented well the flavors of the sausage and the cheese. This, he reckoned quite rightly, was not a coincidence.

Giancarlo took a sip from own glass and settled back.

"So," he said after a moment's contemplation, "you have come at last to the end of your lessons, and it's almost time to fly. Are you excited?"

"I guess so," said Carter with a shrug. "I just hope I don't forget everything next week before I go."

"Don't worry," Giancarlo assured him, "you won't forget anything. Trust me, it's better that you finish your lessons now and take a few days to rest your brain. This way you will have a clear head when it's time to leave."

"A *tabula rasa?*" said Carter.

"*Esatto,*" nodded Giancarlo. "For as much as you might have learned from me, you will learn far more once you are in Italy, things that I cannot possibly teach you." He paused to take an olive and a piece of cheese. "So," he asked, "do you have any plans for what you will do when you arrive in Rome?"

"Nothing definite," Carter admitted. "I thought I would knock around the country for a while, you know, just to get my feet wet. I thought I'd see some of Rome, maybe go to Florence or some other places . . . that is, before I go to Roccasale."

"Ah, yes, of course," Giancarlo nodded sagely, "where at long last you will go in search of your Beatrice, I presume."

Carter gave him a curious look.

"You mean Elena," he said.

Giancarlo grinned at him and gave a little laugh.

"You know," he said, "you have done very well with your study of the language, but someday you really must make a more serious study of Italian literature."

"Well," Carter kidded him, "like you said in the beginning, right now I'm more interested in studying an Italian woman."

At that Giancarlo chuckled again, but then his grin suddenly faded away, and he stared into his glass for a time before looking up at Carter with dark, sober eyes.

"Let me give you a little advice, my friend," he said in a deadly serious voice, "for I know a little bit about the women of my country. I know, for instance, how with just one look an Italian woman can shatter a man into a million pieces. I also know that if she's a *good* woman and she truly cares for him, she will put him back together way better than he ever was at the beginning. But if she doesn't, watch out, because then she'll leave him for dead without so much as a second thought. So be careful."

Despite this ominous pronouncement on his teacher's part, Carter could not suppress a smile.

"Why do I get the feeling that you're trying to talk me out of it?" he said, laughing.

"Hmm," grunted Giancarlo. "Would it matter if I were?"

Had his teacher posed that same question just a few weeks earlier, perhaps then Carter might have wavered, for even he had to admit that at times, as the summer had worn on, his vision of Elena had been like a candle in the wind. There were times when the flame burned so low that it seemed to him all but extinguished. Inevitably, though, whenever he began to despair that it was on the point of dying, it would suddenly flicker back to life, just as it had done in the last few days. Now, with so little time left before he flew to Italy, it glowed more steadily and brighter than ever.

"No," said Carter at last. "Not in a million years." Though he said it with a smile, he meant it with all his being. "Does that surprise you?"

"No, not really," said Giancarlo, his face brightening. "I was once a young man, too, you know, so I understand these things a little better than you might think. But enough of this subject. You have a lesson to complete." With that he picked up his pencil and tapped it against the pad. "*Va bene*," he began. "*Parliamo in Italiano!*"

The two talked for the better part of an hour. In the beginning they discussed a pair of short stories by Dino Buzzati that Giancarlo had assigned Carter to read. With practice, reading Italian had gradually become easier for Carter, and he had enjoyed the stories very much. There were of course, as always, one or two words and turns of phrases that had eluded him, but with his teacher's guidance he quickly grasped their meaning. When they finished with their discussion of the stories, they moved on to more everyday subjects: politics, current events, the weather. Giancarlo often encouraged this more casual form of dialog, for it allowed Carter to speak more naturally, as he would in any ordinary situation. In time the conversation turned to athletics, and the two men shared a lively debate on the question of which was the most demanding sport of all. Carter of course argued the case for American football, while Giancarlo insisted that professional cycling was by the far the most grueling. Neither made much headway in persuading the other man to his side, so the match ended in a draw.

That Carter had spoken so well, however, made it a victory of sorts for both teacher and student. When at last they were finished, Giancarlo fell silent for a time and thoughtfully rubbed his chin. Looking quite pleased with the result, he placed his pencil down and nodded his approval to Carter.

"*Basta,*" he told him. "Enough. I think now you are finally ready for your journey."

"*Grazie, Professore,*" said Carter, bowing his head modestly. "I couldn't have done it without you."

"I know," replied Giancarlo, deadpan.

At that Carter gave a laugh and reached into his pocket for his checkbook to pay for this final week of lessons. Before he could open it, Giancarlo wagged a finger at him.

"No," his professor told him. "This week there is no charge."

"Please," insisted Carter. "It wouldn't be right if I didn't pay you."

"Don't worry," said Giancarlo, getting to his feet. "I'm not planning to let you get away completely free."

With that Giancarlo turned from the table and walked out of the room. He returned shortly, bringing with him the small cloth pouch, which he set on the table before taking his seat again. Loosening the cord, he opened the pouch and let the pocket watch inside slide out onto the table. He considered it for a moment before passing it over to a curious Carter.

Unsure as to just why he was being shown the timepiece, Carter examined it nonetheless with interest, noting the intricate design etched on the watch's cover.

"May I open it?" he asked.

"Of course," replied Giancarlo.

Carter opened the watch and gazed at the young couple and the horse by the well depicted on the face inside. "Does it still work?" he asked, wondering if the figures moved at all when the watch was wound.

"Not in a long time, I'm afraid," said Giancarlo. "Which is why, in a way, I'm showing it to you now. I remember your saying that you were once a Boy Scout, yes?"

Carter nodded his head.

"Good, then I'm guessing that you are a trustworthy sort."

"Well, it is the first point of the Scout Law," replied Carter, quickly reviewing in his mind the other eleven points just to make sure.

"Very good," said Giancarlo. "In that case, I have a small favor to ask of you."

"Sure," Carter told him. "What is it?"

"As you saw that day when we looked at the map," he began, "Roccasale, where you plan to go, is not so terribly far from Castelalto."

"I remember," said Carter. "It was only about an inch and a half away," he quipped.

"Yes, well, perhaps a little farther than that," said Giancarlo, clearing his throat. "In any case, I was hoping, since you will be so close, and if it would not be too much trouble, that you would take this watch and deliver it to someone there for me. You see, I don't care for sending such things through the mail, so I'd feel better if it were in your hands."

Carter did not need to think twice. He had long been curious to know more about Castelalto but had been hesitant to ask, for it seemed his professor had little patience for questions about his hometown or his past.

"Of course I'll do it," he said without hesitation. "It won't be any trouble at all. Just tell me how to get there and who to bring it to."

Giancarlo carefully tugged a sheet of paper from his pad.

"I have it all written here," he said, sliding it across the table.

Carter looked at the name at the top of the sheet.

"Giorgio Rosa," he read aloud, his face lighting up. "Hey, is that a relative?"

"He is my brother," said Giancarlo softly, a faraway look in his eyes.

"No kidding," said Carter, intrigued by this revelation. "You never mentioned you had a brother."

"I've not seen him since I left Italy," his teacher replied, his voice betraying no emotion, "so there really was no need to mention him till now."

"Since you left Italy," Carter said to himself. "Wow, that's a long time ago."

"Almost thirty years."

Carter regarded his teacher for a moment with questioning eyes.

"Um, so I'm guessing that you two aren't particularly close," he said with some hesitation.

Giancarlo gave a shrug.

"I came to America, he stayed in Italy," he explained. "It happens. But it's nothing to concern you. Trust me, you will be very well received when you go there. All you need do when you arrive in Castelalto is ask anyone you happen to meet for the house of Giorgio Rosa. It won't be hard to find."

"Then what?" asked Carter. "I mean, besides the watch, do you have a message or something you want me to give your brother?"

Giancarlo pondered the question for a time.

"Yes," he said at last. "Tell him that he need not send the watch anymore. Tell him it's broken, and it cannot be repaired."

"That's all?"

"I think that should cover it."

Carter sat back, scratching the back of his neck as he tried to imagine how the future encounter would play out.

"Well," he said after a moment's reflection, "I suppose it's going to be a very short visit."

"That," said his teacher, "will be up to you."

With that Giancarlo clapped his hands together once and opened his palms wide, as if to signal there was nothing left to say. Carter took this gesture as his cue that the lesson had come to an end, and that it was finally time for him to leave. He slid the pocket watch back into its pouch and tucked it safely in his pocket. Then he collected his things and followed Giancarlo out to the front hall.

"So," Giancarlo said as he opened the door, "I assume your passport and travel arrangements are all in order."

"Oh yeah," nodded Carter. "All systems are go."

"Then that means there's no turning back now," said his teacher.

"I guess not," chuckled Carter. "Any last-minute advice for me?"

Giancarlo shook his head and looked at him with a smile that struck Carter as almost fatherly.

"No," he replied, "I think you have learned just about all that I can teach you. From now on, you are on your own."

Carter took a deep breath and let it out.

"In that case, I guess it's *arriverderci, Professore*," he said.

Giancarlo nodded and gave him a sly look.

"*Arriverderci, Signor Carter Quinn*," he said with a gleam in his eye. "And *buon viaggio!*"

Then he patted Carter on the shoulder and sent him on his way.

CHAPTER 23

Carter stood in the center of his living room, scratching his head as he stared at the piles of clothes and shoes, travel books, toiletries, and a variety of other items spread about him on the floor. It was early in the afternoon a week later, the day he was to leave for Italy. His flight out of Boston was scheduled to depart that evening at six fifteen, but he was only just now beginning to pack his bag. Where, he wondered, had the week gone? He had planned to pack his bag well in advance, certainly no later than the night before, but there had always been something else to do. His mother had offered to come home and help him, but Carter insisted on doing it by himself. It was a decision he was beginning to regret.

Now, with Jimmy due to arrive in less than an hour to take him to the bus station, Carter's mind was a whirl of indecision as he tried to sort out what he should take and what he should leave behind. How many shirts and slacks did he need? What shoes should he bring? Did he need a sweater, or was a windbreaker enough? What about a sweatshirt? And what if it rained? Should he pack a poncho? He had purchased an oversized duffel bag for the occasion, so by rights this should not have been a particularly difficult project. Nonetheless, he found himself running out of space every time he tried to stuff it all into the bag. Finally, in frustration, he made up his mind to toss out half of the clothes and make do with whatever was left over. That seemed to do the trick, and before long the duffel bag zipped shut without a hitch. Satisfied with the result, Carter hauled the bag out to the front hall and left it next to the small daypack that held his passport, airline tickets, a notebook, a pen, and the like. Then he fled upstairs to take a shower.

"Hey, what are you doing up there?"

It was Jimmy a short time later. He had let himself in while Carter had been showering, and was now pacing about at the bottom of the stairs.

His head still dripping, Carter wrapped a towel around himself, grabbed a second for his hair, and threw open the bathroom door. Rubbing the towel across his head, he rushed to his room to get dressed, pausing for just a moment at the top of the stairs to nod a greeting to his friend.

"Yo, Marco Polo!" Jimmy called after him. "You'd better get a move on up there, or you're gonna be walkin' to Boston."

"I'm hurrying, I'm hurrying!" Carter called back.

A few minutes later, still a little damp around the edges, a barefoot but otherwise fully dressed Carter came racing down the stairs. He sat on the bottom step and began to tug on his socks and shoes as he assessed his luggage. He had never before traveled out of the country, and he was haunted by the thought that he might forget something important.

"You planning on leaving sometime today?" asked Jimmy, who by now was stationed by the door, jangling his car keys.

"Quiet," Carter shushed him. "I'm trying to think. I don't want to forget anything."

His friend gave a sigh and shook his head.

"C.Q., you got your passport?" he asked.

"In here," replied Carter, opening the top pocket on the outside of the daypack.

"Good. And what about your tickets?"

"Same place," said Carter.

"And your wallet?"

"Right here in my back pocket."

"In that case you've got everything you need," said Jimmy.

"The rest is gravy. You need anything else, just buy it when you get there, right? It's not like you're goin' to Siberia, so don't sweat it so much."

Carter saw the wisdom in his friend's advice and immediately began to feel a little more at ease. "I guess you're right," he chuckled, getting to his feet. "I really shouldn't worry so much about—"

Suddenly he stopped and slapped himself on the forehead.

"What now?" cried Jimmy as Carter turned and dashed back up the stairs to his bedroom.

Carter returned shortly carrying a small padded envelope inside of which he had placed the pocket watch his professor had entrusted to his care.

"Almost forgot," he said, breathing a sigh of relief.

"What's that?" inquired Jimmy.

"Just something I promised my teacher I'd deliver for him while I'm in Italy," explained Carter, tucking the watch into the daypack.

"What are you now, the Pony Express?" said Jimmy, rolling his eyes.

Carter replied with a shrug.

Jimmy gave a huff and shook his head again. "You ready to roll now?" he asked.

Carter gave one last quick look around and took a deep breath. Letting it out, he nodded his head. "Let's go," he said.

Later, after Jimmy had driven them to the bus station and Carter purchased his ticket, the two sat in the terminal, waiting for the arrival of the bus for Boston.

"You know," Jimmy said, "I would have driven you up to Logan."

"Nah," replied Carter. "The traffic would be too thick this time of day on a Friday. But I appreciate the offer."

Jimmy stretched out his legs and looked about absentmindedly at the people coming and going in the terminal.

"So, you're really gonna go through with this whole thing," he said, turning to Carter. "I gotta admit, I never thought you'd do it. I figured this Italian broad was just some fantasy of yours that you'd get over after a while."

"To tell you the truth, there were times this summer when I thought the same thing," said Carter, "but it just wouldn't go away."

"So, now that you're finally going, are you nervous?" his friend asked.

"A little bit," admitted Carter, for his stomach was a bundle of nerves. "Actually, a lot. Matter of fact, I think I'm gonna hit the men's room right now." He stood, and gestured to the daypack, which held his passport and tickets. "Watch that for me," he said. "I lose that and I'm up the creek."

"I'll guard it with my life," said Jimmy.

When he came back a few minutes later, Carter found Jimmy relaxing with his eyes closed. He looked down at his friend's feet, where he saw the duffel bag. He was alarmed to discover, however, that the daypack was nowhere in sight.

"Hey," he said anxiously, giving Jimmy a kick in the foot. "Where's my bag?"

"What bag?" said Jimmy, yawning as if he had just awoken.

"The one with all my stuff in it," cried Carter. "The one with—"

"You mean this one?" snickered Jimmy, reaching over the back of his chair and pulling up the missing daypack. He held it up and smiled like a Cheshire cat. "Just keeping it safe," he said innocently.

"When I get back from Italy, I swear I'm going to kill you," vowed Carter, swiping the bag from his friend's hand.

"Just tryin' to get you to loosen up a little, that's all," Jimmy told him with a smile.

Carter grumbled, dropped back into his seat, and stared out through the big plate glass windows to the parking lot, where a bus was just pulling in.

"Hey," said Jimmy, giving him a nudge, "I think this might be your ride."

Sure enough, just then a voice came over the public address system, announcing that the bus for Logan Airport had arrived and would be boarding in just a few minutes.

"Yup," said Carter with a gulp. "It's showtime."

After the duffel was safely stowed in the luggage compartment, Carter and Jimmy stood outside the idling bus, chatting while Carter waited for the final call for all to board. It was a warm, breezy afternoon, and the air was filled with the diesel smell of the engine. By then most of the other passengers had already climbed on board, and the driver was now standing by the door, looking into the terminal to see if anyone else was coming. He glanced at his watch and gave a nod to Carter.

"Well, this is it," said Jimmy, giving him a pat on the shoulder. He paused, and gave a little laugh before adding, "Kind of fitting, isn't it?"

"What do you mean?" said Carter.

"What I mean," said Jimmy, suddenly looking more sincere than Carter could ever remember, "is that you're finally gettin' on that bus. Remember the bus? That same one you told me about that time in the gym? Well, this is it. Now you're going off to do something that most guys only talk about, but never have the balls to follow through on. You're following your dream. And all kidding aside, I think it's pretty awesome, man. So go. Get outta here. Go do like you said you were gonna do. Get on that bus, stay with it all the way, and see where it takes you."

Carter was truly touched by his friend's words. Nonetheless he made a face and rolled his eyes.

"Hey, what are you trying to do?" he said. "Make me cry now before I go?"

"Ha!" laughed Jimmy. "No way."

With that the two shook hands and hugged.

"Thanks for the lift, Jimmy," said Carter, pulling away. "I owe you a souvenir from Italy."

"Make it something good," Jimmy kidded him. "But nothin' too expensive."

Carter gave him a nod and started for the bus. He handed his ticket to the driver and was just mounting the steps to climb into the bus when Jimmy suddenly called to him.

"Hey, Marco," he said.

Carter turned and stuck his head back out the door.

"Forget the souvenir," Jimmy told him. "Just send me a post-card when you finally get laid."

PART TWO

CHAPTER 24

One spring morning, long ago when he was sixteen years old, Giancarlo was sitting at the piano, working through the opening bars of the frenetic third movement of Beethoven's "Moonlight Sonata." It was a challenging piece, even for a pianist as accomplished as Giancarlo had already become by that early age. Nonetheless the music intrigued him, and he was hoping to master it in time for an upcoming recital. It was tough going, though, and he had been at it for almost three hours straight. Now and then, when he grew impatient at his slow progress, Giancarlo would stop and just play his scales for a few minutes to recenter himself before diving back into the music. It was a habit he had learned from his mother, Paola.

"Relax and take a deep breath, Giancarlo," she had always taught him. "When things go bad, just play your scales and arpeggios for a little while to clear your mind until everything comes right again."

Paola Rosa had once been the music teacher at the regional school down in the valley below Castelalto. It had been she who first introduced Giancarlo to the piano when he was just a little boy. A violinist by training, she was a competent enough piano player to recognize true talent when she saw it, and she devoted herself early on to helping Giancarlo develop his. She had of course been equally eager that her other son, Giorgio, also take up the piano or any musical instrument, for that matter. Despite her best efforts, however, she could never manage to get him to sit still at the keyboard long enough to learn the simplest melody. He just had not been born with the patience for it.

Giancarlo, on the other hand, took to the piano right from the start and would spend hours at a time at it, diligently practicing, while his older brother ran off to kick the soccer ball with friends. He advanced rapidly, so much so that by the time he reached the age of nine, he was not only playing an impressive repertoire of classical pieces, but he had already started to dabble in composing music of his own.

Giancarlo's growing achievements at the piano were a source of pride and joy to his mother, but one of annoyance to Giorgio, who naturally resented the fawning attention she showered on his little brother. Sometimes, when Giancarlo was playing, Giorgio would purposely go crashing about the house, making a ruckus to distract his brother from his lessons. Inevitably, Paola would have no choice but to give her rambunctious son a stern talking-to and banish him to the outdoors, reinforcing in his mind the firmly held conviction that Giancarlo was his mother's favorite.

The situation of course was reversed with their father, Roberto Rosa. Though he had fallen in love with and married a music teacher, Roberto himself had never been musically inclined. While he was truly impressed by Giancarlo's skill at the piano and enjoyed hearing him play, his son's gift was one he could not fully comprehend, and he admired it from a certain distance. This puzzled and troubled the quiet young boy, for he longed to earn his father's approbation as well as his mother's. Though his father had never said as much, it had always been obvious to Giancarlo that he was more at ease around his garrulous older son, who liked to talk about sports and was good at soccer. Anyone with eyes could see that the two were cut from the same cloth. Roberto worked for the telephone company, maintaining the telephone lines throughout the valley. Sometimes, while Giancarlo would sit at home playing the piano, he would invite Giorgio to accompany him on a job, and the two would ride off together for the day in his truck. Giancarlo had no interest in trucks or tools or telephone lines. Just the same, he resented the time his father and brother spent together without him, and it reinforced in *his* mind that Giorgio was his father's favorite.

The truth of the matter was that Paola and Roberto were typical parents. They loved both their sons with all their hearts and would have gladly given their lives for either. But as often happens in families, the natural bonds of affection the two adults formed with each of their children were simply different from one another. Though this was difficult for the two siblings to understand, and even harder to accept, it had the effect of creating a sense of balance between them.

Giancarlo and Giorgio were of course typical brothers. At heart, they loved each other dearly, even though at times they were at each other's throats. They alternated between being best friends and fiercest rivals. Always the bigger and stronger of the two, Giorgio often lorded it over Giancarlo at home. He took great pride in being the firstborn son, and he had no qualms about using his superior size and strength whenever Giancarlo needed reminding of just who was boss. Outside the house, however, Giorgio was as faithful and loyal a friend as any boy could hope for. He watched over Giancarlo like a hawk, and woe it was to he that so much as looked sideways at his little brother.

It was a complex relationship, as are all sibling relationships, and it grew only more so when one day Paola Rosa unexpectedly took ill and passed away a month later. Giancarlo, who would never learn exactly what it was that had caused his mother's death, was barely ten years old at the time. It was a devastating blow to the boys and their father, and it seemed that their world had fallen apart. In time, though, the three men pulled together, and with the help of friends and family, their lives went on.

Six years later, Giancarlo still thought of his mother every time he sat down at the piano to play, and he had been thinking of her just then on that morning when he was alone in the house, working on the Beethoven sonata. He had taken a short break and was about to throw himself back into it when he heard a loud bang that shook the front of the house. Giancarlo paid little heed to the noise, for he well knew that it was only his brother, Giorgio, who liked to announce his arrival home by kicking his soccer ball against the front door. As expected, his older brother walked through the door a few moments later and sauntered over to the piano.

"Maestro," said Giorgio, using a nickname he liked to call his brother. "*Cosa fai?* What are you doing?"

"What does it look like I'm doing?" said Giancarlo, without looking up from the music. "I'm practicing."

"I can see that," said Giorgio, "but it's a beautiful Saturday morning, and you're all cooped up inside this house."

"So? What's it to you?"

"Nothing," said his brother. "Except that I was thinking about taking a hike up the mountain. I heard some of the old men talking yesterday about a place up there where some brigands supposedly left their gold, but nobody has ever found it."

"And you believe their story?" said Giancarlo.

"I believe that they believe it," replied Giorgio with a shrug.

Giancarlo smiled. The brigands were outlaws back in the 1800s who hid out in the wilderness of Abruzzo and the rest of southern Italy when they weren't ambushing the forces of the ruling French and Spanish invaders or extorting money from the peasantry. These desperate men came to be feared because of their cruelty on the one hand, but admired for their astonishing boldness on the other. Local legend held that brigands had left behind untold hoards of treasure stashed away in hideouts all over the region. It was all out there for the taking, if one only knew where to look.

To Giancarlo's knowledge, no brigand treasure of any kind had ever been recovered, and he was quite certain that it was all just a myth. Just the same, going out and questing for it with Giorgio had become something of a favorite hobby. Though the two brothers were very different in many respects, oddly enough they shared a great love of hiking and exploring the mountains surrounding

Castelalto, and both had come to know virtually every nook and cranny. It was a particular pleasure for Giancarlo, for it was the one athletic endeavor at which he excelled over Giorgio. Owing to his slighter build, he could easily outclimb his more heavily muscled brother. That this was so was the cause of no small amount of irritation on the part of Giorgio, who at the start of each excursion would insist on taking the lead, only to inevitably find himself falling behind and struggling to keep up as soon as the trail grew steep.

"So, what do you plan to do?" said Giancarlo of the brigands' mythical treasure.

"Go after it of course!" cried Giorgio. "Do you want to come with me?"

"No," Giancarlo had replied. "I want to finish practicing."

Giorgio eyed him for a moment before giving another shrug.

"Eh, have it your way," he said nonchalantly. "I suppose it's better if you don't come, anyway."

Then he turned to go.

"What do you mean 'it's better'?" Giancarlo called after him.

"You'll just hold me up," said his brother, looking back at him with an arch grin. "And I don't want to waste time."

Giancarlo knew that he was being baited. Nonetheless, now that the gauntlet had been tossed down, he felt compelled to pick it up.

"All right," he grumbled. "Give me ten more minutes to play, and then I'll go get my pack ready."

Two hours later, the two young men were up on the mountainside, high above Castelalto. Giorgio had as always led the ascent to the part of the mountain where the brigands' treasure was rumored to be hidden—and as always, there was no treasure to be found anywhere. This of course had come as no surprise to either of them. Still, after a few more minutes of searching, Giancarlo began to feel annoyed at the fruitlessness of the search and complained that it was he who had wasted his time on this fool's errand. At that the two began to bicker, as they were wont to do on such occasions. Sensing perhaps that this might be the time they really found something, Giorgio had felt inclined to press on with the search a little farther. Giancarlo, however, had had enough, and was of a mind to turn around and go back home to his piano before the sun started to set. A great row had ensued, and the two were soon on the verge of exchanging blows.

"Fine!" Giorgio had cried out bitterly instead of throwing the first punch. "You go back if you want to, and I'll go on by myself. What do I care? Go fall off the side of the mountain and kill yourself, for all it matters to me!"

Giorgio followed up these harsh words with an obscene gesture at his brother, who responded in kind before heading back down the trail on his own. Not more than a minute or two later, as he was ascending the trail, Giorgio heard his brother cry out from below in a loud, anguished voice.

He stopped to listen.

"Giancarlo!" he called back.

No reply.

"Giancarlo!" he called again.

Silence, save for the whisper of the breeze.

Wasting no time, Giorgio scrambled back down the trail to find his brother. He soon came to the crest of a particularly steep ledge, which they had only just ascended a short while earlier. To Giorgio's horror, there at the bottom lay Giancarlo, motionless.

"*Dio mio*, what have I done?" he cried at the sight.

Giorgio climbed down as fast as he could to where Giancarlo lay face down on the ground. He knelt as his brother's side and took his hand. It fell limp in his grasp.

"Giancarlo!" Giorgio cried out. "Speak to me!"

Giancarlo did not move and, for all appearances, had stopped breathing. Fearing the worst, Giorgio burst into tears.

"My brother," he wept in torment. "What am I going to tell Papa?" He turned his eyes upward. "God, forgive me for what I said. I didn't mean it! I swear I never—"

Giorgio suddenly quit his lamentations and looked down, for

he was quite certain that he had just heard Giancarlo speak. But no, he was wrong. Giancarlo had not spoken. He was giggling! Giorgio realized at once that it had all been a ruse, and his deep remorse of just a moment earlier vanished in a twinkling. Skipping relief entirely, his emotions instantly sprang to outrage.

"How could you do that?" he screamed, pounding his brother on the back. "What kind of person are you?"

Despite the onslaught, Giancarlo howled with laughter.

"That's what you get!" he shouted back, curling into a ball to protect himself from Giorgio's punches. "Next time be more careful about what you wish for!"

"Next time I'll throw you off the cliff myself!" Giorgio screamed in reply, but his anger soon began to abate, and he relented with the punches. Out of breath from the outburst, he gave Giancarlo one last shove. Then he sat back in the dirt and wiped the tears from his eyes with the back of his hand. By now, Giancarlo had also sat up, but Giorgio refused to even look at him.

Despite his opinion that he had been well within his rights, Giancarlo now felt quite guilty at having played such a cruel joke on his brother. He wanted very much to apologize, to set things right, and he was just about to do so when he happened to glance out at a grove of trees far off the side of the trail. There something suddenly caught his eye. It appeared to be the top edge of the roof of a small building, a hovel of some sort, perhaps, that he had never before noticed. His heart began to beat a mile a minute.

"Giorgio, look up there," he said, poking his brother in the arm.

"Shut up," groused Giorgio, still refusing to look at him. "You're going to pay for that someday."

"Please, Giorgio. Look!"

"No. Look yourself."

Giancarlo jumped to his feet.

"Giorgio," he said with a huff. "I'm very sorry I tricked you like that, okay? But please, just take a look."

"A look at what?" said Giorgio, grudgingly getting to his feet.

"Up there," said Giancarlo. "You see there?'

"Where?" sighed his brother.

"Look there," said Giancarlo. "High over that big rock between those two trees. Do you see it?"

Giorgio narrowed his gaze and peered out to where Giancarlo was pointing. For a moment he saw nothing out of the ordinary, but then his eyes opened wide.

"What do you think it is?" said Giancarlo eagerly.

"There's only one way to tell," answered Giorgio. "Come on!"

A short time later, after a brief but difficult climb, the two brothers found themselves standing in front of a very old stone building, a small rough-hewn house with a single doorway and no windows. To all appearances it had been abandoned for ages. The house sat on the edge of a grassy step on the slope of the mountain. Concealed as it was behind the rock and trees far off the trail, it was sheer luck that Giancarlo had spied it. Though it had most likely been the shelter of a goat herder or a hunter or someone who simply preferred to live high up on the mountain, there was no denying that, for whatever reason it had been built, it made a perfect hideout.

Giancarlo and Giorgio exchanged glances. There was no need to speak, for each already knew the other's thoughts. The two stepped closer and peered in through the doorway. All within was lost in shadows, save for what fell in the path of a slanted rectangle of sunlight beaming in through the doorway and onto the hard dirt floor. Giancarlo looked about at the walls and up at the slanted ceiling with its ancient wooden beams. It looked sturdy enough, but who could tell? For all they knew, the whole place might be on the verge of crumbling at any minute.

"Better be careful," warned Giancarlo as Giorgio led the way inside.

To their keen disappointment, the interior of the house was completely empty save for spiderwebs and a bird's nest tucked up in one corner where the ceiling and walls met. Sadly, there was no brigands' treasure to be found anywhere.

Giorgio kicked at the dirt and looked about with a disconsolate air.

"*Niente*," he sighed. "Nothing. We should have known better than to bother."

With that he walked out to check the grounds around the building, while Giancarlo remained inside, passing his hands over the cold, clammy walls, testing to see if any of the stones would give. He was hoping he might find some secret nook where a brigand might have squirreled away his money. The walls, however, seemed as hard and firm as the day they were built. With a sigh of his own, Giancarlo gave up the search and was just heading out the door when he heard Giorgio cry out in a loud voice. Had he found the treasure?

Giancarlo rushed outside and looked about, but Giorgio was nowhere in sight. Then he heard his brother cry out again, and he realized that his voice had come from somewhere on the other side of the house. Giancarlo ran at once to find him. When he rounded the back corner, he was startled at first to find Giorgio on his knees, his arms spread wide. Then he looked at the ground and began to laugh.

Giorgio was kneeling in the midst of an enormous patch of the largest, most luscious-looking mushrooms he had ever beheld. Giancarlo himself was not particularly fond of mushrooms. But his brother? For Giorgio they were the most wonderful thing in all the world to eat. No brigands' treasure could ever have delighted him more than this serendipitous discovery.

"Look at them, Giancarlo!" he exclaimed with unbridled joy. "Have you ever seen anything like them?"

Indeed Giancarlo had not, and he immediately set about helping his brother collect as many of them as they could carry. When their backpacks could hold no more, the two stood, brushed themselves off, and made ready to descend the mountain while there was still plenty of daylight left.

"Giancarlo," intoned Giorgio solemnly just as they were about to get on their way, "you must make me a promise before we go home. It's the least you owe me after what you did before."

"What kind of promise?" replied Giancarlo.

"You must promise to never tell anyone about this place," he said. "If people were to find out, they would come back here and steal all my beautiful mushrooms. So promise!"

Giancarlo took one look down the steep trail before them and tried to imagine, without any success, why anyone in his right mind would go through the trouble of climbing all the way up here just for a bunch of mushrooms. Then again, he was not a connoisseur of fungi, like his brother.

"Fine, I promise," he said, rolling his eyes. "Now can we please go home?"

"No, not yet," said his brother. "First we must give the place a name."

After a few minutes of debate, Giancarlo suggested *il Rifugio dei Briganti* (the Brigands' Lair). Giorgio loved it. The matter was settled, and Giancarlo and Giorgio began their descent.

The two were in high spirits the entire journey back down the mountain, laughing and joking all the way. In no time they found themselves drawing near to the base of the trail, where the terrain began to flatten out. They were bounding along and just about to emerge from the woods where the trail opened up onto a wide meadow a little ways above the village when suddenly Giorgio stopped dead in his tracks. He abruptly reached out, took Giancarlo by the arm, and pulled him back into the trees. Before he could protest, Giorgio put a finger to his lips to silence him. Then he nodded for Giancarlo to follow him.

Giorgio crept over to the edge of the woods and peered out across the meadow. Turning back to Giancarlo, he put a finger to his lips again and motioned for him to come closer.

"There she is," whispered Giorgio.

Giancarlo looked out to the middle of the meadow, where a young woman he had never seen before sat barefoot on a blanket, an artist's pad resting across her legs. He speculated that she had come out there, from where he did not know, to draw the roofs of the houses below, or perhaps to sketch the mountains in the distance. Whichever the case, apparently she had just finished, for she abruptly closed the pad and got to her feet.

Giancarlo watched her intently as she gathered the blanket into her arms. Even from that distance, he could see that she was a beauty. Her figure was perfectly proportioned and her limbs lithe and graceful, like those of a ballerina. With a toss of her head, her fine dark hair sliding off her shoulder and cascading the length of her back, she started off on her way toward the village. Mesmerized as he was, Giancarlo might have stayed there, frozen in place, had Giorgio not turned and swatted him in the arm.

"Come on," his brother whispered, and off he ran.

Not knowing what else to do, Giancarlo raced off after his brother. Giorgio led him on a circuitous route that brought them down around the far edge of the meadow and to the opposite side of the village. It was not until they raced onto the piazza and stopped near the fountain across from the top of an alley that led back out to the meadow that Giancarlo finally understood his brother's plan. Gazing down the alley, he saw the young woman come into view as she approached the center of the village. By arriving there ahead of her, it would appear that they had encountered her by chance.

By now, Giancarlo's mind was wild with questions, wondering who on earth the young woman could be, but whenever he tried to speak, Giorgio would tell him to keep quiet. And so the two brothers lingered by the fountain, fussing with their backpacks and pretending to tie their shoes, until the young woman came to the end of the alley and walked out onto the piazza. There she paused for a moment, clutching her artist's pad, and glanced their way.

Giancarlo felt his legs go weak beneath him. He had never before seen anyone quite like her. Her face was even lovelier than he had imagined when he first saw her from the distance, and her dark, enigmatic eyes pierced right through him like a lance and left him dazed and bewildered. When she turned and walked away without betraying the slightest hint that she had noticed either of them, it felt as though his heart had been ripped from his chest. In that instant, Giancarlo fell helplessly and irrevocably in love with her, and he knew that his life from that day forward would never be the same.

"What do you think?" said Giorgio excitedly, nudging him in the ribs, when she turned the corner and they could see her no more. "She's a goddess, isn't she?"

"Who is she?" murmured Giancarlo, still gazing after her.

Giorgio took a long, deep breath and let it out. "She's the girl I'm going to marry someday," he said.

Giancarlo turned and looked at his brother.

Not if I marry her first, he thought.

CHAPTER 25

Giancarlo sat at the piano, staring at the keyboard. What was it, he wondered, that had suddenly called forth the memory of that day more than thirty years ago when he and Giorgio had gone up the mountain? He supposed that it had all come to mind because he had been thinking about his mother while he practiced his scales, just as he had been doing on that long-ago spring morning. Even now, after so many years, he still heard the echoes of her voice, gentle and encouraging, whenever he sat down to play. Sometimes the memory of it was so strong, he heard it so clearly that it was almost as if she were still sitting there beside him on the piano bench. Few of Giancarlo's memories were as strong as that of his mother's voice, and it had, he knew, the power to evoke many others. And so it came as no surprise to him that one memory had led inescapably to the next, like the fall of the first domino against the second, toppling all the rest in sequence. Dwelling on the past, however, was not a favorite pastime of Giancarlo's. It only made him weary. So, as he always did, he pushed the whole thing from his mind, just as he pushed himself away from the keyboard.

He glanced at the clock. It was late in the afternoon, the Saturday before Labor Day, and he had to get ready to attend a faculty reception on campus that evening. Giancarlo was not looking forward to the affair. In fact, he would have preferred to skip it altogether, for at the moment he was not feeling particularly enthusiastic about the start of the fall semester. Giancarlo was not one of those people who mourned the end of summer. Just the same, he could not help feeling that this one had passed much too quickly. The tired, burned-out feeling about which he had complained back in the spring was still very much with him, though he tried to ignore it. He wondered if perhaps it had been a mistake to not take a week or two off back at the beginning of the summer, to just go someplace to get away from it all. It might have made sense to do so, but looking back, the thought of planning such a getaway had not seemed worth the energy at the time. Besides, he had committed himself to teaching Carter, and every lesson had counted. In any case, it was much too late to worry about it all now, so he trudged off to his bedroom to change his clothes.

The air was full of lively talk and laughter when Giancarlo arrived at the reception. As he made his way toward the bar for a cocktail, he exchanged greetings with his fellow faculty members, nodding hello and agreeing with them, at least outwardly, that yes, it really was good to be back. When at last he had a drink in hand, Giancarlo turned from the bar and scanned the crowded room for an out-of-the-way spot in which he might station himself. The far corner of the room seemed the most promising prospect, so he began to make his way in that direction. He had not gone far when he saw Henry Sheffield coming his way through the crowd.

"Ah, we meet again, Giancarlo," said the dean, shaking his hand when the two met in the middle of the room. "Good to see you. How was the rest of your summer?"

"A little too short, I think," replied Giancarlo.

"They always are," sighed Sheffield with a nod. Then he brightened, and looked about the room. "But you know, I love the coming of fall. Strange, isn't it? Autumn comes when the year is nearing its end, when everything outside is getting ready to die, but for us in academia it's a time of beginnings."

"You're waxing poetic, Henry," Giancarlo noted, before taking a sip of his drink.

"Ha!" Sheffield laughed. "I suppose I am. It just comes over me sometimes, and I can't resist." He paused, and gave Giancarlo a sideways glance. "So tell me, Giancarlo," he asked, "have you given any thought to that concert in the spring I told you about?"

Giancarlo had known all along of course that the question would come up sooner or later that evening. It was another of the reasons he had dreaded coming to the reception.

"Which concert was that, Henry?" said Giancarlo, feigning ignorance.

"Now, we'll have none of that," replied Sheffield, wagging a finger at him. "You know exactly which concert I'm talking about. And the two of us will talk about it a little more later on. But first I have to go finish making the rounds. You know how it is. Don't want anyone feeling miffed that I didn't say hello. We'll chat later, so don't disappear on me."

With that Sheffield went on his way to mingle with the crowd. Giancarlo was just making for the sanctuary of the far corner of the room when he felt someone touch his arm. He turned around and found himself face-to-face with Patricia. The summer, he saw, had treated her well, for she was looking as tanned and lovely as ever. Her face had a marvelously healthy glow to it that made the blue of her eyes that much more vivid.

"*Buona sera*, Giancarlo," she said with a coy smile. "Where are you off to? You're not leaving already, are you?"

"Patrizia, it's nice to see you again," said Giancarlo in a less-than-convincing voice. It truly *was* nice to see her again. Just the same he had hoped against reason that he might avoid encountering her on that particular evening. He simply was not ready for her yet.

"You know, you're really not a very good correspondent," she pointed out straightaway, confirming his rationale for wishing to avoid her.

"Yes, um, I suppose I must apologize for that," said Giancarlo contritely, staring into his drink. "Honestly, I would have sent you a postcard or something of my own, but you see I never went anywhere this summer, so there really wasn't much to keep in touch about."

Patricia responded by fixing him with a skeptical gaze.

"I see you're starting to let your hair grow back out," he noted quickly, hoping the change in subject might get him off the hook. It didn't.

"So, tell me," she asked, "what did you do with yourself all summer, Giancarlo? I know you didn't spend it writing letters."

"Not much," he said, "other than a little teaching."

"Teaching?" said a surprised Patricia. Then her face lit up. "Wait a minute, don't tell me. The boy who came to you for Italian lessons in the spring, the one who wanted to go to Italy because he was in love, right?"

"That's the one," admitted Giancarlo.

"How nice!" gushed Patricia. "Oh, I'm so glad you did it, Giancarlo. What made you change your mind?"

Giancarlo gave a shrug as if to say he was not quite sure himself of what the reason had been.

"So, how did he do?" she asked eagerly. "I remember you weren't very optimistic because he was a football player or something, and I know how you hate teaching jocks."

"He did very well," Giancarlo answered. "And I don't hate teaching jocks, by the way."

"So you say," she teased him. "But never mind about that. Tell me what he's going to do now."

Giancarlo gave another shrug.

"I guess he's going to go in search of the girl of his dreams," he offered.

"That is so sweet," sighed Patricia. "When will he go?"

"He left yesterday," said Giancarlo. "So he's already in Rome."

"How exciting," she said. "What do you think he will do first? Will he go to her right away?"

"I don't know," admitted Giancarlo. "But whatever his plans are, I'm sure he'll have the time of his life."

CHAPTER 26

At that particular moment, far across the Atlantic in Rome, Carter stood in the bathroom of his hotel room, staring into the mirror. He most definitely was not having the time of his life on his first night in Italy. To the contrary, he was overcome by a profound dread that, for some unknown reason, his life was about to come to an end.

It had all started just a short while ago, after he lay down to go to sleep. Exhausted from the long trip, he had just begun to doze off when suddenly he opened his eyes, for he heard a strange noise in his ears, a buzzing sound, like static on a radio. He sat up and put a hand to his forehead, for suddenly it began to feel very strange, as though something was tightening about it. He felt the same gripping sensation in his chest, and he realized that his heart within was hammering away. A cold spike of fear shot through Carter's gut, and his breath quickened dramatically. He licked his lips and found that his mouth had gone dry. Throwing aside the bedcovers, he went to the bathroom to throw some water on his face.

Now, gazing at his reflection, he saw that his face had gone pale. The skin on the back of his neck and shoulders felt all prickly, and he began to sweat. Something terrible was going wrong with him; he suspected it might be a heart attack. The thought, ridiculous as it might have been, caused him to panic, and his breathing grew even more rapid. He was feeling disoriented, and was certain that he was going to pass out at any moment. He thought of home, he thought of his mother and father, and he thought of Elena. Why, he lamented, had God made him come all the way across the ocean to find her, only to let him die all alone in this cheap hotel room in Rome?

Carter turned on the faucet and brought a handful of water to his mouth before splashing another onto his face. His head was whirling, and his mind raced back over the course of the day, feverishly searching for some clue to what might have brought this on. He tried to get a grip on himself as he thought back, piecing together the events of the past twenty-four hours.

Carter's flight from Boston had departed right on time. With its connecting flight in Milan, it was an uneventful, wearisome twelve-hour journey to Rome. Carter had passed the early part of the trip by reading a rugby magazine, and later he listened to some music on his iPod. When darkness came and the captain dimmed the cabin lights, he closed his eyes to get some rest, but sleep would not come, and he had found himself simply staring out the window into the black sky. Finally, just before the plane flew into the new dawn, he managed to nod off into a fitful sleep for a short while. Soon after, though, some brief turbulence awoke him with a start, and Carter slept no more the rest of the way.

It was midafternoon by the time Carter finally arrived in Rome, cleared customs, and walked bleary-eyed out of the airport to find a taxi to take him to his hotel. The ride into the city proved to be the most stimulating part of the day. No sooner had Carter installed himself in the backseat when the driver abruptly pulled away from the terminal and sped off down the highway with alarming speed. As the driver wove his way through the traffic into the city proper, Carter had the distinct impression that he must have inadvertently bungled his way into a taxicab being used to film a chase scene for a James Bond movie. He clutched his duffel bag and held on for dear life until the car pulled up at his hotel. Grateful that he had made it there in one piece, he practically jumped out of the car when it came to a stop. He paid the driver, and trudged inside to the front desk.

Afterwards, when he had finished checking in and dragged his duffel bag to his room, Carter had collapsed onto the bed and promptly fallen fast asleep despite the steady thrum of traffic below his window. It was just past sunset when he awoke sometime later, opened his eyes, and assessed the interior of his room for the first time. It was a clean but drab affair he found, sparsely furnished with a bed, a night table and a lamp, an armoire, and a small bureau. There was no television, and the telephone could only call the front desk if one wished to get an outside line. The air in the room was still and rather warm, but there was no air-conditioning. The only ventilation came from the window, which at the moment was shuttered closed. Carter recalled that Giancarlo had once advised him that he should not to be too surprised if he discovered that the hotels in Italy were not quite the same as those in America. Now he understood what his professor had meant.

Feeling a bit grimy from the long plane ride, and completely out of sorts from the time change, Carter had decided to take a shower to see if that would perk him up a little. The cramped bathroom had no shower stall, or curtain for that matter, but only a drain in the tiled floor and a showerhead protruding from the wall opposite the toilet and sink. It was an odd space, but Carter had nonetheless felt himself revive as he let the water rain down on his head. When he was done, he took one of the large bath towels hanging on the rack and rubbed it across his body. Curiously, the towel's coarse fabric did not seem to absorb any water, and so Carter wrapped it around his midsection, walked out into the room, and nudged open the shutters. There he stood for a time, letting the air rush in and dry him off, while he beheld Rome for the first time.

In truth, there was not a great deal for him to see. From all indications, the hotel was not located in a particularly picturesque part of the ancient city, but it appeared to be a safe enough neighborhood, and at least the traffic had finally eased. Eager to get outside and take a walk to check out his surroundings, Carter had dressed quickly, grabbed his tourist map, and headed out the door.

Once outside in the fresh early evening air, Carter had ambled about the darkened streets with no specific destination in mind. He was surprised by the number of people still out and about, and he strolled along, letting his feet carry him wherever they would. He had not gone very far at all when he rounded a corner and happened upon a magnificent fountain with an imposing statue of some ancient god at its center and horses rising out of the water. A sizable crowd of people was gathered around. Some sat at the water's edge, admiring the splendid artistry, while others stood nearby, chatting amiably among themselves. Across the way, people sat in the open air of an outdoor café, enjoying the view. It was a pleasant place, and Carter came closer, drawn in by the spectacular sight and the tranquil sound of the water. He stood there for quite a while, simply gazing at the fountain and enjoying it all, before he chanced to look down into the pool and noticed the enormous collection of coins lining the bottom. Just then a young couple came up next to him, and turned and tossed coins over their shoulders into the fountain. Then they kissed and walked away arm in arm.

Wondering exactly where he was, Carter sat at the edge of the fountain and began to open his map. It was just then that he had looked up and noticed a sign across the way that read FONTANA DI TREVI. Carter realized that he had found the Trevi Fountain, one of the many attractions he had read about in the travel guides Sheila had given him. He marveled that he had been so fortunate to stumble upon such a famous site by accident on his very first night in Rome. He had yet to learn of course that in Rome one was liable to come across art and history at any time, on virtually any corner of the city.

When at last he had seen enough of the fountain for that night, Carter responded to the call of his grumbling stomach by walking off in search of someplace to eat dinner. A nearby *trattoria* presented itself, and after considering the menu posted outside on the window and the pleasing aroma wafting from within, he decided to give it a try.

It had still been a bit early for dinner by Roman standards when Carter stepped into the doorway, and he had found just a few other patrons dining inside. He was greeted at the door by the proprietor, a stocky gentleman, with a pleasant face and a mop of curly gray hair. He wore an unbuttoned black vest, and the sleeves of the white shirt beneath were rolled up, revealing a pair of thick forearms.

"*Buona sera,*" he said amiably. Then he gestured for Carter to come inside, directed him to a little table in a corner, and left him with a menu. He returned in a few minutes with some bread and a carafe of water, which he placed in the center of the table. "So, my American friend," he began in English, "what can I give you tonight?"

"How did you know I was American?" asked Carter with a smile.

The owner shrugged his shoulders practically to his ears and opened his palms wide. Then he made an amusing face and grunted, "Eh, how did I know? I just knew."

It was then that Carter realized that he had barely spoken a word of Italian since he landed in the country. In truth he had felt a little intimidated. It was one thing to speak the language when he was in the controlled environment of his Italian lessons. It was quite another to speak it in real life, when it seemed as though everyone was talking a million miles an hour. And so it was that he had been relieved to find that he was able to get by on his English. Somehow, though, Carter had felt challenged, in a friendly way, by the *trattoria* owner's immediate identification of him as an American. He decided, after a moment's consideration, that the time had finally come to put all those hours of study to work. He knew next to nothing about Italian cuisine, so he chose at random from the menu and left the rest to fate.

"*In tal caso, vorrei per il primo piatto gli spaghetti con aglio e oleo per piacere,*" said Carter politely. "*Poi il vitello milanese, se Lei lo racommanda.*"

"*Ma lui parla bene l'Italiano!*" the man had exclaimed, throwing his hands up in delight. "How do you speak so well?"

Carter smiled, and explained with perfect diction that he had taken private lessons from a native Italian before coming to Italy.

"*Bravo,*" said the owner with an approving nod. "In that case, from now on, you and I will speak only in Italian. *D'accordo?*"

"*D'accordo,* but slowly, please," Carter had pleaded with him. "Everyone here seems to talk so fast."

"Ayyy, don't worry, *amico mio,*" the man had laughed. "After a few days in Rome, we'll have you right up to speed."

The spaghetti with garlic and olive oil he had ordered proved to be tastier than Carter had imagined, and the veal was out of this world. He had enjoyed both dishes immensely. Still, it had been a strange experience, for he was not accustomed to dining alone in a restaurant. It was a curious, lonely feeling. The owner had passed by once or twice to exchange a few words, but the place soon got busy, and he had to attend to the other patrons.

After he had finished eating and the table was cleared, the owner brought over coffee. Carter typically drank very little coffee back home, but he was in Rome now, so he had chosen to drink as the Romans did. The coffee, like everything he had tasted that night, had a rich, vibrant flavor. When the owner returned with *il conto* (the check) and refilled his cup, Carter had drunk it without a second thought. By then things were not quite so busy in the *trattoria,* so while he sipped his coffee, the owner took advantage of the lull to chat with him for a few moments. Speaking only in Italian, as he had promised, he introduced himself as Michele and asked Carter for his name.

"Carter?" said a smiling Michele when he told him. "You mean like the president?"

"Yes," chuckled Carter. "But it's my first name, not my last."

"So, tell me *Signor Presidente,*" Michele had asked, "how was your dinner?"

"It was my first here in Rome," replied Carter, "and it was excellent."

"*Grazie,*" said Michele. "I'm glad you enjoyed it. You see, you came to the right place first. So, how are you enjoying your stay so far? Have you had a chance to see any of the sights yet?"

Carter had explained that he had seen very little so far, but that he had at least discovered the Trevi Fountain that evening by accident.

"Ah, la Fontana di Trevi," said Michele. "I hope you tossed in a coin."

"Actually, I didn't," Carter admitted. "Should I have?"

"Of course, you must!" exclaimed Michele. "Don't you know that if you throw a coin in the Trevi Fountain, you are guaranteed to return to Rome someday?"

"No, I didn't know that," said Carter.

"Then again, if you're feeling cheap," Michele went on, "you can always just throw in a *gettone*."

A *gettone* was a token for the pay phone. Michele explained with a straight face that tossing one in the fountain would guarantee that Carter would only have to make a telephone call to Rome one day, which would be far less expensive than airfare from America. At that the *trattoria* owner had burst into hearty, contagious laughter at his own joke. Carter could not help but laugh along with him.

Later, after paying for his dinner and promising Michele he would tell all his friends about his little *trattoria*, Carter had strolled back to his hotel with a full stomach and a contented disposition. Once back in his room, he had lain on his bed for a time, consulting his map and guidebooks to plan out his activities for the next day. Then he had turned off the light, closed his eyes, and lain in the darkness, meditating on what had been a very pleasant first night in Rome.

Now, as he stood at the bathroom sink considering his unsteady hand, the anxious feeling in the pit of his stomach, and his pounding heart, Carter reflected that while it had been a most pleasant first night in Rome, he feared that this might be his last. He wondered if perhaps he was suffering from food poisoning, or maybe he had picked up some strange virus on the plane. He had read about such things happening. Whatever the case, he was seriously considering phoning the front desk and asking them to call for an ambulance, when suddenly he paused and looked at himself in the mirror, for something just then had jogged his memory. What was it Giancarlo had told him that rainy day back in June when he served him the biscotti?

Then he remembered, and suddenly it all made sense.

"The coffee," Carter muttered, recalling the two full cups of the strong, savory brew he had consumed after dinner. "What an idiot."

Carter realized at once that he was not dying, after all. He had simply overloaded himself with caffeine. Given that he rarely drank coffee, never mind the robust type Italians loved to drink, it was quite understandable that his body had reacted as it had that night. With understanding came a profound sense of relief, and Carter felt the nervous anxiety drain out of him like air from a balloon.

Carter might have laughed at himself for his stupidity, but at the moment he was feeling much too weary and spent, and so he staggered out of the bathroom and flopped on the bed. Sleep would be a long time in coming, but at least he now knew with certainty that he would live to see another day in Rome. As he closed his eyes once more and listened to his breathing and his still-racing heart, it occurred to Carter that his Italian professor had been right about one thing: There were some lessons he could learn only by being in Italy.

CHAPTER 27

When Carter opened his eyes late the next morning, he was relieved to discover that his pulse and respiration had returned to their normal rates. He had survived the night! It had taken quite a while, but after tossing and turning for what seemed like hours on end, he had finally drifted off into a deep, dreamless sleep. Still drowsy, he yawned, and rolled over to look at the little clock on the night table. He was surprised to see that it was almost eleven o'clock. The day was already almost half gone, and Carter reproached himself for letting it slip away by staying in bed so long. In truth, he was still exhausted and might have slept even longer if the cars passing back and forth on the street below his window had not awakened him.

Carter sat up and swung his legs off the bed. Setting his feet on the floor, he stretched his arms out wide and rolled his head about to loosen his neck and shoulder muscles. He looked about the room. It was eerily quiet despite the background noise of the traffic outside. It made Carter acutely aware that he was there all alone. How odd this air of solitude felt. That he should perceive it so keenly puzzled and unsettled him. Had he not just lived virtually the entire summer by himself? Why should he now feel so lonely after just one night away from home?

He realized of course that the difference was that he was in completely new and unfamiliar surroundings. Nothing was the same, not the feel of his pillow and blankets, not the way the light switch on the wall or the shower in the bathroom worked. Even the air itself felt different. That, he told himself, was what it meant to go to a *foreign* land. And that was why he felt such a strange sense of isolation.

The best antidote for it, Carter decided, was to dress and get out of the room as quickly as possible. Just the same, he sat there for a little while longer, mulling over his plans for the day. His thoughts turned to Elena, as they often did when he was alone, and he wondered if perhaps he should just pack his things, go to the station, and take the first train for Abruzzo. The idea briefly fired his enthusiasm, but was very soon dismissed. Carter decided that he must stick with his original plan and spend a few days getting to know the country a little before pushing on with his quest to find Elena. He did want to impress her, after all. Showing up in Roccasale in his present discombobulated state was sure to produce something less than the desired effect. With that much resolved, he gave another yawn, got to his feet, and started his day.

The hotel did not have a restaurant, but only a small room off the front lobby where continental breakfast was served each morning from seven to ten. This being Sunday, the breakfast hours had been extended to eleven. By the time Carter came downstairs, however, the tables had all been cleared and the coffee taken away. This troubled Carter only a little, for he had already vowed that morning not to partake of coffee again for at least a week. He was, however, feeling quite hungry. It would be lunchtime soon, and so, with his daypack slung over his shoulder, he dropped his room key at the front desk and headed out the door in search of something to eat.

When he stepped outside, the heat of the noonday sun hit Carter in the face like a blast of hot air from a just-opened oven. It was a bright, clear day with only the hint of a breeze, and a thin sheen of perspiration immediately came to his forehead. Carter brushed it away with the back of his hand, slipped on a pair of sunglasses, and started off down the sidewalk, keeping to the shadowed side of the street as he went. As hungry as he felt at the moment, he was in no hurry to sit alone again in a restaurant, so he stopped at the first open bar he came to and bought a prosciutto and provolone panino—as close to a ham and cheese sandwich as he could find—a packet of cookies, and a large bottle of water. These he tucked into his daypack before setting off again to find a pleasant spot where he might sit and eat his lunch.

Carter meandered his way through the city, familiarizing himself with the local landmarks as he went so he could find his way back later. He took particular care to stay on the sidewalk whenever possible, for it had not escaped his notice that pedestrians were a much-endangered species on the streets of Rome. In the short while since he left the hotel, Carter had more than once found himself springing back from a curb's edge to avoid impatient motorists zooming by who apparently did not take kindly to anyone impeding their forward progress. Car horns blared constantly, often at the last instant, to warn those on foot out of the way. Watching them careen by, he had the distinct impression that Italian drivers, or at least those in Rome, took pleasure in seeing just how close they could come to a person without actually running him over.

At last Carter made it safely to the entrance of the Villa Borghese, one of Rome's largest public parks. Relieved to get away from the traffic and the noise, he ambled straight into the heart of the wooded area and looked about for a suitable tree to sit beneath. An enormous oak just ahead looked like a prime spot, and soon Carter was sitting against its base, enjoying the cool of the shade while he ate his panino. When he had gobbled down the last of it, he opened the bottle of water, stretched out his legs, and settled back against the tree for a time to watch the people coming and going through the park. It was just then, as he was taking a swig of water, that a sign pointing the way to the Bioparco, the Rome zoo, caught his eye. A visit to the zoo had not been on his itinerary for that day, but then again, his itinerary for the entire trip was very much in flux, so he capped his bottle, collected his things, and set off to see the animals.

It turned out to be a somewhat disappointing excursion, not

that this was the fault of the zoo. It really was quite a nice place, in Carter's estimation. The sun, however, was still beating down, and the vast majority of the animals were nowhere in sight. Apparently, to escape the heat, most had taken to the shade, where they lay hidden from view for their afternoon siestas. With few exceptions, the only wildlife he saw were the pictures of the featured animals on display outside of each paddock. As his tour of the zoo neared its end, he was heartened to at least find the lion moving about the front of its enclosure. It was a magnificent beast, and Carter sat down on the bench opposite the cage to watch it for a few minutes, hoping it might give a roar or do something memorable. He was much let down, therefore, when all the lion did was open its mouth wide and yawn before flopping down on its side in the shade. There it lay, panting, with the flies buzzing all about.

The highlight of Carter's day came a moment later, when a little girl of perhaps eight years passed by the cage with her parents. She stopped, took one look at the lion, and turned back to her parents, her eyes wide in amazement.

"Che puuuzza!" the child cried out, holding her nose. What a stink!

Her little face and the sound of her voice were so sweet that Carter could not help bursting out in laughter, as did the girl's parents. She was of course quite right. The animal certainly was giving off a decidedly malodorous air. The king of beasts, however, remained indifferent to her having pointed out the fact. There was not much else to see, so the couple and the child moved on. Carter was ready to leave, as well, for he had had his fill for one day of somnambulant creatures of the wild.

After consulting his guidebook for someplace new to see, Carter left the zoo and walked out of the park in the direction of the Piazza di Spagna and its famous steps. Carter could not imagine what the big deal about an outdoor staircase might be, but according to his map the place was not far away, so there was no harm in going to take a look. Indeed, after just a few minutes' walk he found himself there, standing at the top of the grand, sweeping staircase that was the Spanish Steps. Lined with flowers at every level, the stairs descended to a small fountain at the center of the little piazza below. A collection of people as colorful as the flowers sat all about on the steps or strolled around the fountain, enjoying their Sunday. Down on the piazza, some youngsters were kicking a soccer ball, while others chased each other around. There was talk and laughter and music in the air.

It was a lively place, just the thing Carter needed that day, so he walked down the steps and sat down to soak in the scene for a while. Nearby, a group of teenaged girls were talking a mile a minute among themselves. In fact, as he looked about, it seemed to Carter that just about everybody in the piazza and on the steps was talking—and all at the same time. Even those around him who were sitting alone were yacking into cell phones. Carter settled back and smiled as he listened to them all, trying to understand snippets of their conversations. He found that he rather enjoyed the sound of their voices. He particularly loved those of the Italian women, for it seemed that they sang the language more than they spoke it. It was really quite captivating.

Carter had been sitting there for a time when some of the boys who had been kicking the ball down on the piazza climbed up the steps and sat down near the teenaged girls. One of the boys was wearing an American-style football shirt emblazoned with the insignia of a team called the Dallas Falcons. The boy happened to glance Carter's way and noticed him looking at his shirt.

"Hey, Americano," the boy said amiably, giving him a nod.

"How did you know I'm American?" a curious Carter asked him in Italian.

The boy shrugged and made an expression quite similar to the one Michele, the trattoria owner, had made the night before. Then he laughed, and tugged at the front of his shirt.

"Tell them," he said, gesturing to his friends. "The Dallas Falcons—best football team in all of NFL America, right?"

The boy seemed so proud of his shirt that Carter did not have the heart to tell him that there was no such team back home. There were, in the National Football League, the Atlanta Falcons and the Dallas Cowboys, but alas, no Dallas Falcons. Somebody somewhere, Carter speculated, was probably making a killing selling the phony shirts to people who did not know any better. Still, he did not want to embarrass the boy in front of his friends, or worse, the girls.

"You're right," he told the boy, giving him a thumbs-up. "They're definitely the best."

This pleased the boy immensely, and he proudly nudged his friends to show them that he had been right about his favorite American sports team.

Later, after the boy and his friends had gone on their way, Carter walked down past the fountain to take a picture of the piazza with his digital camera. As he turned and looked up, he got his first good view of the spectacular twin-towered church rising just across the street from the top of the steps. It occurred then to Carter that he had forgotten to go to mass that day, and he felt a pang of guilt about it. He considered climbing back up the steps to the church to see if by chance it would have an afternoon mass, but suddenly the jet lag caught up with him. A wave of fatigue swept over him, washing away any notions of making the climb. Instead, he dropped the camera back in his pack and began to make his way back to his hotel to take a nap before dinner. There would be, he was certain, plenty of other churches along the way. If he could keep his eyes open, perhaps he would stop at one of them to say a few prayers and hope that that would be enough.

CHAPTER 28

"Oh, my God, it's so beautiful!"

Until she had spoken those words, Carter had not noticed the young woman standing beside him, nor the man who accompanied her. He had been far too enthralled at the moment to pay either of them much heed.

It was late in the afternoon the next day, and the three were at the Vatican, in the Basilica of Saint Peter, gazing at Michelangelo's *Pietà*. Even if he had wanted to, Carter could not possibly have found the words to adequately describe the statue of the Virgin Mary holding her dead son, Jesus. He stood there transfixed. The grace and beauty of it filled him with awe, and at the same time evoked in him a profound sadness. Carter, by his own admission, knew nothing whatsoever about art. At the moment he came upon the statue, however, he had understood at once what Giancarlo had meant that day when he said that one only need be human to appreciate some works of art, and that Carter would see things in Italy so beautiful that they would make him want to cry.

This was one.

Carter had missed the statue entirely earlier that afternoon when he first entered the basilica and walked off in the opposite direction from it. It was only by chance that he saw it on his way out. It had been a long day, and at the time he was feeling quite tired. He had arisen early that morning and, after a light breakfast, walked to the Colosseum, where he wandered about the ruins for an hour or two. After lunch he went to the Vatican, and he spent much of the afternoon strolling through the Vatican Museums. He had hoped to see the Sistine Chapel before making his way into Saint Peter's, but for some reason it was closed to the public that day. Not that it mattered. Between the staggering number of works on display in the museums and the sheer majesty of the basilica, Carter had been certain that he could not possibly absorb anything more on that day. Anxious to get back to his room to rest, he had been on his way out the main entrance when he beheld the statue for the first time. The sight of it had stopped him in his tracks and held him mesmerized until just then, when he heard the woman's voice beside him.

It was the first time since he had arrived that Carter had heard another American voice, and his head instinctively turned to her. He saw that she was an attractive woman, a few years older than him, he guessed, with shoulder-length brown hair neatly pulled back in a ponytail. She was holding the hand of her boyfriend— neither appeared to be wearing a ring—who looked to be in his late twenties, perhaps thirty at the most. The two were dressed casually in stylish jeans and loafers, but in a meticulous sort of way, like people one might see in an L.L. Bean catalog. Leaning her head against his shoulder as she stared at the statue, the young woman gave a soft, almost inaudible sigh. Then she pouted, and murmured, "I want it. Will you buy it for me?"

"I would," her boyfriend chuckled, "but I don't think it's up for sale just at the moment."

This was only Carter's third day alone in Italy, but the sudden familiar sound of people speaking his own native language drew his attention like a pin to a magnet.

"I'm guessing the price would be pretty steep even if it was," he found himself saying to them.

"Hey, you're an American," said the man with a look of surprise. "I just assumed you were an Italian when I saw you standing there."

"So did I," said the woman.

"You're the only two people I've met so far in this country who have thought so," said Carter with a grin. "People here seem to know I'm an American before I even open my mouth. I don't know how they do it."

"I think it's your shoes," said the man. "I seem to remember somebody telling me once that that's how Italians can spot an American."

"But I'm wearing sneakers," Carter noted.

"There you go."

Carter glanced down at his sneakers, gave a shrug, and looked back at the statue.

"It is incredible, isn't it?" he said.

"Just looking at it makes me want to cry," sighed the woman.

"I know what you mean," agreed Carter, nodding his head. "It makes you think."

Carter did not know what else to say and was about to walk away when the woman unexpectedly turned to him. She told him that they were from New York City and asked where he came from in the United States. Carter replied that he was from Rhode Island. So far away from home as each of them was, the discovery that they were all northeasterners made it feel as though they were practically next-door neighbors despite being complete strangers. Introductions ensued—Carter learned that their names were Alison and Steve—and a short while later the three were ambling out the door together. As they made their way across Saint Peter's Square, they chatted about their impressions of the Vatican, the basilica, and of course the *Pietà*. Once out of the walled confines of Vatican City, the three stopped on the sidewalk and talked for a few minutes more, before Steve glanced at his watch and mentioned to Alison that he wanted to get back to their hotel so that he might shower before they went to dinner.

Carter assumed that it was time for him and the couple to go their separate ways, and he was about to bid them goodbye, when once again Alison unexpectedly spoke up and suggested that he join them for dinner later on. The offer was a very attractive one, partly because Carter had enjoyed meeting the two, but more so simply because he was not looking forward at all to once again dining alone that evening. He hated to turn her down, but at the same time, he did not want to intrude. He would have said as much if Steve had not agreed that it was a great idea and insisted, as well, that Carter join them. Carter could see no reason to say no, so it was decided that they would meet that evening at Alison and Steve's hotel and look around together for someplace fun to have dinner.

It turned out to be a most enjoyable evening.

Carter arrived at their hotel right on time, and the three strolled over to Via Veneto, where they soon found a restaurant where they could dine outside and enjoy the pleasant night air. When they had settled in at their table, Carter impressed his new friends by speaking perfect Italian to their waiter when it came time to order.

"Maybe we were right after all," joked Steve after the waiter had collected their menus and walked away to place their orders. "You *are* an Italian. You're not an American from Rhode Island!"

"Either that or he has a lot of Italian blood in him," opined Alison.

"Nope, pure Irish American through and through," said Carter.

"But how did you learn to speak Italian so well?" she asked.

"I had a very good teacher," he answered modestly.

Before long the waiter returned with bread and wine, the glasses were filled, and the three made a toast to new friendships. Later, as they talked over dinner, Carter learned that Alison worked for a marketing firm in New York, while Steve was in investment banking. The two seemed to enjoy talking about their careers and were full of advice for Carter when he told them that he had just graduated with a degree in finance. Now and then one of them would suggest some big firm or another in the city to which Carter might want to send a résumé when he got home. He listened attentively, for he appreciated the advice, but something struck him as a bit odd. More than once, for example, when Steve mentioned the name of a particular company where he knew people that Carter might consider approaching, Alison exclaimed that she, as well, had friends who worked there. Inevitably, though, when she asked if Steve knew them, he always answered in the negative. It seemed peculiar that Steve would not have known at least one of her friends. After all, since he had first met them, Carter had assumed that the two knew each other very well. They were quite affectionate toward each other, sitting very close together at the table, holding hands, stopping every now and then to gaze into each other's eyes. They seemed much in love. Despite their outward displays of familiarity, however, Carter began to get the impression that the two were just getting to know one another. This feeling grew only stronger toward the end of dinner, when the talk turned to their travel plans and Steve told him that they were planning to leave for Capri the next day.

"I can't wait to go," said Alison. "I heard it's beautiful. Have you ever been there?"

At first Carter thought the question had been directed to him, but then he realized she was talking to Steve.

"No, I haven't," Steve replied. "I've never been to Italy before. But I've heard Capri is fabulous."

That Steve had never before been to Italy in general and Capri in particular seemed to Carter something that Alison should have already known.

"So, did you two plan this trip together for a long time?" asked Carter, no longer able to contain his curiosity.

"Oh, not at all," said Alison with a little laugh. Then she turned and gazed fondly at Steve before adding, "We only just met at the airport a couple of days ago."

"We saw each other for the first time at the baggage carousel after we landed," recounted Steve. "All it took was one look, and that was it. What is it they say over here? I got hit by the earthquake, or something?"

"I think they call it the thunderbolt," offered Carter.

"Whatever they call it, it hit me hard," chuckled Steve. Then he brought Alison's hand to his lips and kissed it.

"It hit both of us hard," Alison said dreamily, slipping her arm around Steve's. "I've always heard that Italy has a way of doing that to people. It just makes them fall in love when they come here. It's like magic."

"I think she's right," laughed Steve. "So you better watch out, Carter. If you stay here long enough, you're bound to get hit by a thunderbolt, too."

"Maybe," said Carter, grinning, his thoughts drifting far away to Abruzzo, "but for now I'm planning to just stay out of the rain for a while."

After dinner, Carter did not walk with Alison and Steve back to their hotel. He did not need to be told that they were anxious to be alone with each other once more, despite their invitations to have a quick drink someplace before they parted company with him. Saying, quite truthfully, that he was still tired from jet lag, he politely declined. And so, after exchanging e-mail addresses and vows to get in touch one day back in the States, Carter had bidden them a pleasant journey to Capri and gone on his way.

Now, walking along the darkened streets, Carter thought back over the evening he had just spent with his new friends. He was grateful for having had their company at dinner, but finding himself suddenly on his own again only worsened his sense of loneliness. Though he had some vague misgivings about how long their relationship might survive, he envied Alison and Steve for the way in which they had found each other, and for their unabashed bliss. It would not have surprised him if the two were already back in their hotel room, wrapped around one another. He could not help wondering what it would be like to finally have Elena resting in his own arms. The thought gave him an ache, for as far as he had come, she still remained to him a distant vision.

It was then that Carter made up his mind that, although he was not yet ready to go to Roccasale, it was time nonetheless for him to move on. His pace quickening, he resolved to pack his bags that night and leave the city the next day. He liked Rome very much and hoped one day to see more of it, but for now his heart was leading him elsewhere, and he needed to continue his journey. And so it was that Carter hurried back to his hotel room that night, stopping only once along the way to toss a coin into the Trevi Fountain.

CHAPTER 29

While he waited for the pot of water on the stove to come to a boil, Giancarlo peeled a clove of garlic and began to chop it up on the cutting board with a knife. On the burner next to the pot warmed a frying pan lined with a heavy coat of olive oil and a pinch of crushed red pepper flakes.

It was early evening, the night before the first day of classes, and Giancarlo was preparing dinner. His movements almost mechanical from long experience cooking for himself, he stared absentmindedly at the garlic as the knife clopped against the board. Though his hungry stomach growled for attention, his mind was elsewhere. He had been troubled all that day by something he had dreamt the night before. In the dream, he had walked into the kitchen and found his father, Roberto, sitting at the table, the pocket watch dangling from his hand. In that strange way that can only happen in a dream, Giancarlo had watched himself become a little boy again. With a delighted smile, the boy rushed over to sit on his father's knee and eagerly snatched the watch from his hand. He opened the cover and pressed the little button inside to make it play its song, but no matter how often he pressed it or tried to wind the watch, the music would not come. On the verge of tears, the child had looked to his father to make it work. Roberto simply smiled affectionately and shook his head before taking the watch and tucking it back in his pocket. Then the little boy had suddenly disappeared, and Roberto turned stern eyes to the older Giancarlo, who still stood there watching.

"*Basta di pasta,*" he had snapped in a sharp tone, like that which a parent might use to correct a wayward child.

Now, as he pushed the garlic from the cutting board into the pan to simmer, the recollection of the voice still sent a chill up Giancarlo's spine, and he glanced over his shoulder just to confirm that he was indeed still alone in the kitchen. For many years after he first came to America, he had experienced from time to time such vivid dreams of his long-deceased mother and father. This one, however, had been the first in a very long time, and it had been with great unease that he had started his day.

As if the dream were not enough, Giancarlo's disquiet had been further compounded a little while later when he walked across the yard to retrieve the morning newspaper. He had just stooped down to pick it up when he chanced to see a large crow perched on a tree branch just overhead. At the sight of him, the black bird gave a startling *caw! caw!* as if to warn him away, before abruptly taking flight. Giancarlo had been for many years away from Abruzzo, but not long enough to completely dispel the super-stitions of his youth, and so the combination of the dream and his encounter with the bird had left him with a vague feeling of dread. What, he wondered, did it all mean? He supposed it was not all that odd that he should have dreamt of the pocket watch. After all, he had held on to it all that summer before sending it back with Carter. In its own way it had occupied his house like a guest he kept hoping would leave, and it had been a relief to finally see it go. Of the crow, he knew not what to think.

Unable to make any sense of it, Giancarlo shook his head and set about chopping some scallions and olives. These he added to the frying pan along with a pat of butter and, lastly, a small can of tuna packed in oil. When the water came to a boil, he opened a box of capellini and tossed in a handful. The thin spaghetti would take but a few minutes to cook, so he stood there by the stove, stirring them frequently to keep them from sticking together.

As he waited for the capellini to cook, Giancarlo's thoughts drifted to Italy. He wondered where Carter might be at that moment, if his long hours of Italian lessons were serving him well, and particularly, if he had traveled yet to Roccasale. The trajectory of his thoughts brought him right back to the pocket watch the young man carried, and left him speculating on how long it might be before he went to Castelalto. Then some water spilled from the pot and fell hissing to the flames, bringing his attention back once more to the task at hand.

When at last he tested a strand of capellini and found it to be *al dente,* just a little chewy, Giancarlo switched off the gas on both burners and took the pot to the sink. There he dumped the capellini into a strainer, sending up a plume of steam, before he quickly set it back on top of the pot. Doing so would preserve some of the starchy water lest he need a bit for his sauce. Then he pushed the capellini from the strainer into the frying pan, grated some cheese over it, and tossed it all together with the olive oil and garlic and tuna. Rather than make more cleanup work for himself by dirtying a plate, Giancarlo set the frying pan at his place on the table, poured himself a glass of wine, and sat down to eat.

As he helped himself to the capellini, Giancarlo looked over at the refrigerator door, where the postcard from Patricia still hung, slightly askew. He had seen her just that afternoon, when the two crossed paths on campus. Patricia taught French and had been bubbling with anticipation at the thought of the coming new semester. She was like that every fall, Giancarlo reflected. He, on the other hand, had betrayed no such enthusiasm.

"What is it with you?" Patricia had huffed. "You don't seem happy when school begins, and you don't seem happy when it ends. Really, Giancarlo, I don't know how I'm ever going to come to understand you."

"You might try letting me cook dinner for you tonight," he had thought to say.

The words had been right there on the very tip of his tongue—and he was certain she would have said yes—but for some reason he could not understand, he had not been quite able to speak them. Instead he had made some vague excuse for his less-than-buoyant mood by blaming it all on fatigue.

"Oh yes," Patricia had teased him in reply. "I forgot, you spent all those long hours teaching Italian this summer when you could have been relaxing."

"Well, it *was* a factor," Giancarlo had offered in defense.

At that, Patricia had given him a look as if she were about to make another teasing remark, but then her expression changed and she gave a little sigh.

"You know, Giancarlo," she had told him, "life is too short to start hunkering down for the winter when fall hasn't even started yet. Do you know what I mean?"

Giancarlo had nodded.

"No," she had said a little sadly, shaking her head. "I'm not really sure that you do, Giancarlo, at least not yet."

With that she had given him a wistful smile and gone on her way.

Thinking back, Giancarlo himself was not sure if he had truly understood her meaning. There was, however, one thing of which he was quite certain: He had cooked far too much capellini for one person. Looking at it all, he realized that there was more than enough in the pan for two. He would only end up throwing most of it away—and that was the pity of it.

CHAPTER 30

Carter had just stowed his bag and settled into his seat when the train gave a lurch and slowly began to pull out of Rome's Termini Station. He had never before traveled by train, and he was intrigued to see how well he liked this new experience. Turning to the window, he gazed out at the double lines of track that seemed to crisscross haphazardly before branching off in all directions. Closing his eyes for a few moments, he listened to the ringing of the train bell and the metallic scraping of the wheels beneath the car as it changed from one track to another. Before long the train had cleared the station and was clattering along down the rails. As it accelerated, the wheels beneath the car made a rhythmic *clack-claclack-claclack* sound, which Carter found somehow soothing. Unlike with air travel, when every bump caused his heart to skip a beat, he was unperturbed by the movement of the carriage, which rocked gently back and forth like a cradle. It was so different, so less stressful than flying, he reflected, and before he had gone five kilometers from Rome, Carter had already fallen in love with train travel.

Like all things of human invention, of course, this one was not perfect. It was midmorning, and as far as he could see, the second-class car in which he sat was filled to capacity, save for the seat directly opposite him. Indeed, after boarding the train, Carter had been forced to lug his duffel bag through three cars, squeezing through the aisles past other passengers searching in the opposite direction, before he had found an open seat. It had been warm and a bit stuffy inside the train, and by the time he sat down, the back of his neck was damp with sweat. All the same, Carter had felt no reason to complain. After all, buying his ticket and stepping onto the train had been such a simple, straightforward exercise next to the gauntlet one was required to run before boarding a commercial airliner. It had, by comparison, almost been a pleasure.

There were many destinations to which he might have chosen to travel that day. After weighing all his options the night before, Carter had settled on Pisa, where he planned to visit the famous tower and spend the night. From Pisa, he would go to Florence, which would start him more or less in the direction of Abruzzo. The rest of his journey after that was still a question mark, so for the moment he decided to just settle back and enjoy the ride. The train on which Carter was traveling was on a regional line. The trip from Rome to Pisa, with its twenty stops in between, would take the better part of four hours. He closed his eyes, and unlike on the plane from Boston, he immediately dozed off.

When he awoke almost an hour later, the train had come to a halt. As he looked out the window, Carter had a vague recollection of the train having stopped at least once or twice previous to this while he slept. In fact, though he did not know it, the train had already made five stops as it rattled along on its way to Pisa. He consulted his watch, which confirmed that the train must have traveled a considerable distance down the line since he nodded off. Just then the train began to pull away from the station. A voice came over the public address system announcing, he assumed, the next stop, but the words had been spoken so quickly that he had not understood them. Carter looked out, hoping to see if he could catch the name of the town. High up on the side of the station wall was a sign saying USCITA.

"Uscita," Carter repeated to himself.

He did not recall seeing that particular name on the list of stops between Rome and Pisa, but there were many, and he most likely had simply overlooked it. He sat back and closed his eyes again.

A short while later the train pulled into the next station. Once again Carter opened his eyes and was surprised to see USCITA written on a sign high up on the side wall. How could that be, he wondered. They had just left Uscita. He sat up, opened his daypack, and pulled out his map of Italy, but nowhere between Rome and Pisa could he find such a town.

People were getting on and off the train—by now the seat next to him and the two facing him were empty—and it would be only a few moments more before they were under way again. Carter began to get a nervous feeling that somehow, while he slept, the train had turned around and was headed in the opposite direction. How else to explain their consecutive arrivals at Uscita?

When a conductor happened to pass by, Carter gestured for him to stop.

"*Scusa, Signore,*" he said holding up his map. "*Ma dov' è Uscita?*"

Where, he wanted to know, was Uscita?

The conductor gave him an odd sort of look and gestured out the window.

"It's right there," he said. Then he went on his way.

The train once again lurched forward and was soon chugging down the track. Carter now was quite puzzled. He wondered if perhaps he had gotten on the wrong train. There were so many platforms at Termini Station that he might easily have strayed onto a train heading in the wrong direction. But wouldn't the conductor have noticed when he punched his ticket just after they left Rome?

Carter looked across the aisle, where a middle-aged couple was sitting. The man was reading a newspaper, while the woman chattered away on her cell phone. When she finally ended her call and put the phone in her purse, Carter leaned over with the map.

"Excuse me, *Signora,*" he asked in Italian, gesturing to his map, "but could you tell me where Uscita is?"

Though he had asked the question in perfect Italian, the woman looked at him as if she had not quite understood.

"Uscita," Carter repeated, supposing that perhaps she had not heard him clearly. "Do you know where it is?"

The woman shrugged, and pointed toward the front of the train. Carter was about to ask her what she meant, but then her cell phone rang, and she was soon talking a mile a minute once more.

Carter scratched his head. He was beginning to feel as though he were in some sort of dream, like one of those stories where the main character wakes up to find himself all alone on a plane bound for nowhere. He sat there, staring at his map, until the train slowed once more and pulled into the next station. When it came to a stop, the couple next to him stood and gathered their belongings together. Before walking away, the woman looked at Carter and, with a polite smile, gestured out the window.

"Uscita?" she said, pointing to the station wall.

Sure enough, there it was again. USCITA.

At seeing him just sit there with a confused look on his face, the woman said, "Ciao," and then strolled off the train with her husband.

Carter gazed out the window at them as they crossed the station platform and walked out past the USCITA sign. He noticed that all the passengers who had just disembarked from the train were walking out in that same direction.

It was then that understanding began to dawn on the young traveler.

His cheeks burning hot, Carter reached into his pack and pulled out his little Italian-English dictionary. Opening it, he flipped through the pages until he found, as expected, the word *uscita*.

"What an idiot," he muttered when he read the translation.

"Exit."

Someone else might have laughed it off, but Carter wanted to crawl under his seat and never utter a word of Italian again. The woman must have thought him a complete imbecile. How, he wondered, could he have been so stupid? After all the hours of lessons and study, was that what he could look forward to doing when he finally met Elena again? The thought of it made him miserable, until he suddenly recalled the words of Giancarlo that day when he told Carter that he should not be too embarrassed when he made a mistake. So long as Carter was trying his best to speak the language, he had said, Italians would love him all the more for it.

He could only hope that would be the case when at last he went to Roccasale, and so he let out a sigh and flopped back against the seat. Looking across the aisle, he noticed that the man who had been sitting there with his wife had left behind his newspaper. As the train began to move once more, Carter reached over and grabbed it. Obviously there was still a great deal of the language that he needed to learn; reading the newspaper, he figured, could only help.

Carter had just begun to scan the headlines when he heard someone give a little cough. He looked up from the newspaper and saw an elderly man standing in the aisle before him. He was a dapper old gent dressed in a gray suit and carrying a small valise. Holding the top of a nearby seat to steady himself, he smiled and gestured to the two open seats in front of Carter.

"*Permeso?*" asked the man, inquiring if it would be all right if he sat there.

"*Si, Signore,*" Carter replied, pulling his legs in so as not to trip him. "*Prego.*"

The old man nodded his thanks and settled into a seat opposite Carter. There, with his valise resting on his lap, he sat with a very erect posture and looked about at the other passengers with an expression of vague curiosity. For his part, Carter turned his own attention back to the newspaper, but found himself now and then glancing at the old man over the top of the page.

Opening his valise, the old man took out a small thin package wrapped in paper. He put the valise aside and unwrapped the paper to reveal the sandwich inside. He took the sandwich from the paper and held it up to Carter.

"*Ne vuoi?*" he said, offering Carter some of his sandwich.

Carter politely declined, explaining that he was not hungry. It impressed him, though, that the man would have thought to offer part of his lunch to a complete stranger.

Afterwards, when the man had finished his sandwich and wiped the crumbs from his fingers, he crumpled the paper and dropped it back in the valise. Then he sat there as quietly as before, staring out the window when he wasn't looking about at the other passengers. It seemed to Carter that the old man was a bit ill at ease and did not quite know what to do to occupy himself.

"*Lei vorrebbe leggere un po del giornale?*" Carter finally asked, offering the old man a section of the newspaper to read.

"No," he replied in a gentle voice. "I've already read the news today, but thank you for offering."

He sat there in silence for a moment before giving Carter a nod.

"You speak Italian very well for an American," he said.

Carter gaped at the man. Shaking his head, he tossed the newspaper aside.

"How is it that everybody knows I'm an American?" he asked with a laugh. "Is it that obvious?"

The old man smiled and shrugged.

"A lucky guess," he said, bowing his head modestly. Then he asked Carter to tell him from where he came in America.

"Rhode Island," Carter answered. When the man appeared not to recognize the name, he added, "It's a state between Boston and New York."

"Ah, yes," the old man nodded. "I think I have heard of it. You are a long way from home. Where are you going?"

"Right now I'm on my way to Pisa," said Carter.

"I see," he said. "Are you a student?"

"Not exactly," said Carter. "I'm just here on vacation."

"Well, you will find Pisa very interesting," said the man, suddenly taking on a proud, authoritative air. "You will of course want to visit the tower, but did you know that Galileo and Enrico Fermi both taught at the university there?"

"No, I did not," admitted Carter, smiling, for he realized that this was the first real conversation speaking Italian he had yet to have since he arrived in Italy. Encouraged, he asked the man if he was going to Pisa, as well.

The old man's eyes turned sad and uncertain.

"No," he answered, shaking his head. "I'm getting off at Livorno. I'm going to see my son."

At seeing the old man's reaction, Carter regretted having asked what he thought would be a harmless question. Before he could think of something to say to change the subject, the man suddenly began to ramble on in a tired voice about something Carter could not quite understand, for he was talking much too fast. From the little that Carter could make of it, the old man and his son had had some sort of disagreement, but beyond that he could discern nothing else. Whatever the trouble had been, he could plainly see that it was something that pained the old man greatly. On and on he went, the poor soul wringing his hands while pouring out his heart to Carter, as if he were giving his confession.

"*Capisci?*" the old man would pause to say now and then, asking if he understood.

Despite understanding nothing, Carter would nod his head or give a sympathetic shrug, and the man would continue. He tried as hard as he could to follow the old man's story, but in the end all he could do was listen with his heart. Something inside told him that this would be enough, that all the old man needed at that moment was someone to listen to him.

The old man's eyes were wet with tears by the time he finished his tale, and he seemed not the least bit ashamed of it. Turning away to the window, he pulled a handkerchief from his pocket and dried his cheeks. Then he looked back at Carter and let out a sigh.

"*Puo essere dura la vita,*" he said. Life can be hard.

That much Carter understood.

Later, when the train pulled into Livorno, Carter got up to help the old man off. He took the old man's valise and walked down the steps ahead of him, before reaching back to guide him safely down to the platform. Before walking away, the old man turned to Carter, reached up, and gave him an affectionate pat on the cheek. He said nothing more, but simply gave a sad smile and nodded goodbye. Then he turned and made his way toward the exit.

"*Signore*," Carter called after him.

The old man stopped and turned around.

"*Buona fortuna*," said Carter, wishing him luck.

Then he waved goodbye and climbed back on board.

CHAPTER 31

As he had planned, Carter stayed just one night in Pisa. After finding a hotel room near the center of town, he had spent the remainder of the afternoon wandering about the Campo dei Miracoli (the Field of Miracles), where he visited the medieval cathedral known as the Duomo, the Baptistery, and of course the Leaning Tower.

The Duomo, with its massive bronze doors and frescoed dome, was a spectacular sight. Walking about the interior, gazing at the indescribable artistry of the place, Carter had been reminded of Giancarlo's assertion that Italy had some of the most beautiful churches in the world. It was almost overwhelming, which he supposed had been precisely the intent.

At seeing the Leaning Tower for the first time in person, Carter had almost burst out laughing. On the one hand it was obviously a phenomenal piece of artwork. It resembled to him an enormous stack of elaborately decorated cakes. On the other hand, though, it looked completely ridiculous, like the sections of the cake were about to slide off. Standing so close to the Duomo, the tower lent a bit of human frailty to the scene, as if it were bowing before the glorious perfection of God. It had seemed somehow fitting.

In any case, Carter had supposed that it was only right that the tower be located on the Field of Miracles, for it was indeed a miracle that it had not yet toppled to the ground. Before returning to his hotel for his afternoon nap—taking one had already become a habit—he had snapped several pictures of it with his camera before asking a passing woman to snap one or two of him posing in just the right position so that it appeared he was holding up the tower with his hands.

Later that evening, after an early dinner, Carter had taken a stroll around town. The sun by then had fallen far behind the Duomo, and the shadows stretched long across the street as he had ambled along the sidewalk. He rather liked what he had seen so far of Pisa and had briefly considered staying an extra day to see some of the other sights, perhaps even to visit the university the old man on the train had mentioned. He had quickly dismissed the idea, however, for he found that he had been seized by an odd sense of impatience that kept growing stronger, prodding him to not linger too long in one place, but to keep moving on toward his ultimate destination. Inside, he had felt that the time was still not yet right for him to go to Abruzzo. All the same, he knew that it was drawing closer. And so, the following morning after breakfast, Carter had lugged his duffel bag back to the station, purchased a ticket, and boarded the next train to Florence.

Now, two days later, Carter was still in Florence. He was sitting on the curb in the Piazza della Signoria, enjoying a cone of gelato as he admired the group of statues in front of the Palazzo Vecchio. Carter had never been one to eat sweets, but when he had tried gelato for the first time the day before, he had been hooked. The Italian ice cream seemed to him denser but smoother than the ice cream back home. Perhaps it was because of the warm weather, but somehow it had a more satisfying taste that he found irresistible. *Stracciatella*, a sort of vanilla ice cream mixed with shavings of chocolate, had already become his favorite flavor, but there were many more he had yet to try.

Carter liked Florence very much. There was much to see there, and it was brimming with people from all over the globe. He could not quite put his finger on it, but something about the place reminded him of Disney World. Just being there was fun. Across the piazza, for instance, a long, slow-moving line of people was waiting to get into the Uffizi Gallery. Carter was certain that it could not be a pleasant wait, standing out in the hot sun, as they were, but nonetheless he heard few complaints. Most everyone seemed to be enjoying themselves. He had found it was like that just about everywhere he went in town.

When he finished eating his cone of gelato, Carter opened his pack and pulled out his guidebook to Florence to decide where he should go next. Since arriving the day before, he had already seen a great deal. He had visited the Basilica di Santa Croce, the church where the likes of Galileo, Michelangelo, and Machiavelli were entombed. He also saw there the funerary monument to Dante. Later, he had visited the Duomo and found it to be even more stunning than the one in Pisa. It also had the added virtue of the Campanile, the bell tower designed in part by Giotto, which stood next to it, straight as an arrow.

By this time, though, a sort of process of adaptation had already started to take place, and Carter found it increasingly difficult to feel impressed when each new church he entered was more astounding than the last. This particular day, he had decided against visiting any more churches for the time being, and instead had spent the first part of the morning at the Galleria dell' Accademia, where he saw Michelangelo's *David* and the famous unfinished slave statues. Later he strolled across the Ponte Vecchio and visited the Pitti Palace, before making his way back into the center of the city for lunch.

As he sat there on the curb, flipping through the guidebook, Carter looked across the piazza once more at the line of people waiting to get into the Uffizi. Till now he had avoided the place, given that there always seemed to be a long line out front. He was not at all sure as to what was so special about it, but he supposed there had to be something worth seeing inside if people were willing to wait so long to get in. Carter mulled it over for a moment before getting to his feet. He had nowhere else in mind to go that day, so he decided he would take his place in line and find out what the gallery had to offer. Before enduring the long wait, though, he walked off in the opposite direction in search of a second cone of gelato.

By the time Carter finally made it into the gallery quite a while later, he was feeling hot and tired and not at all enthusiastic about spending much time there. He found the air within was hot and stale, heated as it was by the afternoon sun beaming in through the windows that lined the gallery's main corridor. Had he not just spent such a long time waiting in line, he might have been inclined to just turn around and go back out into the fresh air. Since he *had* gone through the trouble, however, there seemed no point in leaving now. He wiped his brow with the back of his hand and trudged on ahead to see what paintings of interest he might find.

Starting in the first room, displaying works from the thirteenth century, Carter diligently walked from room to room, giving most of the paintings only a cursory glance, even though he knew without being told that they were all masterpieces. For whatever reason, perhaps simply because he was tired, few of them seemed to capture his imagination. It was not until he progressed to the works of the Renaissance era that he began to slow his pace and pay closer attention. Even then, he was feeling less than inspired, and was considering cutting his visit short when he happened to come upon Botticelli's *Birth of Venus*.

Carter recognized it at once. Forgetting that he was hot and tired and growing hungry, he immediately stopped and gazed at the painting, as if he had been struck dumb. He understood of course absolutely none of the work's symbolism or classical inspiration, nor for that matter did he care about any of it. What captivated him most at that moment was the tranquil beauty of the naked goddess's face, the eyes, the delicate line of her jaw, the perfect sensual lips, and the long, lovely windblown hair. The longer and more intensely he regarded her, the more he saw the very face and hair of Elena. It was as if he had been transported back to that breezy spring afternoon in May when he had first laid eyes on her and his whole life changed.

Suddenly, Carter now realized that nothing else mattered to him anymore. He had no interest in seeing another painting, no matter how great a masterpiece it might be. He no longer cared to see another statue or visit another museum or behold another astounding cathedral. He had seen enough, and he had learned enough, and now at long last, he finally felt ready to accomplish that to which he had set his heart.

It was time to go to Roccasale.

CHAPTER 32

The train for Bologna pulled out of the station just after seven the next morning.

Despite having passed a sleepless night, tossing and turning, Carter had awakened precisely at six, dressed, and with his duffel bag strapped over his shoulder made his way across the center of Florence to the station. Anxious as he had been to get there well in advance of the train's departure, he had not given even a thought to breakfast. There simply had been no time for it. Besides, he had not been feeling particularly hungry. It was a hot, muggy morning; the clear skies that had prevailed since his arrival in Italy were now gray and heavy with ponderous billowing clouds, and the oppressive sticky air felt like the steamy breath of some enormous beast. Little wonder that he had found himself with no appetite at that hour. To be sure, he had known that it would not be long before his stomach began to rumble, but there would be plenty of time for him to find something to eat later on.

Given the length of the trip ahead of him, and not at all eager to repeat the inevitably tedious search for an unoccupied seat that he had endured on his first two train rides, the normally penurious Carter had decided to pay the extra fare to travel in a first-class compartment. Just the thought of not having to lug his bag down the aisle, squeezing his way the length of the train past the other passengers, had made it well worth the extra expense. After purchasing his ticket, he had strolled at a leisurely pace along the outside of the train until he came to the first-class car. There he had stepped on board and soon found an empty compartment.

Now, comfortably ensconced in his seat as the train was getting under way, his duffel bag stowed in the rack overhead, Carter set his daypack on the seat beside him and unzipped the pocket that held his passport and airline tickets. Next to them rested his train tickets, which he withdrew and clutched in his hand while he waited for the conductor to stop by and punch them.

Carter yawned. Alone as he was in the compartment, he might have stretched out his legs and relaxed. Instead he sat up straight and did his best to stay alert. He was quite tired—the night before was already catching up with him—but for fear of falling asleep and missing his stop, and thereby his connection, he did not dare close his eyes. He would have to wait. The ride northeast to Bologna, the first leg of his journey that day, would only take just over an hour. Once he changed trains and was settled on board, he would have plenty of time to rest.

The train gathered momentum and was soon rushing over the tracks. This was Carter's third time aboard a train in four days, but the novelty had yet to wear off. In fact, the occasional rigors of finding a seat aside, he liked it more and more. He still found himself entranced by the rhythmic clatter of the rails and the gentle rocking of the carriage. That he was enjoying an entire first-class compartment all to himself was an added bonus. Even if the other seats around him had been taken, he still would have been quite comfortable. Carter stood and pulled down the window to let in some air. He rested his elbows against the window frame and leaned out just enough to feel the breeze on his face while he watched the houses and the people and the landscape roll by as if he were watching a movie. All in all, he reflected, it was a very civilized way to travel.

Just then, without warning, another train suddenly passed in the opposite direction with a tremendous *whoosh* that so startled Carter, he jumped back from the window. Catching his breath a moment, he leaned back just in time to see the tail end of the other train as it hurtled away down the adjacent set of tracks. It was then that he realized his train tickets were no longer in his hand. Certain that they must have been blown out the window, he panicked for an instant, until he looked down at his feet and found them lying on the floor. He snatched them up and gave a sigh of relief just as the compartment door opened and the conductor entered with a bright "*Buon giorno!*"

In Bologna, after a layover of almost an hour, Carter switched trains, and the second leg of his journey commenced, this time turning southeast along the Adriatic coast of Abruzzo to the city of Pescara. He was not so fortunate this time around to have the entire compartment to himself. Indeed, the three seats facing him and the seat by the door on his side were taken by an assortment of Italian gentlemen, all of them dressed in business attire. Only the middle seat next to him remained unoccupied. At seeing the perfectly tailored suits and stylish shoes of his fellow passengers, Carter at first felt a bit self-conscious of his own decidedly casual attire. Had one of the others not shot him a dismissive, condescending look over the top of his newspaper, he might have remained so. Instead, emboldened, he sat up straight and proud, with legs crossed to better show off his not-so-stylish sneakers.

The train began to move from the station, and it appeared that the compartment would remain with a complement of five passengers. Two of the four businessmen, including the snobbish one, hid behind their newspapers. The other two immediately pulled out their cell phones and were soon chattering away in self-important voices. As the train was gathering speed, Carter himself was settling back to stare out the window when the compartment door suddenly slid open. He looked up expecting to see a conductor, but instead a beautiful young woman with short brown hair, lovely dark eyes, and shapely slender legs stepped inside. Fashionably dressed in a pink blouse opened at the top and a skirt that stopped a very distracting inch or so above her knees, she carried a sizable briefcase in one hand and an expensive-looking purse over her shoulder.

No sooner had she appeared at the door when both cell phone conversations immediately ceased and the pages of the newspapers were strategically lowered ever so slightly. Four more pairs of eyes fixed themselves on the young woman. It was at Carter, however, whom she smiled and gestured to the seat next to him.

"*Occupato?*" she asked sweetly, inquiring if the seat were already taken.

Carter shook his head.

"*No, signorina,*" he told her.

The young woman smiled at him again, and before he could offer to help her, she hoisted her briefcase up and went to stow it in the luggage rack above. With her arms stretched out over her head, she arched up on tiptoe to drop it in. Pressed so close to him, it was difficult for Carter to avoid staring up into her blouse. Meantime, his compartment mates looked the young woman up and down from head to toe, and exchanged glances and not-so-subtle nods of approval. Just then the train lurched to one side, and the young woman stumbled toward Carter. Instinctively he reached up and caught her by the elbow before she fell onto him.

"*O Dio,*" she laughed when she finally settled into the seat beside him. "*Grazie.*"

"*Prego, signorina,*" he replied politely, sliding closer to the window to give her more space.

Carter turned his attention back to the window, while the young woman, who was no doubt accustomed to being ogled, fussed with her purse. As she did so, she studiously avoided eye contact with the other men, each of whom was dying for her to look his way. Carter glanced back at her now and then. Something in her manner gave him to suspect that she was waiting for him to say something to her. As for the four other men, they took turns looking back in consternation at Carter, trying to prompt him with their glances to say something to engage her in conversation. Were he to do so, it might provide one of them with an opportunity to join in if he botched it. That, at least, is what he supposed their strategy to be. It seemed to madden them that he made not the slightest effort in this regard, and he could not help but be amused by their silent frustration. How, he wondered, could he have made them understand? Yes, it was undeniable that the young woman was indeed quite lovely, and she *had* smiled at him the moment she came in, and then laughed and thanked him in a very telling way when he had kept her from falling. All the same, Carter just was not interested. His heart and his mind were simply elsewhere.

As for the woman, she whipped out her cell phone and dialed a number. Soon she was talking away, and it was like an impenetrable force field had gone up all around her. Someone with keen hearing would no doubt have heard the soft collective groan of the four men despite the sound of her voice and the low rumbling of the train. For his part, Carter closed his eyes and allowed himself to doze for a time.

One by one, the stations ticked by. Faenza, Forlì, Cesena, Rimini. Whenever he felt the train starting to brake, Carter would open his eyes briefly to take a look out the window to see where they were. The stations all looked more or less the same to him, but he loved the sound of the names. He realized that he was rushing through the country, missing so many places that under different circumstances he might enjoy visiting. Perhaps one day he would return and take the time to stop and see some of them, but for now his mind was set on only one destination.

The train rolled on.

Riccione, Cattolica, Pesaro, Senigallia.

At Ancona, everyone in the compartment save for Carter stood and collected their things. The young woman glided out the door and out onto the station platform with the four businessmen walking close behind, enjoying the wonderful view for as long as it would last. The train was soon under way, and Carter once again had a compartment all to himself. He preferred it that way now. As he sat there staring out the window, he had a feeling that reminded him very much of his football days. Before a game, Carter was always a bundle of nerves, to the point of being sick, and he would want for all the world to just run away. At the same time, though, he would be filled with eager anticipation at the thought of taking the field. At such times, he liked to go off by himself for a while to think things over, to reconcile these disparate emotions, and to gather himself together for the task at hand. Only then would he be ready to play.

Carter felt much the same way on this day. His stomach was a twist of nerves, but at the same time he was elated by the thought that he was drawing closer and closer to Elena. And so, with an hour and a half still to go before he reached Pescara and the next leg of his journey, Carter took a deep breath and tried to gather himself together.

When at last the train pulled into Pescara Centrale, Carter jumped up, grabbed his bags, and hurried out onto the platform. The air outdoors by now had grown quite still, and the skies dark and menacing. Carter looked at his watch. There was, he knew, plenty of time for him to find his way to the next train, which would take him inland to Chieti. It was almost noon, however, and he had yet to eat a thing all day. At this point, anything at all would do, so long as he could eat it quickly. Looking across the station concourse, he saw a small bar. Wasting no time, he headed directly to it, intent on buying a sandwich to eat on the train.

The bartender turned out to be a rather plump woman with a round, expressive face. When Carter appeared at the bar to place his order, she took one look at him and pressed her hands to her heart as if she were about to swoon.

"*Che occhi!*" she squealed with pleasure. "What beautiful eyes! Who are you? What is it that you want? Tell me, and it's yours!"

Carter's cheeks flushed bright red.

"I was just hoping for a panino to take on the train," he said.

"No," she said dramatically, pretending to be devastated. "Don't tell me that you are leaving, that you're not going to stay and marry me."

"Sorry," said Carter, starting to laugh. "I really have to go. My train is leaving soon."

"What train?" she huffed. "Where are you going?"

"Chieti," said Carter with a shrug.

The woman broke out in a great smile. "Chieti?" she joked. "That's not so far. We could still get married. What do you say?"

"Well, all I really wanted was a sandwich and a bottle of water," he replied.

"Ayyy, you men," she lamented, shaking her hands at the heavens. "You're all the same. All you care about is your stomach." She let out a sorrowful sigh and shook her head before leaning her elbows on the counter. "Well," she said, gazing at him with lovelorn eyes, "if things don't work out for you in Chieti, at least you'll know where to find me. Promise?"

"I promise," chuckled Carter.

"*Bravo ragazzo,*" she said. "Now, tell me, what kind of panini did you want?"

Later, with his sandwich and water stowed in his daypack, Carter hurried out to find his train. When at last he had climbed on board and settled into a seat, he opened his pack and took out his sandwich. As he unwrapped his sandwich, Carter breathed a sigh of relief. It would be only a short ride to Chieti, he reflected. From there all that would be left was the bus ride to Roccasale. Everything was going exactly as he had planned.

Carter took a bite from his sandwich and looked out the window. The sky had gone nearly black, and he heard the low rumble of thunder from the west. From all appearances it looked as though the train was about to ride into a storm. As the train lurched forward and began to pull away from the station, he settled back and watched to see what would happen next.

CHAPTER 33

The thunderstorm had long passed, but the streets of Roccasale were still wet from the rain when the bus from the Chieti train station rumbled into the center of town. When the door opened and Carter descended to the street, he found a large puddle of water separating the bottom step of the bus from the sidewalk. He turned to ask the driver if he would move the bus forward a bit, but then thinking better of it, he simply tightened his grip on his bags and with one leap cleared the puddle. Before he could turn around to be certain he had not dropped anything on the bus steps when he took flight, the door hissed closed behind him, and the bus rumbled away.

His bags in hand, Carter stood there alone on the sidewalk, looking about for a few moments. Roccasale, he saw, was not a terribly big place when compared to the cities from which he had just come, but it was not so small, either. The main street, on which he had been deposited, was lined with shops. People were bustling in and out of the stores, and cars zoomed up and down the street past him at alarming speeds before disappearing around the corner. Carter was by now an experienced pedestrian. He rightly assumed that the streets of Roccasale were no safer for him than the streets of Rome. As he set off to find a hotel, he reminded himself to keep to the sidewalk and out of harm's way.

There was, Carter discovered, only one hotel in Roccasale, the

Hotel Risorgimento. He found it at the end of the street, near the edge of the town's piazza. It was a very small hotel, run by a lively diminutive elderly couple, who seemed mildly astonished at having a guest when he came to check in. The two made a great fuss over him, marveling at how well he spoke Italian, and asked him endless questions about where in America he came from and how on earth he happened to be traveling through Roccasale of all places. Despite their assurances that he would have the best room in the house, Carter had not been overly optimistic about what kind of accommodations he would find when he finally carried his bags up the stairs. To his pleasant surprise, however, his room turned out to be bright and airy, and the window opened to a nice view of the piazza below. Oddly enough, it was the nicest room he had stayed in since he arrived in Italy, and he could not have been more pleased.

It was edging toward late afternoon by the time Carter freshened up and changed into more presentable clothes than those he had worn on the train. Ordinarily, he would have stretched out on the bed for a nap, as had become his habit, but he was far too excited at finding himself at long last in Roccasale. He was anxious to get out the door and search for Elena, but it occurred to him just then that he hadn't the faintest idea of where to begin. If only he had known a little more about her, even just her last name, it would have been a simple matter of finding her address in the telephone book. His mind was suddenly filled with a thousand nagging, dismaying questions he had never bothered to ask himself those many weeks ago when he first made up his mind to come to Italy. Looking back, he realized that this whole journey had been a leap of faith. He had no idea how many people lived in and around Roccasale, but from the little he had seen of the town, he was certain it numbered well into the thousands. Where was he to start, and how would he ever find out where she lived? Go door to door, knocking like a fool? They would probably call the police on him and have him escorted out of town. And what if she didn't actually live in Roccasale itself, but somewhere outside of town, in one of the *frazioni* Giancarlo had told him about? Who knew how many such places there might be?

Carter sat on the edge of the bed, the questions swirling around his head like a swarm of angry bees, till at last he could stand them no more. With a wave of his hand, he shooed them all away. Of what help were those doubting voices now? No matter what happened, he told himself, he was not going to find Elena by sitting in his hotel room fretting away the rest of the day. He needed to get outside into the open air. Then he would decide what to do next.

Later, after he had strolled about the center of town, peeking into the windows of the shops and restaurants, and briefly venturing down some of the side streets, Carter sat in the piazza. Behind him rose a statue of some Italian statesman or poet or God only knew who—by now he had seen so many. There was no plaque or inscription on the pedestal to tell him who it might be, but that was of small concern to him. At the moment, he was digesting his impressions of the town. From what he could tell, the center of Roccasale was quite old, like just about everything else in Italy seemed to be. Still, he had not needed to wander all that far into one of the neighborhoods that bordered the piazza on all sides before encountering homes and buildings of more recent vintage. He realized that behind the town's ancient facade, there lived and breathed modernity.

Carter looked about at the piazza, wondering if Elena ever came there. Perhaps, if he waited long enough, he would not have to go looking for her, but she instead would come to him. Then again, he thought with a chuckle, he might sit there for days and die of exposure to the elements before he ever encountered her again. He looked across the way to the church on the opposite edge of the piazza from his hotel. He imagined that Elena had been baptized there, that it was there that she had received her First Communion and been confirmed. He wondered if she went to mass there still. Carter could not help himself, but all at once he saw in his mind a vision of Elena in white, of her smiling and taking his arm as the two of them descended the steps from the church together. The pleasant daydream ought to have made him happy but instead had the opposite effect, for it only reminded him of how far he still was from her.

Carter sat there replaying over and over in his mind the memory of the short time that he had spent with Elena that day back in the spring. He was hoping to find some small clue from their conversation, anything at all, that might help him. Nothing. With a sigh, he scanned the buildings walling the perimeter of the piazza, until his gaze fell on the alley between two nearby buildings. Down it he saw the top of a road leading out of town, and just over it the narrowest of glimpses of the Abruzzi mountains rising off in the distance. He gave a grunt. When Giancarlo had told him that one could see the mountains from Roccasale, he had expected a more panoramic vista. Now that he thought of it, he recalled that Elena herself had talked about the beautiful view where she lived, but where was it?

It was then that Carter began to wonder if she had been speaking not of the town itself, as he had assumed, but of the house where she lived. His heart thumping, he jumped to his feet and backed away from the center of the piazza until he came to the church. He climbed the steps, turned around, and gazed back over the tops of the buildings opposite him. From that vantage point he could see for the first time a row of houses on the hill just above the town. Without a second thought, he bounded back down the church steps and set off in that direction to find the road that led there. What did it matter if it took him nowhere? After all, he had no place else to go, and he had to start somewhere.

CHAPTER 34

As he strode down the narrow street that led away from the piazza, Carter felt the inquiring gazes of the people he passed along the way. This was not a city like Rome or Florence, where the streets were always full of strangers from every corner of the world, where a lone traveler such as himself could easily blend in with the crowd and not feel out of place. Here he stuck out like a sore thumb.

Undaunted, Carter pressed ahead through the neighborhood, following the winding, gently rising street until it brought him to a long set of stone steps that ascended, so it appeared, to a road high above. The steps were old and worn down in the middle, the result no doubt of being trod upon for years untold. Carter did not hesitate, but instead vaulted up the first two steps and climbed the rest at a brisk clip.

When he reached the top, where the steps met the edge of the road he had hoped to find, Carter turned around and immediately understood what Elena had been talking about. Looking back over the roofs of the houses below to beyond the far side of Roccasale, he beheld a wide expanse of lovely rolling hills leading away to the distant mountains. All about the sky above it, patches of blue were breaking out amidst the mottled clouds, letting beams of radiant sunlight stream through here and there.

It was almost too perfect to be real, like an imaginary landscape that an artist might paint. Carter would have stood there and admired it for a little while longer had a passing motorist not tooted his horn at him and whizzed by no more than an inch from his elbow. Jolted out of his revery, he quickly turned away from the scenic view and began to follow the road uphill.

It was not very long before he came to an old, rather shabby-looking little house set right at the edge of the road. Carter felt certain that this could not be Elena's home. Nonetheless there was only one way to be sure, so he walked directly up to it and knocked on the front door. No response. He knocked again with the same result. He was about to turn and leave when he heard movement within, and the door suddenly swung open. An elderly woman in a black dress and shawl poked her head out and eyed Carter suspiciously. It was then that it occurred to Carter that he had not yet thought out just what he should say.

"*Scusa, Signora,*" he said politely. "I'm looking for someone named Elena."

"Elena who?" snapped the woman in reply, her eyes narrowed.

Carter of course had no answer for that query. At seeing his hesitation, the old woman informed him that there was no one there by that name before abruptly slamming the door shut in his face.

Truth be told, Carter could not blame her for doing so. He knew that he had sounded far less than forthright, and that he should expect more of the same reaction the next time he chose to knock on a door. Though his heart told him otherwise, he realized that what he was doing was a complete crapshoot that would in all likelihood end in disappointment. Just the same, he could not bring himself to quit, so he decided to persist just a while longer.

The road climbed steadily for a short way before it began to plateau. Up ahead another house came into view, this one larger and far more elegant than the old woman's home down the road. As he drew near, a soccer ball came bouncing off the property onto the road and began to roll toward him. A little boy ran out a moment later to retrieve it. He stopped in his tracks when he found Carter standing there in the road with his foot on top of his ball.

"Ciao," Carter said amiably.

"Ciao," the boy replied in a meek voice, keeping his distance.

With a gentle kick, Carter rolled the ball back to him.

"Does someone named Elena live here?" he asked nonchalantly.

The boy scooped up his ball and shook his head. Then he turned and ran back to the house, crying out, "Mama, Mama! There's a stranger out front!"

Carter knew better than to wait around, so he turned and walked off before the boy's mother came out and sounded the alarm that a suspicious-looking American was prowling the neighborhood. When he came to the next house up the road and walked up to the door, he stopped and stood there, wondering what he should do. It was ridiculous, he told himself, to continue on in this way. He was wasting his time. There were probably dozens of places around the town with nice views of the surrounding landscape. Elena might live in any one of them.

Perhaps it would be better, he brooded, if he just turned around and went back to the hotel to think things over. It seemed the most sensible thing to do, and he was about to go on his way when the door suddenly opened and an adolescent girl of perhaps thirteen or fourteen years appeared in the doorway. She was wearing a set of earphones, and her head nodded back and forth to the rhythm of whatever music she was listening to. Upon looking up and seeing Carter when she went to step outside, the girl gave a shriek and jumped back against the door frame.

Certain that disaster lay in wait for him—perhaps in the form of an angry father—Carter apologized at once for having startled her.

"*Mi dispiace, signorina*," he apologized profusely. "I'm so sorry. I didn't mean to frighten you."

"*O, Dio*," the girl laughed good-naturedly, putting a hand to her chest. "My heart! I thought I was going to faint!"

Then, after taking a dramatic moment to catch her breath, the girl smiled, and looked at him with inquisitive eyes.

"Can I help you?" she asked pleasantly.

Carter saw no alternative but to bluff it out and then be on his way with whatever dignity he could retain.

"I'm sorry," he apologized again, "but I was just wondering if Elena was home."

"Who?" said the girl, her face showing no recognition of the name.

"Elena," Carter repeated softly, knowing full well that it was futile. He was ready to just turn around and leave when, to his surprise, the girl suddenly clicked her tongue and tugged one of the earphones from her ear.

"These stupid things," she huffed. Then, smiling again, "I'm sorry, but who did you say you are looking for?"

"Elena," Carter said with no more hope than he had the first time.

"You mean Elena Simonetta?" said the girl.

Carter's heart leaped in his chest. A last name! Was it possible? Could it be hers?

"Yes," he found himself saying at once.

"You have the wrong house," said the girl, shaking her head. "The Simonettas live in the big house two doors up."

Carter wanted to grab the girl and give her a bear hug, but dared not. Instead he calmly thanked her, and began to back away from the door, stumbling momentarily on the edge of the step as he went. He quickly righted himself, and with a bright "Ciao!" he waved goodbye and hurried up the road.

When he came to the second house, Carter stopped and stood there a brief time admiring it. It was an elegant home with stylish stonework and gracefully arched windows that looked out over the hillside. To the side of the property, a patio and a swimming pool surrounded by flowers afforded the same lovely view. Carter could easily imagine Elena lounging there beneath the sun in that beautiful setting. It was perfect. He knew at once that he had come to the right place, and without a moment's hesitation, he walked straight to the door and rang the bell.

A moment later, a well-dressed, gray-haired woman came to the door. Not recognizing Carter, she gazed at him with severe, suspicious eyes, much the same as the old woman down the road had done.

"Signora Simonetta?" he asked straightaway.

"No," replied the woman without the least hint of cordiality. "I work here. Signora Simonetta is not home right now. Who are you, and what is it you want?"

"My name is Carter," he explained. "I'm a friend of Elena's from America. It is she, actually, that I've come to see."

"Signorina Elena is not here, either," said the woman tersely. "She is away at school in L'Aquila."

L'Aquila.

Carter's heart sank. That Elena might be somewhere other than home was another of those nagging questions he had never bothered to consider back in the spring. L'Aquila, he knew from his lessons with Giancarlo, was the capital of Abruzzo, certainly a far bigger place than Roccasale. How would he find her there?

"Is there any way that I might contact her?" he asked hopefully. "Perhaps a telephone number?"

"I'm sorry, I cannot give you that," said the woman flatly.

Carter sighed in frustration.

"But if you like," she continued, "you can leave a message, and I'll give it to her later on, when she comes home for the weekend."

Carter could scarcely believe his ears.

"*Today?*" he said, wild with elation.

"*Si,*" nodded the woman sedately. "Any minute now."

The words had no sooner left her lips when a sleek silver sports car growled up the road and pulled into the driveway with a screech. Carter stood there as if paralyzed and watched as the driver's door opened and a young woman stepped out.

It was Elena.

Dressed in designer jeans and a stylish blouse, her long golden hair pulled back from her lovely face, she looked down at the ground with a pout and started toward the house with a distracted air. At seeing the young man standing at the front door, she at first fixed him with a haughty, indifferent glare.

Then she stopped.

Elena lowered her sunglasses and regarded him from the edge of the driveway. Suddenly her gloomy expression melted. Her eyes opened wide with surprise, and she broke out in a beautiful, delighted smile that would have dazzled the sun itself.

"Carter!" she cried.

CHAPTER 35

A whirlwind.

Shrieks of surprise and delight.

Elena rushing to Carter.

The two brushing cheeks, first on one side, then the other.

The thrill of having her next to him.

The softness of her cheek.

The scent of her hair.

Pulling away from one another.

Elena taking his hand, leading him inside.

Now, sitting together on the couch, her knees just an inch from his.

Her hand touching his arm when she spoke.

All of it like a dream.

Carter wanting to explode with joy.

"Oh, my God!" Elena exclaimed in English, her eyes still wide with surprise. "I am so happy I see you, Carter."

Carter loved the sound of her voice, so light and sensual, especially the way she pronounced his name. She said it like *Cart-air*.

"Agnella!" Elena suddenly called out. "*Venga qui!*" Then, leaning toward him, she added in a playful, conspiratorial whisper, "I know she's out there listening, the old witch!"

Agnella, the older woman who had met Carter at the door, came into the living room, where they were sitting. Carter had completely forgotten about her. In all the excitement when Elena had come home and recognized him, Agnella had discreetly slipped away and left them to themselves. Her hands folded respectfully, she stood there stiffly with a sedate air, eyeing the two with what seemed to Carter a look of mild disapproval. He sensed that Agnella was protective of Elena, and perhaps still a little suspicious of the young stranger from America who had just shown up at their door completely unannounced.

"*Agnella, cosa fai?*" Elena said to her. Then, turning back to Carter, "This is Agnella, Carter. She was my—what is the word, ninny?—since I was a little girl."

Carter could not help but chuckle, for he was reminded of what Giancarlo had said about how charming people found it when a foreigner made a mistake when trying to speak their native language.

"I think you mean 'nanny,'" he said, smiling.

"Ninny, nanny, whatever," laughed Elena, throwing her hands up. "You know what I mean. Anyway, now I grow up, she still watch me like a mother goose."

Just then Elena's cell phone rang. With a sigh, she apologized to Carter for the interruption, and fished it out of her purse. Frowning when she looked at the number of the caller, she opened it, listened for a moment, and with a terse "no!" snapped the phone shut again.

"*Qualcosa da bere per il giovane signore?*" said Agnella coldly to Elena.

"Carter, she wants to know if you want something to drink," said Elena, regaining her smile.

"*No, sto bene, Signora Agnella,*" Carter said with a slight bow of his head, respectfully declining. "*Niente per me.*"

Elena gaped at him.

"Carter, you speak Italian!" she cried in amazement.

"A little," Carter admitted with a shrug.

"But why did you not tell me this when we met in Newport?"

"Because back then I didn't speak any at all," he told her.

"But how do you speak so well now?"

"I don't," he said, shaking his head in modesty. "Not really. I just studied a little over the summer after I decided to come to Italy, that's all."

"*Bravo*," said Elena, patting his hand, her touch like electricity.

Agnella left them for a minute and, despite Carter having not accepted her offer of something to drink, soon returned with a tray holding a bottle of mineral water and two glasses. She set it on the coffee table by the couch, and retreated once more to another room. Elena poured Carter a glass of water and handed it to him just as her cell phone rang again.

"Go ahead, drink," she whispered to him, reaching for the phone. "If not, she feel insulted."

Carter could refuse Elena nothing, and so he gladly took a sip of the water. He watched her answer the phone with the same frown, and wondered who it was that was darkening her brow. Once again, in an irritated voice, she gave a short "no!" and snapped the phone shut. She had not even put the phone back in her purse when it rang again. This time she simply turned it off and smiled apologetically.

Elena gave a toss of her hair, twisted her body sideways so that she was facing him, and settled back on the couch. She was so close to Carter now, and he wanted so much to reach out and touch her, to feel the gentle curve of her hip.

"So tell me, Carter," she said excitedly. "This is big surprise. What is it are you doing here in Roccasale?"

It was then that Carter realized how fortunate he was that Giancarlo had entrusted to him the pocket watch. Having it had given him a plausible reason for being there, and a graceful excuse for leaving if his reunion with Elena had not gone as well as he had hoped. He explained to her that he was simply passing through Roccasale on his way to a place called Castelalto to deliver something for a friend.

"Castelalto?" said Elena, not recognizing the name. She called to Agnella to ask if she had ever heard of the place.

"*Sta in montagna*," came the curt response. It was in the mountains.

Elena gave a shrug, as if to say it did not matter, and clapped her hands together.

"So, Carter, my friend," she said eagerly. "We must go to dinner tonight and celebrate that you come here, yes?"

Could Carter have possibly said no?

Another whirlwind.

Elena jumping up, taking his hand.

Plans being made.

Being led to the door.

Agreeing to meet her in front of the hotel at seven.

Elena brushing her cheek against his once more, squeezing his hand, telling him that he had made her very happy by coming.

Abruptly finding himself outside once more on the front step, the door closed behind him.

Carter gave a contented sigh and began to walk back to the hotel, not caring at all that Elena had not thought to offer him a ride. What did it matter, he laughed inside. He felt lighter than air and could have drifted the whole way on a breeze. Besides, he had two strong legs to carry him, and it was all downhill from there.

CHAPTER 36

Seven twenty-five.

Elena had yet to show, and Carter was pacing like a caged beast back and forth along the sidewalk in front of the hotel. Cars were zipping up and down the main street through town, and over on the piazza people were strolling about or sitting on the benches, enjoying the warm, pleasant evening. Like Friday nights everywhere, a feeling of lighthearted relaxation prevailed, and the air was full of talk and laughter.

Seven thirty-two.

Carter could barely stand the waiting. He was growing anxious and, truth be told, a little hungry. Everything had happened so fast when he left Elena's house, and he wondered if perhaps somehow they had gotten their plans crossed. He was certain she had said she would meet him at seven in front of the hotel, but could he have misunderstood? Was she expecting instead for him to return to her house at seven? Was she there now, waiting for him?

Seven fifty-three.

Still no sign of Elena. Carter walked back inside to the front desk to ask if anyone had called and left a message for him.

No word.

He was wondering what to do next, if perhaps he should find her number in the telephone book and try calling the house, when he chanced to look out the window and saw, to his relief, Elena's car pull up to the curb outside the hotel.

"*Finalmente*," he muttered, and he started toward the door.

Elena had already stepped out of the car by the time Carter emerged from the hotel entrance. Any pique he might have felt at having been made to wait so long vanished the instant he laid eyes on her.

Her hair falling loose and natural about her shoulders, some simple jewelry dangling from her ears, Elena was dressed all in white, in tight Capri pants and a breathtaking low-cut halter top. The simplicity of the look was all the more devastating because it revealed every delicate line, every tantalizing curve of her figure, while showing nothing. As she sashayed his way, her lovely eyes fixed on him, her face neither smiling nor frowning but serene and simply perfect, Carter saw not just any attractive young woman, but a goddess.

She was Venus.

"Ciao, Carter!" Elena said brightly, walking straight up to him and brushing her cheek against his. "Are you ready to go? Are you hungry?"

"Just a little," he said.

"Good," she said, taking his hand and leading him toward the piazza. "I know good place where we eat well, but first you meet my friends, yes?"

Had she asked him to remove his shoes and walk barefoot across a bed of coals, Carter would have gladly acquiesced. For all the hours upon hours he had spent in the gym developing his well-muscled frame, the simple touch of her hand in his had been enough to make him go weak. He was powerless to resist her, and had no choice but to let himself be dragged along by her like a Raggedy Andy doll.

Elena's friends were gathered together away from the lights, a collection of silhouettes standing around on the far edge of the piazza. Most, if not all, of them were smoking cigarettes, the burning tips bobbing about in the darkness so that, from a distance, it appeared to Carter that he was walking toward a small swarm of orange fireflies. As he and Elena drew nearer, his eyes adjusted to the dim light, and he began to see them more clearly. There were eight or nine young men and women, all of them college age or thereabouts, he guessed.

"Ciao, Elena," called one of the girls at seeing them approach.

"Ciao, *tutti,*" Elena called back.

As if to make a big show of him in front of the group when they walked up together, Elena slipped her arm more tightly around Carter's, and stood there very close to him.

"Listen, everyone," she said in a singsong voice, "I want you to meet my friend Carter. He just came to see me all the way from Rhode Island, where I went to college in the spring. Be nice to him. And be careful. He speaks Italian very well, so no talking about politics and America, *capito?*"

At that, a laugh rippled through the group, and Elena began to introduce her friends to him one by one. Agostina, Gaetana, Vincenzo, Adalberto, and more. The names came too fast for Carter to possibly remember, but that did not concern him, for he was certain he would have more time to learn them all later. What mattered to him most was that they seemed friendly enough, if a bit standoffish. Each of them gave him a polite "*ciao*" or "*piacere*" when introduced, but little more.

One of the young men, Alfonso, did not reply at all. Instead, he gave Carter a quick nod of his head and said aloud for all to hear, "Has anyone seen Armando tonight?"

Elena gave a toss of her hair.

"Who?" she said, as if the name had no meaning to her. Then she released Carter's hand and went off to huddle with her girlfriends. She stood in their midst, all of them talking in hushed voices.

Carter thought nothing of it, for he was of the opinion that women everywhere behaved much the same way whenever they got together. He flattered himself, conjecturing that they were all asking Elena about him. Meantime, the men drew closer and, despite Elena's admonition to avoid talking politics, began to ask him pointed questions about America in general and its Middle Eastern policies in particular. They seemed quite agitated by the subject, and from what he could gather, their opinions of America were unanimously disapproving.

Carter listened politely, trying to understand their questions and respond as best he could, but they seemed less intent on listening to what he had to say than on lecturing him on their own views. For Elena's sake, Carter took it all with good humor. That was, until Alfonso, lurking in the back, gave him a dismissive wave.

"America," he huffed. Then, with marked derision, he added, "George Bush."

Alfonso punctuated this statement by holding his nose, as if he had just smelled something bad.

Now, at this point in his life, Carter had little more than a passing interest in politics and world affairs. Many times back in America, especially on campus, he had heard far worse remarks about his country and his president over the years, and paid them not the slightest heed. Carter had always looked upon them as part of a national family squabble, of sorts. They had rarely bothered him because he had been brought up by his parents to believe that it was all right to say whatever he wanted about his family—so long as he said it at home. Outside the house, however, in front of strangers, that was a different story. There he and the rest of the family were expected to show a unified front, and they stuck up for one another without question, no matter what.

And so, upon hearing his country and his president disparaged in this manner, Carter might have been inclined to look the other way had he been back home in America and had heard it from another American. But he was not back home now; he was away, on foreign soil. The insult had issued forth unprovoked from a foreigner, a non–family member, and it rankled Carter. He took it very much to heart, and he glared at Alfonso in a way that made the others fall quiet and step back a discreet step or two.

"Ayyy, what did I tell you all?" cried Elena, suddenly appearing at Carter's side. She shook her head at her friends. "Didn't I say no politics? It's Friday night, time for fun, so give it a rest!" Then, in

English to Carter, she whispered, "Don't pay them your attention, Carter. All they like do is make arguments about nothing all night long."

With that, Elena seized Carter by the hand and began to drag him back across the piazza toward her car.

"Elena, where are you going now?" called Agostina, one of her girlfriends.

"*A mangiare*," she called back over her shoulder. "We're going to eat dinner. We'll meet you all later at the club!"

Carter had assumed they would have dinner at one of the restaurants right there in town, but at reaching Elena's car she motioned for him to get in the passenger's side, while she climbed in behind the wheel. When the engine growled to life, Elena stepped on the gas and accelerated away from the curb so quickly that Carter's head snapped back against the headrest. Before he knew it, they were tearing down the road at a dizzying speed. Carter's first instinct was to reach for his seat belt, but he saw that Elena was not wearing hers, so he left his unbuckled lest she think him faint of heart. His fingernails digging into the leather of his seat, he did his best to show a brave face as they careened around the corner and flew down the street out of town.

By the time they reached the restaurant, somewhere several towns away, Carter's interest in eating dinner was much diminished. It was not so much the speed at which Elena drove that had unsettled him—he had a heavy foot himself—but her impatience, and the way she swerved the car in and out of traffic on the narrow, poorly lit two-lane roads was unnerving, to say the least. She always blasted the horn the moment she drove up behind a slower-moving car. Worse, she had a habit of pulling out to pass without looking ahead to see if another car might be coming in the opposite direction. Carter had been certain on more than one occasion that they were about to die in a head-on collision. Inevitably, Elena had swerved the car back to her side of the road, but often at the last instant, avoiding catastrophe only by split seconds. All in all, it was not a ride to stimulate one's appetite.

Despite his slightly frazzled nerves, Carter soon regained his breath and was once again in high spirits when at last he was out of the car and strolling into the restaurant with Elena on his arm. Just looking at her, how could he have been anything other than joyous? Before long they had settled in at a little table off by themselves. They placed their orders, the wine was brought out, and finally Carter had a quiet moment with her to confess why he had learned Italian and traveled all the way to Abruzzo in search of her. He longed now to tell her how he had dreamed of her every long summer night since that day in the spring when he first saw her. He wanted to tell her of the connection he felt to her that very moment they met, something that went far beyond anything he had ever known. He needed more than anything else to hear her tell him that she had felt it, too, and that somehow he had occupied a place in her thoughts, as well.

All this Carter had rehearsed untold times over the summer and was prepared to tell her now, when maddeningly, just at the moment of truth, Elena's cell phone rang.

"*Managgia,* this thing," fumed Elena, opening her purse. Upon seeing the number of the caller, she frowned, and followed that remark with an English-language obscenity of the sort that would win a movie an *R* rating from the Motion Picture Association of America.

Carter was taken aback. It was not as if he had never heard the word, or even that he found it particularly offensive. Indeed, it was one that he himself found useful quite often. All the same, it sounded too hard and coarse and crude to have come from her lips. Elena was perfect in his eyes, and he was disturbed by anything that marred his vision of her. That was why he was all the more dismayed when she said it again as she turned the ringer off, sending the call to her voice mail, and snapped the phone shut.

"Ooh, what a day I have had, Carter," she lamented with a pout.

Then her darkened countenance suddenly brightened again. The gloomy clouds disappeared as quickly as they had come, and the sun came out again. She smiled and, leaning closer, took his hand. "That's why I am so glad you are here," she said.

Once again, Carter was bewitched, and his misgivings about her vulgar speech of just a moment earlier evaporated—along with his train of thought.

"I'm glad I'm here, too," he told her. Gazing into her eyes, he had the sensation of falling and losing himself inside them forever. He wanted that moment to never end, but just then the waiter returned with their antipasti, and the spell was broken.

As the meal progressed, Carter tried his best to keep the conversation light, asking her about college and doing all he could to recapture the magic he had felt just a few moments ago. Then Elena's phone had rung again, evoking from her the same brooding look as had the first call. Again she had turned off the ringer, but to his displeasure she left the phone on when she tucked it away in her purse. He was about to suggest that perhaps she might simply turn it off completely when Elena suddenly stood and excused herself to go to the ladies' room. She was gone quite some time, and Carter ate much of the remainder of his meal alone before she returned.

After dinner, Carter paid the bill, and the two walked out to the car. It had been, he reflected, a very puzzling first date to that point. Elena had alternated between brief outbursts of fawning attention and longer bouts of brooding distraction. She was giving him the latter just then, when she perked up once again and suggested they go out dancing.

"We go to fun place in Roccasale," she said brightly. "Everybody will be there."

"Sure," said Carter with a shrug. "Sounds good to me."

Hoping against reason that she would allow him, Carter offered to drive this time. Of course Elena said no, and soon they were roaring back to Roccasale.

Elena's friends were gathered together around three tables near the edge of the dance floor when she and Carter walked into the nightclub. A sizable crowd filled the remaining tables, but at the moment only two or three couples were out on the floor dancing to the music thumping from the sound system. Once again, as she had done earlier that evening on the piazza, Elena entwined her arm in Carter's and walked very close to him as they approached under the watchful eyes of her friends. The two squeezed in at one of the tables, drinks were ordered, and Carter settled back to see what the night would bring. Alfonso, he saw, was sitting at the next table over. At seeing Carter glance in his direction, he quickly looked the other way. By this point in the evening, Carter could not have cared less about Alfonso and his political convictions. His thoughts were too wrapped up in the beautiful young woman sitting next to him. For her part, Elena sat there saying very little to Carter, or to anyone else, for that matter. Instead she looked about the club with impatient eyes. Carter wanted to ask what was bothering her, but then one of Elena's girlfriends sitting on his opposite side tapped him on the shoulder and leaned close to his ear.

"Ciao, Carter," she said, all but shouting to be heard above the music. "I am Agostina."

Agostina was a plain-looking girl with short brown hair and a thin, angular face, but she had bright, playful eyes and a very nice smile.

"Yes, I remember meeting you earlier on the piazza," said Carter, smiling in return.

"Ah, you do speak Italian very well," she said pleasantly. "Do you like Italy? Are you having a good time here?"

Carter nodded enthusiastically. It was simpler than trying to be heard.

"And what do you think of Roccasale?" said Agostina. "Do you like it here, too? "

Carter grinned.

"I do," he answered, glancing back with affectionate eyes at Elena, who by now had her cell phone against one ear and her hand cupped over the other. He leaned back to Agostina. "More and more," he added.

Agostina looked at him thoughtfully for a moment before

smiling again, but this time in a way that struck Carter as a little bit sad.

"I hope you will stay here for a while," she said.

"So do I," he replied.

Agostina smiled in that same way again, patted his arm, and turned to talk to one of the others.

"Carter, what are you doing just sitting there?" he heard Elena cry suddenly. Her cell phone once again out of sight, she jumped up, took Carter's hand, and pulled him to his feet.

"*Andiamo a ballare!*" she exclaimed. "Let's dance!"

Carter had never been one to dance much. For all his athletic skill, it made him feel awkward and out of place. Given his druthers, he would have been content to just sit with Elena at the table and listen to the music all night, but he was powerless to refuse her and so once again let himself be dragged away. Elena's friends followed close behind, and soon they were all out on the floor dancing together. It did not take long for others in the club to get up from their tables, as well, and crowd in around them.

Before Carter knew it, he was surrounded on all sides by a mass of bodies moving back and forth to the rhythm of the music. Though he himself was like a fish out of water, Elena was clearly in her element, and all he could do was watch her and forget the rest of the world.

Tossing her hair back, her eyes closed as if she had fallen into a trance, Elena stretched her arms over her head in the most beguiling way and swayed her lithe, supple body to the music with deliciously sinuous movements. As if knowing that he could not take his eyes off of her, she opened her own once more and draped her arms over his shoulders. Pressing her body against his, letting him feel the warmth of her abdomen and breasts moving against him, she gave Carter a provocative look and ran her fingers through his hair before pulling away and losing herself once more in the dance. On and on it went this way, the music throbbing like a pulse, Elena's body always in motion with it.

Carter was enraptured. It was like gazing into a fire and wanting with all his heart to fall into it and let himself be consumed. Elena was dancing for him, he told himself, for the two of them! Here at last was the reward for his unwavering devotion to her, the discipline, the hours of study, and the long, lonely nights of dreaming only of her. This dance was just a prelude to what the rest of that night would hold, and all Carter could think of was taking her in his arms and making love to her over and over again.

The song was coming to its end now. Elena moved in close to Carter once more. She took his hands and, gazing at him seductively, guided them over the gentle curves of her hips before stretching up to him with moist, parted lips. His heart pounding, Carter leaned forward to accept her kiss, but at the last moment, Elena turned her head and drew back from him. Without a word, she took his hand and led him back to the table. Carter felt on the verge of dying, but he told himself that he must be patient just a little longer, that everything he hoped for would soon happen, when the moment was right.

Elena's friends came back to the tables. Carter was in high spirits and wanted to impress Elena, so he beckoned for the waitress so that he could order a round of drinks for everyone. It was just then, as he was turning away to ask the others if they would like something from the bar, that he heard an angry voice behind him. Carter whirled around to find standing there a young man of his own age with jet black hair and wild, anguished eyes.

"Elena, *venga*," the newcomer snapped angrily. "Come with me!"

"No," Elena said scornfully. She looked away from him and reached out her hand to Carter, but the other man snatched it away.

"Come with me now!" he cried, and he began to pull her from her chair.

Elena gave a shriek of protest.

Carter saw red and sprang from his seat at the man. He grabbed him by the throat and cocked his arm to strike him. The man released Elena, and she slumped back into her chair. Carter turned quickly to be sure that she was unhurt. Then, as he angrily whirled back to confront her assailant, he saw the other man's fist flying toward his face. Carter's first reaction was to duck and shove the man away. He came at Carter a second time, swinging wildly, but missed again. Carter then let loose with one straight punch that caught the man flush on the cheek and sent him sprawling backwards onto the floor.

"Armando!" cried Elena.

To Carter's bewilderment, Elena jumped from her chair and flew past him to the young man's side. Tears streaming down her face, she lifted his head and cradled it in her arms.

"Armando," she wept. "Speak to me. Tell me you are all right!"

Tears streaming from his own eyes, the young man sat up and wrapped his arms around her.

"Forgive me," he cried. "I am so sorry."

"No, it was me," returned Elena, brushing away his tears, and the two embraced.

By now the music had stopped and everyone in the club had flocked to the scene. Carter stood there in their midst, trying to make sense of what was happening but having no success whatsoever.

"Elena," he said, taking a step toward her.

"Get away from me, you stupid animal," hissed Elena, like a lioness protecting her cub. "Go back to America, where you came from."

The rebuke stung Carter, and he stood there stupidly, not knowing what to do, as Elena helped the other man to his feet and the two started on their way out of the club, holding and consoling one another.

"Elena, come back," he called desperately to her.

Agostina came to his side and put a sympathetic hand on his shoulder.

"Forget her, Carter," she said.

"But I don't understand," he replied. "I was only trying to protect her. Who is that guy?"

"Armando," she told him, before gently adding, "*suo fidan-zato.*"

Her fiancé.

"Her *fiancé?*" said Carter, incredulous.

"They had a big fight today just before you came," said Agostina. "You see, she was just using you to make Armando jealous. Don't feel bad. It's not your fault. That's just the way Elena is sometimes."

Carter watched Elena go, and his world crumbled around him. The possibility that she might be involved with someone else was the last of those nagging questions he had refused to ask himself way back at the beginning of the summer. It finally dawned on him then that all he had been doing all this time was chasing a mirage, and that it had all been for absolutely nothing. Everything he had done was a complete waste.

"What a fool I've been," he muttered, rubbing his forehead.

Carter gave a weary sigh and looked around at the people staring at him. One by one, they turned away, even Agostina, who patted him once more on the shoulder and said good night, until only Alfonso remained. As Carter stood there like a statue, his heart dead inside him, Alfonso walked by him on his way out of the club, pausing only to shoot Carter a wry look.

"*Benvenuto in Italia,*" he snickered.

Welcome to Italy.

Then he left Carter there alone.

CHAPTER 37

Carter opened his eyes.

It was morning, and he was sprawled face down, he knew not where, the side of his head resting against something very hard and cold. With great difficulty, as his head was splitting with pain, he rolled over onto his back and looked up. It took a few moments for his vision to clear before he realized that he was lying alone at the base of the statue in the middle of the deserted piazza. He propped himself up on one elbow and looked about.

It was still early; the top edge of the rising sun had only just peeked over the roof of the church. A car passed across the way and disappeared down the main street. Another soon passed in the opposite direction. The town was just coming to life. Carter sniffed the air and caught the scent of bread baking somewhere nearby. Ordinarily he loved the warm, pleasant smell, but at the moment it turned his insides, and he became acutely aware of another, far-less-pleasing aroma. Unhappily, he found that it was emanating from his damp, sticky shirt. Rubbing away the crust from the side of his mouth with the back of his hand, he had a very dim recollection of having recently been sick to his stomach. This unpleasant memory was confirmed by the small, fetid puddle near the stoop of the statue where his head had just been resting.

Little by little, as he gulped back the urge to be sick again, it all began to come back to him. When Elena had walked out of the club the night before and the others had all abandoned him, Carter had stood there like a dolt, not knowing where to go or what to do. It had felt as though a part of him had died, and he felt desolate and empty inside, as if his life had suddenly lost all purpose. Upon the realization that all his discipline and careful preparations that summer had been nothing but a fool's errand, there had seemed only one reasonable course of action. Ignoring the crowd as the music began to play once more, he had walked straight across the dance floor to the bar and plunked down his money.

The rest was a blur.

Now, as he was pondering the wreckage of the hopes and dreams that had led him to that spot, two young boys in soccer uniforms, kicking a ball along before them, crossed the piazza and passed by the statue on their way to an early-morning match. Upon beholding the pitiable sight that was Carter, the two stopped and gawked at him with expressions of distinct revulsion.

"*Schifoso,*" one said.

The other nodded in agreement, and the two hurried off.

Carter had yet to hear that particular word, but the contempt with which it had been uttered gave it meaning enough for him to understand it perfectly. Summoning all his strength and the little dignity left him, he got to his feet.

Strange, but despite the gnawing fatigue, the nausea, the throbbing head, the misery, somewhere deep inside Carter felt somehow relieved. It was as if he had been suffering for weeks and weeks from some virulent infection that at long last had lost its grip on him. The fever had finally broken, and the contagion purged. Yes, he had been laid low and felt truly dreadful, and perhaps there was more suffering to come, but inside he knew the worst of it was over. The most important thing to do now, he told himself, was to leave at once and put this place behind him. And so, taking a deep breath, he staggered back to his hotel to get himself cleaned up and his bags packed.

When the bus rumbled out of Roccasale later that same morning, Carter never so much as looked back even once. Instead he settled into a seat in the back of the bus, closed his eyes, and tried his best to forget that he had ever been foolish enough to go there in the first place. Depressed and exhausted as he was from his misadventure with Elena and the previous night's binge, he soon dropped off to sleep.

When he came to much later, his mouth wide open, Carter sat up and saw that the landscape had drastically changed. Gone were the gently rolling hills, and now the mountains rose all around as the bus motored along the winding road through the valley. Carter gave a yawn and stretched his arms out in front of him. By now his head felt a little better and his stomach not so queasy; it would not be long before he would want something to eat. He opened his daypack and pulled out his map to see if he could figure out where they were. As he traced the route on the map with his finger, he thought back to the morning. His first inclination upon awakening on the piazza had been to travel straightaway to Rome and board the first available flight to America. All he had wanted to do was escape and go home. Had it not been for the pocket watch and his promise to deliver it safely to Castelalto, he would have done so without a second thought. Instead he decided to delay his return a day and to honor his pledge to Giancarlo. Once that was accomplished, he vowed that he would depart at once and leave this land forever.

Carter turned from the window and looked around inside the bus. Besides himself there now remained only three or four other passengers. These few got off at the very next stop. With only one passenger left, the bus driver looked up at him through his mirror, and his assistant, whose job it was to collect the fares, gestured for Carter to come up front.

"Ayyy, G.I.," said the driver cordially over his shoulder when Carter walked forward and plopped down in the first seat. "*Parli l'italiano?*"

"*Si, un po,*" said Carter, indicating that he spoke Italian just a little.

"*Bravo,*" nodded the assistant. "That's unusual for an American."

"How do you know I'm American?" said Carter, puzzled as ever by how the people in this country divined such information without being told.

The driver and his assistant were a jovial pair. At Carter's question, the first gave an exaggerated shrug as he navigated the bus; the second threw his hands up as if to say, who knew? and then the two glanced at one another and laughed out loud.

When at last they quieted down, they asked Carter for his name. The driver in turn introduced himself as Enrico, while the assistant gave his name only as *Il Direttore*, the Director. For whatever reason, this prompted the two to break out once more into another round of raucous laughter.

Once calm returned, the two began to good-naturedly pepper Carter with questions. Where did he come from in America? Was Rhode Island near New York? What did he think of Italy? Was he having a good trip? How had he come to speak Italian so well?

Enrico and Il Direttore were much impressed to hear that Carter had only just taken up the study of their language three months earlier.

"*Ma dica, Carter, cosa fai qui?*" said Enrico. "Tell us, what's an American boy like you doing all the way over here in Abruzzo?

"Just visiting some friends before I go home," replied Carter, thinking the simplest answer would be the best. Then he asked, "How long before we get to Castelalto?"

"Oh, a little while yet," said Enrico. "Why, are you in a hurry?"

"No," said Carter with a grin. "Just wondering."

"Good," said the driver, "because I'm hungry."

With that, Enrico suddenly slowed the bus and turned off the main route onto a roughly paved side road. He drove a short way, until they came to a collection of small, rather rundown-looking buildings next to a gas station. When he brought the bus to a halt and opened the door, Il Direttore stood and hurried down the steps. Before following him, Enrico turned to Carter.

"Carter, *andiamo*," he said, nodding for him to come along. "Let's go."

Carter cast a skeptical look out the window. It was an out-of-the-way place, and he began to get an uneasy feeling.

"Go where?" he asked.

Enrico smiled, as if suddenly understanding Carter's reluctance.

"*A mangiare,*" he said with a laugh. "To eat, of course!"

It was not exactly the Tavern on the Green to which Enrico and Il Direttore led him, but the little *trattoria* in which Carter found himself was a friendly, inviting place with just a few tables, flanked not by chairs but wooden benches. The three sat down at a table, and the proprietor, a squat little man with a shock of thick white hair, poked his head out the kitchen door and nodded to Enrico as if he had been expecting them. A moment later, he emerged from the kitchen with three steaming bowls of pasta and beans. Then he brought out some bread, a bottle of mineral water, and a carafe of red wine. He set these on the table and began to exchange pleasantries with the three of them in some language that, to Carter's ears, only vaguely resembled Italian.

Unable to follow a word of the conversation, Carter turned his attention to his pasta and beans. Having never before eaten such a dish, he took a piece of the bread, dunked it in the zesty red broth, and took a bite. He found it was warm and moist and delicious. It turned out to be just the thing Carter needed. Anything lighter would not have been substantial enough; anything heavier would have only made him sick again. Carter poured himself a glass of mineral water—Enrico and Il Direttore were already draining the carafe of wine—and gulped down a swallow. All in all, it was a simple meal, but as he ate it, joining in the conversation whenever they spoke Italian instead of their dialect, Carter felt just a little bit of life rekindle inside him. He was going to survive.

They did not stay long. The moment their bowls were emptied and the last of the wine consumed, Enrico slapped his hand on the table and announced that it was time to go. When the proprietor brought them the check, Carter reached for his wallet to pay for his share, but Enrico would have none of it and insisted that he and

Il Direttore would pay. Carter was quite surprised by their generosity to a complete stranger. He did not know it, but his two dinner companions had found him to be *simpatico* (good company). It was a pleasure for them to pay.

After having watched his driver consume at least a half carafe of red wine, Carter was mildly apprehensive when the three reboarded the bus and Enrico settled in behind the wheel. It was midafternoon, and though he had drunk not a drop of wine, Carter himself was feeling ready to lie down and take a little nap; he could only imagine how the other two felt. To his amazement, however, Enrico suddenly broke into a loud, bellowing rendition of "La Donna è Mobile." With Il Direttore roaring with laughter beside him, he put the bus in gear and stepped on the gas, and off they went. The two men took turns trading songs, until a short while later when Enrico put up his hand for quiet and told Carter to look up the road.

Carter came closer to the windshield and gazed out. Ahead of them in the distance, he saw what looked like little more than a thin streak of white high up on the mountainside. Having no idea of what it might be, he looked at Il Direttore with questioning eyes.

"Castelalto," he said to Carter, as if that was the most obvious thing in the world. Then he broke out into song again.

The good news for Carter was that the bus arrived at the turn for Castelalto just a few minutes later, thereby saving what remained of his hearing from the auditory assault of the two would-be tenors. The bad news, as explained to him by Enrico, was that the bus was too long to fit around the corners of the narrow, twisting road that led up to the village three kilometers away. As much as it grieved them, they would have to drop Carter there at the base of the road, and he would have to walk the rest of the way. There was nothing to be done for it, so Carter collected his things, thanked the two men for the meal and of course the entertainment, and stepped off the bus.

"Don't worry," Enrico told him. "Somebody will probably come along soon and give you a ride."

"And don't forget to tell them who brought you here," shouted his assistant. "Always remember to say, 'Today I rode with Enrico and Il Direttore!' "

At that, the two men bid him *buon viaggio*, waved goodbye, and broke into song again as Enrico closed the door and began to drive away.

Carter stood there, waving them out of sight, before slinging his duffel bag over his shoulder. Then he turned and began the long trudge up the road to Castelalto.

CHAPTER 38

Enrico, as it turned out, was wrong. No one came along and offered to give Carter a ride. In fact, no cars whatsoever passed by him during his weary slog up the ever-ascending road, and he wondered if perhaps he was climbing to a ghost town. It was not until the road at last began to flatten out and the entrance to the center of the village came into view that he heard a car come sputtering up the road behind him. The driver, an elderly gent in a cloth cap, slowed as he passed and gave Carter a sympathetic shrug, as if to apologize for arriving too late to give him a ride. Carter smiled and nodded at him in reply to let him know that it was no big deal, for the village was just a few steps ahead. With a tip of his cap, the man drove on out of sight.

When at last he walked into the middle of Castelalto, Carter had the distinct impression that he had stepped back in time. It was even smaller than Roccasale, and easily far older. Looking about, he understood now that the streak of white he had seen in the distance while riding the bus was the facade of the stone houses that bordered the little piazza and climbed back from it in clusters up the hill. Carter turned around and looked back at the spectacular view of the valley and the surrounding mountains. Then he leaned forward and peeked over the edge of the piazza at the precipitous embankment that plunged far below. From all appearances, the place was built on a cliff, giving it an isolated, mysterious feel, like some ancient fortress that history and the outside world had long-ago forgotten.

The sound of voices behind him brought Carter back to the present. He turned and saw a group of youngsters walking his way. Here and there, farther back in the neighborhood, people were emerging from their houses. Apparently the place had seemed deserted to him because everyone had been inside having lunch or perhaps taking an afternoon siesta. The arrival of a stranger in town was obviously the cause of some excitement, for the children immediately flocked to Carter to ask who he was and where he was going.

"*Sto cercando la casa di Giorgio Rosa*," he told them. "I'm looking for Giorgio Rosa's house."

"*Si, si!*" the children cried enthusiastically, and before Carter knew it, they were all shepherding him away up one of the little alleys off the piazza. Soon they came to a stone house that looked much like the others. Carter set his bags down and stepped toward the door. One of the children, a wiry little boy, dashed in front of him, gave the door a quick knock, and opened it a crack.

"Signor Rosa!" he called inside. "There's an American here to see you!"

Carter gaped at the child and then just shook his head.

A moment later, a woman came to the door. She was much older than he, perhaps in her late forties, Carter guessed, but quite slender and lovely. Her straight black hair framed a still-youthful face that showed only a few finely etched lines about the corners of her eyes. What struck Carter the most were her dark, intense eyes. When at first she gazed at him, he had almost jumped back for fear that somehow he had angered her. But then she had put him at ease by smiling and gently asking what he wanted.

"I'm sorry to bother you," Carter apologized, "but I've come to see Giorgio Rosa."

"I'm afraid he is still napping just now," she replied. "What is it that you've come to see him about?"

"I've come to deliver something to him," explained Carter.

"And what would that be?" she asked curiously.

Carter reached into his daypack and pulled out the little padded envelope he had kept tucked safely inside this whole journey. He opened it, and let the cloth pouch holding the pocket watch slip out into his hand.

"It's from his brother, Giancarlo," said Carter, handing it to her.

The woman did not open the pouch, but gazed at it with a sad expression for a short time, before giving a little sigh.

"What is your name?" she said after a moment's contemplation.

"Carter," he replied.

She opened the door wider and motioned for him to enter.

"Please come in, Carter," she said, "and I will wake Giorgio for you."

"Are you Signora Rosa, his wife?" he asked, for he was not completely certain.

"Yes," she answered. "But you may call me Antonella."

PART THREE

CHAPTER 39

Her name was Antonella Portinari, the girl Giancarlo had fallen in love with that day so many years ago when he and Giorgio came down from the mountain and saw her pass by on the piazza. In one sense, it all seemed so lost in the distant past that it should no longer have mattered to Giancarlo. It was like a dream of something that had never really happened. At the same time, though, as he stood there in his kitchen, staring out the back window at a gray morning sky, the memory of that day and everything that followed tore at him afresh, reopening a deep, very old wound that had never properly healed.

Giancarlo poured himself a cup of coffee and sat down at the table. In the past week, since he had sent his father's pocket watch back to Italy with Carter, he had found himself brooding more and more about the turbulent times that had been set in motion that day when he had first encountered Antonella. Gazing down into his cup, he let his thoughts drift back to those days and, as if watching an old home movie, began to replay it all once more in his mind.

It had not taken long for Giancarlo and his brother to learn that Antonella had come from another village not far away, where she and her father and mother lived in a house with her grandparents. Apparently she and her parents had come to Castelalto that day to look in on her mother's uncle, Ferdinando, a sickly old widower who lived all alone in a house on the other side of town.

It was the first of many visits the Portinaris would make over the course of the next year, as Ferdinando's health steadily declined. Whenever they came, Antonella would inevitably wander up to the meadow or to the edge of the piazza with her sketch pad in hand. She of course drew the attention of all the boys in town, and the enmity of more than one of the girls, but she remained aloof to them all. For his part Giancarlo would only watch her from a distance, afraid to approach her and make a fool out of himself like the other young men. Only Giorgio, it seemed, had been able to draw her out a little, to get her to talk, and even to make her break into a smile now and then.

Giorgio's success in charming her this way had irked Giancarlo. It was only one of a growing list of grievances he had against his older brother, who, it seemed to him, always took the lion's share of everything. Giancarlo's displeasure in this regard had not been helped much by his father. In his defense, Roberto was a simple man who loved both his children dearly. Having two sons, however, had created for him certain dilemmas. One of these he chose to address with Giancarlo one day not long before the boy turned eighteen.

Giancarlo had been playing the piano one evening when his father asked him to come and sit with him at the kitchen table. Roberto sat there in silence for a while, thoughtfully rubbing his chin, before reaching into his pocket to check the time on his watch. The watch had stopped ticking, so he handed it to Giancarlo to have him wind it for him. Giancarlo had been happy to do so. Ever since he was a little boy, he had always loved the watch— the movement of the figures and the delicate music it played. And he loved the story of how the watch had been handed down to his father from his grandfather, who had won it years and years ago in a card game.

"Someday this will be yours," his father said with a kindly smile when Giancarlo handed the watch back to him. Then his brow had furrowed.

"But Giancarl'," Roberto had continued uneasily, "there is

something you need to know. Look about you. This is all I have in the world—this one little house with a tiny piece of land to grow a few vegetables on. But I have two sons. I cannot divide the house in two, so someday I will have to make a decision, and it's better for you to know right now what that decision will be, instead of finding out later on someday, when I am gone. Do you understand what I am trying to tell you?"

Giancarlo had given a sigh.

"Are you trying to tell me, Papa," he replied softly, "that one day, when you are gone, I will inherit your watch, but Giorgio will inherit your house?"

His father had given a sigh of his own and shrugged in resignation.

"I will do the best I can for you," he promised. "I have found work for Giorgio with the telephone company when he finishes school this year. I will do the same for you next year, when you have finished. I will do everything I can to help you along to get you started."

Giancarlo of course had understood how things were. What his father had told him came as no surprise at all. Still, he had felt embittered. The business about the house had only reinforced the notion that the random accident of his having been born second had condemned him to perpetual subordination to his brother. It was a feeling that had never sat well with him. There had also been the matter of his father's pragmatic plans to find work for him when he finished high school. Giancarlo had been making plans of his own, to continue his education and pursue his love of music. These would inevitably conflict with those of his father, just as his plans to pursue Antonella would conflict with those of his brother.

Not long after Ferdinando died later that same year, the Portinaris, to no one's surprise in the village, moved into the house. At first, Antonella's coming to live in Castelalto had been a cause of great joy to Giancarlo. This soon gave way to dismay, and his resentment of his older brother had only grown worse when Giorgio promptly began to court her before Giancarlo had even summoned up the nerve to say hello. Ironically, it had been Giorgio who would first introduce him to Antonella, when he brought her by the house one day to meet his father. Giancarlo had been at the piano playing when the two had walked in.

"Don't stop. That sounds beautiful," was the first thing Antonella had said to him, her eyes piercing straight to his soul, just as they had on the day he had first seen her. Her eyes had haunted him ever since.

It had been all Giancarlo could do to not jump up and confess his love for her right then and there, to tell her that he dreamed of her every night, but any such ideas had been quickly swept away by the sight of her holding hands with his brother. Giancarlo had done his best to show a brave face, while inside he was dying. Plainly they were already a couple, and all Giancarlo could do was watch and suffer in silence.

The months went by. Giorgio finished school and began training to work for the telephone company. The hours were long, and often he returned home late with his father. Now and then, while Antonella waited by the piazza to greet his brother when he came home, Giancarlo would wander by and say hello before quickly wandering away again. In time, though, he worked up the nerve to stop and chat for a moment or two before going on his way. To his elation, Antonella seemed to welcome his company, and so Giancarlo lingered a little longer every time he passed by. One day Antonella invited him to sit with her while she waited. That had been all the encouragement Giancarlo needed, and soon it became a common sight in the afternoon to find the two of them sitting there together, talking by the fountain.

Antonella loved to talk about art and music and life, and Giancarlo loved to listen to her. With each passing day, she seemed to open up to him a little more, and he rejoiced in it. Her moods, though, were as inscrutable and changeable as the winds across the Abruzzi mountains. Sometimes, for no apparent reason at all, she would suddenly fall quiet and look away with her dark eyes into the distance, her thoughts taking her someplace far removed from their little village. At such moments, Giancarlo would not disturb her, but instead would hold his peace and simply sit with her until she decided she was ready to come back. He loved her more and more every minute they spent together, and it did not matter if they spoke. He was certain that she was warming to him, as well, even though she broke into a delighted smile and jumped up every time she saw Giorgio come into sight. Every time it happened, it was like a knife in Giancarlo's gut.

The following year, much to his father's consternation, Giancarlo refused to go to work for the telephone company, but instead applied for and won a scholarship to study music in Pavia. Roberto could see no practical application for such studies, and he feared that his son would end up in a life of poverty. Nonetheless, against his father's counsel, Giancarlo had enrolled that fall.

It was a mixed blessing. In Pavia, Giancarlo got his first real taste of life outside Castelalto, and he found that it suited him. And musically, he thrived at the university. With no other release for it, Giancarlo poured his passion for Antonella into the music he wrote, and his work impressed his professors very favorably. Creatively, it was the most productive time of his life. Emotionally, however, he was a wreck. Every moment he was away from Castelalto, he missed Antonella terribly, and he would torment himself as he lay awake at night, wondering what she was doing with Giorgio. And so Giancarlo found himself returning home every weekend he could, hoping simply to see her, however briefly, and exchange a few words. Antonella, who herself was busy studying to become an art teacher, always seemed pleased to see him, but their encounters were fleeting. Every time he watched her go off with Giorgio, it only served to make him more miserable.

A year passed this way, and then another.

His second year in Pavia completed, Giancarlo came home for the summer, full of indecision. An opportunity to spend a semester abroad that coming autumn, studying in America, had been presented to him, and Giancarlo had accepted. Part of him was eager to go, for it was the opportunity of a lifetime. Another part of him, though, could not bear the thought of it. He knew without asking that his father was going to object, but that was not what concerned him. It was the idea of being thousands of miles away from Antonella for an entire three months that distressed him most. He was not sure if he could go through with it.

By this time, Giorgio had been working regularly and earned enough to buy his own car. On the weekends, when he wasn't playing soccer for a local amateur team, he liked to dress up and take Antonella out for a ride to show her off. Giancarlo, meantime, got around town on a rickety old bicycle and worked odd jobs, saving like a miser for his trip to America. He felt like a pauper compared to his more steadily employed brother, but he was happy to be home and once again have the chance to spend time with Antonella, who was not working at all that summer. The two took up once more their ritual of meeting on the piazza in the afternoon, and against all reason, Giancarlo began to hope, for he sensed in her a change toward him.

One day, early in the summer, Giancarlo found Antonella on the piazza with her sketch pad on her lap. At seeing him, she beckoned for him to come sit.

"I need practice drawing faces," she told him. "Sit for a while, and let me draw yours."

Giancarlo could refuse her nothing, and so he sat down, and looked away nervously toward the mountains.

"No," said Antonella, shaking her head. "Turn this way, and look right at me."

Giancarlo did as she told him and sat there very still as Antonella gazed at him, studying his face. He could have stayed that way forever, basking in her attention as she began to draw.

"I heard you are going to America," Antonella said after she had been at it for a while.

"That's the plan right now," said Giancarlo. "But I'm still not sure if I will go."

"Oh, but you *must* go," said Antonella, looking back and forth from the pad to his face. "It will be nice for you. I'm glad you are going."

At hearing these words, Giancarlo's heart sank a little, for he had hoped that perhaps she would be disappointed by the news and try to talk him out of it.

"Of course," Antonella went on, "I will miss our little conversations in the afternoons while you are gone."

"You will?" said Giancarlo, scarcely believing his ears.

"Sit still," she told him with a huff. "You have a good face to draw, but I can't do it if you keep moving all around."

"Sorry," said Giancarlo.

For a time neither spoke, and the only sound Giancarlo could hear was his own breathing and the scratching of her pencil against the paper. Antonella's demeanor softened once more.

"You know, I think of your face sometimes," she said in a faraway voice, without looking up from the pad.

"When?" he asked.

"Sometimes at night," she replied, "when it's quiet and I can hear the sound of your piano echoing all through the village. It's one of my favorite sounds."

"I never knew anyone was listening," he said.

"I listen," she answered.

Antonella looked up at him, and in her eyes Giancarlo was certain that he saw the first flickers of true affection. She quickly looked back at her pad, and turned it around for him to see.

"What do you think?" she said, showing him her work.

"I think you've captured me," Giancarlo had answered.

"I know," she said.

Anyone with eyes, and there were always many watching in a little village like Castelalto, could see that there was something happening between the two. At this point it was not yet possible to guess if it was merely friendship or something deeper. After that day when he let her sketch his face, Giancarlo of course was convinced that it was the latter. For too long he had kept his silence about his feelings for Antonella. He decided that the time had come for him to make them known to her, and to learn if she felt the same for him, as he suspected she did. He began to plot exactly where and how he would do it, but as so often happens in life, events would unfold in a way he could not possibly have anticipated.

One night a few days later, Giancarlo had an argument with his father about his plans to go to America, and bitter words were exchanged.

"You are wasting your time," Roberto had told his son. "What kind of living will you make out there by studying music? You will starve."

"I'd rather die starving somewhere out there, doing what I love," Giancarlo had replied in anger. "It's better than suffocating to death here in this godforsaken place, where someday I'll be thrown out into the street with nothing more than a pocket watch to my name."

The remark wounded his father deeply; Giancarlo had seen it in his eyes. He regretted saying it, but he was too proud to take it back, and nothing more was said between the two.

The next morning, before his father and brother arose, Giorgio left early to spend the day in Pescara, where he was training to become a full-fledged technician. Roberto left the house a little while later with Demetrio, a villager who sometimes rode to work with him. For his part, Giancarlo stayed home at the piano, tinkering all morning with a new piece he had recently composed. He took just a short break for lunch and was soon back at work. It was nearing midafternoon when, as he was playing through the new piece, he heard a knock on the door. To his surprise it turned out to be Antonella. She was standing there holding one of Giorgio's soccer jerseys that he had torn in a match. Antonella had mended it for him and had come to drop it off.

"I wanted him to have it for later on when he comes home," she explained, "because he'll be practicing with his team after work. I was going to just leave it at the door, because I'm going out for the afternoon, but then I heard your playing, so I decided to knock. I hope you don't mind."

"No, of course not," said Giancarlo. "Please come in."

Antonella entered, and Giancarlo closed the door behind her. An awkward moment of silence descended on them as she stood there, still clutching the jersey, while Giancarlo fidgeted with his hands.

"What was that song you were playing just a minute ago?" Antonella finally said. "It sounded very nice."

"It's something brand new I've been working on," said Giancarlo, eagerly retreating to the sanctuary of his piano. "Would you like to hear the whole thing?"

"I would love to," she answered.

Giancarlo sat down at the keyboard, and with Antonella standing by his shoulder, his heart pounding, he began to play. It was the first time that he had ever performed for just her alone, and he played with all the passion and intensity he could summon. All the while, despite how lost in the music he became, he was conscious every second of Antonella by his side, watching and listening to him. When he finished, Giancarlo sat back and waited for her reaction, afraid to turn around and face her. At first Antonella said nothing, and he was sure that the music had not pleased her, but then he heard her give a little sigh.

"That was wonderful," she told him. "What do you call it?"

"Sonatina in A," he replied with a shrug, still looking down at the keyboard. "It's sort of a base for a much longer piece I want to compose someday. Did you really like it?"

"I loved it," she said.

It was then that Giancarlo decided that the moment had come.

"I'm glad," he told her, "because, you see, I wrote it for you."

He turned and looked up at her. Antonella gazed back, a teardrop glistening on her cheek.

"For me?" she said barely above a whisper.

"I write everything for you," Giancarlo said.

With that he pushed away from the piano and stood.

Antonella, her eyes suddenly full of torment and confusion, at first backed away, but Giancarlo reached out and gently took her by the shoulders, and she did not resist.

"I love you, Antonella," he confessed to her at long last, the words pouring out of him like the music he played. "I have loved you from the very first moment I saw you, since before time began. I love you, and I live and breathe for you, every second of every day, but I cannot go on living another moment without your knowing it, and without your telling me that you love me, too."

"Giancarlo," Antonella whispered helplessly, dropping the jersey. "Please—"

Giancarlo did not let her finish, but instead swept her trembling body into his embrace.

"Tell me I'm wrong," he said desperately, bringing his face close to hers. "Tell me that you do not love me, and I swear I will go away forever."

The tears streaming down her face, Antonella shook her head and went weak in his arms.

"Tell me!" he insisted, pulling her closer. "Tell me that you do not love me!"

"I can't, Giancarlo," Antonella cried at last in despair.

At those words, Giancarlo felt the very heavens open up inside of him, such was his ecstasy.

"But Giancarlo, you must know something—" she tried to go on.

"There's nothing more that I need to know," he told her.

With that he closed his eyes to kiss her, but their lips would never meet, for suddenly the front door burst open and in rushed Ernestina, Demetrio's wife. At finding the two of them embracing, she looked down at the floor in embarrassment.

Giancarlo immediately released Antonella. There were many women who liked to gossip in Castelalto, and Ernestina was the worst. Giancarlo exchanged glances with Antonella. They both knew what was coming. The word of what Ernestina had discovered would spread like wildfire through the village. Giancarlo knew what it meant for him, and worse, what it meant for Antonella. For the life of him, though, he could not understand why Ernestina had chosen to come through the door unannounced at just that moment.

"Giancarlo," said Ernestina breathlessly, still looking down. "You must come at once!"

"What is it, Ernestina?" he snapped.

"It's your father," she told him. "There's been an accident."

No one saw how it happened, but that afternoon Roberto Rosa fell from a telephone pole and died instantly when he hit the ground. Neither Giancarlo nor Giorgio would learn of his fate until after each arrived at the hospital where their father had been taken. While Giorgio had broken down and wept openly, Giancarlo choked back his tears and hid his grief deep inside his troubled heart. There it would stay buried for a very long time.

In the ordeal that followed in the days ahead—the wake, the funeral, the reception afterwards at the house—Antonella stayed by Giorgio's side, and kept Giancarlo at a distance. It was a time of great anguish for him. Throughout it all, no one in the village breathed a word to Giorgio about how Ernestina had found her together with his brother, and indeed no one ever would. All the same, Giancarlo could see it in their eyes, the looks of recrimination, and he felt the walls of Castelalto closing in around him.

For three days after the funeral Giorgio and Giancarlo barely spoke to one another, but instead sat about the house in somber silence. Then one night, while he sat at the table lost in thought, Giorgio suddenly gave a sigh and said, "Basta." Enough. Then, as if he had come to a resolution about something, he slapped his hand down on the table, got to his feet, and hurried out the door. When he returned sometime later, he asked Giancarlo to sit down and talk with him.

"There is something I need to tell you," said Giorgio.

Giancarlo had already anticipated the coming of this conversation and was not of a mind to take part in it.

"Don't waste your breath," he said bitterly. "I already know all about the house. What's yours is yours, just as it has always been. What do I care?"

"What?" said his brother with a puzzled look, as if he had not understood, but by then Giancarlo had stormed out of the house.

Giancarlo walked the streets that night, turning things over in his mind, until at last he came to a resolution of his own. By the time he returned home, it was well past midnight and his brother had already gone to sleep.

The next morning, Giorgio arose early and returned to work while Giancarlo still lay in bed. No sooner had his brother left the house, than Giancarlo jumped up and got himself dressed. He had not spoken alone to Antonella since the day his father died, and he was frantic to see her again. Not caring what anyone thought, he walked straight across town to the Portinaris' house.

Antonella was home alone when she came to the door and opened it to find him there. Giancarlo stepped up to the threshold, but did not enter.

"Giancarlo, what are you doing here?" said Antonella in a hushed, anxious voice as she looked past him out the door to see if anyone was watching.

"I had to see you," he said, "and tell you that I'm going."

"Going *where*?" she said.

"I am going to America, just like I planned," he told her, "but I'm not coming back, and I want you to come with me."

"What do you mean, come with you?" said Antonella.

"Come with me, Antonella," he begged her. "Let's get out of this place and go to America, where we can live like we want and do what we want."

"But Giancarlo, you know I cannot go with you," she said.

"Please," he implored her.

"Giancarlo, my life is here," she told him. "How can I go with you?"

"What life?" he scoffed. "What is there to keep you here?"

Antonella put her hand to her mouth and closed her eyes. Then she breathed a sigh, and looked at him again.

"Your brother has not spoken to you yet, has he?" she said.

"Spoken to me?" he answered. "About what?"

"Giancarlo," she told him gently, "last night Giorgio came here and asked me to marry him."

Giancarlo felt the very life drain out of him.

"And?" he gasped.

Antonella looked at him, her eyes filled with compassion.

"And I told him yes," she said.

No one came to see Giancarlo off the day he left Castelalto. It was early in the morning, and the rising sun had not yet cleared the mountains when he stepped out of the house with his two bags in hand. As he made his way across the sleeping village, Giancarlo stopped only once, at the piazza, where he gazed off into the distance one last time. Then he went on his way and began the long descent down the mountain, never once looking back.

Now, almost thirty years later, the memory of that lonely march and the sad days that preceded it was as fresh in Giancarlo's mind as if it had all happened only yesterday. Pushing away from the table, he got up and brought his coffee cup to the sink. He stood there for a time, gazing once more out the window. The dark gray skies had suddenly opened, and it began to pour. The wind beat the rain against the window, and as he watched it come down, Giancarlo wished that somehow it could wash everything away, all the heavy memories he carried around inside himself like those two bags he had carried with him out of Castelalto. Perhaps he *had* never looked back that day when he walked away from home all those years ago, but deep in his lonely heart, Giancarlo also knew that he had never learned to loosen his grip and just let it go.

CHAPTER 40

While he waited for Antonella to rouse her husband, Carter stood in the kitchen, looking about at the bright interior of the little house, the high ceilings above, the beautiful marble floors beneath, and the stylish modern furnishings throughout. He marveled at how sharply the inside of the home contrasted with its ancient, rough-hewn, almost bleak exterior. By now of course he was becoming accustomed to discovering that in Italy, the face of things and what lay behind it were not always one and the same. How many more times, he wondered, would he have to be taken in by facades, bleak or beautiful, before he learned?

Antonella went to the back of the house and shouted up the staircase.

"Giorgio, *alzati!*" she called. "Get up! There's someone here to see you!"

A minute or two later, a yawning Giorgio Rosa came down the stairs, walked into the kitchen, and stood before Carter, scratching his side. He was a solid-looking man, stockier than his more slightly built brother, Giancarlo, and with a fuller, rounder face. Nonetheless, Carter could see right away that the two brothers still bore an unmistakable resemblance to one another. At the same time, he also perceived that the two possessed markedly different personalities. Giorgio seemed to exude a relaxed, easygoing air, which was in striking contrast to his brother's reticence and cool reserve. He gave Carter a friendly smile, and shrugged as if to ask why he had come.

"Giorgio, this is Carter," said Antonella. "He has just come from America."

"Yes, I can see that," said Giorgio.

By this point, Carter was not of a mind to bother asking how.

"He comes from Rhode Island," Antonella said with a furtive look. "He was sent here by Giancarlo."

Giorgio passed a hand over his stubbled face and gave another yawn.

"I'm sorry," he said. "I've been taking a little siesta. What did you say your name was again?"

"Carter," Carter answered. "Carter Quinn."

"Well, then, Carter, Carter Quinn," said Giorgio, gesturing to a chair at the table, "please sit, and tell me how you know my brother."

Carter smiled.

"Actually, it's just Carter Quinn," he explained. "You know, one 'Carter,' not two."

"Carter? Like the president, right?"

"Yes," Carter nodded.

"But what kind of first name is that?" said Giorgio with a curious look.

"It's an American name, you buffoon!" cried Antonella, swatting her husband in the arm. "Just go sit, and listen to what the boy has to say."

"I was only asking him," Giorgio said good-naturedly, defending himself, "because it's not an Italian name, but he seems to speak the language very well."

"I learned to speak Italian from Professor Rosa," Carter told him.

"From my brother?" said Giorgio with surprise. "All this time, I thought he only taught music over there."

"He gives Italian lessons at his house sometimes in the summer."

Carter explained that he had recently finished college, and that he had taken lessons from Giancarlo throughout the summer in preparation for his trip to Italy.

"Well," said Giorgio, sounding impressed, "he obviously taught you very well."

Carter nodded his thanks at the compliment.

Antonella, meantime, brought a plate of grapes to the table, then a bottle of mineral water and two glasses. She poured Carter a glass of water and motioned to the grapes.

"*Prenda*," she told him. "You look tired."

Carter gave a sheepish shrug.

"I stayed out a little later than I should have last night," he confessed, before taking a sip of water. "*Grazie.*"

"*Prego*," she said.

"So, I take it you are here in Italy on vacation, yes?" said Giorgio.

"Yes," Carter told him. "I've just been traveling around for a while, seeing things."

"And how did my brother ever talk you into coming all the way to Abruzzo, to such a little out-of-the-way place like Castelalto?" said Giorgio with a laugh.

Carter handed him the pouch with the pocket watch, and Giorgio stopped laughing.

"He knew I was planning to visit a friend in Roccasale," said Carter. "Since it's not that far away, your brother asked if I would deliver that to you while I was still in the area. It was no trouble, so I said yes. Anyway, I was there last night, and I left just this morning."

As he slid the watch out of the pouch and into his hand, Giorgio exchanged glances with Antonella, who turned and looked the other way.

"Did my brother, Giancarlo, have anything to say about it?" Giorgio asked as he looked over the watch.

"He just said to tell you not to bother sending it anymore," Carter told him. "He said it's broken and cannot be repaired."

"Nothing else?" said Giorgio.

"That was it."

Giorgio squirreled up the side of his mouth in a look of consternation, gave a grunt, and glanced again at his wife.

"That sounds just like Giancarlo," he sighed.

Antonella replied with a roll of her eyes and a shake of her head.

Giorgio sat there for a moment, quietly contemplating the watch before tucking it back in its pouch.

"Well, then," he said amiably, reaching out to pat Carter on the shoulder, "what can I say, after you've come all this way to bring it to me? *Tu sei un bravo ragazzo.* You're a good boy. *Mille grazie!*"

Then Giorgio turned to Antonella and said something to her, of which Carter could not understand a single word. When she replied in kind, he realized that they were speaking in dialect to one another. It seemed to Carter that they were talking about him, but he could not be sure. Whatever the case, he had delivered the watch. Now it was time for him to move on, and so he began to get to his feet.

"*Ma dove vai?*" said Giorgio abruptly at seeing him stand. "Where are you going?"

Carter was taken aback and did not know what to say.

"Um, I just thought it was time for me to go," he offered meekly. "You know, to find a hotel for the night."

"A *hotel?*" Giorgio laughed aloud, throwing his hands up in the air, as if this was the most preposterous thing he had ever heard. "In Castelalto?"

Carter stood there stupidly, quite confused as to what he should do.

"*Aspetta*, Carter," Giorgio reassured him once he had composed himself. "*Calmati.* Relax. Now tell me, are you planning to go back to America tonight?"

"No," said Carter.

"Tomorrow?"

"Well, no, not exactly," he admitted.

In truth, Carter had originally planned to stay in Italy at least another week. After his debacle of the previous evening—he was not at all anxious to discuss this—he was more than ready to go home a few days early. It was simply a matter of returning to Rome as soon as possible and exchanging his airline ticket.

"*Bene!*" exclaimed Giorgio with a big grin, before Carter could try to explain. "Then there is no hurry."

With that, Giorgio slapped his hand down on the table, and stood.

"*Venga,*" he said, taking Carter by the arm and directing him toward the door. "Come. Let's take a little walk."

"*Grazie, Signora,*" Carter said over his shoulder to Antonella, who simply nodded in reply as she watched the two men leave.

Before Carter knew it, he was out the front door and being led by Giorgio down a side alley and back out into the other side of the village. There they emerged in front of a little neighborhood bar. Giorgio parted the beads that hung in the doorway, and the two walked in. It was, Carter discovered, a simple, one-room place, with a small bar, a few tables and chairs, and some benches pushed up against the wall. There were several men inside. Three grizzled characters sat at one of the tables, playing cards, while the others lounged about, talking and drinking. Almost all of them were puffing cigarettes. Apparently the nationwide prohibition against smoking in public establishments had not yet reached this particular outpost in Abruzzo, or if it had, no one was particularly concerned about it. At seeing Giorgio walk in with a stranger, all conversation stopped.

"*Ascoltate,*" Giorgio said to them. "Listen, everybody. This is my friend Carter. He just came from America to visit Antonella and me."

Carter gave a little wave to everyone.

"*Carter?*" said one of the old men playing cards. "You mean like the president?"

"Yes," Giorgio answered for him, "but it's his first name."

"Hey, that's okay," said the old man with a shrug. He raised his glass of wine. *"Al Presidente,"* he said straight-faced. "To the President."

"Al Presidente!" the rest chimed in, and they all had a good laugh.

Henceforth that afternoon, Carter would be addressed as *Il Presidente*. He took the honorary title with good humor, and installed himself on one of the benches while Giorgio ordered two beers for them. By then everyone was talking and puffing their cigarettes again. Immersed in the smoke and the laughter and the nonstop spoken Italian, Carter did his best to understand what everyone was saying. From the snippets of conversation he was able to catch, he understood that some were talking about sports, others about politics, and the rest about women, pretty much all the same things men talked about in barrooms all over the world.

When Giorgio brought over Carter's glass of beer, he raised his own to him and said, *"Benvenuto,* Carter. Welcome to Castelalto."

"Benvenuto!" the others joined in.

"Grazie," said Carter, raising his glass to them all. *"Salute."*

"Salute!"

Carter took a sip of beer. Despite still suffering to some extent from the ill effects of the previous evening, he found the taste of it to his liking. All the same, he promised himself to drink it at a judicious pace.

"Hey, *Signor Il Presidente,"* one of the men called to him. "So tell us, what do you think of our country?"

"È bella," Carter answered. "It's beautiful."

At this the men murmured their approval.

"But which do you prefer?" the man asked him. "America or Italy?"

The room fell suddenly quiet, and Carter got the distinct impression that he was being put on the spot.

"Italy is beautiful," he replied cautiously. Then he put his hand to his heart. "But America is . . . it is . . ."

Carter hesitated and frowned, for he could not remember how to translate the word he was thinking of into Italian.

"*Patria?*" one of the others offered.

"*Si, grazie,*" Carter nodded in relief. "*America è patria.* It's my country, and it's my home."

A love of one's country was something the men all seemed to respect, for they once again looked at one another and nodded their approval. Then to Carter's surprise, one of them raised a glass.

"*A l'America,*" he said. "To America." And everyone joined in the toast.

Giorgio sat down next to Carter and gave him a pat on the knee.

"You know," he told him with a smile, "I think you've made some new friends."

Later, after they had been there quite some time, Giorgio gave a nod to Carter to let him know that it was time to leave. By then it was growing late. They walked home through the gathering shadows by way of the piazza, where Carter paused and gazed out across the valley. There, framed between the darkening mountains, the light from the setting sun glowed like a chalice of embers.

"Come on," said Giorgio, giving him a tap on the shoulder. "Antonella will have a little dinner waiting for us."

"That's very nice of her," Carter called after him. "But where will I stay tonight?"

Giorgio turned and gestured for Carter to hurry up and follow.

"Where do you think you will stay?" he laughed. "At Hotel Giorgio!"

CHAPTER 41

Carter awoke the next day to the discordant sounds of church bells and intermittent gunfire echoing through the valley. It was Sunday morning, which explained the former well enough, but the latter, if not cause for alarm, was something of a puzzlement. Still drowsy, Carter yawned, and stretched his arms over his head. He had slept quite soundly; it had in fact been the best night's sleep he had enjoyed since he came to Italy. There was something snug and inviting about a home, even one strange to him, that made it far more conducive to repose than even the most agreeable hotel accommodations. Of course, after having slept face down on the piazza the night before in Roccasale, Carter would have found it an improvement if Antonella and Giorgio had made him sleep in the bathtub.

Carter gave another yawn, and pulled the covers more tightly about him. It was a cool morning, and he was inclined to remain in the warm confines of the bed for just a little while longer. It was not long, though, before the aroma of freshly brewed coffee came wafting up the stairs. Despite the memory of his near-death coffee experience on his first night in Rome, and his resultant aversion to all things caffeine, Carter found the smell irresistible. Throwing the covers aside, he set his feet on the floor and began to get dressed.

Antonella was sitting at the kitchen table, perusing the newspaper and sipping her coffee, when Carter came downstairs. A clean mug and spoon were set out across from her in anticipation of his awakening.

"*Ayyy, finalmente,*" said Antonella when he walked into the kitchen. "*Buon giorno!* We were beginning to think that you were going to sleep all day."

As much of the language as he had learned, Carter still found it difficult to speak Italian first thing in the morning, so it took him a moment to translate in his head what she had said and to formulate an appropriate response.

"I think I could have slept all day," he finally yawned, "but the bells woke me up." It occurred then to Carter that he had once again missed mass.

"That's our church, La Chiesa della Madonna," she told him.

"I heard something else," Carter added. "It sounded like guns to me." There came the report of another gunshot. "There it is again," he said.

Antonella put the newspaper aside and gestured for him to sit. Then she took his mug and went to the coffee pot on the stove to fill it.

"*I cacciatori,*" she told him as she set the steaming brew before him. "It's the hunters. They like to go out in the valley on Sunday mornings. Giorgio is out there with them now."

"Really?" said Carter. "What does he like to hunt?"

"Who knows?" scoffed Antonella. "He never brings home anything. I think he just likes to go out there and shoot his gun in the air just for the fun of it. As long as he doesn't shoot himself in the foot, that's all I care about. But he should be back anytime now."

"Professor Rosa never mentioned to me anything about hunting," said Carter, before taking a sip of his coffee. "I wonder if he liked to hunt, as well, when he lived here."

Antonella gave a little smile and sat down once more at the table. "I don't think so," she said. "He was never really that type." She sat there for a moment, staring pensively into her cup. "So tell me, Carter," she asked, looking up at him with eyes full of curiosity. "How is your professor? Is he doing well? Is he happy?"

"I think so," said Carter with a shrug. "But honestly, it's hard to say. I still don't know him all that well, and he doesn't really say very much about himself."

Antonella gave a little sigh, and nodded. "Yes, I know," she said. "He has always been that way."

Carter could not help being a little curious about his professor's past.

"He did tell me once," he said delicately, "that he has not seen your husband since he left Italy and came to America. I took that to mean that he has never returned here at all."

"*Mai,*" said Antonella, shaking her head. "Never."

"It made me wonder what happened between them," Carter went on. "If maybe they had a falling-out of some kind."

Antonella nodded sadly.

"Giancarlo had a falling-out with the world, I think," she said. "You could not know it, but that pocket watch he sent you here with is just his way of saying that nothing has changed for him. The watch belonged to his father, you know, and it was supposed to be Giancarlo's when he passed away, but Giancarlo keeps sending it back. It's no wonder it doesn't tell time anymore. It's as stuck in the past as he is."

"It seems an awful long time for it to have gone on," mused Carter.

Antonella gave a little laugh.

"You don't know Italians very well, Carter," she told him. "No matter how much it hurts, we can hold on to grudges longer than anyone else in the world. We can keep them going for generations, if we feel like it."

"I guess that was something we just didn't get around to talking about during my Italian lessons," he said with a chuckle.

"Eh, believe me," she said, waving her hand for emphasis. "There's a lot to learn."

As Antonella predicted, Giorgio returned home from the hunt empty-handed a short time later.

"Ayyy, there he is," he said with a big smile at finding Carter at the table. "I was going to ask you to come along this morning, but you were sleeping like a baby."

"I was a little tired," Carter admitted.

"Then you need to rest," said Giorgio with great conviction. "You should stay here in Castelalto a few days. It will be good for you."

"Oh, I couldn't do that," said Carter.

"Why not?" said Giorgio with mock indignity. "What's the matter? You don't like it here?"

"Oh, I like it very much," Carter hastened to explain. "It's just that I don't want to impose, that's all."

Antonella held up her hand to silence both men.

"Carter," she told him, "you are no imposition at all to us. You came here out of friendship for my husband's brother, and we are very grateful. You can stay with us as long as you like, and of course leave whenever you are ready."

"But not before dinner," added Giorgio, holding up a finger.

"Dinner?"

"Of course," said Giorgio. "It's Sunday. You *must* stay for dinner. No questions. *D'accordo?*"

Carter could hardly refuse.

"*D'accordo,*" he said, nodding his head in agreement.

To pass the time before dinner, Carter went for a little walk around town with Giorgio. As small a place as it was, everybody knew everybody in Castelalto, and Giorgio said "*Buon giorno!*" to virtually everyone they passed. The children scampering through the alleys. The old ladies in the doorways. The other men out for a Sunday stroll before dinner.

As they ambled along, Giorgio put a hand on Carter's shoulder and renewed his invitation for him to stay a little longer in Castelalto.

"Carter," he told him, "you really must stay with us for a day or two more. Tomorrow I have to work, but the day after I can take off so that we can all take a little ride and show you the area. I think you would enjoy it."

Carter was still not sure of exactly what his plans should be for the remainder of his trip. Part of him was enjoying his stay there, but another part was ready to go home. Given his indecision in this matter, he responded with a noncommital nod and shrug.

Eventually the two wound their way past the little piazza. It was a bright, sunny day, the sky over the valley so blue that Carter thought he could almost reach out and touch it. He was enjoying the view for a minute when Giorgio tugged on his shirt to get him out of the way of a line of cyclists coming up the road.

"*Sta attento*," said Giorgio. "Be careful. Those guys would rather run you over than slow down."

The line of cyclists, perhaps thirty strong, crested the hill and pedaled across the piazza at a brisk clip, before exiting through the opposite side of the village and beginning the descent back down to the main road. A few moments later, a pair of stragglers appeared at the top of the hill and rolled across the piazza at a more leisurely pace. As they passed, Carter noticed that they were older men. Judging by their voices and the gestures of their hands, the two were more interested in conversing than keeping up with the others. They nodded hello as they went by, and contentedly pedaled off, gabbing away the whole time.

"I take it cycling is popular in this country," said Carter.

"Oh yes, people love to ride their bikes here," said Giorgio with a nod. "Cycling is a great sport. But of course, not as good as soccer!"

Carter smiled, for he recalled his debate that summer with Giancarlo about which was the tougher sport, football or cycling. He considered asking Giorgio where he thought soccer fell in the mix, but he did not want to stir up any more trouble than he suspected already existed between the two brothers. He kept the question to himself, and the two went on their way home.

Antonella's mother and father, Silvana and Paolo, who still

lived in Castelalto, joined them for dinner that afternoon. They were a sweet old couple, and Giorgio called them Papa and Mama, just as if they were his own parents. Upon meeting Carter, Paolo shook his hand enthusiastically, while Silvana gave his cheek a healthy pinch and a gentle slap before exclaiming, "*Che bravo ragazzo!*"

They all ate together in the dining room, which was more or less one end of the living room, where the television was set up so that Giorgio could watch the afternoon soccer match while he ate. As they sat down at the table, Giorgio pointed out for Carter the upright piano against the far wall, the same one upon which his brother, Giancarlo, had first learned to play long ago. To all appearances no one played the piano any longer; its primary purpose seemed to be as a place to display the family photographs, of which there were many.

The meal surpassed by far any Carter had yet experienced in Italy. It began with the minestrone, a savory vegetable soup that Silvana had cooked that morning. It was almost a meal in itself. When the soup bowls were cleared away, Antonella brought out the cannelloni, slices of rolled pasta stuffed with beef and pork and covered in what Giorgio called "*un bel sugo,*" a rich, zesty tomato sauce. By the time this course was completed, Carter was already feeling as stuffed as one of the cannelloni, and so it astonished him when Antonella brought out a leg of roast lamb and a platter of broccoli rabe. Later on, for dessert, they nibbled on fruit and nuts, before enjoying a cup of coffee with a piece of chocolate cake sprinkled with almonds. Lastly they sipped amaro, a thick liqueur that Paolo explained was good for one's digestion.

Fortunately, the meal had been served at a slow, leisurely pace, which allowed for lively conversation as well as adequate time for one's stomach to recover between courses. Nonetheless, when it was finally over, Carter could barely stand, and happily admitted to as much.

"That was nothing," laughed Giorgio. "You should have been

here last week, when my daughters, Giulia and Daniela, were here with their husbands. What a feast we had!"

Carter could scarcely imagine it.

Later, the five of them went out for a *passeggiata*, a little walk in the open air, which ended at the piazza. There they sat on the wall, chatting with the other families that were out doing the same. As he sat there by the fountain, soaking it all in, Carter breathed a contented sigh. It was, he found, a simple, satisfying way to spend the rest of his Sunday afternoon. He let his gaze alternate between the people and the ancient village and the surrounding mountains. It struck him how all three seemed to form a harmonious whole that was almost idyllic. It was simply nice to be there, and he could easily see himself remaining another day or two, as Giorgio had implored him to do. Why, he wondered as he looked around, would anyone ever want to leave?

CHAPTER 42

"Hey, *Il Presidente!*" someone called.

It was late the following morning, and Carter had been out walking around, exploring the outskirts of the village. In truth, there wasn't a great deal to be seen, but it was something to do to pass the time. He had been making his way back down an alley, beneath lines of drying laundry flapping in the breeze overhead between the houses, when he heard the voice calling to him from up above.

Shielding his eyes from the sun, Carter looked up and saw that its owner was Domenico, one of the men he had met in the bar his first day in town. Domenico was standing atop the roof of one of the houses, a crowbar in hand.

"*Buon giorno!*" Carter called back to him. "What are you doing up there?"

"What do you think? I'm fixing the roof," Domenico called back.

Carter looked over to the side of the house, where he saw a collection of broken roof tiles next to a ladder leading up to the roof. Having spent the entire summer working as a construction laborer, and having nothing else in particular to do at the moment, he was interested to see how things were done in Italy.

"Hey," he called to Domenico. "Do you mind if I come up and take a look?"

"*Come no?*" answered Domenico, gesturing for him to come up. "Why not?"

Carter climbed to the top of the ladder and stepped off onto the edge of the roof, his foot slipping a little before he found his balance.

"Ayyy, be careful, *Presidente*," quipped Domenico, waving his crowbar at him. "If you fall off the roof and get hurt, there'll be war between our countries!"

"Don't worry, I'll be careful," Carter promised with a smile.

With that he sat on one of the exposed beams and watched as Domenico went back to work, carefully prying up the tiles that needed to be replaced. All the while, Domenico talked away a mile a minute, speaking so fast that Carter could barely understand a word. From his gestures, however, Carter inferred that Domenico was explaining to him how the roof was made and how he needed to go about repairing it. It was no small job. Even with his inexpert eye, Carter could plainly see from the condition of the roof that Domenico had a great deal of work ahead of him.

Carter had never been one of those people who could watch someone else toil away while he sat around taking it easy. And so, after a few minutes, he surprised Domenico by asking if there was a spare crowbar. Domenico nodded to his toolbox, and a few moments later Carter was hard at work by his side, ripping tiles up with such gusto that a laughing Domenico had to tell him to slow down. Carter relented only a little, for he found the work rather therapeutic. It helped him vent some of the lingering ill feelings from his visit to Roccasale, and was in many ways the most fun he'd had since he came to Italy.

The fun came to an end, however, when one of the neighbors spotted Carter and called Antonella to inform her that her young American houseguest was up on the roof, risking life and limb.

"*Mannaggia!*" Antonella had cried when she rushed to the scene and saw Carter on the roof. "*Ma tu sei pazzo!* You're crazy! Get down from there, *subito!* What am I going to tell your poor mother if you fall down and kill yourself?"

Antonella's impassioned pleas, which were met with a mere smile and wave, did little to dissuade Carter from continuing to assist Domenico. When these failed, she turned to the ever-reliable standby of food to lure him down from the roof. At the mention of lunch, Domenico agreed that perhaps it *was* time to take a break—and that was that for roofing for the rest of the day. When Carter came down the ladder and brushed himself off, he stood there smirking for a moment, before Antonella grabbed him by the ear like a wayward child and dragged him yelping back to the house.

Lunch turned out to be a simple meal of sliced tomatoes drenched in olive oil and served over bread like an open sandwich. After the previous day's feast, it was more than substantial enough for Carter, who ate his fill before obeying Antonella's order to go to his room and rest from the morning's exertions.

Giorgio laughed heartily when he returned from work later that afternoon and listened to Antonella's account of Carter's perilous activities that day. Despite his wife's opinions of the inherent dangers of working on a roof, he found Carter's industriousness admirable and worthy of a little treat.

"Come, Carter," he said, leading him out the door. "We must go see Demetrio."

Demetrio, Carter learned as they walked through the village, was an old friend of Giorgio's father. Now long retired, he had once worked with Roberto for the telephone company. From the way Giorgio spoke of him, Carter could tell that he held Demetrio in high esteem. Nonetheless he advised Carter to be a little careful about what he said in front of him.

"Demetrio is a good friend," Giorgio explained, "very *simpatico*. But he talks to his wife, Ernestina, and she's a *cacchieressa*, a real chatterbox. She blabs everything."

When they came to Demetrio's house and knocked on the door, his wife, Ernestina, answered. She was a little woman with a wrinkled face that for some reason reminded Carter of a squeezed lemon. Her husband, she informed them with a wave of her hand, was out back, making his wine.

"That is exactly what I had hoped he would be doing when we came," said Giorgio with a big smile.

Demetrio was a wiry old man, with a thin, angular face and sinewy arms. When Giorgio and Carter found him, he was rolling an empty wine barrel up the walkway to the little stone shed that was built into the back of his house. Giorgio rushed over to help him, and the two set the barrel on its end just below the level of a second barrel that stood just inside the shed's open door.

"Demetrio," said Giorgio. "This is my friend Carter. He's here visiting from America."

"Ah, *si*," replied Demetrio affably. "My wife told me that there was a young American boy in town. *Piacere.*"

"*Piacere*," Carter replied as the two shook hands.

Giorgio gave Carter a quick wink, as if to say "See what I told you?" Then he turned to Demetrio and said, "Carter has come to watch how you make the wine."

"Ayyy, there's not much to see today, I'm afraid," said Demetrio. "All I'm doing is moving the wine from this barrel into that one." Then he gave Giorgio a knowing look and added, "Of course, while I'm doing it, we might have to taste a little of it to make sure everything is going as it should."

Demetrio went on to explain to Carter how he was planning to rack the new wine, to move it from one barrel into the other in order to filter out the sediment, the dead yeast, and the fruit debris from the grapes. This he would accomplish by siphoning the wine from the first barrel with a thin hose. To get the process started, Demetrio sat down next to the full barrel, put the hose into his mouth, and drew out the air like he was sucking on a straw. Soon the wine began to gush forth in a splash of red. Demetrio quickly wrapped a cloth over the end of the hose to filter the wine, before bending the hose to halt the flow. He motioned for Giorgio and Carter to sit next to him, and soon the three men were taking turns drinking the wine straight from the barrel. Carter had never tasted anything so sweet and robust, and it filled him with a deliciously warm sensation. The hose was passed around again, and Carter took another healthy gulp.

"What do you think?" said Demetrio. "Not bad, eh?"

"*Delizioso*," said Carter.

"Better even than last year's," opined Giorgio. He nodded to Carter. "Demetrio makes the best wine in Castelalto."

Their verdicts pleased the old man, and he let them pass the hose around for one last taste before he stuck it into the empty barrel. While they waited for the barrel to fill, the three men settled back and stretched out their legs.

Giorgio let out a contented sigh, and gave Carter a wink.

"What do you say, Demetrio?" he asked. "Can you buy wine like that in the store?"

Demetrio gave a solemn shake of his head.

"Ha!" laughed Giorgio. Then he turned to Carter and gave him a nudge.

"So tell me, Carter," he said. "Did you enjoy dinner yesterday?"

"Of course," Carter replied. "It was incredible."

"What did you eat?" asked Demetrio with sincere interest.

Carter recounted the menu for him

"Ahh, *che bello pranzo*," sighed Demetrio. "What a nice meal. What was your favorite thing?"

"The lamb," said Carter without hesitation. "It's one of my favorite things to eat."

"Really?" said Giorgio. He sat back and gave another sigh. "Mine is mushrooms," he said wistfully. "I love mushrooms. I could eat them every day. If they had mushroom-flavored gelato, I would buy it! Someday I will show you how to cook them. I'm a pretty good chef, you know."

"I didn't know that," said Carter with a smile. "But do you know how to make gelato? That's something else I love."

"No, I don't make gelato," confessed Giorgio. "But I know a good place where we can get some tomorrow, when we go for our ride."

When the barrel was full and stowed away in the shed, Giorgio clapped his hands together to signify that it was time for them to go.

"*Basta,*" he said. "*Basta di pasta—*"

"*Andiamo ad Aosta?*" Carter finished for him.

Giorgio regarded him with astonishment. "Yes," he said, nonplussed. "I guess my brother really did teach you well. You'll have to tell me all about it when we get home."

With that, Giorgio and Carter thanked Demetrio, bid him *buona sera*, and started off for home.

"Food and wine," mused Giorgio as the two ambled along. "Besides love, what else is there to life?"

"There's gelato," noted Carter.

"That's right!" laughed Giorgio. "And tomorrow I will take you to the best *gelateria* in all of Abruzzo!"

It sounded great to Carter. What he could not know, however, was that it would be a very long time before he ever tasted gelato again.

CHAPTER 43

The next day Antonella was at the table as usual, enjoying her morning coffee, when Carter came downstairs and walked into the kitchen. At seeing him, she motioned for him to sit, and went to the stove to pour him a cup.

Carter slid into a chair, rolled his head around a little, and gave a yawn. Owing perhaps to Demetrio's wine, he had slept exceedingly well and was still feeling pleasantly drowsy. Just the same, when Antonella set the cup of coffee before him, one whiff of its rich, warm smell was enough to perk him up. Before taking a sip, he looked about for Giorgio, and was puzzled to see that he was nowhere to be found.

"Where is Giorgio?" he asked. "Did he change his mind about taking a ride today, and go to work instead?"

"No," said Antonella. "He got up very early this morning, before the sun was even up, and went out, I'm not sure to where. But before he left he woke me and told me not to worry, that he would be back before lunch to take us all out."

"Where do you think he went?" asked Carter.

"His walking shoes and backpack are gone," she replied, "so I think he must have gone out for a little hike."

"A hike?" laughed Carter. "Why this morning?"

Antonella gave an exasperated sigh and rolled her eyes.

"Who knows," she said with a shrug. "You don't know my husband, but he has always been like that. Giorgio has hiked all around, up and down these mountains, ever since he was a boy, and he still loves doing it today. Every now and then, for no reason at all that I can see, he just wakes up and decides to go. I think sometimes he just likes to go up there and get away from everything for a little while to think. But I'm surprised that he didn't wake you this morning and ask you to come along. I'm very sorry about that. I'm sure it would have been fun for you."

"That's all right. Don't worry about it," said Carter easily. "He probably just wanted to be alone."

"Well, whatever he is doing," said Antonella, "he had better get back good and early, like he promised, or else I'll box his ears when he comes home."

Carter rubbed his own ear.

"Yes," he said with a wry grin, "I know how you can do that."

After, when he had finished his coffee, Carter took his cup to the sink and glanced at the clock. It was still early. If Giorgio would not be back until lunch, then Carter had a few hours to kill before they all went out. Carter could see no point in just sitting around waiting all morning, doing nothing, so he turned and began to head out the door.

"And where are *you* going now?" said Antonella suspiciously.

"Just out to the piazza," said Carter, trying with little success not to sound too evasive. "It looks like a nice day out, so I thought I would get outside for a little while, until Giorgio comes home."

" *Va bene,*" said Antonella, fixing him with a skeptical gaze. "But don't let me find you up on top of any more roofs this morning, *capito?*"

"Of course I understand," said Carter. And then he was out the door.

"Hey, *Presidente,* I hope Antonella doesn't know you're up here," said Domenico when Carter climbed up the ladder. "I appreciate the help, but if she catches you again, she's liable to blame it all on me and give *my* ear a twist like she gave yours yesterday."

Domenico tended to work at a far more conservative pace than his energetic American assistant, so there remained from the previous day a large section of old tiles still to be removed before the new ones could be set in place.

"Don't worry," chuckled Carter, getting straight to work. "If she finds out, we'll hide out in the mountains with Giorgio. I think he's up there right now."

"Ayyy, what's that one doing up there today, when he's supposed to be working?" laughed Domenico.

"He took today off," Carter explained. "Antonella said he got up and went off on a hike this morning."

That Giorgio had done so seemed to surprise Domenico no more than it had Antonella.

"Eh, Giorgio loves those mountains," he said as he pulled up another tile. "He knows his way around up there better than anyone, you know."

"Good, in that case he'll know some good hiding places for us if we need them," said Carter.

"*Veramente*," nodded Domenico. "But in the meantime, try to keep your head down*, per piacere*. Safer for both of us. Antonella is a beautiful woman, but I would not want to cross her."

Carter and Domenico worked for a good long while, making steady progress on the rest of the tiles, before stopping to take a break. The two sat on a ceiling beam and let their legs dangle down. Domenico lit a cigarette and breathed a puff of smoke into the air.

"So, *Presidente*," he said, wiping his sweaty brow with the back of his hand, "what do you think of our little town out here in the Abruzzi, eh?"

"I like it very much," said Carter truthfully. "I'm looking forward to seeing some more of the area this afternoon, when I take a ride with Giorgio and Antonella."

"Eh, what's to see?" joked Domenico. "Mountains, valleys, people. You can see it all right here in Castelalto."

"Yes, but I was hoping to get a cone of gelato today," noted Carter.

"Ah, you have me there," sighed Domenico. "We don't have a

single *gelateria* in town. It's one of a lot of things we don't have in town, as a matter of fact. Castelalto, as you've probably already guessed, is not the most exciting place in the world."

The words had no sooner left Domenico's lips when Carter suddenly sensed a strange vibration rising up through the foundation of the house. It began as a mild shudder, but quickly grew in intensity, until it shook the entire house with such force that some of the loosened tiles on the roof cracked and fell off by themselves. Fearing that they would fall, as well, Carter and Domenico each instinctively grabbed the other by the shoulder, and the two hung on for dear life. As quickly as the event began, it peaked and died away, like the reverberation of a passing train.

When calm had returned and all had once more grown still, a blanch-faced Domenico tossed away his cigarette and made the sign of the cross.

"Whoa, what was that?" said Carter, whose own face had gone pale.

"*Terremoto*," said Domenico nervously. "An earthquake. A little one, thank God."

Just then there came another low rumble, echoing in the distance like the sound of an approaching thunderstorm. Like the tremor, it lasted but a few moments, then died away.

"*Terremoto?*" said Carter, not at all anxious for a repeat performance.

Domenico looked out with puzzlement at the surrounding mountains and rubbed his chin thoughtfully.

"No," he finally said, shaking his head. "That was something different, but I don't know what. But whatever it was, I think that's enough work for today, eh?"

"*D'accordo*," said Carter, not needing to be told twice, and the two scrambled down from the roof.

"*Va a casa*," Domenico told him when they were back down on the ground at the foot of the ladder. "Get back home."

Without another word, Carter hurried away.

By this time, of course, people all over the village had already spilled out of their houses and run into the streets to see what had happened. At that hour on a weekday, mostly women, old retired men, and children too young for school were at home. With hands over their hearts after the fright they had just received, the women all stood about in groups, talking in loud, excited, almost frantic voices. To all appearances, though, other than having had the wits scared out of them, no one was hurt, and the village had sustained no real damage. The expressions of fright soon gave way to relief and nervous laughter when it became clear that everyone was all right.

Antonella was waiting at the door, looking about anxiously, when Carter finally made it back to the house. At seeing him come into view, she put her hand to her heart like the rest of the women in town and breathed a sigh of relief.

"Finalmente," she said when he came to the door. "You're not hurt, are you?"

"No, I'm fine," Carter told her. "And you?"

"Si, si, I'm fine," said Antonella. "But I must go check on my mother and father."

"And what about Giorgio?" he asked. "Is he back yet?"

"No," said Antonella. "But don't worry, I'm sure he is on his way. Come in. Stay here now, and when I get back we will wait for him to come home."

CHAPTER 44

Noon came and went, and Giorgio did not return.

Antonella sat at the kitchen table with her pad and pencil, sketching in quick succession the coffee pot on the stove, a cup and bowl on the counter, and the salt and pepper shakers on the table. If she was at all perturbed by Giorgio's delay in coming home, she did not show it to Carter. If anything, as she sat there drawing, she exuded an air of calm. It seemed to him that, instead of worrying, she had chosen to simply withdraw into herself and focus all of her attention on her sketch pad.

Carter himself was not overly concerned at first, but with each passing minute, a palpable sense of uncertainty began to hang in the air.

"Carter, I told you, do not worry," said Antonella at seeing him look out the window. "My husband knows those mountains like the back of his hand. Trust me, he will be home soon."

"But what about the *terremoto*?" said Carter.

"That was nothing but a little shake," she assured him. "We get them every now and then around here. If anything, Giorgio was probably safer up on the mountain in the open air than he would have been at home in this old house."

Carter could only take her at her word. If she wasn't concerned about Giorgio's whereabouts, he reasoned, why should he be? It was obvious that there was nothing else to do but wait, so he picked up the newspaper that had lain unread on the counter all morning. He sat down at the table with Antonella and opened the paper to the back page to try his hand at an Italian crossword puzzle. Now and then the two exchanged idle chatter, as if nothing was amiss. That it was well past one o'clock and neither of them had yet to eat all day seemed to have escaped both their notices. Food, at that particular moment, was the farthest thing from their minds.

An hour passed, and then another.

By this time, Antonella herself had gone to the window and was standing there, rubbing her hands together. For his part, Carter had long since given up on the crossword and was pretending to peruse the sports section of the newspaper. He peeked over the top of the page at her and watched as she gazed outside with eyes that showed, if not worry, then at least the first hints of real doubt.

Antonella was just turning away from the window when suddenly, from outdoors, came the whirring thrum of a helicopter passing close overhead. The noise of it shook the house with almost as much force as the morning's tremor. The helicopter passed just as quickly, and the sound faded away in the distance. All the same, a feeling of dark foreboding descended in its wake.

Carter folded the paper and put it aside.

"Does Giorgio carry a cell phone?" he asked hopefully, for he had not considered that possibility before.

"Yes, usually he does for work, Carter, but he hates it because he can never get away from it," said Antonella.

"Have you tried calling it?"

"No," she replied with a shake of her head.

"But why not?"

"Because today he left it in the bedroom, charging," she explained. Then, with a sigh, she added, "He is so thick sometimes. I don't know why he didn't just take it with him even if it was not completely charged."

Carter scratched the back of his neck, wondering how long they should wait before reporting Giorgio missing. He was certain that Antonella was fretting over the very same question. Until she made up her mind, there was nothing for him to do, so he stood, stretched his arms in front of him, and started for the door.

"I think I'll just go outside for a few minutes to get some air," he said.

Antonella did not protest, but remained at the window, keeping silent watch.

Carter had no idea how many people lived in Castelalto, but it seemed to him that all of them must have been gathered there on the piazza when he walked out of the house and into the center of the village. Everyone had come out to talk about the tremor, the young and the old, the mothers and the grandparents, the children, and the fathers, who had rushed home from work the moment it struck to make sure that their families were safe. Everyone was talking and laughing. A lively, almost carnival-like atmosphere prevailed, as the frightening event had obviously now taken on the status of a shared adventure.

Carter wandered into the midst of them, nodding hello to people as they greeted him. After four days in the little village, everyone, even those to whom he had yet to be formally introduced, knew who he was. He quickly learned that the tremor had been felt in a very large radius around the region, but it caused no serious damage anywhere, and none in Castelalto, as far as anyone could tell. There was, he supposed, good reason for their lightheartedness, but as he turned and surveyed the landscape, he was troubled to see a helicopter, most likely the one he had just heard fly over, hovering in the distance over one of the nearby peaks. At seeing Domenico, Carter walked over to get his take on what had happened, and to ask if he knew what was going on up on the mountain.

"*Ciao, Il Presidente*," said Domenico lightly. "What do you think? I guess we had a little excitement in Castelalto after all, eh?"

"Yes, we certainly did," replied Carter with markedly less enthusiasm.

At seeing the distracted look on Carter's face, Domenico eyed him with concern.

"Everything all right at home?" said Domenico.

"Oh yes," said Carter, assuming quite rightly that it was not his place to raise any alarms just yet about Giorgio. "I was wondering, though, what was happening up on the mountain where the helicopter is."

"Didn't you hear?" said Domenico incredulously. "It's been all over the news on TV all this afternoon."

"What news?"

"Remember that rumble we heard this morning right after the *terremoto* stopped?" said Domenico.

"Yes," said Carter. "What was it?"

"*Una frana*," replied Domenico. "A big landslide way up there on the north slope of the mountain. I guess the quake shook things loose, and it all went crashing down the side, like a freight train."

Carter went cold inside.

"Was there anyone up there when it happened?" he asked. "Do they know if anyone was hurt?"

"Ayyy, I don't know for sure," said Domenico with a shrug. "I heard they rescued a couple of hikers who managed to get out of the way when it happened. Now they must be up there with the helicopter looking around to make sure there was nobody else up there. Hey, *ma dove vai, Presidente*? Where are you going?"

Carter did not turn around, but simply waved over his shoulder as he hurried back to the house. When he threw open the door, Antonella was no longer at the window, but pacing about in the kitchen.

"What is it?" she said anxiously at seeing the look in his eyes. "Did you hear something about Giorgio?"

"I think we had better turn on the television," he said.

CHAPTER 45

Time, reflected Carter as he stood with Antonella watching the television, was a very changeable thing. Just a short while earlier, when they had been waiting for Giorgio to return, the minutes had crawled by at a ponderously slow pace. Now, however, as they watched the news coverage of the tremor and the resultant landslide, and it was all but certain that Giorgio was in some kind of trouble, he felt time suddenly accelerate. Carter had hiked enough in his scouting years to know that there were a thousand ways a man on his own could go wrong in the mountains and suffer a serious mishap, never mind wandering into the path of a landslide. Finding Giorgio as soon as possible was critical. From now on, until they did, there would not be a single moment to waste. Each precious second would pass much too quickly.

Antonella gasped when the television flashed the images of the landslide. There was of course no footage of the actual event, but before-and-after photographs of the mountainside showed just how dramatic it must have been.

"*O, Dio*," Antonella murmured. "Giorgio cannot be there. Please tell me he cannot be there." Unable, it seemed, to turn her gaze from the television, she stood there beside Carter, wringing her hands. "*Che faccio io?*" she said. "What do I do now?"

"We must report him missing at once," Carter told her. "*Subito.*"

Her hand trembling as she put the phone to her ear, Antonella dialed the number for the provisional police and informed them that her husband had gone off on a hike, possibly in the area of the landslide, and was long overdue in returning. She remained on the phone for some time, speaking so quickly and with such urgency that Carter could not quite understand what she was saying. When at last the call ended, Antonella stood there with a hand to her forehead, as if she were feeling faint.

"What did they tell you?" asked Carter, taking her by the elbow to steady her.

"Someone will be here shortly," she said. "They said they will need to know as much as we can tell them about Giorgio and where we think he might have gone."

"Do you have any idea at all?" Carter asked.

"No," she said. "I've wracked my brain trying to think if he said something else to me before he left, but I can remember nothing."

"In that case, we will have to ask everyone in town," he told her. "Maybe someone saw him when he left this morning."

Antonella took a deep breath to compose herself.

"Yes, you are right," she finally said, her eyes suddenly darting back and forth as she contemplated how this would be best accomplished. "First," she said, "I must tell my parents what has happened, before they hear it from someone else."

"What about your daughters?"

"Both of them live in the city," she said. "I called them this morning after the quake to make sure they were all right. I'll call them again later, when we know more about their father."

"What can I do in the meantime?" said Carter.

"You can start spreading the word," she told him.

"Where should I begin?"

Despite the circumstances, Antonella's face broke into a thin, rueful smile. "You remember Demetrio," she said, "the man you and Giorgio drank wine with yesterday?"

"Yes," said Carter.

"Go to his house first, and tell his wife, Ernestina," she said with a mildly sardonic air. "Start there, and by the time you get home, the whole village will certainly know."

Later, after the police had come and gone, and the news about Giorgio had spread all through Castelalto, people began coming to the door. The women rushed straight in and gathered around to console Antonella, who had stationed herself on the living room couch, with her mother and father beside her. It was not long before her two daughters, Giulia and Daniela, arrived with their husbands, Michele and Nunzio. The two couples had met up in Pescara and made the drive to Castelalto together. After being introduced to the four, Carter excused himself and went outside to wait with the men of the village, who had gathered outside. All were talking among themselves in somber voices, trying to decide what they should do. No one, it seemed, had seen Giorgio go off that morning. He might have gone anywhere, but it was agreed that the likeliest place to look for him was near the area of the landslide. Night was already falling, however, and few if any of the men were equipped for hiking during the day, never mind in the dark. They would have to wait until morning to organize themselves and ascend the mountain to assist in the search for their friend. And so it was decided that everyone able to make the climb would meet on the piazza at first light. Till then, all they could do was pray that, wherever he had lost himself, Giorgio would survive the night.

There was no question in Carter's mind that he would go along with the rest of the men in the morning. In fact, he was anxious to begin the climb at once, but he knew that they were right. To go out unprepared, stumbling about the mountainside in the darkness, was a recipe for disaster; it would only put all of them at risk. Impatient as he was to go, there was nothing to do till morning, so as the men drifted home one by one, he went back into the house to tell Antonella of their plan and to see what news, if any, there might be on the television.

Upon hearing Carter tell of the search for Giorgio being organized for the next morning, Nunzio and Michele instantly vowed to go along. Antonella, however, would hear none of it. She pointed out that neither of the two had any climbing experience at all, and in any case they were completely unequipped for such an effort. All they would do is cause the family even more worry and, worse, risk serious injury. If they insisted on taking part, she told them, they should confine their search to the paths all along the lower elevations around the village. There was every bit as great a chance that Giorgio might be found there as there was higher up the mountain. Her adamance in the matter left no room for negotiation, and the two sons-in-law were wise enough not to argue with her.

When the hour grew late and the women of the village began to go home, Antonella asked Giulia and Daniela to escort their grandparents home. Nunzio and Michele went along, leaving only Carter behind. No sooner had they left when Antonella made him sit down next to her on the couch. She looked at him for a moment, rubbing her chin thoughtfully, as if she were not sure of what to say.

"*Cosa?*" said Carter. "What is it?"

Antonella looked him squarely in the eye.

"Carter," she told him, "I must ask you, too, not to go up the mountain with those men tomorrow."

Carter was dismayed by her request. Already in his short stay with them, he had grown very fond of Antonella and Giorgio. They were like old friends to him. Carter was as worried as anyone in Castelalto about Giorgio, and he felt an obligation to do all he could to help find him.

"But why would I not go?" he protested. "What good will I be doing anyone just sitting around here all day?"

Shaking her head, Antonella sighed in frustration and muttered something in dialect that he could not understand.

"Listen to me," she finally said tersely. "If you go up to the top of the mountain tomorrow, Michele and Nunzio will think they have to go, as well—out of pride. Do you understand what I am saying?"

"Yes, but—"

"*Ascolta!*" snapped Antonella, cutting him off. "Listen to what

I say! If you want to help Giorgio, if you want to help us all, you will stay close to the village and look after those two. They want to help, and I am proud of them for that, but they are city boys. It is dangerous up there, and they won't know what they are doing. Keep them safe down below, on the lower part of the mountain. And don't look so disappointed. I meant it when I said there is just as good a chance of finding my husband there instead of way up on top."

"But Antonella—"

Antonella seized his hand.

"Carter, listen to me," she pleaded. "Forget your pride, and do this for Giorgio. Help take care of his family. That is what he would want you to do. Do you understand? Will you do that for Giorgio? Will you do it for me?"

Carter did not answer, but gave a sigh and bowed his head.

When the men of Castelalto left the piazza at daybreak and started up the mountain, Carter reluctantly kept to the back with Nunzio and Michele. At an early juncture, the three broke off from the others and began their search of the lower part of the mountain. It did not take Carter long to acknowledge Antonella's wisdom in keeping her sons-in-law close to the village. The two had shown up at the piazza with no backpacks and no provisions whatsoever for the hike. Worse, they were both wearing casual dress shoes, which might have been appropriate for strolling through a shopping mall but were of little use when it came to trekking across rugged terrain. It was a rare five minutes that passed without one or the other of them losing his footing or stumbling over a rock. These minor mishaps grew in frequency as the morning wore on, and the two began to tire. Although he admired their tenacity, Carter feared that it was only a matter of time before one of them turned an ankle or fell and broke a wrist. As much as he would have liked to push ahead harder, he was forced to keep the pace slow and steady.

The hours passed.

On they went, tracing a zigzag course through the trees and across the lower slopes of the mountains around Castelalto, always keeping the village in sight, for the last thing Carter wanted was for one or all of them to get lost. Now and then they would pause and call out Giorgio's name, hoping for a response, but none ever came. It was a tedious march, and Carter made frequent stops to let his companions rest. Given that neither of the two had thought to bring food or water for the journey, he was obliged to share his own. Carter had packed more than enough to get himself through the day, but had not planned on having to divide his food and water three ways. Come early afternoon, he ran out of both, and the three had no choice but to head back to the village.

By the time they reached home, Nunzio and Michele were dejected and worn down. For his part, Carter was ready after a few minutes' rest to refill his water bottle and head back out. No word about Giorgio had yet come from up on the mountain, and he was eager to resume the search, with or without Nunzio and Michele. Antonella, however, prevailed on him to wait. It would not be long, she pointed out, before they began to lose the daylight and the men started to return. Decisions would have to be made then, and she did not want to have to worry about Carter being off in the wilderness, wandering around by himself.

As Antonella predicted, a few hours later, with the sun quickly dropping below the horizon, the men began to trickle back through the shadows into the village. Exhausted and dispirited, they gathered outside the house to let her know that they had searched everywhere but had found no sign of Giorgio. It had been for them a long, frustrating, disheartening day.

"We looked everywhere up there near the landslide, but nothing," lamented Domenico, who had taken part in the search. "We haven't given up, and we will try again tomorrow, but we have no idea where Giorgio could have gone to, or where we should search first. Maybe he went off in some other direction. We just don't know, but we will try, we promise!"

After Antonella had thanked them profusely for their efforts and the men had gone on their way home, Giulia and Daniela, who had shown brave faces throughout the ordeal, broke down and began to cry. Stern-faced, Antonella motioned for Nunzio and Michele to console her daughters, while she herself paced back and forth, lost in thought. She seemed, to Carter, to be turning something over and over in her mind. What it might be, he could not guess. At last, though, she stopped, and gazed blankly out the window, as if she had finally brought her deliberations to a resolution. Then she turned to Carter and gestured for him to follow her outside. Once the door had closed behind them, she turned to him with desperate eyes.

"Carter," she began in a hushed, urgent voice, "I did not want to talk in front of my daughters and upset them any more than they already are, but there is no time to lose. Giorgio has been gone for a day and a half. God only knows what has become of him. He might be lying up there injured, with no food or water, and no way to let anyone know. He might die before he is ever found."

"I know," said Carter. "But where could he have gone?"

"The men of the village are doing their best," sighed Antonella, "but they don't know the mountain like my husband, or what he might have been thinking of when he went off on his own." She paused, and put a hand on his shoulder. "Carter, there is no one else here that I can turn to, so I must ask of you a favor."

"Anything," said Carter.

Antonella paused again and took a deep breath.

"*Bene,*" she said at last. "Here is what I want you to do. . . ."

CHAPTER 46

Giancarlo was sitting at his desk, preparing to eat the sandwich he had brought for his lunch, when the telephone rang.

Having hung up the phone just a minute earlier, he was not inclined to pick it up again. It was Henry Sheffield who had called before, to cajole him once more about performing in the charity concert in the spring. Apparently momentum for the event had already started to build, as had the growing consensus that Giancarlo should take part in it. Since the idea first arose back in the summer, Giancarlo had been doing his best, to the point of obstinacy, to politely decline the invitation to play. At the same time, Sheffield had been doing *his* best, to an equal degree of obstinacy, to politely insist that he accept it.

Sheffield, Giancarlo well knew, was too much the diplomat to ever come right out and demand that he agree to play. Still, Giancarlo was fully aware that the dean had his own subtle ways of exerting pressure. Giancarlo had seen him in action more than once. It's not that he considered him to be devious, but Sheffield was a consummate backroom politician. He had a way of pleasantly implying that a request accepted would be considered a tremendous favor, and rewarded as such sometime in the future. Left unsaid, but always understood, was the assurance that a request denied would most likely precipitate a contrary result. Such being the case, Giancarlo suspected that it was Sheffield calling once more to employ some new carrot or stick he had suddenly found at his disposal.

The telephone rang again.

Giancarlo ignored it, for there was no point in talking about it anymore. How, he wondered, could he ever explain to them all why he could no longer compose music or perform it at the piano? He himself was at a loss as to why it had happened. It was like asking a golfer to explain why he had lost his putting touch, or a gambler to explain why Lady Luck had suddenly chosen to abandon his side. The magic had left him, that's all there was to it, and no amount of prodding, pleasant or otherwise, could bring it back. It was beyond anyone's control.

The phone rang a third time.

Giancarlo sighed, and looked out the window. It was a lovely September day, warm and dry. As so often happens, the transition from summer to fall had brought with it the best weather of the year. Outdoors, students were strolling about in shorts and T-shirts, or lounging about on the grass, enjoying the sunshine. Giancarlo envied the carefree air they all seemed to exude, and he berated himself for not having had the sense to take his lunch outside when he'd had the chance and avoid his office altogether.

A fourth ring. Two more, and the call would be directed to his answering machine.

Giancarlo had every intention of letting it do so. What did he care? It would not be the first time in his tenure at the college that he had hidden behind his voice mail. Lots of people he knew did the same. Then, however, his determination to avoid the call began to waver. What if it really was Sheffield calling? By avoiding him, Giancarlo knew he would only be postponing the inevitable. Sooner or later he would have to confront the issue head-on, instead of politely dancing around it, as he had been doing. Perhaps the time had come, he thought, to make it absolutely clear, in no uncertain terms, that he would not play at the concert, and damn the consequences. Knowing Sheffield's resilience in such matters, he realized that even an outright refusal would probably not put an end to it. Most likely the dean would simply retreat for a while to formulate some alternate strategy to win him over. A firm no at this juncture was only a temporary fix, but it would buy Giancarlo a little time, and hopefully allow him, at least on this day, to finally eat his lunch in peace.

A fifth ring.

Giancarlo let out a groan of consternation. It occurred to him that it might not be Sheffield at all, but possibly Patricia. He had been promising to have lunch with her one day soon—and indeed he had been looking forward to doing so—but for some reason even he did not understand, he kept putting it off. He felt bad about it, and would not have blamed Patricia if she was calling to voice her displeasure over his managing to avoid her another day. If it was Patricia calling, Giancarlo knew that the least he owed her was the courtesy of answering the phone. Whoever the caller was, Sheffield or Patricia, Giancarlo dreaded the thought of the conversation that was about to take place, but he could think of no remedy for it. Before the telephone could ring again, he took a deep breath and picked up the receiver.

"Giancarlo Rosa," he said.

No answer came.

"Hello, Giancarlo Rosa here," he said again.

He heard a garbled sound, like static on a radio, but still no one replied.

"Hello?" he said a final time.

"*Professore?*" came a voice over the line just as Giancarlo was about to hang the phone back up. "Are you there?"

It took Giancarlo a moment before he recognized the voice.

"Ayyy, Signor Quinn!" he exclaimed. "Is that you?"

There was a moment of silence.

"Where are you?" said Giancarlo. "Are you back in America already?"

"Yes, it's me," said Carter.

Another delay.

"No, I'm still in Italy," he answered to the second question.

Giancarlo immediately understood the problem. Very often when calling overseas, there was a short delay between when a person spoke and when his voice came through to the person on the other end of the line. He knew he would have to speak in a deliberate manner and allow enough time for a reply.

"How are you doing?" he asked. "Are you enjoying your vacation?"

"Um, pretty much," Carter answered. "I've had quite a trip so far."

Despite the poor quality of the line over which they were talking, Giancarlo could detect the hint of strain in Carter's voice.

"Where are you now?" he asked.

"I'm in Castelalto," he replied.

Giancarlo was surprised, for he had not expected him to go there so soon.

"Well, I'm glad you found your way there," he said uneasily. *"Bravo.* But why have you called? Is there something wrong?"

"Yes," said Carter, "there is. I will tell you all about it in a second, but first I have been asked to give you a message. It is from Antonella."

At the sound of the name, Giancarlo froze.

"What is it?" he said.

"Just one word," said Carter. "She said to tell you '*Venga.*' "

Come.

CHAPTER 47

When his plane landed in Rome some seventeen hours after he spoke to Carter, there was no time for Giancarlo to go into the city and sit around Termini Station waiting for a train to take him to Abruzzo. He had known this would be the case before he had made the hurried trip to Boston that previous afternoon to catch the only available flight to Italy. Giancarlo had briefly considered renting a car, but upon reflection rightly concluded it would be safer and quicker to hire a driver, and so he had made arrangements to have a car waiting to take him to Castelalto directly from the airport.

Now, as the car sped down the autostrada away from Rome and Giancarlo stretched out his legs in the backseat, he saw the wisdom of that decision. As bleary-eyed and exhausted as he was from the time change and the whirlwind of travel that had brought him there, he was glad for the time being to leave the driving in someone else's hands. It was one less thing for him to worry about.

Looking back on the day just passed, it all seemed like a blur: booking his flight, arranging for the car, cancelling his classes, informing Sheffield of the situation, saying a clumsy, hurried goodbye in passing to Patricia, rushing home to throw a suitcase together, making the slow, frustrating drive through the afternoon traffic to Boston, waiting in line at the airport to clear security, and finally sprinting to the gate to board the plane. Just thinking about it all left him out of breath.

Giancarlo settled back and stared out the window, his thoughts drifting back to that day all those years ago when he thought he had left Castelalto for good, vowing never to return. For a very long time after he had gone to America, he refused to even speak the name of the place, such was the bitterness and resentment that had driven him away. All the same, as much as he tried to shake it off, Giancarlo had never been able to completely rid himself of the lurking suspicion that, somehow or other, time and circumstances would one day conspire to bring him back. Of course, precisely what would motivate him to return, and how it would all play out once he did, were till now things about which he could only imagine. The present scenario was one of which he could never have possibly dreamed. Recalling how resolved he had been to never return to his hometown, it astonished him that, in the end, all that had been required to draw him back was a single word from Antonella. That in itself was far more powerful than the earthquake that had shaken the mountain. So much time had gone by, so much had happened, and so much had changed for Giancarlo, but as he watched the landscape rushing by, he realized that things inside his heart were still very much the same.

It was not long before Rome was well behind them, and the flat terrain gave way to rolling hills. Away to the east, Giancarlo could see the mountains begin to rise like a dark wall across the horizon. His driver took note of them, as well, and glanced at him through the rearview mirror.

"*Signore,*" he said, gesturing into the distance. "*Abruzzo.*"

"I know," said Giancarlo softly.

Then he closed his eyes to rest for what was to come.

When he awoke with a start sometime later, Giancarlo found that they had left the autostrada and were now traveling through a valley along a two-lane road, the mountains looming on all sides around them. He sat back and looked up through the rear window at the sun, relieved to see that the skies had remained clear. Rubbing his eyes, he yawned, and leaned forward onto the back of the front seat.

"*Un mezz'ora di piu*," said the driver before Giancarlo could ask. "Another half hour."

Giancarlo sat back once more and looked out the windows, searching for a familiar landmark by which he might get his bearings. It was not until much farther along, when the car rounded a long bend and the road led them to a wide-open panorama of the mountains ahead, that he finally knew for the first time exactly where he was.

It was an odd moment. The realization that he had truly returned to his native land began to set in on Giancarlo, and he found it at once comforting and troubling. He could not deny that he felt a certain rush of expectation at the prospect of soon walking once more in the place of his birth. At the same time, he was filled with a sense of dread. He felt it at the thought of his lost brother lying dead or injured somewhere off in the wilderness. He felt it, as well, in the painful memories that were closing in around him once more, as dark and ponderous as the mountains themselves. It had all come about too fast, this abrupt, unanticipated flight into his past. For all the years of brooding, he had not been ready for it.

Ready or not, the minutes and the miles ticked inexorably by, until at last Castelalto came into view on the mountainside not far ahead. At the sight of it, Giancarlo gave a slight nod of recognition, as if to acknowledge that whatever was about to transpire was as inevitable as a raindrop falling from a cloud. Forces of nature were now at work, and all he could do was let them have their way.

A forlorn-looking Carter was sitting by himself next to the fountain on the piazza, gazing up at the mountains, when the car drove up the hill and into the center of the village. Giancarlo did not get out right away, but sat looking at the young man for a moment. How strange it was for him to encounter his pupil in these remote surroundings. Save for the day they met at his office, he had never once seen Carter outside the confines of his home during one of his Italian lessons. That the two should find themselves in Castelalto at the same time seemed so improbable as to be almost ridiculous, and yet here they were.

At seeing the car approach and come to a stop, Carter got to his feet and eyed the car uncertainly. When Giancarlo stepped out, a look of relief came over his face, and he hurried to the car to greet him.

"*Ciao, Professore*," said Carter. "Welcome back to Castelalto."

"*Ciao, Signor Quinn*," replied Giancarlo with a slight bow of his head as the two shook hands. "You know, I must admit I never expected to ever meet you in this place. Now that we have, I know that I was right the day I met you when I said that I would regret taking you on as a student."

"If it would help, you could always charge me for that last lesson you gave me for free," quipped Carter.

Giancarlo gave a grunt.

"I suppose," he replied unamused, "we can discuss all that some other day."

When Giancarlo had collected his belongings from the backseat of the car and his luggage from the trunk, he paid the driver and sent him on his way back to Rome. Then he turned back to Carter and gave him a questioning nod.

"So, tell me what you know," he said. "Has there been any news about my brother?"

"No," said Carter, shaking his head. "They've found nothing so far. Not a clue."

Giancarlo turned his gaze to the mountain, and let out a sigh.

"That means he is still up there somewhere," he said.

Giancarlo looked back at Carter and then all around at the empty piazza. Things were curiously quiet, even for Castelalto.

"Where is everybody?" he asked.

Carter gave a shrug.

"Most of the men are up on the mountain," he said. "The kids are in school, and I guess everybody else is in their houses."

"And where is my brother's wife?" said Giancarlo.

"At home," Carter told him. "She's been waiting for you."

"In that case," said Giancarlo, taking hold of his suitcase, "let's not keep her waiting any longer."

As the two marched through the village toward the house, Giancarlo gazed straight ahead, ignoring the stares of the old men and women sitting by their doorways. He knew that, despite being away for so long, some of them still recognized him, and he was not surprised to hear someone whisper, "Is that Giancarlo, come back after all these years?" as he passed.

When they came to the house, Giancarlo stopped, and regarded the front door. To his eyes, at least on the exterior, very little of his boyhood home had changed. He knew full well, however, that behind the door he would find things much different. It was another in a string of strange moments for him, for he realized then that he was not sure whether he should knock before entering the house or not. He stood there, debating what to do, until Carter stepped in front of him and opened the door without hesitation. Giancarlo took a deep breath and followed him inside.

Antonella was alone in the living room, sitting by the telephone, when Carter and Giancarlo walked into the room. At seeing them come in, she immediately stood and folded her arms, striking a pose that was equal parts defiance and supplication. Antonella looked weary, like a soldier who had been at the front for too long. Her face was drawn, and the dark circles under her eyes bespoke the anxious, sleepless nights. Despite it all, she was still beautiful.

"Carter," she said in a terse voice, "I would like to talk to my brother-in-law in private. Would you mind leaving us alone, just for a few moments?"

"Of course," said Carter. With that he turned and walked out at once.

Giancarlo lingered sheepishly by the entrance to the living room, keeping his distance. He tried to look Antonella in the face, but instead found himself staring down at the floor, until they heard the front door close and they knew that Carter had gone outside. Slowly, he lifted his gaze to hers.

"Let's get something straight," said Antonella, wasting no words and no time. "I don't know what you have been thinking all these years, but whatever it is, I did not marry your brother because he inherited the house and you didn't. I did not marry your brother because he got that little scrap of land at the bottom of the hill and you didn't. I did not marry your brother because he had a job at the time and you didn't. For all these years since you ran away, I have had to listen to the whispers going round and round behind my back all over the village, all because of a single kiss that never even happened between us. No one knows the truth, not even you, but I am going to tell it to you now, whether you want to hear it or not. Yes, I did love you then. Part of my heart belonged to you, but still I married your brother, and I did it for one simple reason. I loved him more. That's all there was to it. Nothing more, nothing less. I'm sorry that it hurt you, but that is life. You can't choose the people you love any more than you can choose the color of your eyes. It just happens. Can you comprehend that? Can you get it through that thick Abruzzese skull of yours once and for all, and let the past go?"

Giancarlo's only reply was a nod of his head.

"Good," she said, spent, it seemed, from her outburst. "Now, if you don't mind, go, *per piacere*. Find my husband, if you can, wherever he is up in those mountains, and bring him back to me."

"I will," said Giancarlo, at last breaking his silence. With that he turned to go, for he knew that there was really nothing more for him to say that she would want to hear. All the same, he paused, and looked back around.

"It's good to see you, Antonella," he told her. "You're looking well."

"Eh," said his sister-in-law with a weary shrug. "So are you. Now go."

Then she waved him away, and collapsed back down onto the couch.

CHAPTER 48

"Did you get everything together I asked for yesterday?" said Giancarlo.

They were in the kitchen, hurriedly looking over their equipment. By now it was growing late in the afternoon, and they both knew there were only a few precious hours of daytime left before they would start to lose the sun.

"It's all here," said Carter. "Backpacks, sleeping bags, first-aid kit, plastic tarp, rope, water, food, walking sticks. Everything. I've checked it twice."

"And for communication?"

Carter pulled something from his back pocket and held it up for Giancarlo to see.

"Giorgio's cell phone," he said. "Antonella gave it to me this morning. She says it might work up there—but then again it might not."

"It will have to do," said Giancarlo. With that he sat down on a chair, pulled a pair of ancient-looking leather hiking shoes from his suitcase, and began to put them on.

Carter looked at the shoes with great skepticism.

"Are you really going to wear those?" he asked.

"These shoes are old friends to my feet," said Giancarlo, pulling the laces tight. "They've carried me many miles. I trust them, and that's important now."

After he finished tying his shoes, Giancarlo took the backpack

Carter had procured for him and stuffed into it the nylon jacket, the sweater, and the other hiking clothes he had thought to bring before he left home the day before. When everything was packed, and he was satisfied that he had all that he needed, he sat for a moment in silence, listening to his own breathing, to clear his mind and to gather himself. Then he stood, and nodded to Carter to let him know that it was time to go.

A short while later, as they were crossing the meadow above the village, Giancarlo stopped, leaned on his walking stick, and gazed up at the mountain.

"Where did you say the landslide happened?" he asked.

"Up there," Carter pointed, "on the north side of the mountain. That's where everyone has been looking for your brother."

Giancarlo looked with puzzlement at where Carter was pointing. Then he rubbed his chin and shook his head.

"What on earth were you doing way up there all alone, Giorgio?" he said to himself.

"Antonella says that sometimes he likes to go up in the mountains just to get away from things and think for a little while," said Carter. "Does that give you any clue?"

"No," replied Giancarlo.

"So what's our plan, then?" asked Carter.

"I guess we start in that direction," replied Giancarlo. "It seems to make the most sense for now. We'll climb up as far as we can before it gets too dark to go any further, and sleep on the mountain tonight. At least that way we'll already be up there and have a head start when morning comes. Then we will decide where to go next."

"Are you sure you still know your way around up there?" inquired Carter with a sideways glance.

Giancarlo responded by fixing him with a withering glare.

"Just asking," said Carter, quickly looking the other way.

Giancarlo gave a harrumph.

"Are you sure you want to come with me?" he asked peevishly. "You don't have to, you know."

"Yes, I do," said Carter.

Giancarlo's gaze softened

"I thought as much," he said at hearing the quiet determination in the young man's voice. "In that case, if you're ready, *andiamo!*"

With Giancarlo in the lead, the two began the ascent. The path through the woods that began at the edge of the meadow at first climbed at a gentle grade, but it was not long before it began to gradually steepen. Carter was a well-trained athlete. The moderate pace Giancarlo set taxed him only a little. Nonetheless he was not accustomed to the particular stresses hiking up a mountain with a full backpack put on one's legs, and he was soon feeling the first hints of a burn in his quadriceps and calves. He watched Giancarlo closely as he followed him up the path, amazed at how effortlessly the older man climbed. There was a discernible precision in each step Giancarlo took, a practiced efficiency of motion. His focus was always on the trail just in front of him, his walking stick tapping out a methodical rhythm. Regardless of the terrain, his pace never varied. He neither sped up nor slowed down, but simply pressed on with quiet, relentless intensity. Carter had no particular trouble keeping pace, but he knew he was working, and he was not disappointed when Giancarlo stopped from time to time to take a break.

For his part, Giancarlo was experienced enough to know his own limitations, and he was careful not to exceed them. To be sure, he felt entirely at home on the mountain. With every step, he reacquainted himself a little more with the terrain he knew so well in his youth. All the same, it had been a very long time since he exerted himself in this way. He had to be cautious not to tire too soon, so despite his desire to move quicker, he made certain he maintained a sensible pace.

Now and then, at various junctures as they progressed up the mountainside, Giancarlo would stop and survey the landscape. As he cast his gaze about, it seemed as though every bend in the path, every rocky ledge, held at least one memory, however faint it might be. Letting his thoughts dwell on them, he hoped to jog some recollection of the past, some clue that could provide a hint as to where his brother might have gone.

The day started to wane, and the sun at their backs cast a warm, orange glow over the mountain. Soon, as they climbed higher and higher, Carter and Giancarlo began to encounter the men from Castelalto descending in groups of three or four in the opposite direction, back to the village. When they came upon each other, it struck Giancarlo how readily everyone greeted Carter. Apparently his young student had made a favorable impression on the townspeople. As for himself, an introduction was usually required before anyone finally recognized him. In spite of his prolonged absence from Castelalto, none of them seemed particularly surprised to see him. That this was so was of little concern to Giancarlo. What he was most anxious to hear was their accounts of where they had been on the mountain and what they had seen. When he had gleaned as much information as he could from them, he would abruptly bid them all *buona fortuna* and promptly resume the climb.

On, Carter and Giancarlo went, until all that was left of the sun was a purple smudge over the western edge of the world, and darkness began to fall in earnest. By then the two had ascended above the tree line and could now look down with an unobstructed view at the cluster of lights glowing in the windows of Castelalto, far below them. The rest of the valley was a vast bowl of shadow, punctuated here and there by the lights of other villages off in the distance.

With the vanishing of the daylight, Giancarlo called for them to stop. The two took a moment to find a suitable spot, and within a few minutes they set up camp for the night on a reasonably soft patch of ground. Neither of the two had carried a tent, which was why Giancarlo had requested the plastic tarp. He opened his backpack, pulled it out, and opened it up across the ground. He set his pack and sleeping bag atop it, and gestured for Carter to do the same.

"We'll sleep on top of it during the night," he said. "It will be a little cool, perhaps, but not bad."

"And if it rains?" asked Carter.

Giancarlo sighed and gave a shrug.

"If it rains," he said, "we sleep underneath."

With accommodations for the evening secured, the two men unpacked the sandwiches Antonella had made for them and sat down to eat their supper. For a time the two ate in silence. Indeed they had spoken very little since they had taken to the mountain late that afternoon. Giancarlo had done so to conserve his breath during the climb. Carter had done so partly for the same reason, but more so because he did not want to disturb his teacher's concentration with idle chatter.

When he had finished his sandwich, Carter stretched out his legs, settled back against his pack, and looked up at the night sky.

"*Professore*," he said, "the stars don't look as bright to me as they should out here in the country. Why is that?"

As he took a last bite of his own sandwich, Giancarlo gestured over his shoulder with his thumb. Carter turned around and saw the top edge of a full moon just beginning to rise over the mountain behind them.

"I guess that explains it," he said.

"Yes," said his teacher. "And by the way, anywhere else you may call me *Professore*, but up here I am simply Giancarlo, *capito*?"

"*Capito*," said Carter.

Giancarlo settled back against his own pack and stared out at the valley.

"So, Carter, with all this hubbub, you have not yet told me anything about your vacation," he said. "Have your Italian lessons proved worthwhile?"

"Oh yeah," said Carter with a nod, "especially down there in the village. I've learned a lot. But it's a relief to have someone here I can finally speak English with again. To tell you the truth, I was starting to get a headache from trying to think in Italian all day long."

"I can well imagine," said Giancarlo. "But tell me, where have you been, and what have been your impressions of Italy so far?"

Carter recounted for Giancarlo his first sleepless night in Rome and his later wanderings around the city. He described how much he enjoyed train travel, and talked about the old man he had met that day on the way to Pisa. He raved of course about the food, and he acknowledged that Giancarlo had been right about the artistry of the churches in Italy, but confided that by the time he left Florence, he had seen quite enough of them. He told Giancarlo about the singing bus drivers he met on the way to Castelalto, and lastly about his brief stint working as a roofer down in the village.

"Well," said Giancarlo when he had finished, "it seems like you have had quite an adventure."

"You know, I haven't been in Italy all that long," said Carter with a smile, "but it seems like I've been away from home for ages."

"A lot has happened since you arrived," noted Giancarlo. "But it seems to me that there is one thing you haven't mentioned at all yet."

The smile drained away from Carter's face.

"You mean, what happened in Roccasale, right?" he said ruefully.

"Yes," said Giancarlo. "Did you find your Beatrice?"

"Elena? Yeah, I found her," said Carter.

"And how did things work out?"

Carter did not reply at once, but instead straightened up, gave a disdainful sniff, and spit out a pepper seed from his sandwich that had been stuck between his teeth.

"I got left for dead," he said.

Giancarlo was little surprised by this revelation. He did not need to be told that it was not a subject the young man wished to discuss, so he simply gave an understanding nod and looked away into the darkness.

Later, as they were unrolling their sleeping bags and preparing to settle down for the night, Giancarlo discussed with Carter what he thought their strategy should be when daylight finally returned. Left unsaid to that point, but much on the minds of both, he well knew, had been the distressing fact that come the morning, Giorgio would have been missing for three days. The question of whether they might already be too late was one that had weighed heavily on Giancarlo all that day.

"Do you think we can find him in time?" asked Carter unexpectedly, as if he had read Giancarlo's thoughts.

"My brother is a strong man," said Giancarlo after a moment's contemplation. "I don't know what has happened to him, but no matter what, I know he will fight to stay alive. The most important thing you can do right now is to search your memory to see if you can think of something he might have said, anything at all that could tell us where he went."

"It's all I've been doing," said Carter wearily. "I keep coming up with nothing."

"Then give it a rest," advised Giancarlo. "Go to sleep, and maybe the answer will come to you in the night."

Just then a baleful howling rose from somewhere in the mountains around them. Giancarlo seemed to pay it no heed, but Carter stopped what he was doing to listen.

"Wolves?" he said.

"Yes," said Giancarlo with no more concern than if it had been a herd of sheep. "They roam all over this area. Bears and wildcats, too."

Carter shook his head.

"Why am I not surprised?" he said.

While the wolves kept up their serenade of the moon, Carter crawled into his sleeping bag and stared up into the sky.

"This has been a very strange trip," he muttered.

Then he burrowed down into the bag as far as he could and squeezed his eyes shut.

CHAPTER 49

Giancarlo opened his eyes and looked up into a shroud of gray. It was morning, the next day, perhaps a few minutes past dawn. It was impossible to tell for sure. A blanket of clouds had moved in over the mountains during the night, obscuring the sky above and the valley below. Giancarlo propped himself up on an elbow and looked about. Save for the rugged terrain within his immediate surroundings, the rest of the world was lost behind a wall of mist.

Giancarlo sat up and surveyed what he could see of the landscape. A nervous knot twisted in his stomach. The odds of finding Giorgio in time had never been very much in their favor, even with the perfectly clear weather that had prevailed to that point. Now, with the mountain lost in fog, the odds against them had increased exponentially. It was discouraging, almost to the point of hopelessness, but there was no time to dwell on that just now. Regardless of the visibility, the chances of finding his brother were zero if they sat around waiting for better weather to come, so he reached out across the tarp and gave Carter a poke in the back.

Carter awoke with a grunt. He sat up, rubbed the sleep from his eyes, and gazed about at the misty surroundings. The look on his face told Giancarlo that he understood at once the predicament presented by the changed skies.

"Do you think this will burn off?" he said with marked apprehension.

"It might," replied Giancarlo. "It might not."

"So what do we do?"

"I was hoping you might have some ideas," said Giancarlo. "Did anything come to you in your dreams?"

"Nothing but wild animals," griped Carter. "And none of them had anything to say."

"Think," Giancarlo prodded him, the same way he might have done during one of their lessons. "Think hard! What was the last thing you remember talking about with my brother?"

Carter grimaced as he strained to reconstruct in his mind the events of the day before Giorgio disappeared.

"We talked about taking a ride the next day," he said in frustration. "That's all. He was going to show me around the area. He didn't say anything at all about going up into the mountains."

"There must have been something," Giancarlo insisted. "Think. Was there any place in particular that he wanted to take you?"

Carter closed his eyes for a few moments and concentrated again, before giving up with a sigh.

"He said he knew where the best *gelateria* was in all of Abruzzo," he said at last. "Other than that, he didn't mention anywhere else. Trust me, I've gone over this again and again in my mind."

Now it was Giancarlo's turn to sigh in frustration.

"I'm sorry," said Carter, a forlorn look coming over his face. "It's all that I can come up with. So now what?"

"Now, I guess we do our best to find our way up to the north slope," said Giancarlo, "and hope we get lucky along the way."

It did not take long for the two to collect their gear and prepare themselves to get back on the trail. When their packs were buckled and secured on their backs, they took their walking sticks in hand and set off toward the top of the mountain.

As he had the previous day, Giancarlo stayed at the lead. He remained there not only so that he could dictate the pace, but also because of the fog. Given the poor visibility, it would be quite easy to lose their way and blunder onto dangerous terrain. If any misfortune was destined to befall one of them, he preferred that it happen to him.

Up and up they climbed through the mist, neither man ever completely certain that they were headed in the desired direction—or indeed if the desired direction was where they really needed to go. At times they would encounter a fleeting break in the clouds, one just large enough to afford a brief glimpse of the top of the mountain. Giancarlo would instantly reorient their ascent in that direction, before the clouds once again closed over the scene, like the curtains on a stage.

It was slow going, and as he carefully picked the way forward, Giancarlo began to wonder if they were wasting their time, trekking to where everyone else had already searched. The higher they climbed, the less it seemed to make sense to him that Giorgio would have come this way. At first he passed these doubts off as fatigue, for he understood how it had a way of slowly eroding a worried man's resolve. As hard as he tried, however, the thought would not go away, but continued to gnaw at him more and more with every step he took. When at last he could ignore it no more, he held up his hand to signal that it was time to stop for a break.

Giancarlo remained standing, leaning against his stick. Carter, meantime, took the opportunity to sit down on a rock and open his pack. He pulled out a bottle of water and gulped down a few swallows.

Giancarlo kicked pensively at the dirt.

"Tell me something," he said. "That sightseeing trip you told me about. Did Giorgio say at what time he thought you would leave?"

"No, I don't think so," replied Carter. "But the last thing he said to Antonella was that he would be back before lunchtime, so I guess he planned for us to go around then. Why, what are you thinking?"

Giancarlo scratched his head.

"Let's assume he left the house at six o'clock that morning," he said, "or maybe even a little later."

"Okay," shrugged Carter. "So what?"

"That would give him less than six hours of steady hiking to go wherever he planned and then come back home, yes?"

"Makes sense," said Carter.

"If that's the case, why would Giorgio hike all the way up here, when he must have known that there was no way on earth that he would ever get back home on time?"

Now it was Carter's turn to kick pensively at the dirt.

"That's a good point," he said. "But if he didn't come this way, where could he have gone?"

"I don't know," said Giancarlo, beginning to pace back and forth. "But there's something else I've been wondering about. What made him want to take you to a *gelateria*?"

"We were drinking wine made by a man named Demetrio," Carter told him.

"Yes, I know him," said Giancarlo. "Go on."

"Well, there's not much to tell," said Carter. "We started talking about Sunday dinner, and I said that lamb was one of my favorite foods, and then . . . I don't know . . . somehow I must have mentioned that I liked gelato. That's when he told me about the *gelateria*."

"And that was all?" asked Giancarlo.

"Pretty much," said Carter. Then he gave a little laugh.

"What is it?" said Giancarlo.

"Nothing," replied Carter. "I was just remembering that your brother made me laugh when he said he wished they made mushroom-flavored gelato."

Giancarlo stopped, and gaped at him.

"*Mushroom?*" he said.

"Yes," said Carter. "He said mushrooms were his favorite thing in all the world to eat."

Giancarlo's head was suddenly awhirl, and his heart began to pound in his chest.

"Of course," he gasped, slapping a hand to his forehead. "*Il Rifugio dei Briganti!* How could I have been so stupid?"

With that Giancarlo abruptly turned and set off at once across the mountain, away from the path they had been following.

"The *what*?" Carter called after him as he jumped up to follow. "*Rifugio Briganti?* What does that mean?"

"If I'm right," Giancarlo called back, "it means that everyone has been looking in the wrong place!"

CHAPTER 50

Giancarlo stopped at the foot of the incline and looked up at the grove of trees that still stood near the edge of the grassy step above. He was certain that he had led them to the right place, but he saw no sign of the ancient stone structure that he expected to find.

"Is this the place?" said Carter.

"I think so," said Giancarlo, his eyes nervously scanning the ridge up above, "but something's not right."

If his memory of the place was correct, they ought to have been able to see the corner of the roof through the branches of the trees. Perhaps, he speculated, the building was further back than he remembered, or the trees had grown thicker, or maybe the mist was obscuring their view. There was only one way to be sure. Though weary from the long, arduous trek to reach that spot, Giancarlo gave Carter a nudge, and the two began to scramble their way up.

Carter made it to the top first, reached back to give Giancarlo a hand, and pulled him up over the lip of the ridge. When Giancarlo straightened up and surveyed the scene, he realized that he had indeed brought them to the right place, but as he stood there panting, he felt a terrible sinking feeling in his gut.

Il Rifugio dei Briganti, the brigands' lair that Giancarlo and Giorgio had discovered that long-ago day when the two went up the mountain in search of forgotten treasure, lay in ruins. Half the roof above where the doorway used to be had caved in, and the rest looked about to fall at any moment. One of the side walls was completely crumbled, and to all appearances little more than a passing breeze would be all that was required to do the same to the others.

Giancarlo stood frozen as he gazed at the devastation. He could not bring himself to draw any nearer to the place for fear of what he might find inside. For a moment, time stopped, and all he could hear was the sound of his own breathing and the whisper of the wind drifting over the mountain. Then suddenly, to his utter astonishment, he heard something coming from within the shattered refuge. At first he could not believe his ears, but then he realized he was not imagining it. It was the sound of someone, in a low, weak, almost pathetic voice, struggling to sing, but ending in a fit of coughing.

Carter looked wide-eyed at Giancarlo and threw aside his walking stick.

"Come on!" he cried, sprinting ahead.

When he reached the outside of the ruined shelter, Carter placed a hand on the wall and cautiously leaned in to have a look, just as Giancarlo caught up to him. The two hazarded to step inside together and peered through the shadows. It took a moment for Giancarlo's eyes to adjust to the dimness, but when his vision finally cleared, the sight he beheld lifted his spirits, but at the same time broke his heart. There on the floor, pinned on his back beneath a pile of wooden beams and rock, lay Giorgio Rosa.

"Giorgio!" cried Giancarlo.

At hearing the voice, Giorgio lifted his head. Clutching a small knapsack to his chest, he squinted in the dim light and gave a feeble cough.

"I don't know who you are," he rasped, "but I am very glad to see you."

Then his head promptly dropped back onto the dirt.

Giancarlo's heart was flooded with a thousand emotions, but there was not a single second to consider any of them. He dashed to his brother's side, brought a bottle of water to his lips, and cradled his head to help him drink a few gulps. He poured out the water across Giorgio's bruised forehead and face to revive him a little, before gently setting his head back down again. Then Giancarlo jumped to his feet and began to help Carter, who was already furiously pulling away the rubble to get at the enormous beam that had trapped Giorgio's legs.

As the two men worked in a frenzy to free him, Giorgio lifted his head once more and peered up at his rescuers.

"Carter?" he said in the same rasping voice. "Is that really you?"

"*Corraggio*, Giorgio!" Carter urged him. "We'll get you out of here!"

Giorgio gave a deep, rattling cough that bespoke some terrible internal injury.

"But how on earth did you find me?" he wheezed. "No one knows about this place."

"Almost no one," said Giancarlo with a grunt as he and Carter put their backs into it and lifted the wooden beam that had kept his brother pinned. They set it aside, and at last, after three long days, Giorgio's cracked and bloodied body was free.

If he had felt any relief from his sudden release, Giorgio did not show it. Instead, as his two rescuers set about tending to his wounds as best they could, he gazed in confusion at Giancarlo's face, until the light of recognition showed across his own. Then he grinned despite the pain.

"*Giancarlo?*" he gasped, his eyes welling up. "Is it really you? Have you really come back?"

"It's really me," said Giancarlo, squeezing his hand.

"*Dio mio*, Giancarlo, I am so happy to see you again!" cried Giorgio. He nodded to the empty knapsack by his side. "I came up to get mushrooms."

"I thought as much," said Giancarlo. "You and your silly mushrooms."

"I picked a nice bunch to cook for this one," Giorgio went on, gesturing to Carter, on his other side. "And then I came in here to get out of the sun for a minute. Before I knew it, the ground started to shake, and everything came down on top of me."

"You're lucky to be alive," Giancarlo told him as he wrapped a bandage around a nasty cut on his brother's arm.

"Eh, I'm lucky I had my mushrooms to keep me going," said Giorgio with a weak grin. "Though I must admit, as much as I love them, after three days of eating raw mushrooms, a man gets sick of them."

Giorgio paused, and put a hand to his head, gaping at his brother in wonder. "But Giancarlo," he said, "after all these years, I can't believe you came back to find me."

"I didn't," Giancarlo told him with a half smile. "I came to get my watch back. This time I plan to keep it."

"That's the way it should be," said Giorgio with a laugh that ended in a cough. "That's the way Papa wanted it."

At the mention of their father, Giancarlo's own eyes began to well up.

"I'm so sorry, Giorgio," he said, his voice beginning to crack. "I've been so stupid for all these years."

Giorgio reached out and gave him a gentle pat on the cheek.

"Forget it, *fratello mio*," he said kindly. "It was not your fault. It wasn't anyone's fault."

Then Giorgio gave a terrible groan, and his face became contorted with pain.

Giancarlo and Carter exchanged worried glances.

"It's time to use that cell phone," said Giancarlo.

Carter gave a nod of agreement and pulled out the phone. He pressed the numbers and waited. Nothing happened. He tried again with the same result, and let out a curse.

"I can't get a signal!" he cried in frustration.

"Eh, those things never work up here," said Giorgio with a weary sigh. "That's why I never bother bringing mine. Don't worry about it. It doesn't matter now, anyway."

"Don't talk *stupido*," Giancarlo told him. "Save your breath now."

"I don't think I have many breaths left, my brother."

"Don't say that!" cried Giancarlo.

Giorgio gave another heavy sigh and beckoned for Giancarlo to lean closer.

"I have to tell you something," he said, speaking to Giancarlo in dialect so that Carter could not understand. "There's something I want you to know."

"What is it?" said Giancarlo, taking his hand, terrified at how weak and fragile it felt to him.

Giorgio gazed up into Giancarlo's eyes.

"I wasn't blind, you know," he said. "I knew about you and Antonella back when you left Castelalto. I knew all along. I could see what was happening between the two of you from the very first day. I saw it coming even before either of you did." Giorgio was suddenly wrenched with another deep cough. "It was not her fault, either," he said when it had passed. "She had to choose, Giancarlo. Do you understand? You must forgive her. There was nothing else for her to do."

"I know," said Giancarlo, hanging his head. "I know."

"What you don't know," said Giorgio, his voice growing ever weaker, "is that if she had chosen you instead, I would have given *you* the house, no questions asked. I would have given you everything, whatever it took to make her happy, to make the both of you happy. You see, I loved her. And I loved you. And in the end, what else matters?"

Giancarlo felt his insides tearing apart. There was so much he wanted to say, so much to tell him before it was too late, but before he could say a word, he felt his brother slowly letting go of his hand.

"Stay," Giancarlo begged him.

"Take care of her," Giorgio whispered.

And then he closed his eyes.

CHAPTER 51

The tears came.

After thirty years of keeping it all locked deep inside, all the useless bitterness and resentment that had colored his life black at long last spilled out of Giancarlo, like rain in a downpour. His brother was gone. He had squandered away all the chances he might have had to come home and reconcile with him. Now it was too late, and all he could do was weep.

Paralyzed with grief, Giancarlo gazed down at Giorgio and let it all go.

"What have I done?" he sobbed, squeezing his head between his hands. "My brother! What a fool I have been! God, forgive me, what have I done with my life?"

Giancarlo trembled, and wept openly like a child. He wept for his father, releasing the tears he ought to have shed for him years ago. He wept for his mother and his brother, and he wept for himself, for now only he remained, and he felt more lonely and lost than ever without them.

"What do I do now?" he lamented. "I have nothing left. Where do I go from here?"

The tears streaming down his own face, Carter came to Giancarlo's side and put a hand on his shoulder to console him.

"Learn from me, Carter," cried Giancarlo, shaking his head in misery. "Don't waste your life, as I've done. Don't——"

Giancarlo abruptly ceased his lamentations and looked down at his brother, his jaw dropping open. He stared in disbelief, for unless he was greatly mistaken, his supposedly deceased brother was wearing an unmistakable smirk. Worse, as he leaned over to take a closer look, he realized that Giorgio was struggling not to giggle!

"You're alive!" cried Giancarlo, not sure if he was elated or outraged.

Giorgio could contain himself no more and burst into laughter despite the obvious pain it was causing him.

"Of course I'm alive!" he exclaimed. "Did you really think a few rocks and wooden beams could kill me?"

Giancarlo looked at him aghast.

"But how could you do such a thing?" he screamed.

Giorgio only laughed all the more, even though it really was killing him. Then he looked over to Carter and held up his hand to him.

"*Scusami*, Carter," he pleaded. "You must forgive me. I know that was cruel, but if you only knew how many years I have waited to do that, to pay my brother back for the scare he gave me one day a long time ago."

His eyes wide in amazement, Carter looked back and forth between the two brothers and just shook his head.

"You guys have some issues," he said, deadpan.

"You have no idea," grumbled Giancarlo.

With that Carter got to his feet and wiped the dirt from his hands.

"Now what do we do?" he asked.

"Since we can't call for help, I suppose we'll have to carry him out. Do you think we can manage it?"

"Sure," said Carter with a shrug. Then he gave Giorgio a sideways look. "That is, if you still want to."

Gazing down at Giorgio and seeing the look of true affection in his brother's eyes, Giancarlo realized he could no longer stay angry at him. After all, what would have been the use of it?

"Why not?" he finally said with a smile. "I guess it's time for all of us to go home."

* * *

Later, when Giancarlo and Carter finally descended out of the mist, bearing Giorgio on the stretcher they had fashioned from their walking sticks and tarp, someone on the piazza caught sight of them, and a jubilant cry went up all over Castelalto. Within moments people from all over the village came rushing out to help. Giancarlo and Carter, their faces white with fatigue, were only too glad to hand over the stretcher when at last the joyous throng reached them. Their arms resting across each other's shoulders, they staggered behind like battle-weary soldiers while the other men carried Giorgio back to the piazza, where an ambulance was already waiting. The rest of the crowd pressed in around the two and escorted them home, cheering for them the whole way, like they were conquering heroes.

It was a chaotic scene when they reached the piazza, everything happening in a whirl, as if in a dream. By then word had reached Antonella and her daughters, and the three came running from the house, wild with relief and joy. The tears streaming from their eyes, they rushed to Giorgio's side as the rescue workers transferred him to a real stretcher and prepared to put him into the ambulance. Antonella, who had stayed cool and collected through it all, was now so happy and yet so distraught at the pitiable sight of her injured husband that all she could do was sob uncontrollably, while Giulia and Daniela cried, "Papa! Papa!"

Giancarlo stood with Carter in the midst of the crowd, watching with a smile the reunion of his brother and wife and their beautiful children. It was not until they were putting Giorgio into the ambulance that Antonella finally turned Giancarlo's way and gazed at him for a fleeting moment with eyes full of gratitude. For now there was nothing more that needed to be said between the two, so Giancarlo simply smiled and nodded in reply. Then Antonella climbed in with Giorgio, the doors closed behind her, and soon the ambulance took them away.

As he watched them go, and the people gathered around to shake his hand and pat him on the back, Giancarlo found the tears once again welling up in his eyes, but this time they were not tears of sadness. Something inside him had changed, like he had been freed from a great weight that had been holding him down all these years. Suddenly he felt lighter than air, and for the first time since he could remember, Giancarlo Rosa felt truly happy.

EPILOGUE

Giancarlo and Carter stayed two more days in Castelalto. By then the doctors were certain that Giorgio would recover from his injuries. He would be in the hospital for quite a while, but in time he would mend.

The day they were to leave, Carter came downstairs with his duffel bag in tow and lugged it out to the piazza, where a car was waiting to take them to Rome. The driver, who introduced himself as Giacomo, took the bag from him and stowed it in the trunk next to Giancarlo's suitcase. Carter looked around. It was nearly time to go, but his teacher was nowhere to be seen.

"Don't worry. He'll be here soon," said Antonella, who was waiting over by the fountain.

"Where is he?" asked Carter.

Gesturing for him to follow, Antonella walked to the edge of the piazza and pointed down below, to the village cemetery. There Carter saw Giancarlo kneeling before a gravestone.

"He went to mass this morning," she said softly. "Now he's saying goodbye to his mother and father."

Giancarlo walked out of the cemetery and returned to the piazza a few minutes later. Though his eyes were red-rimmed and swollen, he walked with his head held high, and he looked very much to Carter like a man who had finally found peace.

For his part, Giancarlo truly did feel as though the world had finally been set right again. This strange, unexpected trip, the end really of the one he began thirty years ago, had led him through the darkest chambers of his heart, but along the way he had learned at last how to throw open the shutters and let the light back in.

By now, many of the villagers had turned out to see Giancarlo and Carter off. They all bid their farewells, before retreating a discreet distance to let Antonella say goodbye to them by herself.

Antonella looked at the two men and pressed her hands together in a gesture of gratitude, before opening her arms wide.

"What can I say to the men who rescued my husband?" she said with a smile.

With that she came up first to Carter, gave him a warm embrace, and brushed her cheek against his.

"Ciao, Carter," she said. "Remember, you are always welcome here, so come back again anytime you want."

"I will," promised Carter with a mischievous smile, "but next time I'm definitely going to want a cone of gelato."

"Ha!" laughed Antonella, giving his cheek a pinch. "You'll have to take that up with Giorgio someday."

At that Carter stepped aside and drifted over to the car to wait.

Now it was Giancarlo's turn to say goodbye to Antonella. He had known of course that this moment was coming, and he had struggled all day to think of words that would be adequate to the occasion. None came, and all he could do was shrug and smile as Antonella came and stood there before him, gazing at him with warmth and affection.

"Thank you for bringing him back to me," she said. "Thank you for bringing back my Giorgio."

"*Prego*," said Giancarlo, bowing his head.

Then to his complete and utter surprise, and that of all the villagers watching, Antonella stepped up to him, took his face in her hands, and kissed him full on the lips.

"There," she told him gently, stepping back from him once more. "Now I owe you nothing."

Giancarlo flushed bright red as a murmur of laughter at the look on his face rippled through all the onlookers.

After all the years of hearing whispers behind her back, Antonella whipped around with defiant eyes and stared every one of them down.

"What's the matter?" she challenged them with hands on her hips. "Can't you see I'm just saying goodbye to my brother-in-law?"

Then she spun back around and gave Giancarlo a wink.

"That will keep them gabbing for at least another thirty years," she said. "So go now. You are free. Go start your life over again. Go home to America, where you belong, and don't come back here again unless you come with a wife. *Capito?*"

"Understood," nodded Giancarlo. "*Arrivederci,* Antonella."

With that Giancarlo turned away, and he and Carter climbed into the car. When the doors were closed, Carter looked at Giancarlo for a moment with curious eyes.

"You know something?" he said with a shake of his head. "This is a nice country, but the women here are a little hard to figure."

"So I take it you are ready to go home, then?" said Giancarlo with a chuckle.

"Anytime you are."

Giancarlo leaned forward toward the driver and patted him on the shoulder.

"*A Roma,* Giacomo," he told him. "To Rome."

"*Si, Signore,*" said Giacomo.

With that he put the car in gear, and soon Castelalto was behind them.

Later that afternoon, when they boarded the airplane in Rome, Carter and Giancarlo settled into their seats and made themselves comfortable for the long flight home. As the plane pulled away from the terminal and began to taxi toward the runway, Giancarlo took out a pen and a piece of paper and, humming to himself, began to draw closely spaced lines across the page.

"What's that you're drawing, *Professore*?" asked Carter, leaning over to see.

"Just a few bars of music," said Giancarlo. "They just came to mind, who knows from where."

"I thought you didn't write music anymore."

Giancarlo gave a shrug.

"Well, I guess now I do again," he mused. "I suppose it's about time. I do have a concert coming up in the spring." He paused, and tapped the pen against his nose, before breaking into a smile. "But first I owe someone back home some piano lessons."

"Sounds like you'll be busy," said Carter.

"Oh yes," replied Giancarlo. "And how about you? Are you planning now to settle down a little and start your career when you get back?"

"Actually," said Carter, "I've been thinking that I might like to learn how to speak French when I get home."

"*French?*" said a surprised Giancarlo.

"Sure," said Carter. "How hard could it be? I mean, look how fast I picked up Italian."

"But why?" asked Giancarlo.

"I don't know," said Carter evasively. "It's just that I was thinking I might take a trip to France one day soon. You know, I've always been kind of interested in French culture."

"Ah, I see," said Giancarlo, putting the paper and pen aside.

He smiled at the young man, and settled back into the seat as the engines roared and the plane started its takeoff.

"So, tell me," he said, closing his eyes. "What was her name?"